AT THE CENTER

AT THE CENTER

Norma Rosen

Boston

HOUGHTON MIFFLIN COMPANY

1982

Library of Congress Cataloging in Publication Data

Rosen, Norma Gangel, date
At the Center

I. Title.
PS3568.O77A79   813'.54   81-7099
ISBN 0-395-31263-9 AACR2

Printed in the United States of America

P   10   9   8   7   6   5   4   3   2   1

With dearest love to my children
ANNE and JONATHAN
who enliven and rebuke me
with their never-ending excitement
about books and ideas

Urge and urge and urge,
Always the procreant urge of the world.

. . . .

A child said *What is the grass?* fetching it to me with full hands

. . . .

. . . I guess it is the handkerchief of the Lord,
A scented gift and remembrancer and designedly dropt,
Bearing the owner's name someway in the corner, that we may
    see and remark, and say *Whose?*

. . . .

Enough! enough! enough!   '
Somehow I have been stunn'd. Stand back!
Give me a little time beyond my cuff'd head, slumbers, dreams,
    gaping,
I discover myself on the verge of a usual mistake.

—Walt Whitman,
Leaves of Grass

Book One

One is tempted to ask why a society, which has failed . . . to protect . . . already existing child life . . . takes upon itself the reckless encouragement of indiscriminate procreation.

— from Margaret Sanger's
Pivot of Civilization,
as memorized by Nana

A little abortion of a man hurried before us . . .

— from Nathaniel Hawthorne's
French and Italian Notebooks,
as recorded in Selig's notes

1

"HELLO, DARLING." Ellen Bianky studies, with practiced eye, the face of her husband, Edgar, to see what kind of day he's had. Handsomest of men when they married fifteen years before: olive-skinned face darkly tanned, brilliant smile. Worry has crept over, blurring. Not that he's a ruin at fifty — far from it! Down-sloping eyes of dark clarity, nobly shaped head with no gray yet, still imposing. Still makes her heart stop in the street — stop here, on the wide gray sidewalk beneath the deep canopy with its distinctive lettering. Her body, though — trim, elegantly clothed — goes on evenly walking: discipline.

"How was it, darling — today?" Ellen will ask, but not yet.

Edgar takes her elbow at the curb — they have arrived within moments of each other's cab, straight from hospital and clinic — and escorts her into the Pigeon Roost, he dark and heavy-shouldered, she blond, small, bone-delicate.

But it is Ellen who feels she escorts Edgar. She is the protector. She lifts Edgar in her arms and carries him in to where it is warm, her female slightness struggling with his heavy male bulk, and sets him down inside. There! She pants, staggers. It's worth all the effort. He is safe — safe!

In reality, Edgar's hand is on her elbow. In reality, they walk — handsome couple! — into the Pigeon Roost, where they are known.

It is Ellen's idea, this nightly arrangement at the Pigeon. Edgar and she, both busy physicians, enjoy the convenience of a restaurant in Manhattan's East Sixties, a comfortable stroll away from their apartment. The food is delicious, the prices high. Here Ellen struggles inwardly — her strong democratic preference makes her loathe exclusivity, yet the manners and judgments of her background and class make her dearly love its effects. Pigeon equals peace, privacy.

Though not lately. Since the restaurant critic of *Gourmet Living* has translated into print some of the Pigeon's mouthwatering dishes (prices were also mentioned, but seemingly more in admiration than warning), the restaurant's patronage has doubled. Of course Ellen preferred the early Pigeon — emptier and quieter, heavenly! But a thought nags her: these waiting, not-so-well-behaved cocktail-sippers who now crowd the bar, these newly moneyed citizens, no doubt spring from the former poor. Toward what do her democratic preferences lead if not to dinners at the Pigeon Roost for all? Yet she can hardly help her feelings — the noise! The show! The middle-classness of these crowds! Her preference swings back to the struggles of progenitors. Like a pendulum that is blocked, she thinks — like some faulty windshield wiper! — the arc of her sympathy, greatly narrowed, returns again and again to the deprived, present or past, and withholds from their more prosperous progeny the extended curve of her concern. But why — she demands of herself — do I do that? So unfair. She casts a clear eye at her own inconsistency. Then she blankets it with a portion of irony from a naturally abundant supply, as if an excellent housekeeper, noticing a spill, snatches from a well-stocked linen cupboard some deep, dry toweling and with a brisk patience, more amused than irritated — "You see . . .? Careful as I am . . ." — lays it over.

Now the maitre d' comes forward, smiling amid the delicious smells of *veau d'or* (tantalizing with white wine and olives) and *volaille en croûte*. In that moment when he so warmly beckons them — when they detach themselves from the waiting crowd and follow him to their secluded table laid with crimson linen, and with small white chrysanthemums arranged in a gleaming glass bowl — Ellen again confronts her conscience.

But when she looks at Edgar — handsome, harried, worn! — then her heart flames up. Her face, though, keeps its composure. Her posture, rhythm, stride remain unbroken. Ellen, you're a fraud! She thinks that, yet at the same time thinks: He must have it, I can't let him wait.

If there were no table! If one night they came and the restaurant were full and somehow M. Henri were not there to greet them, and the new man didn't know them and so there were no table — she knows what she would do. She would march to their regular place and say to the strangers sitting there, "Get up! Dr. Bianky has had a trying day. He must sit down. He must eat his dinner. Get up! Get up!" And when they had fled before her — because her voice, so quiet and strong, was her hospital voice, accustomed to command, and in fact was the voice she had found was her voice anyway — she would turn to Edgar: "Sit down. Sit down, my love, and eat."

Strain. There are marks of unmitigated strain on his face. She fears he is heart-attack prone, like his father. She knows from her practice how incapable men are of resting themselves. They pushed and pushed until they fell down.

"Get up at once," she would say in a strong, stinging voice to the astonished couple. "We have priority!" They might even be sprung from the recent poor, from the newly moneyed ones — there are thousands!

Numbers in general are not lost upon Ellen Bianky. She observes how very large they have grown in this present society. If millions of Americans have a higher standard of living than ever before, millions of people are also starving in the Far

East. In a century only two-thirds over, several genocides have already taken place. "Estimated deaths" is a phrase Ellen often finds in the *Times*. "Estimated deaths run to four million, sometimes five . . ." "The estimate of six million deaths is occasionally disputed . . ."

Ellen hears the soundless crash that follows these phrases. It is difficult to live with such numbers vibrating in the recent air. Millions of people, already fully formed, living lives, thinking and feeling . . .

No one can assimilate these huge numbers. The world — even that segment of society that dines well along with Ellen and Edgar Bianky — feels itself to be in a permanent state of intellectual and emotional indigestion. In the last few years since abortions were legalized, millions of them have been performed. Ellen's husband, Edgar, is responsible for a portion of these millions. Often he seems to bear upon his handsome head the heavy weight of these numbers.

Because of all this, Ellen now monitors carefully the first conversations of their dinner while she cuts her food with her surprisingly strong-looking hands. It is midweek. If it were week's end, they'd be dining with friends (these days Ellen selects their most cheerful ones) and going to the theater afterward. But now they chat lightly through the meal. No real shop talk yet. Ellen tells funny anecdotes, if there are some, about her hospital staff. Edgar never has any. They may take in an early movie after that. Usually they head home, as now, to read before bed.

Upstairs, all is restrained elegance and comfort, twenty stories above Madison Avenue. Yet once in their apartment, a change comes over the tone of things. All day Edgar has, with his thick neck and abstracted manner, held up his dark, handsome head while the cares of the Center stormed about it. Now he lets his head sink frankly downward. He pours out what plagues him: "Charlie claims we make too much of the patients' feelings. He'd like to lock them up when they arrive, I think. Not let them change their minds!"

"He may have a point," Ellen answers.

"There are subtleties he won't look at," Edgar goes on. "And Paul. Trying to make a doctor-patient relationship. Those women don't want it. In and out safe and fast is what they want."

"Some of them might like it."

"I don't feel the equilibrium I want to see there!" Edgar's passionate outbursts, uttered in a deep baritone, are taken at first by some newcomers to the Center for boiling temper. But he is gifted with resonance, not choler.

Ellen, on the other hand, lets into her voice a kind of steady pizzicato — clear, even. It is compounded of the New England tone she was raised on, plus a technique evolved from her own work as physician. Ellen is a radiologist. There is bad news, often, in those x rays. The hardest part of her job is to whisk patients past the news and into treatment. What she wants is to apply words like little dabs of caustic, useful for emotions that threaten to pus up and infect everything.

"Now, that's useless worry." Ellen dabs often and briskly at Edgar. Meanwhile she plucks up a clear, reliable tone: "Those men have the steadiest hands in the business."

Ellen understands that she is called upon to be short, almost stinging, with Edgar's fears. She was brought up to be controlled — no display, either of dress or emotion — and this is one of the qualities Edgar values her for. But she longs sometimes to fling her arms expressively, in joy or sorrow. When she visited Edgar's mother she had watched the way the old woman, in one evening's time, lived through the range of emotions — weeping for the dead daughter and husband, hugging and kissing those who remained, laughing with tears, scolding with unabated concern, calling upon the saints to shower blessings on them all.

Ellen has caught an Italian fever from Edgar's mother and brothers, but not from Edgar. He struggles to become more like what she has been, to keep tight rein on his emotions. It is as if, lacking children, some cross-fertilization, some genetic mixing, has gone on within each of them. But nothing of Ellen's part in this can be revealed to Edgar, who chills himself in her coolness as if existence itself is too hot for him.

Ellen begins to rub Edgar's back, moving her small, strong fingers along the stripes of his pajamas. With her thumbs she outlines the contours of vertebrae as cleanly as if her eye saw them on her x-ray illuminator, and works into the nodes of nerves along the margins.

"In the early days you were all heroes, in spite of the chaos," she says. "For three years before the rest of the country came around, New York was a haven for the continent. Now you're settling into routine — all of you, Women's Clinic, Parkmed, Planned Parenthood — it's the story of every movement. Naturally it makes you nervous!"

She ends sharply, as if the subject were finished, though she knows it is only beginning. Edgar protests that he's not complaining of routine, only about the members of his staff. He thinks them the best in the world, yet he wonders aloud if they are capable of sudden betrayal — not through meanness, but through the sheer burden of their own troubles. Most often, he voices fears about his partners. About Paul, for the instability of his life. About Charlie — for a hundred reasons.

"And now Charlie's illness," Edgar says. "His troubles finally burst through his gut" — with Ellen he allows himself unscientific lapses — "that's a showing-forth in the flesh, all right. Poor bastard, my God!"

"What a wonderful world if no one had problems." Ellen's tone plucks a little faster and stings a little more. "No one would need your Center. Teen-agers wouldn't pretend that contraceptives are for the middle-aged and the middle-aged wouldn't pretend to be teen-agers. A world without self-delusion, think of it!"

Edgar's healthier self revives under the healing bite of the caustic. Yet often he feels that he is bracketed, as in some operatic trio, by the two partners. Paul, the one on his right, the one who feels so deprived, sings with tenor desperation, straining after everything life can offer: relationships, work, wealth, meaning, joy. Each day at the Center is an act that robs him again of a world he came too late to inherit.

The one on his left — Charlie — is all renunciation and nihilism. With his dry, downward-driving bass he hammers into the earth everything that Paul strains to grasp. Life is nothing but dust and ashes. Best never to be born. If birth does take place it had better be under optimum conditions or not at all. For Charlie every procedure they do is an act of affirmation that contributes to the void he imagines is better than the life he sees.

And here is Edgar in the middle, *upholding yet another center,* singing with all his might — his lungs nearly bursting — of human aspiration and error and tragedy and hope and forgiveness and reconciliation and, above all, of fresh chances.

It is very tiring. He would like, often, to lie down. Now it's delicious — his face deep in the pillow with Ellen working at his vertebrae — but most of the time he cannot rest. He sleeps badly many nights now. Responsibility burns like grit under his eyelids. Too painful to close them. Open-eyed he sees sketched on the dark ceiling the particulars of his recurrent fantasy. Ellen knows it. Everyone on the staff at the Center knows it. But Edgar experiences it alone.

It's always the same. The woman's name is Genevieve. He knows her first name is Genevieve. The last eludes him. Strom? No, that had been a colleague of his. Muller? That doesn't fit his dream rhythms. It's something a little off. Smoth? Jeens? Whett? Bluck? Brewn?

She's X. Nothing else feels right, and she lies on the procedure table for nearly an hour. After the first few minutes, she develops breathing difficulties. She had been crying before the anesthetic, maybe that caused it.

His thoughts always jump here to the inquest. His best aide, Mary, the one his staff calls "the Reassurer," testifies that the doctor performing that day (Charlie Brodaw? Paul Sunshine?) seemed . . . distracted . . . Or it's the Indian doctor, Lal, who comes on Tuesdays and Fridays, or the Korean, Gen-Lee, who moonlights on Thursdays, his day off from the hospital. Or anyone!

After nearly completing the procedure, the doctor — Brodaw? Sunshine? Lal? — makes the grave mistake of piercing the uterine wall. Because of the patient's breathing difficulty, the operating doctor compounds the first error with the second — far worse — of not calling him, Bianky, at once, as is the rule, and tries in haste to finish the job. Or the doctor is oblivious to the perforation — the stories vary, depending on how much punishment Edgar is inflicting on himself.

"Oh!" Sometimes Edgar lets out an involuntary groan, and then Ellen knows what place he is at.

The next part of the fantasy never varies. Within a few seconds, a portion of the woman's bowel is sucked up into the waste bottle and she's off into shock. The anesthetist shouts for aid, the other doctors rush in to do chest incision and heart massage.

Edgar himself stands paralyzed.

"Stop it!" He frantically cries out to people pushing past him. "Stop it! Stop it!"

Too late. Genevieve X is the first maternal death in the four-year history of the Bianky Family Planning Center.

"Just dark fancies." Ellen says it firmly. She's right, of course. In beautiful, sunlit reality, the Center is thriving — doing a thousand procedures a month, in addition to counseling, checkups before and after. Who knows this better than Edgar? Why in God's name should he suffer such fantasies? The dream is now reality!

Except that issues now are not as clear-cut as they once were. There have been astonishing developments. The Center, it appears — from the hate mail he gets and the news he reads — is not for blacks because that's a form of genocide.

Not for Jews because they must replenish themselves. Not (as of course he always knew) for Catholics because of mortal sin. Then who is it for? For women. They still come in the millions. Blacks. Jews. Catholics. Of course they come!

And of course there are millions of people who give support to their coming. But also there are millions crying out against!

Sheer volume has begun to tell on some of his doctors. His own fantasy of Genevieve X is a horror to him, and there are others among the staff who have bad dreams. Edgar tells himself: None of this matters! Nothing can subtract one iota of the good done at the Center. He will let no one harm it. But it is wearing, wearing, and the forces against them, it seems, are tireless.

Besides all that, something else has happened. Someone at the Center had sent Edgar a note: "Your confidence in your wife is a miracle of faith. If you knew what she's up to in her lunch hour."

He is pretty sure who it must have been — a nurse he had fired, totally wrong for the job, one of his rare bad choices. It was an act of malice, that was all. The note is in the breast pocket of a little-used jacket. It is signed "From the Center," and he felt for a while as if something vital *had* been withdrawn from his core. Sometimes he looks at Ellen when she cannot see him. Does he believe it or not? Is it possible? No — impossible!

Yet sometimes he pictures how it might be with Ellen at lunch time. She is in one of those apartments near her hospital that so many doctors keep for their late nights, or so they say. She is lying on someone's bed. She is propped up. He is kissing. She is fondling. With a thunderous shout, Edgar bursts through the door!

All this comes because of worrying about Genevieve X, Edgar tells himself. And Genevieve X comes because of the Center. And how has the Center come about? Never as a boy had he thought of becoming a doctor. What he had loved was ball. "Play ball, play ball," his mother complained, "every day." When he came reluctantly home at dark the phonograph was always going. "Opera, opera," he said in retaliation. But he could feel his mother was proud of his strength, smiling half-bashfully at the sight of his muscular body in his purple high school trunks and shirt. After he'd left home it astonished him to discover how much of opera had crept into him. He distrusted that swelling-up of feeling, like a boil on the heart.

In the first month of his freshman year at an upstate college — he'd won an athletic scholarship — he received a midnight call. A woman's voice said his sister Mimi was sick and couldn't stay where she was. It whispered an address in eastern Massachusetts. Edgar borrowed a car, and all night, driving, he heard arias from *La Bohème* in his head. He pictured his beautiful sister propped against a pillow, coughing like that other Mimi. But there was no opera written with a scene like what he saw. First, he was let onto the decayed porch of a shabby house that stood alone at the edge of a field. Then a stout woman led him up dark stairs to a top-floor room. No words, only her harsh breathing, a frightening sound in the otherwise silent house.

What was it like? What was it like? The room swam in a terrible mist of fear. His twenty-year-old sister — Mimi — was hunched into a corner on the floor. Her long hair, always worn up, was spilled to one side where she had ground her head at the wall. Never before had he seen her naked body. Now he saw it. Her heavy breasts were — They rested on her knees like — Oozing there from — A tremor shook his bones. This blood-spattered page from the Book of Bad Girls, this hideous caricature of the Bad Girl's Hell — this could not be Mimi!

In her delirium she whispered. He had had to dress Mimi with the stout woman's help and drive her to the hospital — the woman would not permit an ambulance to come to that address. A nurse told him afterward that what Mimi had whispered over and over was something about "the Portuguese fisherman in the white Cadillac." Edgar thought it hallucination. But after her death he drove to Cape Cod, slowly, slowly, along the coast, looking. Not hard to find in those narrow streets in the dead of winter, out on the very spit of the land, itself curved like a fishhook. Much harder to resist the impulse to wait beside the car and kill its owner! Edgar set the police on to it and soon they had him, the fisherman, septic fishhook in hand, ready to pierce some poor creature on the back seat of the Cadillac, which he had driven onto the deserted winter beach.

The screams, sobs, curses of his parents had nearly driven him mad. They still echoed in his head. His father had never relented in his shame and disgust for his daughter — only to his mother had Edgar been able to tell his ambition. But even that he had kept vague. She had died — he had almost thanked God — before the Center opened.

The white Cadillac drove Edgar to medicine. Then for years he had lobbied, with physicians and other groups, to repeal the antiabortion laws. He and a handful of enlightened colleagues tried to redress the wrong done by earlier physicians, who had not liked that the pleas of the desperate were answered by lay women — a kind of midwifery of abortion. Those jealous physicians campaigned by crying out against maternal deaths. The deaths in childbirth at the hands of the medical profession itself they ignored. Thus the deaths multiplied, as abortions were driven further underground.

Long before his goal was realized, Edgar began to plan the Center. "For Mimi," he said. "For poor Mimi, and all like her "

The permutations of grandparent-generation immigrating had altered the spelling of the family name from the Italian Bianchia to its present form. Edgar would have liked to change it again to the anglicized Banks, and to call the Center that, the Banks Family Planning Center. So unforgiving had he felt about Catholic strictures that had forced his sister to a literal end of earth to meet her death.

He had not altered his name. Could never bring himself to join the ranks of background-changers, ashamed of forebears. He was a heavyset, swarthy man, taken for Jew or Armenian. That was all right with Edgar. Blond Ellen, with her deceptive look of delicacy, was prize enough from the Protestant world. And so, as Bianky, the Center opened. Edgar was staggered by the response. A thousand women every month. All together — at his own and other clinics — a million women a year. Where would they all have gone? To the Portuguese fisherman?

Sometimes, in the midst of the cleanliness and freshness of the Bianky Center, Edgar's nostrils again filled with the penetrating odor of Mimi's death place, the farmhouse where the smell of mold seemed to rise from some earth-deep corruption.

As soon as possible after the liberalizing of the New York State abortion laws in 1970, Edgar quit his obstetrics practice and opened the Center. He put into it nearly every penny he and Ellen had saved. When it was done, he was satisfied — the humane design of its space! Procedure rooms. Recoveries. Lounges. The whole Center staff knew how much more had been done than was needed. They marveled at the altruism. Whatever had been buried before in darkness and fear was now redeemed by beauty and light.

Edgar — "Bunky" to his colleagues — couldn't have swung the financial investment or handled the volume of patients, responsibility, alone. He regretted having to take on as partners two brilliant but erratic men. There they were — Charlie Brodaw and Paul of the ironic surname: Sunshine. Teacher and pupil.

Edgar had made the largest financial investment and had final say in policy decisions. Charlie had put in a sizable chunk of money, but left management to Edgar. Paul had no money at all, and so contributed all his time. A contingent of doctors who gave one or two days a week to the Center completed the roster. Some of them still behaved like horses' asses, hiding their Center activities from their "respectable" gynecology practice.

Once it had even happened that a patient, intimidated by her doctor's public disapproval of abortion on demand, had concealed her secret from him as he his from her, and had then encountered him in one of Edgar's procedure rooms. A comic bit of dialogue, just before the anesthetic took, had escaped from under the tent of melodrama:

"Dr. Medlar! *You!*"

"Miss Lovestone! You *here!*"

Edgar defied the mentality of the horses' asses. With emotion, he spoke these stubborn words shortly after the Center opened its doors one bitterly cold November day: "We will be a national byword for safety and the highest type of medical practice. Not the first or the biggest clinic, but by God the best!"

Charlie had listened with that unnerving half-smile of his.

Paul had said, "They'll still call us a mill, Bunky. It will never be the Harkness Pavilion."

Edgar knew which way Paul's bitterness cut. Nevertheless, the words had stung. He had then hired special aides. Motherly women who soothed the clients and helped to avert — Edgar prayed — catastrophe. He worried about everyone, about his partners almost more than the rest.

In fact, everything is going splendidly. Yet Edgar suffers. When he thinks of what can happen! Worried, becoming fat, made nervous by the responsibility and guilty by the amounts of money that pour in despite his efforts to keep fees down, Edgar imagines disasters. He feels them in his bones, sees them projected under his eyelids at night, in the darkness, away from the rational white lights of his sane, life-giving procedure rooms. Ellen, trying to probe through at his back, cannot prevent what goes on behind his shut eyes.

He imagines that his beautiful Center, which depends on word of mouth for its large practice even more than on doctor's referrals — he has scorned the slimy practice of linking up with one of those "free" consulting agencies that are no more than self-referral fronts — shuts down permanently.

First a shaken aide has to go into the waiting room and announce repeatedly "All appointments are canceled!" to a disbelieving crowd of women. There are in all at that moment (he decides) one hundred women waiting in various stages of pregnancy.

Some have waited for weeks to be placed on the appointment schedule. A similar wait elsewhere would mean, in many cases, going beyond the first three months of pregnancy. The abortion would then have to be done in hospital by injections of saline solution to kill the fetus and produce hard labor in the mother.

Edgar then outdoes himself in imagining a scene of catastrophe. It is worthy, in the terribleness of its crashing, of *Don Giovanni*. Though a few who know about it think it closer to Olsen and Johnson, or some other team of comic ineptitude. Not that the fantasy itself could ever be funny — no, it is horrifying enough. But *something* about it is funny, because this dedicated doctor, giving everything he can to the task at hand — this doctor, sweating and getting fat over it — *he* is somehow funny, as overconcern and anxiety in others are always funny. They strike comically on the cruel part of our natures, that cruelty which itself springs from the terror and hatred we feel for our own fears, and for which the best we can do in the way of a civilized coating is to temper cruelty with affection. Who at the Center does not amuse himself *affectionately* with Edgar's disproportionate pain?

A shrieking goes up. Women grab flowerpots from the window ledges and fling them through the glass, which falls onto the shoulders of two ambulance attendants and an intern below, just entering the building in response to the emergency call. The intern's neck artery is lacerated by plunging glass, and emergency treatment must be given to him on the floor of the lobby. The ambulance then rushes him back to the hospital, leaving Genevieve X to be retrieved later.

Now some of the waiting women are making their way along the corridors, through the recovery rooms, where fifty women occupy beds in various states of stupor, past the conference alcoves — all of these rooms so beautifully, quietly appointed; soothing music is still being piped in — and on to the procedure rooms. There they discover the dead woman lying in blood-soaked sheets, her chest slashed open, a portion of her entrails extruded from her vagina.

Without his knowing how or why, his beloved Center has turned into the Portuguese fisherman's white Cadillac. "How did it happen?" Edgar whispers.

Ellen smiles in affectionate knowledge. "You feel guilty because you've made money from work you wanted to give your life to, that's all it is. You don't *need* to feel that way but you do. All it is is *ironic,* darling!"

She reasons, his beautiful wife, as coolly as she speaks. But Edgar has other sounds in his ear, other scenes in his eye. His mother sits in his memory, screaming, screaming — the neighbor women put cloths on her head, his sisters hold her hands to keep her from tearing her hair, her cheeks. His father, having groped his way into a rage more bearable to him than grief, pushes the women aside and shoves with the hard heel of his hand at the soft sweating flesh of his mother's arm. "What did you teach her? What did you make her? A whore!" Edgar hits him — his father, dead many years. He feels the bone in his father's nose crack, and the old man, worn out with grieving, falls away from under his fist and lies on the floor like a corpse. More blood, more screaming. They all go mad. Much, much later they were able to give each other heartbroken kisses. His mother survived to old age, his father became prosperous — a fleet of fat-bellied cement trucks rumbled over the roadways of northern New York. But the screams of his mother! The curses of his father! Not all the coolness in his wife's well-shaped hand can tamp down those fires, or make *piano* those grand, *forte* cries in his soul.

So he sweats and sleeps and wakes and sleeps and wakes more. Through it all a woman's voice (coloratura) shrieks repeatedly from behind the closed office doors, "You're all abortions yourselves!"

Now and then, thank God, the old joy of life reasserts itself. Edgar and Ellen take a ship's cruise to the Mediterranean. Edgar at once tans a beautiful mahogany-brown, wins at shuffleboard, draws admirers to poolside with his powerful racing-stroke swimming, and tries a rusty Italian with the stewards. A doctor of his acquaintance tells him of a two-week archeological dig in Sicily among Etruscan ruins, and Edgar books Ellen and himself into the next session. He has a wonderful time, wears shorts and wields a shovel, grows hard-muscled again, shouts and runs about the trenches happily picking up pottery shards that his guide has planted there like fish in a stocked pond. It never occurs to Edgar — though it does to Ellen — that he has not gotten so far from his métier, and that in his free time he is digging treasure from another kind of womb. Ellen stays beside the hotel pool and reads. When Edgar proudly shows his calloused palms, she kisses them. He feels like a boy again. Physical workout is uppermost; the worried mind goes happily to sleep after the pickax sings.

Edgar toys with an idea: he may abandon the whole painful enterprise on Sixth Avenue. He may slip into some child's play like sex therapy, as some of his obstetrics colleagues have done. There is even one, Gorman, an uncertain gynecologist at best, who has foisted himself on television audiences with his wife, formerly a junior high school counselor. A sex team! She chatters happily away at a stricken-looking couple; he puffs his pipe and asks a single question near the end: "Now are you folks willing to give it a shot?"

But it takes very little to bring Mimi back to Edgar's mind. Soon he is in New York on Sixth Avenue in the Fifties, up on the seventh — the lucky — floor, walking everywhere in his rumpled white coat, keeping eyes on everyone, and nearly crushed by concern.

Ellen, watching him droop now, seeing the handsome head lower itself in weariness and worry, feels surge up inside her a heated protectiveness. She rubs, strokes, caresses his heavy body. Keeps up a constant flow of soothing, scolding, stinging advice, uttered in restrained, low-key tones. And often she wonders: From where have these disguised, heated passions come? From Edgar's mother during their stay in her house before her death, years ago? Was it possible to learn the fervor of a whole culture in a single week? And then to translate it into the voice of another culture?

Ellen is, to Edgar's conscious mind, bracing in her detachment. She is also warmly, deeply concerned for him in a way so like his mother that he has never noticed it. He is, everyone at the Center agrees, a man doubly blessed in his marriage. Unless, of course, those rumors, spread by a few disgruntled ones as they left the employ of the Center, are true. In that case, what a curse! As much as anything else at the Center, this tantalizing doubleness of possibility about Edgar's private life prompts more than one nurse or aide there to reflect, about her years of experience with the human drama, "Oh, I could write a book!"

And then in the evening, Edgar groans to Ellen, "Can you imagine if Genevieve X really happened? What would the world say? The whole right-to-choice effort would be tainted. And the Jews there! Brodaw, Sunshine. People would say: Jews! what do you expect? They'd say, A Jewish doctors' plot to do away with babies."

With her bright, brisk, enlightened brain, Ellen will not tolerate the tolerating of slurs. "Do we listen to what the cretins say? I call that waste of energy. Better to channel it elsewhere." Ellen's voice at its most caustically stinging. She begins to rub the back of his neck with long deep strokes.

He sighs. "And I have a feeling there are a few love affairs going on there, among the staff."

"*Who?*" Ellen forgets her tone is meant for medicine. It changes to open curiosity.

But Edgar cannot be diverted to gossip. "Can you believe it? Right there, they actually have the strength, the drive to make love!"

"Is it so draining to work there?" Her voice now appears to take on a different, special edge. He notes it sadly, and then goes on, pretending to have heard nothing but the question.

"Totally." He feels himself asleep, but then adds, "Do you know what Rothenberg, who comes in on Tuesdays and Thursdays, told me? He said when the aspirator is vacuuming he hears this nonsense going round and round in his head: 'The wages of sex are thin.' "

"What does he mean, 'thin'?"

"He means as it gets sucked up the tube."

She rubs harder at the knots in his shoulders. Amazing, the strength in her slender fingers . . . He drifts into sleep again and wakes with a start.

Ellen must know his broken sleep patterns all too well. How can he expect her to put up with it? At the same time — if only Paul could have a wife as loyal as Ellen, he thinks, it might make all the difference. Charlie, thank God, has Sylvia, a staunch woman.

Was it one of the physicians at her hospital? Was it icy-cold men, he wondered, that Ellen would pick?

He is out of bed and heading for the kitchen. Ellen follows. "My desk is heaped . . ." he says.

Ellen knows what's coming. The wound to which she applies caustic at one end continues to ooze at the other.

Daily on Edgar's desk the pile of envelopes, folders, flyers. Antiabortion brochures bombard him. Even now he sometimes brings them home, finds they've hopped into his pocket like fleas. There's one now in his pajama breast.

" 'God does care about all the seed that gets wasted!' " Edgar removes it, rustling, reading it aloud.

"That explains why God has no time to care about anything else," Ellen snaps.

" ' — But most of all, don't dare to uproot the seed that takes hold. God's will is in that seed . . .' "

"I hope not, thinking of some seeds I've had the misfortune to know."

" 'Suppose' " — Edgar skims another — " 'the seed that got aborted held a Savior?' "

"Or a Satan? A Hitler. A Genghis Khan."

" 'Tiny little feet,' they say. They show pictures of little feet. At ten weeks."

"Those little feet" — Ellen cries it out, letting her passion at last come through — "they wouldn't lift a hand to help those feet once they're out of the womb!"

"But I even understand their fear. If they think there's no necessity, no inevitability about birth, no *had to be,* then nothing stops them from the thought 'There is no God and there doesn't even have to be me!' "

"Don't be so understanding!"

Having forgotten why he came to the kitchen — it was to drink tea and read more medical journals — Edgar now follows Ellen back to the bedroom. If she feels how much she loves him, if even her flesh does, does she still fear that if it makes do with a steady diet of only him, it may lose hold of its possibilities? Do the icy-cold men, he asks himself, arouse her more?

She embraces him. She is much smaller than he, and her arms reach only halfway around his ribs. Through the pain of his doubt, he feels delight at the touch of this small strong woman who roots herself in the world like a giant tree.

"Has-to-be-you and has-to-be-me will go to bed now, darling. And after that we'll get some sleep."

When he closes his eyes he can see the Center in its perfection. Pearl-colored walls. Sea-blue panels. He had craved some tone of the coast, of that lovely seashore where his sister had gone expecting life and had found death. Pure horizon light comes into the rooms. Drapery threads spin themselves of air and sun. Sixth Avenue in the Fifties, its dingy reality, is shut out as surely as the pain and humiliation of the dark pre-Bianky Center days. Mini-gardens instead — flowering geranium and begonia and violet. And to ensure the keeping of gardens and the adjusting of draperies and reed-woven shades, he employs one more orderly than is really needed. His job also to stagger in daily with filled produce bags. The smell of fresh fruit in the recovery rooms is now sacred custom. Here the women wake. Some euphoric and ravenously hungry. Some self-punishing, wanting to deny themselves even a taste of anything good. The fruit is there — bowls of it. Edgar sees, smells it. Apples, bananas, oranges, pears as fat and yellow as butter, or crisp and long, their skins a tan silk. Grapes cluster like miraculous offspring. As if to murmur — those everlasting shapes — to the waking women on their cots: "Why lament a few blasted buds? There can be no end to fruitfulness!"

The women wake; Edgar sinks toward rest. Harmony, as in the great reconciliation scene at the close of *Le Nozze di Figaro*, rises to embrace him, and he can — though he knows it is not to be trusted and won't endure — end his bedtime performance in the silent applause of sleep.

2

NOW AND THEN the strongly muscled arm of one of
the orderlies reaches across at the next table for something. Or a nurse, for emphasis, flings a hand up into
the breeze they're all shooting. Light streams over the lunch
room, enriching skin tones from bleached to black. Felicity of
design. The lunch room shares it with the rest of the Center.
Staff members eat with gusto amid an anecdotal din and fra-
grances of fine seasoning. Bunky is a generous employer. Paul
Sunshine, who figures they could all have lived without the
fancy slanting shades here — sunlight is Bunky's balm —
unconsciously shifts his chair to bask, and goes on speaking:
"You know how much I respect and admire him, Bunky. But
how much of his own life can a man throw away and still live?"

"A father figure," Edgar murmurs. "Naturally you're concerned."

Paul shakes his head. A flopping lock of black hair catches
behind his glasses, which he wears for reading but sometimes
also — memories of a deprived boyhood make him want to
bring whatever is tasty into nearer focus — for eating. He
grabs out the hair with nervous fingers, very clean from repeated scrub-ups, only now a bit sticky from the marinated

artichoke hearts. Or the three-bean salad. Or the peperoncini vinaigrette. Condiments clot the surfaces of the tables. Paul thinks it waste, but piles his plate gratefully, like everybody else.

He sets Bunky straight. Bunky is the father figure. Charlie the brother one. Fortunate older, better-endowed brother. Now in some kind of mortal danger — but he doesn't plunge into that yet.

Instead he blurts, "Naturally, I envy him too. Till *I* got to be a doctor! Spanish anatomy. *El caudal sanguineo. La cabeza. Enfermedad del corazón.* But I *know* that!"

Paul's tone is still overexcited. On his way to the lunch room, minutes before, he had seen the face of a young woman walled into the wall. The face was pretty, heart-shaped, young. Brown ringlets cascaded down on either side of the face. A hand brushed at the ringlets while tears trickled onto the round cheeks.

Oh my God, Paul had thought.

The face was in the wall because a one-way window has been set into the corridor outside the waiting room. On the window's reverse side there hangs a mirror. Though all the woman sees is her trouble, she can be looked at by any passing member of the staff.

Naturally, Paul thought, it's me.

As he caught sight of the glass-framed face, it was faintly shadowed by the reflection of his own — long, pale, with a dark wave of hair falling forward. Paul wished that Bunky's vigilance had not taken this clever turn. He wished neither glass nor faces — not hers, not his — were there.

At the bend in the corridor he had stopped, drawn uncomfortably back. By then the woman's face was gone. No point entering. Needle in a hairstack. One of the counselor aides would catch her anyway.

He peered through the window. The women sat in their rows. They are always there. With the smell of cold on their coats, snow on their boots in winter. With bare arms and legs in summer. Like fields or trees, always there. Motionless. Planted.

As he walked on he held them in his mental eye: the stoical silence with which so many, all at the same time, endure their waiting! He admires them — strong, resilient. *I* should be so resilient! He feels continual astonishment.

But that was not what was on his mind when he hurried toward the lunch room. What he had to tell was about Charlie. Urgently. So that Bunky could use his influence. Before whatever Charlie had in mind to do was done, and everything too late. If he was lucky, he'd thought, hurrying, he'd catch hold of Bunky for a talk. And maybe even beautiful Hannah, the new counselor aide.

He had found the first. He has yet to achieve the second.

Edgar listens with drooping, skeptical eyes. He is waiting out Paul's excitement, to interpose a subject of his own: Wouldn't Paul like a week's vacation?

"Charlie's going to kill his wife, I think," Paul blurts. "Poor Sylvia!"

"Charlie?" Edgar gives him a startled stare. "Has another woman?"

Paul is startled in turn by the practicalness of the question. He says Charlie hasn't.

Edgar's creased, heavy face turns fully toward him. Paul gazes at this large, anxious-looking man who is smitten by responsibility as other men are by love, who spoils digestion with worry, fattens himself on care. Paul would like to tell Edgar that he admires him for bearing humbly in public, like a woman in late pregnancy, the fruits of what smote him.

"Come, then!"

Paul can't believe Bunky doesn't understand.

"He wants *her* to be free."

"That may be, but . . ."

"Or he'll drive her to suicide with his nagging. I've been witness."

Edgar shakes his big head. Cannot repress the brilliant smile in his dark face. The trouble with your deep worrier! He knows he overdoes it in certain areas, so he'll underdo in others. Edgar is robust for once, Italianate. Someone else's fears bring out native, life-embracing optimism. Besides, none of this directly touches the Center.

"Charlie's good sense will prevail. And Sylvia — that even-natured, modest woman? Paul, relax! Why not think positively? We all ought to. Our work should teach us, if anything, to believe that, Paul. If it teaches anything. If anything does teach that."

Edgar's desire for clarity of language sometimes causes him, like a composer working out his themes, to repeat, invert, or counterpoint his comments, an anxious music.

"You ought to take" — finally Edgar says it — "a little vacation. Fly off somewhere for a week. Steal seven days and run away."

"I can't break the pattern of visits with my kids, Bunky. You know Margaret. She'd snatch them back if I missed."

Edgar pushes away his plate as if to leave. But Paul won't let him.

"And now" — Paul is plunging on again — "with Sylvia it's all part of the same idealism. But it's almost — no — it *is* unbelievable! How Charlie's trying now to get rid of such a wife!"

Paul gestures excitedly. His long fingers send careening the small vase of fresh flowers (fortunately with little water) as well as the pot of sweet chow-chow. Both spill some of their contents onto his cheese-and-mushroom quiche with a side of veal and lemon sauce. A sharp mustard smell settles over the table. He decides to continue eating as if he hasn't noticed. Bunky, who notices everything, looks away toward the next table. Paul hopes the sight of his staff there will restore him.

After a silence, Edgar speaks in a voice that is sometimes

more, sometimes less, agitated, like a man before an interesting but precipitous view. "Canary-colored uniforms on the aides. It *is* cheerful, Paul! Those women are a special triumph. Everyone chosen for a pleasant countenance, a ready, sympathetic tongue, and the maturity of years. Except for Selig, of course." He lowers his voice. "Selig is the first *young* woman I've ever hired. Twenty-five years old. Though something about her seems older. On the whole I've been well enough pleased with her to hire another young woman aide. She won't be coming for a while — " Abruptly, Edgar cuts himself off and a flush darkens his face. He resumes, "I hired Selig on a hunch."

"What hunch, Bunky?"

"That some women who come here would prefer to shed their tears before the lonely and displaced. But I now and then have doubts."

"What doubts?"

"Is her displacement too much for women already feeling displaced? Feeling their own displacement, will they resent hers?"

After a silent moment, in which Paul offers no hint of answer, Edgar goes on, "It may add an ugly note."

"But she's a beauty, Bunky!" Paul blurts it before he can stop.

A crease in Edgar's forehead registers a new complication.

"In need of repair, of course . . ." Paul tries lamely to cover his tracks.

Bunky veers off. "We insist on freedom. It's the glory and curse of modern life. What some call freedom others call . . ."

Believing that Bunky has returned to the subject of Charlie and Sylvia, Paul can't resist breaking in with passion, "And what a sweet woman, Sylvia! And patient. And loving. She waited up for Charlie in the old days, no matter how late. With a hot dinner — you know I was practically a boarder even after my internship. She tells me now she misses those days. Misses them! God, to have such a woman. To count on such care!"

"Well — you see — though I was speaking of Selig — it's not everything for some. Some make nothing of it."

"But she was happy! Not complaining! Do you understand it? — it's Charlie! He's the one who's trying to break it up."

Edgar smiles with shocking unperturbableness, enjoying a mistaken moment of serenity snatched from other troubles. That note about Ellen, he is positive, is a lie. "These women" — he says it with calm warmth — "will educate us yet."

"Dr. Bianky! Dr. Bianky!" The loudspeaker cries out as if with Paul's own anguished inner voice. Hearing himself paged, Edgar leaves in a hurry. Paul sops Edgar's paper napkin into the puddle on the table. He feels he has made an equivalent mess of the conversation.

✦ ✦

Now that he is eating alone (on a fresh plate, banana- and cranberry-bread slices are sloped together like the walls of a house, a blueberry muffin on top for a plump chimney: Paul meditatively demolishes house and chimney; he eats like this and his rangy body looks, if anything, undernourished), he is penetrated by sound.

Hubbub of voices and accents at nearby tables. West Indian, Spanish, Irish — plus a din of dialects, American-born. After the manner of nurses, the aides call each other by their last names. Warner. Bomstein. Selig. Only Mary is Mary, in the mysterious ways of naming among colleagues.

Someone from time to time breaks into a recollection from an earlier nursing career. To which, in chorus, aides, orderlies, and nurses never fail to respond "You ought to write that down in a book!" Variously accented.

If Bunky were here they wouldn't joke so boldly. Volumes under way, you'd think, to hear them give out encouragement. Paul knows these jokes. All hot air, according to Charlie. They'd rather yak than write. Thank God.

He wonders all the same if he would come out well in their works.

He feels Hannah looking. Intense, pale, engrossed. He sees from memory. Everyone in the place says, "Poor Selig." Something about her life he doesn't know. He finds her ravishingly beautiful. Amazing gray-green eyes behind the glasses. And beautiful hair. Though it sucks color from her makeupless cheeks. All vividness is in the gold-orange that radiates about her head. Somebody could teach her makeup, clothes, colors. And she doesn't take advantage of Bunky's good food. Her elegant slimness borders on fragility.

It's pleasant; it gives him pleasure that she often looks at him. He turns and catches her at it sometimes. All the same, when he had asked her to dinner she had refused. "It would not work out well," she had mysteriously said. Yet he feels her interest. As she must feel his.

He is boyish-looking for thirty-eight, he knows. A confused and irresponsible personal history has kept him from showing age. It's like a dividend from tainted money. What can he do? Accept whatever dividends come.

Men can take their time, women can't. How come Hannah doesn't know that?

The hundred waiting women. An awed sense of them again comes over him. And a hundred more each day, caught in a dimension of time beyond what's common to the species. Time-ridden as well as -bound.

He starts on his chocolate cake. With a sweetened tongue, he reflects further on his hopes. His ex-wife, Margaret, had made his character lapses clear. She'd been on the receiving end of them long enough to get a good look, he supposed. He meant to change!

Had Hannah been trying to tell him that he should first be one hundred percent wholehearted? Was that when things would work out? When had he ever been one hundred percent wholehearted about anything? How farseeing were those amazing eyes?

When he listens again, she has the same nothing to say. Before long, someone cries, "Warner, love! *You* ought to write a book!"

"I ought to. I should. With all the stories I know. On the terminal wards for years. That's where you see human nature. Some of the relatives begrudge the poor patient his last five minutes!"

Like a threat, Bomstein ominously adds, "If I ever put the things *I've* seen into a book . . ."

"Why don't you?"

"How once I saw a nephew — he stood to inherit — messing with the plug! And a poor vegetable stewed in its own mucus for two years because the wife liked the companionship of the ward!"

"Put it down!" they cry.

"And what goes on here," Bomstein says. "The world does-n't know the half."

She lowers her voice, and the chorus, lowering theirs, an-swers, "Put it down. You ought to."

"I often think it's funny to think of it, the Center. You know what I think's the center? Two by two, where it all begins, is where."

"Two by two, is that the center?"

"No, it's one with one."

"Man and woman?"

"Man and man, woman and woman, or any one with an-other. That's what I mean."

"Start with that then!"

"I'm definitely starting. Oh, you can see the whole thing laid out plain when you start with one and one, which is at the center. There's nothing can escape you then if you know how to look at one and one!"

"Selig too, aren't you?"

She headshakes no.

"You can't see much, mon — your eyes love-blurred."

Shielding his glance under the fallen lock of hair, Paul sees how Hannah's look travels — with interruptions, with cautious eye-lowerings and resumptions — over him sprawled there.

The eyes are extraordinary. Behind outmoded narrow black harlequin glasses, of the sort foisted on female patients fifteen years before, are the large gray-green irises, roundly curved, alively staring. Her mouth is full-lipped, tender, though the lips are whitened and chapped, poor lips.

In another sneaked look, Paul sees the aides and nurses grinning wickedly at him. Selig's fingers twitch with small writing movements on her uniformed knee.

Paul notes all this with pleasure, but then must leave disappointed. There is no chance to talk to Hannah.

◦§ §◦

Once more a woman in the wall! Dry, wide, stoical eyes. Bitter down-turned mouth. Why does he look? She withdraws.

As he is about to divert his gaze from the window, the elevator door opens. Charlie Brodaw passes through into the waiting room.

Paul marvels again at the change in Charlie since they'd met in interning days. The pudgy son of the famous doctor-father has vanished. In its place is a lean, slight figure in a well-cut suit. His partly bald head is close-cropped. His skin tanned. His face, once a puffy ball, is elongated, with a hard vertical crease in each cheek. Bony jaw. Long blue eyes. After his illness, the small body frame is visible for the first time. He looks elegant, delicate yet impressive.

Capable of anything?

If I were in a play, then just about now, Paul thinks, I'd make a pact with the Devil. Say into the air, "If I can have that part — the real medical practice, the doting wife, the self-assurance — then I'll take it all. Sickness too. Obsession."

He shudders. Happiness without demons, he'd meant! He vows to leave off "fixating" on Charlie — Margaret's word. He had his ex-wife's word on most of his faults. More truth in a bad marriage, probably, than a good one.

I'll take pride in the work. Limited but necessary.

Paul loiters in the corridor outside the ladies' room. He traces with his forefinger a delicate pattern of white scallop shells hand-blocked onto sand-colored wallpaper.

A woman emerges with a green coat thrown over her arm.

"Good afternoon!" He hears himself professional and brisk, feels his smile comically stiff and possibly lopsided.

"Good afternoon." She looks startled and stops in her tracks.

"Just try to relax." Paul's fingers move in the pocket of his white coat, hoping to find a folded stethescope. But his pockets, naturally, are empty.

"I do try." She faces him now attentively, as if it occurs to her this encounter may be part of the free therapy sessions the Center offers. The coat on her arm begins to dip toward the floor. "I am relaxed."

Her dark hair is cut short and is well brushed. Her age seems about twenty-three or -four. She has just applied fresh mauve lipstick.

"Well, that's fine." He plumps up his voice with what he recalls, from when he was in residence, of Dr. Bodein's special hospital-renowned bedside manner. Slow rhythms, round vowels, tender tones, homey, short words. "It may seem like a lot of waiting. But your turn will come up soon."

She looks at him curiously. "I already had it."

"Ah," he says. "Then — good luck."

He walks on abruptly, hoping that no one besides this puzzled person has seen or heard him make an ass of himself.

Even Dr. Bodein might have had trouble with a stand-up bedside manner. Though Charlie probably wouldn't. He's back to Charlie!

The trouble is, he knows Charlie's life in a way better than his own. First, envy motored him to note every scrap. He had lived with Charlie and Sylvia while interning, before he married. Again for a while after his divorce from Margaret. Then Charlie became his friend, talked about his life in that peculiar, careless way of his. As if he had no personal interest in it. Or no — as if personal interest itself led to mocking self-appraisal. Then Paul, in defense against Charlie's own careless recital of events, memorized and took under his protection the naked unchampioned bones of biography.

By degrees Charlie's life, career, troubles — childhood and otherwise — became more to him than his own, which bears no thinking about. Yet it is somehow in connection — in contrast — with his own life that it is now a source of fascination and pride to him that he works with two altruists — Bunky and Charlie — the one a worried father to the world, the other a cool scientist, scraping away at human tissue before it rots. In short, he prefers Charlie's past to his own. The lows and the highs. Having seen Charlie through the distancing lunch room window brings it all back . . . Especially, of course, the highs . . . Charlie's noble act on that May evening in 1969 . . .

3

PAUL MORE THAN THINKS about Charlie's noble act. He makes it his own on his way to the procedure room. Once there, he glances briefly and, he believes, tactfully at the tense-faced woman lying on the table. Her legs are cramped into the stirrups, her thighs opened into a sheet-covered V. Her arm is extended to the anesthetist, who has already inserted the needle attached to the drip tube. Concerned with nothing but the tube, the drip, the arm, and the monitoring gauge, he waits, at the doctor's nod, to release a clamp.

Paul withholds the nod. He moves up toward the head of the table and speaks to the woman lying there.

"How are you doing?"

"Scared." She whispers through barely moving lips.

"There's nothing to be scared about."

The woman's teeth begin to chatter. He feels her chill seep up at him through the sheet.

"Maybe if you know what I'm going to do" — he begins again — "you won't feel there's anything strange or frightening. It's just that this suction machine here . . ."

"Oh, God! Don't tell me!"

Paul swallows the rest of his words and gives the anesthetist the nod.

He, poker-faced, releases the clamp: the drip flows, the patient sighs herself unconscious.

Paul begins the seven-minute routines of safe, sane, legal abortion.

All the while, behind his strict, exact attention, a comforting scene unfolds. The romance of the old days. He makes it his. Charlie's heroic act.

It is late afternoon. Charlie's father, himself a physician, stands in Charlie's own waiting room, fiercely whispering.

"Is this what you call sane?"

It is hoarsely, passionately repeated.

An ironical tilt to the right of Charlie's pudgy head, with black ringlets and waves that bounce on the tilt.

His father chews a furious cigar. Obese, short of breath — and why else but because of all those years of running, running, in behalf of his patients? Never eating or sleeping right, he has proved devotion and has every right now to shout.

He shouts. "Let this one do what the others do. She can put a pillow on its face after. Or give it to adoption."

An ironical tilt to Charlie's left.

His father flaps his hands toward the corners of Charlie's office.

"If you throw this away you help nobody!"

Spacious. And always filled. Empty now except for the two nurses, straightening things up in the examining rooms before they leave. And all ears you can bet.

His father gasps like a runner. "You don't have to do what everybody asks you!"

Beat, beat, in his father's neck. Half-smiling on Charlie's face.

"I don't?"

His father never liked Charlie's ironic bent. Bent against

himself. A father scorns to respond to that. Plus what physician, exalted by the reverence of women in thousands, some of them blessing in Yiddish his golden hands, his remarkable head, wants an ironical son?

"How could she ask?" Charlie says. "She doesn't know enough to. She just came by to see if it was so."

"Then why, why, tell me why . . .!" His father's veins pump up ancient exasperation, rusty red on his neck. Charlie, till he looks again at his father, wants to shout. Then old age, the parent-punisher, takes away his rage.

"You always said" — half-smile — "a doctor is father and mother to the patient."

His father stares. Looks sick. "Father and mother don't make this kind of work."

"Only because it's not legal yet."

"Legal yet?" It's a chance for his father to recover from his own words. "Two *days* before it is legal is the same as two *years!* This tramp will tell the world. She'll send her cousins. They squat under every bush. If you don't take them on, they'll blackmail with police. When your patients find out you broke the law, do you think they'll think, 'Such a good man — he terminates pregnancies for the poor and the underage?' "

His father's speech mixes medical detachment and choler, in the manner of self-made immigrant sons — steady strivers whose rage breaks out at baffles.

"No!" His father thunders at him. "They'll think, 'Why should I trust him? If he broke one law he'll break two.' I don't agree with the Park Avenue crooks. I don't agree with the AMA that thinks the whole system will collapse if a patient knows the doctor farts. But I agree in one thing. A doctor obeys the law!"

Riva and Golda in the back keep their ears open but do not comment to one another about the conversation they are overhearing. They move about the examining rooms. They collect and label urine samples, blood samples, vaginal smears. They clean and store in the proper enamel drawers the fitting-diaphragms, the metal instruments and lubricants. They prepare each of the cotlike tables for the morning with a fresh cotton sheet and a runner of heavy paper. They wipe, at the base of each table, the iron stirrups and leggings. (Paul's hand shakes with an instant's tremor, grieving for the lost articles of his lost profession.)

Unlike his father, Charlie knows how women feel about those tables. Knows how they feel about the introduction of the doctor's gloved hand, the penetration of the metal speculum and other instruments into the vagina. Women confess their feelings to Charlie. They are right to do so, Paul concedes. It is as if they sense his altruism, his efforts on Sylvia's behalf, his noble act of May 1969 . . .

Meanwhile, Paul's hand expertly guides the nozzle of the aspirator through the cervix, which resembles a million other cervixes, of this woman whose name he has no interest in knowing.

Next to the nurse's desk in the antechamber stands the father's oak armchair. Since his retirement, his father has come to Charlie's office each morning to occupy that chair. On the seat, a black leather cushion is depressed at midcenter from his bulky weight. The influence of Charlie's father on Charlie has been great. Nevertheless, this night in 1969, Charlie disregards it. He dismisses Golda and Riva (faithful Golda taken over from his father's office; Riva, Charlie's own peppery-tongued discovery), and receives in his office the fifteen-year-old girl whom he knows only as Maria.

She comes alone. She wears tight jeans with rolled-up bottoms and high-heeled vinyl boots and a round-necked T-shirt. Imprinted on the T-shirt is a tropical scene of flamingos and palms.

Her face is thin and dark, her eyes lit up with fear, her lips bitten bloody.

Charlie speaks to her in a quiet voice. All trace of his mocking disguise has vanished.

"Did you tell your mother and father about this, Maria?"

She shakes her head of rich black hair. "My father beat up my sister once when she wanted to do it." Her voice has a child's hoarseness. "Then he made her and her boyfriend get married."

"Do you want to stay single for a while, Maria?"

She looks down. A fury she didn't dare express when she met his gaze escapes her.

"Why shou-int I?" She makes an extra elision in the contraction. Its effect is to deepen Charlie's sense (Paul's also, reimagining it) of the deprivation of her life. No luck or leisure even for a syllable.

After a moment she says, "I told my mother I was goin' to sleep at my married sister's and wou-int come home tonight. My sister knows."

She flashes up an alarmed look.

"It's all right," Charlie says. "I know you had to tell your sister."

He waits. After some minutes she lifts herself from her passivity and cries out, "I don't care what nobody says!"

Charlie stands. "Then come with me."

She is motionless.

"What's the matter, Maria?"

Her face is shrouded by forward-rushing hair. "My friend says it hurts like anything!"

She gasps, and covers her soft baby-mouth. Above purple-polish-tinted fingers she darts a swift sideways look at him.

His father is right, he sees. She has told her friend, and the friend's friends will come clamoring. He waits to feel the sickening spill of fear. There is none. Instead, a kind of triumph that rises, clotted, into his throat.

"You won't feel pain, Maria," he says. "Afterward, you might have something like bad menstrual cramps. You can stand that, can't you?"

"You mean like every month?"

"Yes."

"Every month I climb the walls. But I don't care." Her thin pinched face bears a look of desperate will. She has not cried.

When she lies on the examination table, he tells her to turn on her side for a moment and curl up. "Like a baby, Maria," he deliberately says, because he wants to watch what she will feel. But she makes no response to that, only obeys. He sinks the needle in.

(Paul inserts the suction tube.)

Her thighs are narrow and smooth. The pubic area looks childish — small, pale pink within — not yet the deep womanly scarlet.

Charlie leans between the forced thighs. Parts the swollen labia. Penetrates the vagina with his dilator, spreading it, stretching the vagina, reaching in and in. He pries open the shut mouth of the cervix that hangs in the vaginal throat. He plunges in. Brutally scrapes with sharp metal what the hidden tissue has tried to nurture. The soft, secret tissue has no protection against his sharp scrapers. He reaches with all his skill to scrape out the child's child.

After forty-five minutes, he is drenched with sweat, and the results of his scraping are piled in a little heap on the towel. A blob of tissue and mucus and tiny jellied bones.

Maria's eyes are still clenched tight when he finishes. Her face is small and shocked. He tells her to sleep, it's all over. Her forehead is damp, her hair clotted like an infant's.

Charlie sinks into a chair and watches her fall asleep. He feels the euphoria of the rescue.

Paul, on the other hand, finishing the procedure, snaps off his gloves without even noticing how anesthetic and procedure have been perfectly timed. The patient, awaking, is helped into a chair, wheeled to recovery.

Now instead of feeling his usual gloomy boredom, Paul with a certain eager anxiousness narrows his eyes at his mental canvas. Was that how it had been with Charlie? Had he imagined right?

He moves on to the next procedure room. Where through

the next careful extraction, he refines his dramatization of Charlie's old triumph. He combines all versions heard over the years — Charlie's, Riva's, Sylvia's.

Until, snap! The gloves again peel off like skin. Another patient, half-sedated, is wheeled back toward daily life.

Without wasting motion, Paul procedes to the next room where he disinfects himself, dons new gloves, gazes at the patient's unprivate parts, floodlit, framed by a sheet squared off like a proscenium arch.

He relives again in his mind Charlie's heroic act. He thinks now that what he most deeply envies in Charlie's life may be not what Charlie has. Self-denial — that transcendent luxury to those who feel themselves already denied by life — is what secretly draws him. Even — why not? — to risk his life to save somebody!

❧ ☙

It is Paul's turn to check the "assembly room." He has no hardness against this sight:

The bits of fetuses are to be fitted together. To make sure nothing has been left behind. No juicy bone unsucked by the vacuum aspirator. The ball head. The infinitesimal hands. Fingers. Toes. The spine of Homo erectus, glory of evolution. Two and a half inches long, and crushed.

"God, those women out there hope for a better life after what they're here for. I hope also. Change my luck! Change my life! You invented something to relieve them, why not me?"

In this new de-Creation, he feels entitled to a new Eve.

He thinks of Hannah.

❧ ☙

"I heard what you said before." Hannah suddenly appears in the coatroom at the end of the day, her cheeks pale, her eyes and hair alight. "About men and women — they should share a pregnancy. A noble, beautiful idea!"

Paul is delighted, but also inwardly shamed. Another of his ill-advised jokes. He had said at the midafternoon tea break that the best contraceptive science could develop would be to find a way to double the pregnancy period. Then, at horrified looks from nurses and aides he'd added that science should also find a way to enable fathers to be part-time carriers. "Transfer fetus in utero," he'd said hastily, "for the second bearing."

The others had spotted it at once — his forgetfulness about women. Hannah had leaped over all that to a "noble" idea. Though he wonders why she *hadn't* spotted it, he feels grateful. Her way of seeing is balm after sharp-eyed Margaret.

"I'm glad you liked my idea," Paul says.

"One day science will find a way. It's conceivable."

Conceivable! She doesn't hear herself.

"There is so much still mysterious." Her English strangely stilted. As if she's translating herself into some idea she has of what conversation is supposed to be. As if she hasn't had much of it.

"I feel it a privilege to work here. At the very conception of things."

Conception again. Marvelous! She has no idea what she's saying! What Bunky means by displaced. But she is smiling a tiny smile, lips closed. Maybe she *does* have an idea? Does or doesn't — if that's how she has to be in order to think well of him, let it go. And my God, she's a beautiful girl! The full lips, with the smallest curve modeled into the smiling corners. The fine modeling visible everywhere in the face — in the small loop-turns at the inner corners of the great eyes, in the delicate imprint, the crisp shallow crimp at each nostril tip. Is he the only one who sees it? Is that possible? Her hair — so full of life. Streaming away from her head in fiery wavelets. Beautiful. Because it is red and unusual, he supposes. Why doesn't she start with that and make herself . . .? He would like everyone to see it.

Treading carefully, as if afraid he might tilt her into a worse view of him, he suggests again that they have dinner. She says no.

"Don't you like me?"

She ducks her head in answer. And again: "It wouldn't work out."

"You said that before. Can't you say why?"

She considers that, adds nothing. Then a minute after, "Would you like to see?"

It startles him. It sounds like a lascivious enticement as he is about to leave for the day. But all she holds out is her battered blue notebook.

Her marvelous green eyes stare.

"Take it, please. What else" — she asks it with sudden, astonishing pride — "could I share with you?"

He feels a certain reluctance. If she has been writing about all of them here, he will be forced to read about himself in all his incompleteness. He will be a character invented by someone so unfinished she may need inventing herself.

He unwillingly lets his fingers close over the blue notebook boards, stuck with jam and other cafeteria messes. He shoves it into his coat pocket and heads out.

4

KAREN AND HELENE jump up from their chairs and come flying toward him at the sound of his step.

"Daddy! Daddy!"

The long braids of Karen flog his cheeks, the thick braces of Helene dig into his chin. They kiss and hug him with chubby eight- and nine-year-old arms. They love their daddy. His eyes mist with tears.

Paul is rounding a familiar corner, turning into a familiar street. Nearing home, not-home, in the lovely late afternoon.

"Dr. Paul Sunshine, impeccably dressed, busy physician, approached the house where his delightful children were looked after by a competent woman. His visits were eagerly awaited . . ."

He can't help himself. On the way to his ex-wife's apartment to pick up the girls, he always feels physically sick.

Children, for all their warm, sweet hugs, have a knife-edge grasp. Can you blame those women who come into the Center, he asks himself, who want to rid themselves of children before they can lay their hooks into their mothers' hearts?

Seconds later, with disappointed insight he sees: Of course he has blamed them! When he thinks of them — so many

— doesn't he sometimes secretly fill with revulsion? Child-abandoners! Though the child has no existence.

Aha! Now the record is going!

He feels the reproach of the abandoned child for its mother. Even though it was his father who abandoned him. Yet wasn't it true — for his vanished father his heart had reserved tender, romantic, forgiving feelings? Blushes and heats of love. Stronger, almost, because secret, than the intense love he bears his daughters. For his poor mother, contempt.

His father had not abandoned *him* — wasn't that how he had figured it out? — only his madwoman of a mother. *She* had driven his father away — that wonderful, dashing, adventurous man! But where had he gotten such an idea? He hardly remembers his father. Had invented the form to piece out scattered images of a man restless, jumpy, inattentive, and short-tempered. She had driven him away, he had told himself, with her dirty, sullen, black waters. All these years!

"I plan to be a doctor."

Dirty, wild-haired, looking in need of a doctor himself, he'd announced it to schoolmates. A dybbuk might have spoken through him — where else had the idea come from? A teacher of high school chemistry, a subject in which he dreamed answers to questions not yet even asked in class, had rescued him.

"I'll recommend you to Dr. Ritchie's special honors class. Anybody who wants to be premed after that gets right in. But doctors" — a smile to lighten the shame — "have clean nails."

After that, Paul, his nails scrubbed — no one had to tell him twice about getting ahead — had leapt and leapt — schools, jobs, scholarships — right through Columbia College, enough even to pay his dorm board. By the time neighbors called the police to come get his mother he was living away from home, rescued by fate and Dr. Ritchie.

But even Dr. Ritchie's fame foundered on Paul's applications to American medical schools. South America, that soggy continent, allowed Paul to sink in. From there he threw desperate ropes to New York hospitals, and Charlie Brodaw had grabbed one and pulled him out. His mother, meanwhile, sank toward an institution death.

Piercing memories break through. She had sat up nights with him in sickness. And for no reason he can recall she had made a party for the two of them when he was very young and had constructed one paper hat for him and one for herself of oaktag and gold stars. They sang songs and ate ice cream. The intsy-bintsy spider went up the water spout. His sinuses clog with unshed tears. Oh, good Lord!

He remembers, as he walks, the happiness of that day. It is the matrix for all his dreams of joy.

Oh, my, how it goes! The familiar record that turns and turns. Someplace where it is hard to get at to shut it off. There had been record-making places, when he was a kid, where you could stand and recite or sing, and deathless grooves would be carved by your own voice. He must have found such a place — a cheapshop of his childhood — and had set the record on some timeless turntable so that it always revolved, but the mechanism for shutting it off was missing.

And now anything could set it playing, any tremor — but he could turn it off only by a great effort of will.

Stop, stop! — he strains at it. But it goes on. A sorcerer's apprentice must have made it — it should have been worn through long ago, but it keeps its miraculous strength, grows its own layers, tough as horn. The little box at the bottom of the sea that grinds out salt. The porridge pot that boils up enough to feed a village and then overflows all its streets and houses. "Stop, little pot, stop!"

From where have these children's tales come? From his mother's lips. When not drowning, she had read him nursery tales, bedtime stories.

His breath catches in a sob. "Look how she tried!"

The thought of being a man — a physician, a father —

walking in his respectable suit with its gold chain and with what he feels is a certain measured tread (it is more a loose-kneed nervous lope), and of moving all of it — the suit, the chain, the watch, the fob, the head filled with medical knowledge, the heart full of fatherly concern — all to the relentless rhythms of that child's record carved years ago — makes his throat ache and throb.

What I need . . . I need an analyst. Somebody who'll listen while I get it all out. Somebody like Philip Roth's patient guy: "So. Now vee may perhaps to begin . . ." Or Woody Allen's. Twenty years I read he said in an interview.

But that costs. In the old days — a baby born a minute. I could have earned enough to open a practice. That and the Center, together. But now, my luck, I fell into the abortion enlightenment . . . Oh, don't start that again . . .

For rescue, he pulls his thoughts once more to his daughters. Karen and Helene. Margaret had named the girls for two female psychiatrists. If they'd been boys she would have wanted, maybe, to call them Sigmund and Carl Gustav. Thank God they'd never had boys. Though he'd thought it life's bad joke that he was surrounded by females at home as well as at work, he's also thankful. What would he do with a son? He can't see himself with a son. Set him the example of going now in humility to consult with the ex-wife because, after all, she knows him best and he can, oddly enough, trust her?

His long arms hang down in his formal suit jacket. Beneath it the vest, festooned with antique watch chain as if heirloomed to him, but picked up at a pawn shop. He has worked hard on his appearance but feels suddenly that he cuts a foolish figure. The aides who teased Selig know *how* foolish.

But now, when he listens again, he believes he has been successful. Has it stopped? He thinks so. He has managed — yes — to stop the record.

Paul rings the apartment buzzer and waits. Margaret agreed he could come earlier, while the girls are in the park with the maid. She had even moved up a patient for him. A good sign — maybe.

If only he were carrying something! The sacred black physician's bag! He could rush in breathless. "Double-parked, Margaret. Due at the hospital for surgery soon!"

A neat black bag would help.

She admits him by buzzer and he takes the elevator to his old apartment. Helpless to stop the flood of homecoming feelings. Michael, the elevator man, greets him warmly and turns his homely uneven-eyed face about to him while the elevator rises. "How's it going, Dr. Sunshine?"

"Couldn't be better, Michael!"

With one small eye, one big one, Michael sees through the hearty borrowed voice (whose is it this time?).

Margaret receives him in her studio office, where she sees clients. A transparent ploy. The office is filled with plants, hung with impressive-looking modern prints, gold-framed. Photography, unlike obstetrics, is expanding, especially when combined with Margaret's trained insights.

She tilts back in her swivel chair, smokes, and tries to make him feel the advantage of her position. She has taken to horn-rimmed glasses instead of the no-color ones she used to wear, and allows her dark brown hair, well threaded with gray, to hang long now.

"I'm bushed, Margaret. I get so worked up by the end of a day, all I want to do is rest, but I dream and toss." He is being conversational. Plus it doesn't hurt for her to know how hard he works.

But she is turning her most penetrating look on him. "What kinds of dreams, Paul?"

Suddenly he is reluctant to tell his own dreams. He substitutes Bunky's.

"Bloody," he says. "Straight from the butcher's. Hacking meat. Filling up basins with blood, tissue."

"Whose blood, Paul? Whose tissue?"

"I don't know." He shifts in his chair.

"Any special anxieties," she asks — with a certain conde-
scension, he feels — "other than the usual?"

He shakes his head unconvincingly.

"You've had no maternal deaths, have you?" She asks it
briskly. "Any close calls?"

"No deaths. One or two close calls. Everybody has them.
Thank God they worked out. Everybody perforates occasionally. I have once or twice. Bunky's a genius at this. He has a
strict rule. Disconnect the aspirator and call him. He personally does the D and C. The most patient, full, forty-five-minute
scrape-out. He deserves his success with the Center. He cuts
no corners, takes every precaution. He's even put on another
aide."

Secretly, his hopes light up. Hannah. He hides it from Margaret.

"He uses them to spot anyone who feels too upset to go
through the procedure safely. Some of those broads think
they're supposed to have a big reaction to a seven-week-old
fetus."

Instantly, he regrets his choice of language. How come he
always does this? Bad jokes with the aides too. Women must
bring on some kind of death wish.

Margaret throws him a battering look.

"And you — *you!* — have decided their reactions are bullshit? This incredible, complex thing they are experiencing
— hope, guilt, shame, relief!"

Doesn't he think the very same thing himself each time he
passes the woman in the wall? Yet he feels he must back up his
idiocy.

"I know you thought you had the right to insult me before,
Margaret. What's your right now?"

"When I see a consciousness down on its hands and knees
I try to raise it up. You've got daughters!"

"All right, all right." In fact, he agrees. The two little girls have softened him. He sees baby-faced teen-agers at the Center and he thinks of Karen and Helene. As Edgar says, "For Mim," and thinks of his sister, so he says in his heart, "For Karen and Helene," and thinks of his daughters.

"Anyway — that's it in the surgical department — all in good shape." He hopes that will finish it.

She tilts back. Lights a fresh cigarette. Gives him a powerful sphinx look.

"If you don't talk to me openly, I can't help you."

Uncanny! She reads his mind. But she herself had warned him once — long ago — "Don't ascribe magical powers to me, or to any woman. Your woman-worship makes you fear every female. That's what makes you a bastard. You're so afraid of being overpowered. That's what killed our marriage . . ."

He doesn't accept all that. Since the divorce, a little more, maybe.

He feels the words dragged from him: "I'm losing my physician's art, Margaret. All those things I studied so long and hard to master. I do ten-minute procedures all day. I've become a technician, servicing women. An unfilling station."

He thinks achingly of Charlie's private practice, forever beyond him. Then decides now is not the time to complain about that.

To his own surprise, he complains anyway. "Some people are luckier. Charlie is luckier. He has his practice in the mornings. He actually delivers a baby now and then. He comes to the Center only in the afternoons."

"Whatever the patient needs. Isn't that what it's supposed to be?" Margaret flushes with anger. "Are you sorry you can't go back to the fine art of amputation now that antibiotics are here? The field of medicine exists so that the doctor can have a variety of experience, is that it?"

Among other things she has developed since the divorce — she has found a tongue and a voice! What a silent female she had been when they married. Now words pour like water. And how in awe she had been . . .

He should have known she'd misconstrue. What the hell, he can't allow her to intimidate him.

Recklessly, he continues. "It's not a life for a doctor. Nothing but procedures all day. If I'd had the money, or the father, I could have opened an office, like Charlie. Or if only women had gone on having babies so that an office could pay for itself. You know my liberal views on women's rights" — he throws a sidelong glance, but sees from her set face that he's earned no points. "Still, there's something about presiding over death all day — "

For a minute, he thinks she gazes startled and human, almost with sympathy. The next, a professional mask closes over.

"Guilt, Paul? Repressed hostility to women? You are scooping out their fruit."

"Cut out the automatic psychological crap. Can't there be some dimension of real dilemma here? Must it always be neurotic?"

"Must you always conceal personality inadequacy under some grandiose universal bullshit!"

Incredible how it always ends like this! She takes down his pants, humiliates him. He longs to give way to his fury. Curse her, storm out. Even — he savors it in his muscles: they lunge against his bones like checked horses — more than that!

Checked. He is checked. An iron band clutches his bowel and his arm. The disappointment of the girls. His own guilt and grief after he leaves. He stays in his chair, as stubbornly silent as Margaret, reflecting.

Once upon a time he had given way to terrible tempers. He had actually struck this woman numbers of times, early in their marriage. He had been scrabbling for position, frantic and mean. As people think, "Only the rich can afford philanthropy," so he had explained to himself that unlike Charlie he could have no time or taste for altruism. Did that make him the Scarlett O'Hara of the medical profession? If I had been better provided for emotionally, I'd be as virtuous as Ashley Wilkes? Or Charlie.

Except that Charlie was not rich emotionally. Only that he'd made the decision not to grab for himself. In that decision lay all the difference.

Margaret meanwhile had pulled herself up and out. Had taken an old interest of hers, involving nothing more than an index finger and an eye, and against all odds had turned it into a going business. She had augmented photography with psychology — Jung, Horney, Adler, Freud: what books didn't she bring home from those exhausted nights at school! — and now had the reputation, lucrative, of being a filmic portrait painter who, after spending many sessions in intimate conversation with clients, went on to capture the essence of personality and character in a click. Every public face was in her files; magazines checked her first when they planned articles . . .

Was it seeing through him that had sharpened her eyesight?

She had been a trusting vulnerable girl when they met. Had he turned her into this hardened version? Maybe she was still soft with others. The girls adored her, they had late night talks, popcorn . . . Was her hardness only against him, because she feared for Karen and Helene? Didn't he fear for them too, and distrust himself?

She had hung out her shingle and got rid of him. He couldn't believe the speed with which his life had turned around. He felt like a man moved by religion.

He wanted, in God's name, to feel himself capable of some selfless act. But what? Where? How? The world in its new openness was closing in — there were no more fifteen-year-old Marias. No more lives to save.

He and Margaret now sit together, smoking and silent, in a terrible, cozy enmity itself like a marriage. To comfort himself, he thinks of Hannah. Relishes the slight clumsiness in her words. Compared to Margaret's ironic looks and knowing tongue. The strangely free way Hannah moves her body — none of it learned, all of it natural to the sinews and bones — moves him profoundly. He smells, when she is near, a flower of South America whose name he has forgotten. Hannah liberates the lost scent from the wretchedness of his South American adventure into its rightful fragrant loveliness. So she sets him right!

A delicious warmth and happiness fills his chest sometimes as he listens to Hannah's voice coming from another room and pictures how she must look, in her charming canary-colored outfit, on the other side of the wall.

It takes all his strength to keep from blurting out to Margaret that somehow, in this human cauldron or whatever it is that cooks up its tissue and blood each day, he has, in a kind of delirium, fallen in love.

When he hears the key fitting into the front door, he knows he has lasted out to his reward. He jumps up to meet the girls, upsets his chair, knocks with his flailing arm at the high wooden box that stands like a mysterious door on Margaret's desk but does not, thank God, overturn it, and is pursued and pinned by Margaret's voice: "If I so much as see a sign that you're tampering in any way with the self-image of my daughters — I mean even one peep about 'That's a man's job, you're just a little bitty girl . . .' I warn you, Paul. You won't see them again!"

All evening in his seat in Madison Square Garden, with one loving daughter on either side of him touching his cheeks with excitement, pleading sweetly to have a monkey on a stick, a little light that can swing on a leash and somersault through the dark like a circus acrobat, Paul feels relief and joy. The record is off, he is behaving like a grownup, giving gifts to his daughters, cautioning them not to eat what will make them sick.

Even so, while the clowns tumble and the trapeze artists

hang from their toes, thoughts about Charlie still touch Paul's brain for seconds at a time. When the elephants lumber past, carrying the clowns' suitcases in their tough, wrinkled trunks, they remind him of Charlie's father. They are like a procession of weary, gray-suited obstetricians, beasts of burden of the old-time deliverers' trade. Paul's heart winces with regret, but that is not enough to start the record playing again. He puts his arms about his daughters and hugs them to his sides like a man squeezing a life preserver against himself, and does not let go until the girls complain that they cannot *see*.

When he says good night in the living room of Margaret's apartment, his daughters excitedly fling their warm arms about his neck and burst into tears. He is nearly moved to tears of tenderness himself.

Margaret follows him to the door and all but sinks her teeth into him.

"Bastard! What did you do — cripple them with your complaints of how lonely Daddy is without them?"

Clairvoyant! She has powers! He flees from that house of females, even while he knows he cannot flee far: Next day at work he will again be surrounded.

And to crown all, one of these nights at home he has to look at Selig's notes!

5

TOO RESTLESS for sleep, Paul lies on his bed, opens Selig's notebook, and has a shock.

"I've held haunches of men and women — great beef hocks — in my hands. If I can plunge into their bodies' openings, why not into their thoughts as well?"

Great God, he thinks: another barracuda!

"Don't I know their thoughts? Haven't they talked and talked at me? Haven't I heard and heard?"

Selig? he thinks, wondering. *This is Selig?*

And the notebook answers: "A possible voice, though not mine. Mary's?"

His face flushes hot — he is being parodied! Though whether on purpose he can't tell. He experiments with spoken tones of voice; his own inner scale is never firm but constantly sliding up and down. Selig experiments with written voices.

He reads warily on.

"You can call me Y or Z. X in this place is reserved for someone else."

Who is she talking to, Paul wonders. Who is "you"? He eagerly skips ahead to find out. Then his eye is caught.

"We believe in the Center," he reads. "But the Center isn't

Paradise. It alleviates a part of human hell, a big part! But other hells intrude here too. Human beings belong to an ascending-descending species. The primordial ooze renews itself — within! Oh, I'd like to believe that spirit imitates the bodily organ we know so well here. What is the uterus? The place, it's said, where evolution is re-enacted in the developing fetus. I'd like to believe, as well, that each soul re-enacts the race's spiritual evolving. Ascent not to human *form* this time, but to human *consciousness.* I'm tempted to believe it! That in each life evolving spirit can, like the developing physical organism, grasp its own higher reaches and from there flower upward. But I see — am afraid to see — periodic descents to whatever spiritual equivalent there is for — how else can I put it? — the fetal pig!"

He shuts the book but keeps his forefinger inserted in its crotch.

"Selig was a poor Williamsburg girl." Paul mutters this aloud. "She learned no style in dress, no grace in manners, had nothing but the barest fundamental and fundamentalist education. I recognize all that from having grown up around my own low-class corner from Selig's life. Where then did she — who can barely open her mouth to speak — get these high-flown allusions, this high-falutin prose style?"

Since he is making a comparison between them, he wonders whether she might have grasped at books the way he has at dress (his pawn shop watch fob, his impeccably tailored suits). But through awe of the unaccustomed, both of them have stuck fast in formality.

"From where else this port-winey British sauce to cover up Williamsburg hash?"

He moves his finger sideways.

"What," he reads, "can anyone prove?"

He snaps on lights, and walks about his three-room apartment. For the sake of Karen and Helene he had been determined to find a good place. Of course he couldn't compete with their mother — now she's planning to buy a brownstone with a garden in the back — she earns more than he does: unfair! Psyches have complications and are expensive to portray, gynecology has been reduced to maid's work. *Oh, don't start that,* he begs his inner complainer.

At the door of his balcony he stops and thinks of going out to smoke a cigarette under the moon. But he sees that though the evening has been clear, a light rain now has begun to fall. He watches it slowly soak the metal balustrade. It is more a mist than a rain, more a foggy dripping breath than a mist. He feels that Selig's notes catch him like that. Breath by breath she is misting every part.

He begins to feel curious — what more can she have to say? — and returns to her book in bed.

He finds a hodgepodge of disconnections. Unassimilated reading, philosophy, remnants of yeshiva-wisdom, allusions to people at the Center and some he never heard of. Now and then an insight that startles him with its truth.

He comes upon a description of himself that he finds too painful to read attentively. Though upset, he can see it is sympathetically, even lovingly, done. His attachment for his children is stressed. He is described as a "repenting man," longing to become a "just man." That is flattering. There are also pages of conversations, remarkably like some of his own, that she could not have overheard. She has guessed at what he talks about with Bunky and with Charlie and with Margaret. He flips a page. Next, this:

"Those who are practical psychologists say: Because we died in great numbers — in millions — we ought to oppose any view that makes death easy. If *they* become accustomed to killing the fruits of their own bodies, how much more easily will we be killed? But when we were killed they *treasured* the fruits of their own bodies.

"And those who are political will say: When the walls of morality collapse, it is always the Jew who is buried under them. In Law is our defense. But the Laws of Nürnberg?

"Or finally and most thunderingly: God wants all the babies! To which I respectfully answer that we do not know what God wants. God is like some great poet who has written lines so perfect they bring forth tears of gratitude from us. Yet when the poet visits the house, he may be as cruel as a peasant, assault the host and kick the furniture to pieces. This is no doubt another sort of poem, but what is its meaning?"

And further on:

"Human seed's a penny a trillion. More gets spilled than planted. Human eggs drop out of us like rain. Even the pious can't avoid it. And though they fast and pray to atone for spilled seed and dropped eggs, they can never bring them back. Think of it — a Niagara of sperms, an ocean of eggs! Who are they, in potential? Who, what, has been lost?

"Suppose any two lovers. They have a child. Who will it be? Suppose they don't have a child. Who would it have been? Why this seed not that seed? What is spirit? Comes from? Goes where?"

Lower down on the page, Selig has added, "This is how I will address them. All of them in New Jersey."

"In *New Jersey?*" Paul mutters it aloud. For God's sake, New Jersey? Is that what she thinks the *world* is? Is there anyone more confused than Selig?

And why does her confusion fascinate him?

His telephone rings. He does not want to stop reading. A glance at the clock tells him it is after midnight and he decides it must be a wrong number. He continues with his face deep in her book.

The ringing stops. Paul's scalp loosens. He feels he has removed a hat. He reads on, then skips and reads at random, and comes upon Selig's own overeager, rushing speech in the small, neat, near-print script.

"I know now where to begin! Also where to finish. But everybody's walking around outside my notes. I have it all planned for them (good and noble acts!) but I'm afraid they — the real ones — are going to do wrong things and make me lose faith in what I planned. I ought to leave but — I'm afraid I'll miss something!

"Bomstein won't try to make what she writes come out better than life. She'll put down all the terrible things. She's never at a loss!"

Bomstein, he thinks. Bomstein too?

In another entry, the language is again high-toned and literary. Selig trying out her other voice.

The phone starts up again. He lets it ring. It keeps on ringing. He thinks in sudden panic of Karen and Helene. Lifts the phone, but it has gone dead. He frowns to get his concentration back.

"To read the notes of a book in which you are a character is to see yourself not only mirrored but enclosed. You look into an empty room and see a hand that writes. A fragile hand, unequal to the task, makes notes that cannot fairly plead your case. This is the pain of all judgment — that no act can reveal a person's whole truth and yet no act is a wholly false indicator."

He shudders — where does she get this stuff? — and skips more pages, reading bits in fascination.

"Bomstein's book. Negative images. I won't settle for that. Imagine what Bomstein will do with Paul!"

Enough is enough. She thinks he is an open book. He bangs *her* shut, and at that moment hears the doorbell ring.

A face white with cold and wearing fogged glasses looks out from under its hood like an egg from an egg cup. Selig at his door in a blue duffel coat.

"Did you already read some of it?"

He hides his astonishment in an elaborate yawn, and manages to shake his head.

"Keep it a little longer." A compassionate librarian, she by this time has entered his apartment and has begun unlatching the clumsy toggle loops. The blue duffel coat drops to his carpet.

The canary uniform has been replaced by a sort of woolly jumpsuit. Although the color, pale tan, wrings all natural tone from her skin, she looks adorable to him — fresh, strange, also cuddly, if you could get near. As if some semitame animal, a fawn — even though his apartment is seventeen stories up — has come to his door in dead of winter. He is about to offer her a lump of sugar and hot coffee and brandy to go with it if she wants, when suddenly, with a long, buzzing sound, she unzips herself from throat to crotch and steps forth naked from her chrysalis, flamboyantly lovely. Oh! — he thinks with dazed wits — not a deer, something with wings!

She removes her glasses — he hastily removes his also — and extends her arms to him, as silent as her notes are wordy.

He feels enchanted, under a spell. Or she is.

She leads him by the right hand to his bedroom, as surely as if following a blueprint. He follows her slender naked back — or more exactly, the two dimples above the plump, creamy-skinned buttocks. Meanwhile, he feverishly undoes his pajamas with his left hand, stumbling out of his pants. She leads serenely on, without looking back.

From the moment they lie upon his bed, she dominates the scene. She carries his hands to her breasts that hang above him as deliciously full as the fruits in the recovery room and sits sticky on his belly, rotating her divine spread-out ass until he wonders if he is supposed to give up ocean, like a drowned man. She arches herself back like a cat and sheathes him.

I won't make conversation, he thinks — like a compromised girl on a date — when they afterward lie resting side by side, Selig quietly contemplating the ceiling. Let her talk first. He awaits revelations from enchanted and enchanting Hannah, is ready to receive love-confidences.

But instead she is at him again, swinging herself upside down and flipping them both to their sides.

She moves her kisses downward along his body, blunders a little (if she had thought to look at things from a self-interested point of view) by lapping lightly with her tongue at what should better at that moment have been left unlapped. What in fact she does is to stick her face between his legs and lick at the soft part of his jointure, down the seam, between asshole and rod, the place where, if he'd been female, her tongue could have gone clear in. After that, she seems to want to suck out marrow, all his news from within. His pleasure is intense, and when she is done he is exhausted, but also faintly humiliated. He feels he has been marionetted, made to speak and cry certain cries, as if she is the ventriloquist of his bed.

While he lies spread-eagled and done in, she, a fastidious guest careful not to overstay, quietly rises and, having retrieved her jumpsuit from the next room (trailing it childishly along the floor, one-armed, like an ectoplasmic teddy bear), zips herself up again. At the doorway of his bedroom, he hears her utter the first words since entering — hears as if under water.

"I hope in this I'm not too timid for you. I have to learn everything from books." She looks suddenly pale and shaken, like a student who has crammed all night before and now, after the examination, is frightened to realize how little she remembers of what she did or didn't know.

"Books?" He repeats it slowly, to hide his astonishment. He has assumed transports of love.

A fearful doubt crosses his mind. "Do you have any idea about" — he searches for an old-fashioned word — "precautions?"

She answers that on this subject, also, she has read up — using, of course, the Center's own literature.

"How can you," he bursts out, "be such contradictory things!"

Her expression now appears so clear-eyed and knowing, so open and hidden at the same time, so deep and so steady, with a surface so full of love and with suggestions of layers and layers of more of that below, that he feels pass through his chest an answering something that is itself like the light breath of love.

"I hope you don't mind that I write about you," she says.

She gazes at him with the full, loving look he feels upon him every day at the Center, then says good night.

"Don't come to the door," she adds. "It's chilly." And clicks the lock behind herself.

He looks around after that and sees that she has changed her mind. She has carried the notebook away with her. Otherwise he would have checked, exhausted as he is, to see whether this is a scene she has already confided to paper.

By chance or design a leaf has drifted to the floor, like a feather from a great, rushing bird. He recognizes a few high-flown words from a passage he had mostly skipped. Sinking onto his bed, he studies it now.

"I want to be sure you understand me. Not for a minute do I think we ought to worry about those babies we miss having in our midst. Poor creatures, if we can't welcome them, what hope is there for them? They are like butterflies born into arctic snows." (She writes like *this,* he grumpily thinks, and can't get out two words of explanation to me?) "They are like José's sister's children." (Who, Paul wonders dizzily, is José?) "Without them we may be lacking some glorious specimens. Imagine what wonders might unfold their feelers and wings if butterflies could survive Antarctica! But they can't, so we must make do. And take good care of what we've got in the world in the way of short-lived iridescence. We must make each of us count!"

And neatly on the back, a recapitulation of a thought:

"To read a book in which you appear is to see with the eyes of pulsing raw material the meager model that has been made. Enraging it must be to see all darks and deeps so shallowly lit. Yet terrifying. You look into a room and see a hand with a pen in it. It writes slowly, on a single sheet of paper. You are judged."

It's strange — this time around he's not bothered by that idea. He feels a sudden, almost uncontainable joy. Why? Why? Because of this slip of paper about which he feels such nervous doubts — after all, is she a loony? After all — to whom is she writing? And about what? About people at the Center? Others in New Jersey? About life and death? Arguments for and against just about everything? *Poetic* arguments in favor of a process that ought instead to be presented in a cut-and-dried, scientific way. And *matter-of-fact* presentations of behavior that could only appear wildly unlikely — not to say, to use her own favorite word, "inconceivable" — to whatever audience she is notating all this for. And yet, she is writing about him too! The attention of Selig's notes — it feels like love turned language. Feels as if the writer's pen is a hand that caresses him, soothes him, salves him . . .

He folds the paper and places it with almost tender care beneath his pillow. Then he lowers his head, which feels nearly bursting, to the exact spot, as if onto a healing poultice.

6

A ND EVERY TIME, in the taxi from office to clinic,
from the old world to the new, I talk to Pop. I speak
with my dead father."

Charlie looks straight ahead while he tells it. His handsome
face is profiled against the car window as he drives toward
Westchester and home. Compared to him, Paul thinks, what
am I but a baby?

"Sometimes I say," Charlie goes on, " 'In ten minutes I
undo what took you twenty-four hours, on call all through the
night!'

"Or I say, 'You think you helped women? What did you do
but add to their burdens? I unburden them. I give them freedom! I loose the dumb ox from the plough!'

"Then my father answers" — Charlie's voice now takes on
a deep, dragging sound, weighted with barely suppressed rage
— " 'When in my life did I ever call a woman a dumb ox except
if she failed to keep a baby's circumcision clean?' " Charlie
turns from traffic to face Paul for a second. Paul is pinned as
always by Charlie's special combination — words terrible,
manner charming. Mild. Sweetly hopeless.

" 'Now there's no circumcision to worry about, Dad,' I say.

" 'Murderer!' he yells. 'What are you doing to Jewish babies!'

" 'I'm democratic,' I say. 'I'd do it to all. I'm no murderer! I let the mothers live! Something you never gave a damn about!' I time the conversation and the trip so that I have the last word." Charlie's eyes widen in mock innocence. And his lips — handsome, full, well shaped — thrust into a one-sided smile.

Even his good looks, Paul thinks; he's ready to throw them away.

"Glad you're coming for dinner tonight," Charlie says. "Easier for Sylvia when we talk in front of you." When he is not practicing imitations, Charlie's speech is clipped, impatient.

"To tell the truth, I don't think it is, Charlie. I'm a distraction for her, maybe, because she sees I get uncomfortable and she tries to make me feel better. But two people sharing pain don't divide it in half."

"Sylvia's pain's conditioning," Charlie answers, not for the first time. "Surprised you don't see it."

It is not an argument Paul wants to pursue now. He lets it drop and struggles silently with his feelings. Charlie wants nothing less than liberation for Sylvia. Yet Paul often pities her. She is the stunned and manipulated partner in that marriage as he had been (he now likes to feel) in his own.

He gazes again with Charlie at the flowing traffic. In each car there is a driver with no doubt a life of inner complications. Also signs of outer adhesions of humanity — there are passengers. Each car becomes for Paul a whole galaxy of separate bodies — spinning, circling, attracted, repelled, and moving on in the lemming tide toward the extinction of that day's events in the fresh woes of home. Oh! — the dream of happiness must be the cruelest there was. Where had he gotten such an idea? Where had Charlie? Or anyone?

For Sylvia, happiness is to be left alone in her illusion that the life she stumbled into was what she had desired.

But Charlie won't allow it.

From time to time Charlie wracks his brains (and Paul is supposed to help by wracking his) for new words to dislodge Sylvia from her old life. It is a drop-by-drop process, and Charlie has been working on it since his illness began.

Paul's luck, he has been present, a witness too many times, to these drops.

"Shrouds everything with veils!" Charlie's voice rises to an unaccustomed pitch of heat. "Coarsest necessities of her life. What she said — still says, now, when I can get her to speak at all about her unwanted and premature pregnancy — 'Something in me couldn't wait to love Daniel.' "

Rarely, Charlie allows a strong passion to escape him, but a reply in kind is difficult. By the time Paul speaks, Charlie is ready to cool his fire with the mocking half-smile.

"That's touching in her!" Paul protests doggedly. "It makes life happier, sweeter!"

Charlie swings off into a service road to avoid a traffic tie-up ahead. A young couple, arm in arm, crosses the street when Charlie stops at a light. Each drags along by broad khaki-colored straps an enormous blue cloth suitcase to which tiny wheels are attached. The suitcases wobble. The couple staggers in their laughter, as if drunk.

"Ah, yes, vacation!" Charlie's dry voice again comments. "Sylvia and I took one after I joined the Center. Decent hours at last. An unremitting view of each other then, for the first time. Without interruption. Without necessity. Do you know how we felt? Appalled! Christ, we couldn't even make it in bed. We were embarrassed about so much naked time. We needed breathlessness, the drunkenness of doing good till all hours. We decided to be worried about Daniel. He was fine with a friend, but we had to come home sooner."

Paul stares at the passing couple. The young woman, whose hair is completely hidden under a bright yellow cotton scarf, puts out a hand to steady the young man's case, which wobbles worse than her own. As she brings her hand back, she caresses his cheek, then lets her hand fall slowly down his arm. The young man wears a torn plaid shirt, and his forehead, when his laugh subsides, shines with a look of pure joy. The same look shines below the yellow kerchief of the girl. Paul is astonished at himself: the jealous pang, the one he would surely have felt before at such a scene, has vanished! Is it Hannah's doing?

His relationship with Charlie is reversing itself. Charlie is the one who is — or is determined soon to make himself — bereft. Paul now has richness for the taking — Hannah's love.

Guiltily, as though Charlie's loss is somehow his own envy's doing, Paul renews his attention to what Charlie is saying. He is shocked to hear how this idyllic little street scene has roused Charlie to sneering: "The women! The whole world sheds tears over them, yet they feel nothing! They never say, 'I'm carrying a helpless eight-week-old fetus whose life depends entirely on me — ' "

"Why should they?" Paul protests. "How could they?"

"They say, 'I'm two months pregnant, help me!' "

"Of course they do! If a wild animal is at your throat, do you scream for help or do you describe its biological beauties? I know it's a poor analogy — this is no wild animal — but probably that's how it seems to them, life-threatening! Even though their emotions tear — "

Charlie gives him an amused, half-pitying look. "There's no tearing, I assure you. Never mind; don't bother defending. It's the same in the end, even better. If there's any doubt, out! That's the only way."

When Charlie gets like this it seems as if a door opens in Paul's soul. Behind the door, leering, are all his own, old idiocies about women. He sees them clearly whenever Charlie talks this way. He resolves mentally, at that instant, every time, to get rid of them, to change. But then, of course, afterward, he forgets about it. The best he can hope is that because he repudiates these idiocies so many times — even for an instant — they will somehow melt away. Or that with better influences — Hannah? Hannah? — he will be rescued from them.

Very quietly now, Charlie says again, "Glad you'll be there tonight."

But Paul does not have the feeling that things are better when he is with them. Or that his presence makes Charlie's message less frightening to Sylvia. In Paul's recollection, such conversations have always been filled with Sylvia's cries of pain. Charlie had begun lightly, ironically: "Now that I'm on a nine-to-five schedule, you see what a slave you've been all your life. Keeping supper hot till midnight. Washing dishes at two in the morning."

"I never minded it!" Sylvia's slight, trim figure would sometimes tremble when Charlie began this way. Her short, waved hair was always carefully groomed now. She had begun to go gray two years before and asked Charlie if she ought to dye it.

"Live!" He'd answered with a dramatic flourish of his arm. "Why not?" He kept after her. "You never had time for a life of your own. A maid could have done what you did but you wouldn't have it."

"A maid couldn't do it with love," Sylvia answered stubbornly.

"For God's sake. Free yourself! You shouldn't want slavery."

"I never thought of it as slavery, Charlie!"

"No reason now to hang around the house. Go back to school. Get a profession. Anything you like. Lovers. A new life!"

Since illness had bound him, Charlie had turned with a ferocious benevolence toward Sylvia's life. And there was no way Sylvia could hold out against him. She was Chekhov's compliant "Darling" come again in a new generation. In this case, the Darling's husband said, "If you love me, you'll leave me!"

Understandably, the Darling's will was utterly stymied. She stood as aghast as a caged mouse whose nose has led it not to food but to a nasty electric shock.

Sometimes Sylvia regained, God knows how, an almost heroic balance.

"I like to be here when Daniel comes home from school," she might then say. "There are always errands, problems, things to discuss. Don't talk nonsense, Charlie — about lovers."

"Only a few months left of that. He'll be off to college." That had been over a year ago.

"I'll *see* what I want to do!" Though it made her frantic, she would always answer Charlie point for point.

After Daniel had begun college, Sylvia wanted to *see* again how things went for him: it was such an adjustment! When Daniel dropped out in his freshman year, Charlie blamed not his own repeated idea that little in most people's lives meant anything, but Sylvia. "He knows you're waiting at home to serve him; why *wouldn't* he come back?" Sylvia patiently cooked, consulted therapists, wrote letters to see who would accept Daniel's credits if he decided to return to school.

Tirelessly, Charlie pursued her.

"You and I never did anything ourselves. My father led me and your mother led you by the nose. You married who she said you should marry. Then you folded up your life."

Paul had witnessed and winced with double agony. First as a pained spectator, exposed to every cut. Next, his own impoverishment dug him deeper each time Charlie prodigally cast off Sylvia's rich devotion.

"I admit I was a stupid girl, Charlie," Sylvia had cried out. "I wouldn't do the same if I were starting today! But I want to make good at least on what I did choose!"

Once, in a fury, she had pounded Charlie's chest with her fists and sobbed. "I don't feel like a failure until you start on me!"

The light changes. Charlie resumes his homeward drive.

"Charlie, you're Lear! You give up your best possessions too soon. Why not hang on to Sylvia?" Paul pleads as if, strangely, for himself. "She wants to be your slave, for God's sake!"

"Can't stand slavery." Charlie kills it off with an exact, half-measure smile.

"The things you throw away are what I'd give eyeteeth for. I could understand if there was somebody else, but there isn't as far as I know, and maybe — "

"Never will be," Charlie breaks in.

"I didn't say that! I can understand a drive for happiness. I can understand even — yes! — those jokers, doctors with drugs always handy who do their wives in and sprint for foreign parts with Nursie and the diamonds. But you — I must be missing all the main facts about you, Charlie! I know a lot but I don't know you. 'Conditioning' isn't enough to explain wrecking your own world!"

Charlie drives silently and shifts himself against the rich red leather of the upholstery. His elegantly cut navy blazer shines with brass buttons. His tie is flecked handsomely with red and gold threads. He glances at his watch, a fine gold one that Sylvia gave him several birthdays ago. Paul had been there then too. Jacket and shirt collar and gold-banded watch all hang loosely on the body made spare by illness.

"It's six-forty. We'll be home by seven. Do you want twenty minutes' worth?"

Curiosity and heart-sinking together. Must his nose always be rubbed in? He feels he has gone over every inch of the terrain, but wonders what Charlie will choose to tell.

"Sure!"

Charlie is silent again. Paul sees that his expressive mouth moves about its own fullness, his half-smile coming and going, as if Charlie rehearses mentally some event about which he feels irrepressible mockery.

Paul shudders at the first words — "A small boy hears *'shi-vah'* " — though Charlie's voice is light, ironic, laughing — "and thinks 'shiver'! You understand that?"

"Why shouldn't I?"

"My aunt Frieda explained it. Not to me, to a neighbor. Why my father couldn't sit and shiver with me for my mother."

Paul has heard all this! From Sylvia — her voice choked with tears for Charlie's pain. From Riva. From Bunky. Who hadn't he heard from? But when Charlie raises his voice to a nasal shriek, Paul admires the mimicry.

" 'He's too *bu-sy!* His office hours are in the *bel-lies of wo-men!* How can he take the *time?'* She'd scream it out the window to the neighbors and over the phone. 'He's the *King,* I'm telling you! Of all those fancy doctors. They call him up when the cord twists around the poor baby's neck, or the position isn't just right! Or the mother is lazy and don't push! He gives advice and takes no money! Runs all the time. Busy morning till night till morning again. I cook but he don't eat!' "

Charlie subsides.

"What about Aunt Frieda?" Paul knows Aunt Frieda by heart, but he wishes to escape the pain of obstetrics practice.

"Aunt Frieda! She came to take care of skinny little Charlie. But what could she do? There was her doctor-brother, the King! She saw self-denial without connecting it to self-infla-tion. Continual giving to the world. Give! Give! Give! She never connected it with depriving. She felt her brother's power and served him. When the doctor came home, the house had to be deathly still, in case he wanted to sleep. He liked to eat boiled chicken and soup. So that was what she prepared every day. In case he arrived home to eat it."

Charlie bursts into the dry exploding sound that is his laugh.

"You can't believe how much noise that woman made! Ter-rified the doctor would arrive unexpectedly. Nervous noise all day. Farts. Belches. She dropped ladles and slammed pot lids and yelled on the telephone."

"You laugh like a bystander," Paul nervously says.

"I *was* one! I watched it all, continuous performance! At seventeen, do you know what I said to my father?" Charlie strikes the wheel in time with his short dry laugh. "Crazy things! I wanted to go to India and work among the poor. I wished to serve. Like my daddy! Or if not that, I wanted to study acting, to lift up hearts and minds from the stage."

"You said that to your father?"

"The wishes came forth in pieces. You can imagine!"

Charlie, who almost never stutters when he is with Paul, then begins to imitate himself stammering. Paul looks out the window.

"Pop was by then very paunchy. Short of breath. Heavy-cheeked. He shifted his cigar in his mouth. He set down the black bag he'd been checking into. He said" — here Charlie draws forth his father's deep, draggy voice — " 'You're not *going?* ' "

"Instead of saying, 'I have to be someone else,' the kid gagged. Like this: 'A-a-a-a-a-a-a-a-a . . .' "

After the terrible choking sound subsides, Charlie again takes the role of his father. "The father breathed in shallow gasps!" Charlie gasps raspingly. "He stared at his son!" Charlie turns away from traffic to drill at Paul a heavy-lidded stare of disapproval. Paul looks nervously away. "Who was already jigging, hopping, dancing in his fright!" Charlie bounces up and down in his seat, beating on the wheel and laughing his dry Hungh! Hungh! Hungh!

"A look of disgust settles on the doctor's face. He opens his bag again. He gazes inside, as if looking for a remedy for the affliction of this abortive birth, his son. He closes the bag with a snap, shifts his cigar once more, and leaves the house without a word."

"God, Charlie . . . !" Paul begins.

Charlie lifts a silencing hand, smiles crookedly, and continues.

"They never discussed it again. When Charlie was eighteen, he told his father he would become a doctor. He was rewarded with his father's touch, the first he'd received in years. His father dropped one of his golden hands on Charlie's shoulder.

" 'I always wanted you to be a doctor.' " Charlie again imitates the dragging pace. " 'I wanted for your own good. I can't see another job for a person. What, in business — arguing? Or in a store? Or with snotnoses in a school? Or some kind of a job with a boss and with' " — Charlie puts heavy contempt into it — " 'with *hours?* You'll see yourself how good it is,' the doctor said. 'To these people you're a father and a mother.' " Charlie lifts a hand and smooths Paul's shoulder. " 'I'll help you,' he said."

Charlie's touch wakes Paul. He had without warning slid into a daydream of Hannah. They are lying naked on his bed, arms clasped about each other. No feverish love-making: an exchange of warm kisses.

Clearing his head hastily, Paul prods, though Sylvia had pumped him full, "And Sylvia?"

Bunky's words come back to him — "These women will educate us . . ."

But Charlie has dropped out of school, along with his son. "Ah!" he says with manic malice. "How Sylvia came into Charlie's life! Charlie joined his father's office after he finished training" — Charlie turns to give his lopsided grin — "an opportunity much admired by some . . ."

"But Sylvia — Sylvia!"

"She answered an ad for a three-week vacation replacement for Pop's receptionist. Shyly pretty. Soft-spoken. Eager to please. Stayed late without being asked. Volunteered to look after the books. On the one hand, the senior Doctor Brodaw pronounced her good doctor's wife material. On the other" — Charlie's dry laugh rattles out again — Hungh! Hungh! Hungh! — like a dead man's refrain — "the stupidest reason of all: she was the first woman to kiss Charlie since his mother had died."

"Don't call that stupid!" Paul remembers Sylvia's account. Veil-covered? Endearingly so.

"Let's say they cast emptiness into each other's arms and called it love. Sylvia discovered she was pregnant. A poor girl. Working toward a degree in Early Childhood Training and nothing but grim years of second grade ahead. You get the picture?" Charlie's laugh nails up the picture. "She let it be known she had always hoped to marry a doctor. So their bargain was made. And each kept it. Like the King, Charlie never vacationed. Busy and needed. Sylvia too! Busy and needed! Even her complaints, if she complained, which was seldom, were proud. His aunt had become his wife."

"I don't think that's fair, Charlie . . .!"

Charlie ignores him.

"After a while, his own office. Working around the clock! Like the King, he got chubby. He fended off exhaustion with endless containers of sweetened coffee, endless portions of Russian coffee cake. Prodded sluggish bowels with endless pieces of prune Danish. He became his father! Though not, of course" — half a smile stretches into one lean cheek — "a King!"

"The alternatives," Paul says glumly, "were worse."

He remembers, though, that the interns struggling for places under Charlie had not liked him.

"Gentlemen do you know why you are here?" Charlie would half-smile at their wretched looks.

The interns had pulled their lips about and privately mimicked his stutter like schoolboys.

But Paul had from the first been fascinated by this aristocrat of renunciation, his opposite in every way, who practiced an idealism close to heroic, with a scorn close to contempt. To Charlie's private patients Paul had heard him say, when the mood took him, "This is a pompous trade. If a doctor won't give you a reason for doing something, go somewhere else. Nobody has a right to treat you like a dog. Doctors are ordinary! Not kings or gods!"

Sometimes he challenged patients on their subservient ways.

"I call you Ruth. Why do you call me Dr. Brodaw?"

"I like," came the humble reply, "to call a doctor Doctor."

To which he might give the reply for which he had become notorious at the hospital: "What's a doctor? Just a plumber, working with the plumbing. Do you want me to put the pipes here or put them over there?"

Still there poured out to him the loving trust of women — nothing stemmed it. When they told him, not questioning, of friends who had had breasts cut off and wombs cut out, he hissed at them, "Don't be that shit-bitch dumb! Get ten opinions first!"

Charlie's voice cuts into Paul's reverie.

"Ah, the bursting-open days of the nineteen sixties! Oh, the great social upheavals of youth! The liberations! Choose joy! 'Surely,' Charlie thought, 'there's a liberation movement for me?' A Diogenes lantern burned day and night in Charlie's gut. He searched!"

Charlie swivels his head to mimic an inept searcher.

" 'Where is my joy? Where was my youth? My life imitates my father's. When I die I won't have lived!' "

Charlie shakes his head, still humorous.

"By the time Maria came to me, I had already delivered thousands of children. Thousands!"

Despite his effort to control it, a deep sigh escapes Paul.

"I was an accomplice to humanity's malign fate."

"Why is all of it malign? Look at some — "

"It didn't matter," Charlie interrupts, "if the parents were jubilant. Or resentful. Or indifferent. I never failed to observe some trait that meant misery for the child. It was a rare one that didn't make me think, 'Better if it had never been born!' Women came to clinics to have babies and give them up to adoption. I asked them why we couldn't rescue the children too. But I only terrified them."

"So by the time frightened little Maria walked into your office" — Paul is excited to find his fantasy corroborated — "there was no power that could make you refuse her request! You proved your father wrong!"

"No, Pop was right. He predicted a stream of the desperate would find their way to my office. They did. Somehow the rest of the prediction never came true. The abortion bill was made law a year later in New York. You remember what happened then?"

Flinching from the memory, Paul hastily says he does. Charlie nevertheless continues. "How they flew to us? And also by van, bus, train, auto? Slept on cots, sleeping bags, the floor of my waiting room? Came with lovers, sisters, mothers? Or alone? Riva and I stayed all night with them. We gave them sedation and started early in the morning. 'Better not to be born,' I said with each scraping. Then it all settled down. Abortions by appointment during daytime working hours nine to five. A chance for a new life."

"For me it was the end of the world."

"My father thought so too. He didn't stick around to see it long. A new life was out of the question. You know for who else?"

"No, not Sylvia!" Paul protests. Though he has seen for himself what Charlie means. At first Sylvia had been strangely distraught, thrown off balance, when Charlie began arriving home at seven every evening. She, who had stood in her bathrobe night after night and served Charlie from the stove, at midnight or later, was now restless. Those other nights, before the Center — Paul had often been there — Charlie had talked in exhausted snatches. After the Center opened there was nothing to report. They had no conversation. Passion for Daniel. Sylvia's antiques. It seemed too late for them to slow down. They had already been overwhelmed by quantity. Sylvia had amassed tables and chairs. Charlie had delivered thousands of babies.

What drove Charlie to despair was just what Paul admired. A woman so filled with devotion and love for her marriage that she refused to question it, through all its permutations.

"That's when I began to see it," Charlie says. "That's when I began to have my idea about Sylvia."

"That's when you began to torment her," Paul says.

"It drove me wild to see her still placid, passive. The world had turned around!"

"She doesn't want to travel. She doesn't want to meet men. She says the idea of flirting — of sleeping with another man — makes her sick. She's used to you, Charlie!"

"Used to! Used to! It's all conditioning! And why should we allow ourselves to be conditioned away from freedom and happiness for all our lives by one second of misery?"

Paul anticipates what is coming now and hopes the thickening traffic will distract Charlie from the telling. But Charlie goes on. "When I went to see Moe Stricks about stomach pains" — his stiff smile is back — "I actually thought my father had reached out from the grave. To say 'No, no freedom for you!' When a doctor says, 'I'd rather bite off my tongue than tell you this,' you know he plans to cut off some vital part of *you.* They wanted me to walk around with a bag in place of a bowel."

"Thank God it didn't come to that," Paul says quickly. "Thank God you didn't have to submit to such an operation. Thank God it remitted, Charlie!"

"It lasted long enough to blast my idea. It added to Sylvia's guilt about leaving me in the first place. Now there was all the extra about *leaving a sick man!*"

"Of course there was — she loves you! And your own unselfishness inspires her!"

"There is no unselfishness!" Charlie talks through ground teeth. "But of course Sylvia accuses me of deception in that, of *pretending* to selfish motives! The middle-aged Pollyanna — if I kick her it must be for her own good!" Charlie shakes

out his dry rattling sound again, the laugh that is terminal
— Hungh! Hungh! Hungh!

"Well — whatever it is — "

"Now everything's changed. This thing that we do —
a 'procedure' — the whole thing — we see that it's nothing!
And how many women have gone down in shame over this
— nothing!"

Baffled, Paul says, "But I thought you hated — you said they
never thought about the fetus — you just said . . ."

"It doesn't *matter* who feels what. Nobody's life should go
down the drain!"

"Not even the fetus's?" Paul asks that in a sullen moment
that springs from his bafflement, his resentment at being
pulled here and there by what seems like Charlie's inconsistency.

"I mean cognizant life," Charlie answers evenly. "The only
life that matters."

"Okay, okay. But what about Sylvia? She doesn't want to
go."

"She'll go. Because I'll make her go. I'll scrape her out of
that cozy life one way or another. Rotted into it. Sickening!"

"But if — she — won't — go — Charlie! What then?"

"I'll strangle her." Charlie's flat words are free of any tone
of comic hyperbole. He flexes his fingers on the wheel and
then grasps the rim tight. As if coming to certain conclusions
about those small, weak-looking hands, he adds, "Or if no
strength for that — then strychnine — injection of air while
she's asleep — anything!"

"For God's sake, Charlie, don't talk like that!"

Charlie turns to grin at the panic on Paul's face. "Never
mind," he says, dryly. "Dismiss it from your thoughts."

After a moment, Paul adds, hesitantly, "In the end Sylvia
always does what you ask, Charlie."

"Not quite, this time. I asked her to take a trip to Europe,
to find her own apartment in the city, to find a lover —

and she appeases me by enrolling in a course at the New School. Dilemmas of Modernity! A literature course!"

"Couldn't you let it go at that?"

"Don't you see I made that mistake too many times? Gave in to Sylvia's conditioning the same way I gave in to my own and Pop's. Otherwise Pop might have seen he could love a son who wasn't in his image. He went to his grave wrapped up in his own thick hide. I was the only one in the world who could have punctured it. I could have lanced that conditioning of his that he wore like a hardened abscess. I won't make that mistake again!"

Without Paul's having noticed, they have arrived. Charlie pulls into the driveway of the large Victorian house with bays and balconies, whose wrought-iron scrollwork has been carefully restored around the peaks and pitches of a small garrison of rooftops. A rose light glows in the west windows.

"And here we are now," Charlie says. "Heartbreak House."

Paul sits stubbornly. So many painful conversations with Sylvia before! How many are there — dizzying thought — recorded in Selig's notes?

"Let's go in," Charlie says. "Help me save Sylvia."

"We're here!" Charlie calls it out when they step into the hall through the front door, always left unlocked.

Paul is amazed to hear the sudden lift to Charlie's voice. Sylvia's muffled one comes to them from the back of the house.

Charlie's forehead opens and smooths, his movements — putting their coats into the hall closet — are quickened, he rushes forward, eager — so it seems to Paul — toward the sound of Sylvia's voice.

Idiot! Paul thinks it in amazement. How is it I didn't see before? He needs her! The next minute he wonders if he is, like Sylvia, concocting a "beautifying" lie. Could Charlie's agitation be caused by something else?

They walk toward Sylvia, through rooms crowded with furniture polished to a mellow shine. Delicious cooking aromas waft toward them. In the dining room, pale green candles, already lit. Crisp linen laid on the table. Flowers. Silver. A blue-and-green mallard duck of carved wood is the centerpiece, with ornamental grasses cleverly arranged about it. In the midst of the table, a small glowing garden complete with suggestion of pond.

Sylvia is in the kitchen. Cooking always agitates her. She kisses Paul, then moves nervously back and forth for the last touches to make the meal ready. Her hair, with its delicate blond wash, falls over her flushed cheek. She is wearing a pale blue skirt and a pale blue matching sweater, with a flowered shirt collar neatly peeping out.

They have their drinks in the kitchen. Then there is leg of lamb studded with garlic and glazed with currant jelly, roast potatoes, whole string beans picked by Sylvia from her garden and kept in the freezer to be served deliciously now with oval slices of almonds. Dessert is fresh fruit compote, with thick slices of lemon-roll and nut cake, baked by Sylvia. Paul eats hearty, grateful portions; Charlie picks.

Through part of the meal, they discuss the field of journalism, because of their tall, handsome son. Daniel, bored at home, is wondering whether he might be interested in it. He wants to go to Northwestern to study. Sylvia says it is far away. Daniel, who had come home unbidden from college in Maine, replies — now that he is asked to stay close by — that he will certainly not hang around the city to go to Columbia just because his mother thinks that would be nice. Paul, adopting an avuncular tone, says that well, now, there is the telephone and there are airplanes, and that seems to end it. Daniel excuses himself at the end of the meal to change his clothes before going out with friends.

It is the moment Paul dreads.

They three sit suddenly silent. To Paul's horror, he sees that tears are trickling down Sylvia's cheeks. He begins again to say that Chicago is not so far away. Sylvia pushes back her chair, stands, clutches her arms, then abruptly controls herself. She says, "I'm sorry," and smiles tightly. Then she grasps her chair and, before Paul can jump up to help, pulls it over next to his. She sits down quietly, lowers her head onto his shoulder, and begins to sob.

For a startled moment, while Paul puts his arms around her, he has an outlandish idea. She might have overheard snatches of Charlie's terrible judgment of her in the car. That is followed by another outlandish idea. She might somehow have eavesdropped on Charlie's account in the car of his pain-filled childhood and now, wonderful woman that she is, she weeps for him.

Both men bend over her and hear her whisper through her sobs, "No more, no more!"

She collapses in tears on Paul's neck. It is Paul's fate in that house. The message is filtered through him.

"Dilemmas of modernity, Paul!" Sylvia sobs with her face half-buried in his shirt. "It's not so funny after all. I feel ashamed . . . not just that I went to bed with someone . . . with Simon . . . but Charlie might think I felt impatient because he couldn't . . . because the effects of that treatment . . . that I could be that cruel, that greedy . . ."

It takes Paul some seconds to understand what Sylvia is announcing — half in tragedy, half in triumph, hiccuping, weeping — about herself and some fellow student. And then, to quell any doubt, she sobs out, over the white rice-pattern Rosenthal bowls holding the soft lumps of the fruit compote, "I didn't *want* this to happen! All we were going to do was go for coffee after class!"

Paul can well believe it. Awed at Charlie's power, he tries clumsily to comfort Sylvia.

"But oh, Paul, the rotten timing!" Sylvia moans it.

For God's sake, he wants to say, don't torment yourself! It's not even your timing, it's his!

Charlie is patting her shoulder. He seems strangely agitated, very pale. Yet he keeps insisting that Sylvia must join Simon. Who is Simon? A shadow figure whom Charlie at once places at the center of their lives. When Sylvia protests that it is out of the question — she will not move into Simon's bachelor apartment, Simon might not even *want* her to, and even if he did *she* wouldn't — Charlie agrees that she should retain her independence: they will find her a place of her own, he says, in the city.

Sylvia makes efforts to compose herself. She rinses her red eyes at the kitchen sink. They follow her there.

Charlie's trauma increases. He stutters, nearly totters as he talks. "We'll look for a p-p-place . . . this w-w-weekend . . . it shouldn't be hard . . . don't c-c-cry . . . it's all f-f-fine . . ."

Daniel comes to stand in the kitchen doorway.

"Couldn't you wait to play your games till I went away to college?"

He cries it out in fury and disgust.

"I only have a few more months till I go away, out of your lives, and won't bother you again!"

Sylvia weeps; Daniel slams doors; Charlie trembles and stutters. Paul moves from one to the other, trying to restore sanity to his friends' lives, and trembling himself from the lack of it in his own.

Next day at work, Charlie's face seems to have increased its gauntness. But he keeps to a light tone.

"Now that it's accomplished, that part of my idea," he tells Paul, "I don't think I'll follow Sylvia's lead after all."

He is suffering! The thought crosses Paul's mind and he feels anger mixed with his pity. Arrogant! Incredible! Giving away treasures, thinking himself above need, not like others. Making himself a King after all . . .

"What about your idea applied to your own new life?" he asks Charlie.

"No heart for it. Potency that returns erratically seems spurious. No faith in it."

"But Moe told you . . ."

"Moe assured me I'd be fully potent in time. With a complete sperm count. 'You want to be a father?' Moe said. 'You can become a father.' I think that's what makes me indifferent."

Charlie summons a half-smile for his indifference.

It's trying — Paul thinks, shocked — like some wounded animal, to raise itself again. And he's indifferent!

7

CHARLIE'S WAITING ROOM keeps the old appearances. Still the office of a doctor who brings life into the world, although it mostly isn't.

Daily in the decade of his practice, Charlie has stared hopelessly at those lies, the pictures on his walls.

Sylvia had hung them there. Picasso's *Mother and Child*, chalk and pastel. Blooming firm-fleshed woman and her infant: good health is all. Käthe Kollwitz's mothers and children stare starkly next out of charcoal eyes. The grasp of mother and child on one another is tight, intense, even hysterical. Kollwitz's intentions are to make antiwar posters. But here they represent an anxiety of motherhood that stands by itself. Another Picasso — the artist's blue period: emaciated mother feeds her child at starving breast. Easy, in Charlie's waiting room, to disregard political purposes and contemplate with simple acceptance, as thousands of women who have sat here in impending motherhood have done, the numbed, sacrificial union.

He had complained — "Jesus! Add some woman all by herself!" — but Sylvia had never found anything appropriate. Just as Charlie leaves beside the nurse's desk the oak chair with its cushion still dented by his father's former bulk, so he leaves the pictures, leaves his office in its schizophrenic décor: the pictures entirely of motherhood, the practice three-quarters antimotherhood.

He now passes under a painting of a black woman with shiny taut skin, hugely pregnant among tropical flowers, and enters the inner office.

His nurse, Riva, a short, plump woman in her early thirties, with a skeptical smile that closely resembles his own, greets him with bantering. "Late, late!" She shakes her finger, though it isn't late.

Ten years before, Riva had been fired from another office for impertinence, and she is unrepentantly impertinent still. Charlie considers Riva indispensable for the very tone that makes her unemployable elsewhere. She is his bulwark, he often says, against doctor's pomposity, should he be tempted to it.

Charlie removes his jacket and puts on his white doctor's coat. Meanwhile, he tirelessly teaches pitfalls of pride.

"The doctor's moment of theater, Riva! Doctors put on arrogance with the white jacket."

Riva is adept at ignoring his sallies. She puts forth her own. "I'll bet you don't remember!" She challenges him. "A patient you delivered your first year of practice."

He says she is right — he doesn't.

"I thought you wouldn't!" She crows with triumph. "I do! She's in the waiting room now."

"F-f-f-first?"

"No, three others first."

Charlie seems relieved. Now Riva gives him a sharp look. "Sylvia called before. She said to tell you to bring some of her Chopin music from the piano bench. She's renting a piano."

"Chopin! Perfect!" Charlie laughs. "The melancholy exile!"

Riva laughs uneasily with him. She would like to ask him questions, but somehow can't. Brash Riva is suddenly shy. "Is this going to be permanent?" She would like to ask. "Is this what you want?" She would like to remind him that for such a long time she has gone along with each of his moods, his sarcasms, his teachings, his pain, his wit . . . If he cared to see it, he would know how she feels. She would like to say "If you ever feel lonely . . ."

Brash Riva goes quietly back to her desk.

⇛ ⇝

The woman complains of pain when Charlie examines her, ankles puffy, breasts tender. He observes the darkened nipple areolas. Soon there will be brown streaking on the belly, as if a rich inner river had forced silt onto its shores.

"I vomit in the mornings," she says in a disgusted voice.

"Omit salt from your diet."

"Why not tell me to eat straw?"

"It's not for long."

"Nine months — not long!"

"Too long?"

"Did you think it was my dream to get pregnant in the first six months of marriage?" Her small-featured, pretty face looks somehow pinched in its anger.

Charlie waits. Nothing more.

"Only two missed periods." He speaks carefully, turning his back.

"I wish to God there was none."

He more excitedly says, "You talk as if n-n-nothing had changed!"

She looks blank, her narrow face sullen. Then she says, "Oh!" and all the sullenness is wiped out by fright. "I couldn't do that. I would if I didn't have a husband. But I do, so there's no good reason . . ."

"I'm not going to d-d-draw that line!"

"I'm going to get dressed."

"You have less than a month."

"I'll be back in a month."

Charlie stalks out of the examining room.

"That woman in there doesn't want that b-b-baby!"

Riva leans her face on her hand.

"I c-c-couldn't talk her out of it! She's clamped on. Not through love, through sh-sh-sh —— "

They fall silent as the woman emerges. She hurriedly takes her appointment card from Riva, who gives her a brisk smile, and leaves.

"How do you know" — Riva turns to Charlie — "she doesn't want it? Or if she doesn't today, how do you know she won't tomorrow?"

"No today, yes tomorrow, no the day after?"

Riva puts her hands on her hips and announces with spirit, "I'd like a little leeway for my emotions, thank you, when I get pregnant!"

"What I should have done was throw her on the table, knock her out with a needle, and siphon the stuff into a w-w-waste jar."

Riva accepts, as she has always done, her quota of outrageousness with the daily job; it drives out boredom. "Go on, go on." She laughs. How many years, she thinks, has she gone along with his pain, his wit? Does he have any idea? If he were lonely would he come to her?

Now Charlie's behavior is exemplary.

A new patient sits up on the table after her examination, draped in a sheet, hardly able to keep her smile in check. Now and then it escapes into a downright laugh. Her cheeks glow with color.

"Am I supposed to feel this marvelous, Charlie? Where's the heaviness, the drowsiness, the sickness? I feel great."

"Good, Sally. Who said you're supposed to feel sick? For some women, it's the healthiest time of their lives."

"I must be one of them."

"I can see it in your eyes. Also, your urine. A-One. Go forth and multiply."

She laughs. "I'll have my quota — two."

Charlie reports to Riva that he feels nothing but pleasure in Sally's pregnancy.

"Don't try to convince me you're not a freak!"

~§ §~

"Ready for Mother Tovah?"

Charlie, his familiar half-smile in place, nods to Riva and moves to the next examining room.

At the sight of Tovah Melnick, something imprisoned in Charlie's life seems to screech, giving him a headache.

"How are you, Tovah?"

She hesitates. "I missed two times in my cycle, Dr. Brodaw."

"Two!" Charlie pretends to marvel. "Good work! Now your ten children can have a little brother or sister."

She regards Charlie with pleading eyes. Her waist is already thickened. Her body's springs, trained by repeated accommodations, sag swiftly into the outlines of pregnancy. Her shabby black dress, her heavy chestnut wig with a black kerchief tied around it, seem a uniform made for nothing else.

"You remember," she begins in a timid voice, "last time when I came to the eighth month how my legs swelled up?"

"I certainly do."

"I wondered, in that case, whether you would speak with Rabbi Tarn."

"I'd be honored to speak with him. What would you like me to speak with him about?"

She stares at him for a second, then lowers her head and humbly weeps into her hands.

"Say it!" Charlie commands.

Her expression is flat and dull. She shakes her head, wiping her eyes.

"You want me to speak to your rabbi. You want me to tell him it's a medical necessity — you'll also quote me to your husband, or maybe your husband will want to come himself and hear me say it. And all of that you want without ever yourself pronouncing the word abortion?"

She covers her face with her hands again, nods in wordless imitation of the very state Charlie has described.

"Why not?" She wails it up, muffled, from her hands.

"You have to say you want it."

"It's the same thing."

He shakes his head.

"But I get so sick!"

"Your varicose veins, your aches and pains, are normal for a woman who's had ten babies. It won't kill you to have another. It will help to ruin your life though. Acknowledge it. Admit you need help for the sake of your own life, that your own life is worth something too!"

"I can't," she whispers. She lowers her hands to just above her lips. The shocked eyes, the covered mouth, give her the look of a woman witnessing an accident.

Now Charlie keeps doggedly silent.

"Don't say no," she begs, extending her hands. "Don't make it so hard for me. I'm a religious woman. I can't do what would make me an outcast in my own community!"

Tovah Melnick, her hands clasped and extended before her as if praying, sways so violently in her chair that she appears to be drunk.

"You can always go to another doctor." Charlie's half-smile shocks her.

"How can I? You delivered seven of my children! Your father delivered the first three. Everyone would know I went elsewhere just for — that."

"Then say this to your husband: 'My body and my spirit are tired of giving birth. The law says I can get a safe abortion. I want one.' "

"But Jewish Law says no."

"Jewish Law can adapt. Jewish parents no longer stone disobedient sons."

"That was never done, the rabbis tell us!" She speaks up with quick conviction.

"One hundred years from now they will say, 'It was never done, that when a woman had ten children and wanted no more, she was forced to have another!' Teach the law to the Law!"

"You don't understand that it is impossible. Only if I am sick . . ."

"Suppose it is impossible for me to be a hypocrite and a liar?"

She flushes deep red, then rises so hastily, for all her heavy body in her confining clothes, that the chair falls over backward with a single sharp report. She turns and in her thick shoes runs heavily from him.

Charlie waits till she is almost to the end of the corridor, almost to the door of the waiting room, before he yells after her, "All right, I'll speak to him!"

She stops, turns, walks slowly, heavily back. She lifts up her white face under its ugly wig, straightens her thick body in its heavy, ugly clothing, and asks, "Why did you make me suffer so much before you said yes?"

This spark of truth and dignity flies like a hot flame from the quenched woman.

When she has gone, Riva comes into the hall, gives Charlie a piercing look, and asks, "What was all that about?"

"I know what it is to be a dead soul, led by the nose!" Charlie is white-faced. "I was one all my life. It's because of my life that I spoke to her that way."

As if to check on him, Riva stays through the examinations of the next two women. Charlie had delivered one child to each of them, and Riva had, over the years of checkups, developed easy relationships with them.

୶ৡ ৡ৶

"At least" — Riva salvages the morning with her tough humor — "you weren't knocking them down and sucking anything out! Watch it, Charlie, power corrupts!"

"I hope," Charlie answers mildly, smiling his half-smile, "that this time when I happen to have some it won't corrupt me."

"Probably already too late!" Riva speaks sternly but looks with affection. "Anyhow, I still have some funny feelings myself."

"Funny how, Riva?"

"I would never want to go back to the way it was — never! But when Sophie wants to abort because it's inconvenient timing, or May wants to because she's found out she's carrying a boy and she's got a thing against raising a son because she's so deep into feminism, then I feel funny, that's all."

Charlie frowns.

"Say it's like civil rights, judicial protection," Riva continues. "I don't want to change that, even though some who are guilty escape back into society. Because I say there are abuses doesn't mean I want to wreck the whole system."

"There are no abuses."

"Very funny, Charlie."

"No. It's a perfect system. Marvelously self-controlling."

"But you heard — "

"No matter. As soon as a woman suspects she may want to be rid of the fetus, that's good grounds for doing it. I'd say more. I'd say mandatory."

"You're getting fanatic, Charlie. There's your father in you, whether you know it or not."

"You may be right. But I tell you, Riva, if there's any d-d-doubt — out!"

Instead of keeping up the argument, Riva chuckles, having long ago decided that she would bind them together with banter.

◦⧉ ⧉◦

"You were my f-f-first delivery, my nurse tells me. I think I remember it, too. My father was busy on his own case. I was sick with f-f-fear because of your long, slow l-l-labor." Charlie consults her file. "I wouldn't have remembered your name. But I remember you."

The last patient of the morning is a handsome woman in her late thirties. "Do you feel sentimental about the marriages you sealed with babies?" She asks it in a low voice.

"I'm never sentimental about marriage." Charlie smiles his no-expression smile and keeps his eyes wide open with neutral interest.

"I feel a little ashamed of what I want to ask, isn't that funny?"

"Don't feel shame. It's only conditioning."

She takes a deep breath, then veers off the subject with visible effort, as if she were driving horses to one side.

"We've both changed. You for the better."

Charlie says it hasn't been exclusively for the better. After that, she is ready to say what she came to say.

"I'm divorced from the husband you met in the labor room ten years ago. Do you remember a guy who cried with joy when the baby was born? Or do they all do that, then it wears off? Five years after that he left me. I've fallen in love with someone again, at last. We're going to be married. But he feels we're both too old to start a new family. That's why I'm here."

"Here's the place to come."

"But sometimes I think I'd like to keep this baby — a seal for the relationship between my friend and me."

"Children aren't supposed to be used as sealing wax or glue." Charlie keeps his eyes on her, as if she might dart out if he didn't. Meanwhile he lifts the phone and reaches the Center. After a moment, he covers the mouthpiece.

"I can get you an appointment in two weeks. Well within the time."

"But I have more time than that?" She sounds alarmed.

"You have till the end of the first trimester. That will be in under two months. After that, if you delay that long, you'll know you're giving birth — but there'll be only the killed fetus. That would be a dumb move."

"I'll make it in time. I have to come to a point where I feel there's no choice, then I do a thing. Like my divorce."

"Don't be tempted to use it for glue!"

"I won't change my mind."

"I h-h-h-ope so!"

He launches one more persuasion, gets through it all smoothly, with no stutter. "At the Center where I work there's almost a superstition about someone people there call Genevieve X. They say she'll let things go till the last minute, then try to change her mind on the procedure table itself. She spells trouble — for herself and everyone else. I'm telling you this so that you'll know how important it is, if you insist on waiting, to spend the time getting yourself into the right frame of mind. No reversals!"

"Don't worry, there won't be any."

He leaves the office together with his former patient. At the door he stops and turns to look back at Riva, who calls, "I'll lock up."

"When you first came to the office," he asks his patient, "did you see my f-f-f-f . . .?" He is stuck.

"Famous bedside manner?" The patient supplies it with a nervous smile, trying not to look pained.

Charlie frowns. F's shake through him again. "F-f-f-f . . ."

"Fashionable clientele?"

"Father!" He births the word.

"Oh, yes! He sat in that seat!" She points to the oak office chair, the black leather cushion thinned out in the center from the old man's weight.

Charlie seems not to notice that her eyes fill with tears. He nods, satisfied.

8

H OW DID IT HAPPEN? When did you break out?" Paul
asks it in the taxi going over the Brooklyn Bridge to
Hannah's apartment. He feels a small disappointment.
The notebook, Hannah has been explaining, is not meant for
him. It is written for some others she refers to as "the community." "So you were," Paul says, "this pious, sheltered girl?"
"I might once have been that." She answers in a low voice.
"Now I educate myself in other things."
In the act of unfastening her blue duffel coat in his apartment this evening, Selig had remembered an important letter
that might be waiting for her in her mailbox. Her car —
the junk heap she had impulsively bought with her first earn-
ings at the Center — is in the repair shop. Paul offered the taxi
ride to her apartment and back to his.
"If I don't come early to my mailbox," she says now, to
explain further, "sometimes vandals get in. Then they tear
open everything to see if there is a check."
"A letter from — someone very important to you?" Paul's
voice shows some nervous concern.
"From a rabbi," she replies.
He looks blank.

"This is the rabbi," she begins with patience, "who moved away with the whole congregation to New Jersey."

"How come they did that?"

"Bad things happened in the neighborhood. Terrible things. The old people . . . they were . . ."

She is unable to finish.

"What? Bothered?"

She silently nods.

"That happens all over New York," he says. "People shouldn't run away."

"It was very bad."

"Even so — they could have asked for more police protection. Look at Crown Heights . . ."

The taxi has stopped at her door. She sees he is gazing through the window while she prepares to get out. He is looking at the filth of the street. Mary has told her that Paul grew up not thirty blocks away from here, in an apartment with his sick mother. Maybe he is transferring to there the refuse he sees here. Dirt on the walls. Bad smells.

She says, speaking very low, "Two people were killed."

"Were they so vital to the community that it couldn't have gone on functioning here?"

"Vital? While they were alive they were vital . . ."

Ahead of time she knows that it will be almost impossible to go on. But there are certain things she cannot allow him to believe about her.

"Father and mother . . ." she begins.

She feels dizziness and fumbles for the strap to hold on to. Then she is sorry for the look of horror she has brought to his face. By this time she has released the strap and has dug her nails into the flesh of her palm instead. It relieves the dizziness. She says quickly, "It was a war."

"A what?"

"What else do you call it when God kills people because another person broke an agreement?"

"Are you the one who broke it? Is that what you think?"

"Our own teachers give the idea that every destruction is the fault of sin. Innocent children for the sins of their parents. In my case, innocent parents for the sin of the child."

"My God, what was your sin?"

She is silent so long that he thinks now she will leave the whole thing in mystery, but then she begins almost inaudibly.

"My parents survived death camps in Europe. And came to America nearly crushed by what was lost. A beloved child and a beloved rabbi. Rabbi Pinchas, who led the community here, they found they could love almost as much as the saintly one who perished in Hungary. But I, who was born here, could not replace the beloved child, a son. Of him they would have made a rabbi. Year after year I had no idea what to do except to refuse whom they chose to marry me. Finally I was twenty-two years old and I wished to leave the community. Not to marry at all. To study at a university."

"Do you actually believe . . . ?"

"Do you see the cleverness? I was the one who was left. By parents. Community."

"Do you *believe* this?" Paul looks frightened.

She thinks, He has been more sheltered than I. "No, I don't believe it." She makes her answer gentle. "Since they have all moved away to New Jersey I argue sometimes in letters to Rabbi Pinchas, in my notebooks. God, I argue, gave free will. What kind of free will is it if God steps in with destruction if you use it?"

She opens the taxi door. "Will you come in?" she asks politely, without urging.

He shrinks to the back of the cab, shakes his head. She would like to stroke his unruly dark hair. "Don't be afraid," she wants to say. But chooses restraint. It is out of the question, she understands, that Paul would want them to make love in her apartment. That would frighten and depress him.

"If you would like to read something," she says, "while you are waiting . . ."

◄§ §►

After she enters the dim doorway of her house, Paul, waiting in the cab, shuts his eyes. A mistake. He sees, as if climbing stairs with her, the dark, smeared hallways. Her loneliness seems to seep like a dank smell into his shirt and up to his nostrils.

He opens his eyes and stares down the darkening street. Her own community ran away. Now there's no one to save Selig. No one but him. He feels fear — and elation.

He looks down. She has left a notebook in his lap.

◄§ §►

Hannah opens her mailbox with difficulty — vandals have bent its door — and finds the envelope with the New Jersey postmark and the familiar jagged handwriting. She carries it up the stairs to her apartment.

At the door she flinches for one moment, just before she steps inside. But of course now there is always nothing. Everything that can happen here that matters has already happened. She is not afraid to live on in her old apartment, with its worn wood floors, its peeling walls, its shabby chairs. The evil that had swept over it feels like a guarantee forever against a certain kind of harm. Like a fire that burns the ground so that nothing can creep upon it.

After the old neighbors moved away, she had come to know a Puerto Rican family upstairs. The mother had once sent down a pot of meat and rice, spicy and rich-smelling. She had wanted to eat it, and had tasted it. But her stomach had rebelled against the rebellion of her will. She had had to throw the food out, feeling the sin of waste.

In gratitude she had done what she knew how to do — she'd baked a Shabbos *challe* for the family, brushing the high curves of the twisted dough with egg yolk to make them shiny. The mother upstairs had exclaimed with pleasure over it. Her middle son had come good-naturedly down to show her how he had split it along its length, packed ham and cheese in it, and made a giant hero sandwich to take to work.

Another son, a strangely wizened unmarried man, sometimes waits for her on the stairs.

"He like you," his mother said sadly to her one day. "You no Católica, too bad. But he don't like too much girls. My son good. He could be priest. Maybe 'cause you got lotsa sorrow."

The good son, waiting on the landing, stares at her with glistening eyes. Once she had said sternly, "Don't feel sorry for me anymore, José!" To which there had been no reply.

Hannah thinks it must be as his mother said — he should have been a priest instead of a project security guard, because he cannot separate love and grief. His wet lips seem marinated in misery.

Not, Hannah hopes, on her behalf.

"You should fight back anyway," she had said to him one day in the hall. "Poor man, don't be afraid."

In the kitchen, Selig takes a drink of water and then listens, waits to hear if there is the sound of hoarse breathing behind her. Yes, very faint. Then no, gone. Had she heard it at all, this time? She keeps her face turned toward the sink until the sounds — the ones she always thinks she may be hearing — stop. For a long time she had heard them distinctly, horribly clear, whenever she entered her apartment, especially near the kitchen — the rasping of her father's and mother's last breaths. The two old people had been tied to kitchen chairs, back to back. They had choked on rags thrust roughly down their throats. Selig's own throat had closed — no scream could come forth when she had opened the door that evening, two years before, and saw them. Poor, trussed bodies, lifeless drooped heads . . . those struggling survivors whose painful task had been to say no to the death that had been willed for them . . . they had been made into rag dolls. She had squeezed the grocery bags she held till the cans and fruits thudded to the floor. The smell of raw meat — what would have been their dinner slid from butcher's paper and splattered over her feet — could still make her vomit.

"So if you missed this time Rosh Hashanah, you'll come in time for Succos."

The rabbi — whose letter she has carried up the stairs with her today — had at first telephoned from New Jersey with coaxing messages. Later there were urgent notes: she would surely celebrate with them, please G–d, one holiday or another. They missed her, and wondered and worried about her. *Soon,* she must come. The terrible thing that had happened must not be allowed to exert its dominion any further. The beloved parents must be remembered and named among the newborn. As with the Holocaust, so this. She must join them, marry, have children. Selig detected embarrassment, as well as sincerity, in the notes. The community even before going to its remoteness had been unable — oh, very unable! — to produce a husband for her. In their eyes she was an *alte moyd,* pitiable to them, she knew.

On what fated day had she decided to answer the Bianky Center's advertisement? She had been attracted by the queerness yet rightness of the language. "Individual sought with feelings of sympathy for other people's sorrows. Personal acquaintance with grief preferred." What Bunky had meant, it turned out, was someone who'd had an abortion. But many women who might have responded didn't; their experience had seemed to them not a grief but a triumph. So Bunky had settled for Hannah. The sympathy was what counted, he'd said.

"Goodby, Rabbi Pinchas," Hannah had written. "I am breaking my ties with the community. Please don't write me any more letters. I am going to work at the Bianky Family Planning Center. It is an abortion clinic."

The rabbi had replied at outraged length. Hannah's reply to him in turn lengthened itself, and in the end she had not sent it; it became a part of her journal. After a time Rabbi Pinchas wrote again, a briefer and more restrained note. Hannah was busily replying — in her notebooks. But when he heard nothing, he repeated the process: after a wait, he wrote — four more times.

Finally Hannah found a way to answer him. She had read always, read hidden away in her parents' apartment, walking back and forth to the library, cooking and keeping house for them, not thinking of running to a life of her own because to do that would have been to rob them of their last possession — enough that she robbed them, by her not marrying, of grandchildren . . . Since the death of her parents, she had read in a new way. She had begun her notebooks and discovered that she had a gift for mimicry.

Because she was fond of Rabbi Pinchas, Hannah did not write of the war that raged in her house. She had come upon the letters of Lady Mary Wortley Montague and had made use of a little of the letter-writer's sleight of hand, which could sometimes make getting your own way seem like yielding it.

"I know you feel it is your duty to change my mind," she wrote. "But you are so busy with everything you have to look after there. How hard it must be for you to find time to write even one letter! Won't you please allow me to save you this time? I beg of you — do not place on me the sin of drawing away even one ounce of your precious attention. Those who can profit from your advice should have nothing taken from them."

It was the reply to this letter that Hannah anticipated. Though she expected little from it, she felt bound to save it from vandals if she could.

The white-faced, dark-coated Jews had been replaced by dark-faced men who wore clothes of bright colors. No longer was there a synagogue in the neighborhood. The Jewish stores had closed. She let her observances lapse — those which she did not retain for purposes of her own — and God did not at once strike her dead. She had known He would not proceed in that way with her.

It is Friday. She has come not only for the letter but because she remembered the day. She squeezes two fat white candles into green glass holders from Woolworth's — the low brass ones her mother used had been taken with the other things. Downstairs, in Paul's taxi, the meter is running, but there is no help for it. She puts a match to the wicks and says the blessing in Hebrew. "Blessed are You, Lord our God, King of the Universe, who has sanctified us with commandments and commanded us to light the Sabbath candles."

Those little flames are supposed to draw God's spirit closer to earth. She watches a moment, then sits at the table and writes quickly in her notebook by their light, doubly transgressing. When God came close, He would have a slap in the face.

She had performed these bitter rites over and over, and others like them. But this war had gone on so long now that she begins to have doubts. The strength of it, the hot, bitter rage, is receding. She is no longer so sure of the messages she is flinging out, or of the recipient. She makes efforts to feel everything as she used to, but it is becoming harder. Not just because, for instance now, Paul is waiting. It is simply receding, that's all — it is threadbare.

When she is finished writing, she thinks that Paul may want something to eat. Luckily there are fresh vegetables. She prepares a sandwich for him, moving from refrigerator to sink to rinse off the vegetables. For all her resolve to break the Law, she can eat only dairy now. She regrets that this eliminates challenges of meat and milk. Sexual purity is another problem — how to flout it truly when there is no ongoing sex in a woman's life? She had, however, before her first visit to Paul, squatted in her tub and murmured a prayer. A virgin till that night, she had pierced her own hymen by her leap, like the leap of an Indian woman, a suttee leaping — as she herself leaped onto Paul's erection — into fire.

In Biblical times the man and woman lay together at first meeting. Rebecca and Isaac, she remembers very well, while she cuts bread for Paul's sandwich. And that was their betrothal. In the magazines she picks up on Forty-second Street — no, that does not happen.

She had educated herself there. At street-corner stands, and among illustrated manuals of erotica piled on bookshop tables where sexual techniques had been flung like infant animals that someone wishes to drown. From the pulpy, roiling seas of newsprint, Hannah innocently retrieved this drenched pathetic fur, these hairy pelts matted flat, and brought them to Paul's astonished bed.

God — she had once argued with Rabbi Pinchas — does not care about rabbinical inventions surrounding our lives. See how little the Bible had to say about food — only do not seethe a kid in its mother's milk! A restraint to greed and a reminder, even in feeding, to respect the sorrow of the mother of the butchered animals. Necessity must not make brutes of people.

Yet the time came when she was glad of these rabbinic elaborations. The more Laws, the more to flout.

She cuts into a tomato and remembers what she had started to tell Paul. Does he believe her? That there has been a war raging in her kitchen between God and herself? She mixing up meat and milk utensils: God slicing her finger; she writing on the Sabbath and riding to libraries: God sending her leaping imagination and visions of possibilities that run from her pen — only to deny them in life, one by one; she lying with her lover when it is clear there is no betrothal — will God turn away the lover's heart? She has fallen not into the marriage bed, but into deep love.

What would she tell Paul if she spoke of this again? "I hardly believe this any longer myself," she would have to say. "Yet it is better to believe God is responsible than that no one is.

But the terribleness of that . . ." There was her own guilt too, because some hidden part of her may have felt relief when her parents died — because she was released . . .

From time to time when she is not scribbling into her notebook about people at the Center (the immersion in new types opens up in her mind a seam of imagination she had not known was there), she writes instead about her community as lost in the woods as she is in the city. The thought has come to her that she would have had to discover notebook-keeping there as well, if she had joined them instead of refusing to go. There she would be an outsider too. One day the notebooks will explain her life to the community.

She chops at the vegetables with a knife while she rehearses in her mind the newest Center incident, which she will record in her notebook. This afternoon a tall, handsome, light-skinned black woman had, when Hannah sat with her to take information, bitterly complained, "Three o'clock! My God, what a time to give for an appointment!" "What's wrong with the time?" Hannah had asked. "It reminds you — kids coming home now from school . . . !"

The woman was wearing a beautiful beige suit with a navy turtleneck and matching navy everything — stockings, pumps, purse. Her manner was collected and cool. But when she said that last thing, suddenly her eyes filled with tears and abruptly she stood up. "I have to telephone," she said.

Hannah led her to a small office off which there was another room where she could stand near the open door and observe. Because she had been warned. The aides had told her and Bunky had told her to be on the lookout.

The woman spoke in a steady clear voice, and the man to whom she was speaking used a strong, confident, convincing tone. Just by lifting the extension receiver on the desk, without raising it to her ear, Hannah was able to hear the conversation.

"It's Alexandra. I'm here," the woman said. "The appointment is made, okay? First visit's a checkup. It's not today. *That* day it will be at three o'clock, what a time! Kids coming home from school . . ."

"No, it's a *good* time," the man said. "Think of it, Alexandra — *have* to be home, *wait* for them — I'll be with you on that day, babe."

"No you won't be! I don't want you to come, Brody. I won't even tell you the day. You'd hate it, sitting with all those pregnant women. I'd worry more about you than anything else. After it's all over, then you'll know."

Hannah saw that she had removed a thin, tooled-leather wallet from her purse and had opened it to a picture. Hannah could not see it where she stood, but from the way the woman caressed the face, Hannah guessed that the woman's — Alexandra's — heart was bending and crumpling around that picture of the man. Who now laughed.

"I'm going to be with you anyhow in my thoughts, baby. Nothing you can do about that!"

She didn't answer this time, and he impatiently asked, "What is it?"

"Why do you think there's anything?"

"Because I don't hear *something.*"

She was quiet again and he said, "It's not a baby!"

"Not yet it isn't. It's just a little piece of you and a little piece of me."

"Hell, not even that! Just some damned growth! Jesus, millions of women do it!"

They are both quiet, and then the man, Brody, starts again. "How often have you told me what you thought about your mother, Alexandra? What did you say she was?"

"I said she was a doormat, she was nothing."

"And when she was forty, how old did you say she looked?"

"She looked sixty."

"And her legs?"

"Yes."

"And her sloppy worn-out clothes?"

"Yes. Sloppy. Worn out."

"And her figure from having all those kids? What did your daddy say about that? Before he *left,* I mean!"

"He said he saw better figures on the slips of paper the numbers runners handed him."

"And you — great job, great clothes, great looks! Right?"

No answer again. " — And your father," the man said impatiently.

"Yes, he had women. Young, pretty ones."

"And you said — ?"

"I know — what I said!"

"Just don't blow it, is what I'm saying!"

"It's my own life, I can blow it if I want," she said, and when he answered, "Hey, baby, what'd you say?" she laughed apologetically into the phone.

"I love you like you are, baby," the man whom the woman called Brody said, "and I mean — *no changes!*"

Hannah had waited a few minutes and then had gone in.

"You can't imagine the conversation I've just had," the woman said, wiping her eyes.

"I may have heard most of the conversations there can be in a place like this," Hannah answered. "So you'll have your checkup and then you'll go home and think things over, won't you?"

"I have thought myself," the woman said, "to the end of thinking."

And truly, Hannah thinks now, what could the woman do but toss back and forth between her own wanting and her fear of what she wanted? Hannah has heard about Genevieve X. Mary had told her, with a ringing Irish laugh, that Bunky didn't have enough on his mind and so he'd had to invent Genevieve. But Hannah thinks that Bunky's story of Genevieve X has its own compelling logic to it. A recognizable ring. Have you achieved what you worked hard for? — a Center, a haven, a place where your sister's death can be redeemed by the rescued lives of a million women? Why then, Genevieve X will be sent to you! And for what reason? Don't even ask! Rabbi Pinchas might have an idea that Genevieve X would be sent to punish for what Rabbi Pinchas does not approve of. But what of all the punishments inflicted on those the rabbi does approve of? What about the good and the gentle? For what reasons do those happen? Rabbi Pinchas would admit he doesn't know. But if you don't know all, you don't know any!

⋘ ⋙

Waiting in the taxi, Paul looks into Hannah's notebook and then whistles softly to himself. My God, with *this* she's going to argue down the rabbis in that community — with Joe the orderly? He thinks that what has happened is that, released from her cloister, Hannah has gotten drunk on the world — the Center, Joe the orderly, bookstores, books! Or else — now he reverses it completely — what has happened is that *before this* she was drunk in her cloister, drunk on all those God-high people, and now she is sobering up, dazed by the difference.

What he reads is this: "Now I hear someone objecting: 'God has a part in the conception of each child. We snuff God each time we kill a fetus, at whatever week . . .' To which I answer in the words of Joe the orderly that God is snuffed every day in the living. Joe is a devout and thoughtful West Indian man who has worked in hospitals. He has seen things. 'Don't talk to me about snuffing,' he says, getting angry. 'Because then I might talk to *you* about snuffing! About the lives I've seen of children destroyed inside so they can't reach out to another human being except to want to kill *it*. First they are locked into a torture chamber from the days of birth, and then into a madhouse or a jail — and where's God in that? God doesn't make us Himself, you know,' Joe says. 'It's God with father and mother. And I notice one thing: if father and mother bow out, God does too.' "

Paul stops reading to muse that of his two theories he prefers the first: that she is escaped from her cloister and is now dazzled, drunk on the world. For him it is like encountering a wild child — a beautiful, nubile, wild, gentle girl who has stepped out of her meadow onto Sixth Avenue. He feels a quickening in the rhythm of his breathing. Soon he will share in whatever it is — that erotic drunkenness of hers, or that dazed wildness.

He looks down again at the page. Drunken? Wild? The writing is neat, precise. It speaks of some determination he has not yet fathomed and which for the moment he feels a strong desire not to know too much about. He lingers deliciously instead with his image of the wild girl on Sixth Avenue, and shuts the notebook, whose cover falls, like the lid of some blue-tinted Pandora's box, on Hannah's opinions.

⋙ ⋘

At the last bit of green pepper, Hannah sees without surprise the blood dripping from her thumb. She washes the blood from the vegetables and finds a Band-Aid. She keeps a supply — is always cutting, scraping, bumping herself. It is as if the knife — her mother's meat knife — understands her intention to use it to combine the vegetables with cheese, and under orders, had bitten sharply down. Now she washes the blood from the knife, then uses it resolutely for the cheese. She rinses the knife again and puts it carefully away in the splintery wooden meat drawer, contaminated.

Before all of that had begun to recede from her, she had considered such cuts to be wounds from the war. Small-scale smitings, nothing at all compared to the grand-scale ones of which she had proof.

Once or twice a great rabbi of the past had argued with God. One, after a bloody destruction, had even thrown stones up at heaven. But women? They were not on record as doing anything much but beseeching and weeping. When Biblical Hannah prayed in the Temple for fertility, swaying in her fervor, the priest had pronounced her drunk.

If once in a while (or often) women wanted to curse God, they must have done it like Job's wife — told their husbands, who prayed for them, to curse for them as well.

Let Him hear for a change a woman's voice, she had said to herself, before all this receded. Her pen, like Balaam's tongue, somehow pours out only praise and hope. Therefore her voice would be in the kitchen, slicing cheese with a meat knife; under the Sabbath candles, writing about the Center; in the lover's bed. And a kind of message comes back. A message of pain that she calmly accepts. Or had done, before the receding.

Arguments with men God sometimes seemed to enjoy — with Abraham, with Moses, with Lot, with Jonah. Up to a point. But with women? About this there was no news. She would see, she had thought, what the end of her argument would be, and had meditated stoically on possible endings before all this had begun to recede from her.

Meanwhile, now, she prepares Paul's sandwich and reflects that some might think her belief that she could engage the Deity in dispute had been no more than self-delusion. But is what I thought so different, she asks herself, from what men do? They take off their prayer shawls and tell themselves they've had their say!

She feels a moment's pang — a sharp but *bloodless* cut this time: all that is receding from her!

When she has finished carefully wrapping the sandwich in aluminum foil, she wipes her hands and opens the letter.

Rabbi Pinchas' note today is terse but fierce. The sharp European daggers with which he forms his letters tower high and plunge deep with rabbinical passion and splattered ink: "Think of your father and mother!"

To this note she will never reply. For what reason should she? He must surely know that everything she does now she does because she thinks always of the fate of her father and mother.

Outside her door, some of Sorita's children are loudly playing. One is hammering a shoe on the iron railing of the stairway. The five-year-old twin boys are punching each other with serious, flinching faces. The baby sits perilously close to the open stairway in a soaking diaper, blinking at the scene.

"Here you are too, José!" Hannah greets him almost gaily. Sorita's brother, unemployed now for a long while, stands watch over Sorita's children while she is inside with her man. He stares intensely out of his dark eyes. His short, wiry body seems to rebound from the wall against which it leans. He is thinner since his mother has gone back to Puerto Rico with the younger children. Only his sister, with so many children of her own, remains.

"I'm going to visit my friend, José," Hannah explains carefully. Although he never answers her in words she can understand, she always speaks to him. He is like me, she sometimes says to herself. His community has left him.

He breathes heavily, and a cold smell of garlic surrounds her. He is like someone who has run from somewhere with a message. What is the message? She watches him closely for a response, but there is nothing except his glossy stare.

Sorita emerges from her apartment. She is young and pretty but looks bad. Deeply shadowed eyes, yellowish pallor in the cheeks. Her hair is not too carefully combed. She shuffles in men's slippers.

"Sorita! I haven't seen you in so long," Hannah says. "How are you?"

"I been gettin' sick in the mornings again. That's why I dint come out to see you."

"Not this time *again*, Sorita!"

"Yeah. What can I do? He likes it better when it makes a baby." While she self-consciously laughs, she shields with three fingers the bad front teeth of which she is ashamed.

"I told you, I told you — you can come with me."

"Oh, I wanna have this one. Once it starts I gotta go through with it, that's how I feel."

"All right, but you shouldn't have more after this, should you?"

"Oh, no, I never want another one!" She laughs again, shakily. "I know that's what I said before, too."

"Come with me to the Center, then. They'll tell you, show you, everything you need to prevent the next one from starting."

They have been speaking low, but the door opens and a man's angry face peers through the opening.

"Sorita!" he calls so sharply that the name is almost a single syllable. She calls to José to pick up the soaked baby, grabs the hands of two of the kids, and hurries inside without another word to Hannah.

◄§ ❧►

The cab at once, at Paul's word, takes off. Hannah hands Paul the sandwich, the paper napkin, and the small can of cold apple juice.

"You might be hungry. You have had a long wait."

She turns slightly away from him to give him privacy to eat, and pulls still another notebook from a worn shoulder bag.

"Why do you write so much?" He has taken a mouthful of her food. What is it — something not bad on dark, dense bread. Crunchy. With some kind of cheese. Goat? He is impressed with what he has read, yet feels nervous about it. "Why not just say what's on your mind?"

"The reason I write" — Selig speaks with a quiet force that surprises him — "is that it comes out better on paper. It must be that I like to perfect — to see progress. Speaking is wind — it blows over. On paper it's still there if you like to have another listen and to make changes. It's the same for me with people. A person who corrects himself, who wants to make himself better and goes over and over and crosses out and puts in where he was lacking before — such a person goes to my heart."

She gazes at him with an expression of such deep and open love, yet without in any way moving toward him, that he feels as if a decision to love him has been made and settled without demand of response from him. When he stops chewing, he finds that it is difficult for him to swallow. His chest is full of emotion. But now moved by God knows what spirit of compassion mixed with self-preservation, he blurts, "Marriage isn't my line, I'm convinced. One bad one was enough."

"We'll see what God permits," she answers quietly. "To marry is not my first business."

In the quiet intimacy of the taxi, racing cozily away from the dirty sprawl of these Brooklyn streets, there comes over him some clear open feeling toward Hannah. Again, as once before, he feels touched by a breath from the fanning wings of love. One wing, anyway. Later in bed, he exerts effort to give Hannah pleasure and hears her utter a cry that has not come from her before. In an interval of peace and well-being she gets up and walks to his kitchen. She brings, with an expression of deep love on her face, a cup of steaming liquid to him in bed, with a chunk of lemon from his refrigerator on the saucer. She walks naked and unselfconscious, carrying the tea cup high and close to her lovely breast from carefulness, not modesty.

"You're bringing me tea?" Though he hates it, he is touched.

Maybe because she hears he doesn't want it, at the bedside she stumbles. The searing liquid sloshes back over her skin, just above the nipple, and she screams.

"Cold water! Right away," he orders, jumping up and seizing her by the arm.

But she refuses. "It's all right."

"It must hurt. It *will* hurt. Just for one minute it's desensitized!"

"Not so much." Mystifyingly, she smiles.

He sees the skin of her breast grow fiery red. He insists; he brings ice; he makes her lie down while he applies the coldness. All the while she is smiling. As if someone had played a joke. A joke?

"For God's sake, Hannah, don't smile. I know how it hurts!"

She kisses him lightly. Amusement, sadness, patience play over her lovely, intelligent features. She says, "A message is better than silence."

A second wing beats strongly over his head and then — how could he have doubted it? — he is enfolded by both powerful wings of love. He feels the feather-soft though crushing embrace on his heart, and pictures a medieval painting: seraphim with front-folded wings, each as large as a separate body, strange and frightening and wonderful on the otherwise human form. As the angel holds him, so he holds Hannah. And begins to murmur to her, thinking that is the message she means — about his love. His heart is full.

But then her reply is so strange that that very same heart, by now almost used to her ways, gives a triple-thudded jump. He can hardly separate the thrill of love from the shock of Hannah.

"Though it may be a message," she says softly, reflectively, "that lost itself in time and arrives out of turn. Just as light comes late from stars receded from us, already extinguished — " She cuts herself off abruptly and then smilingly says, "You mustn't mind. An old habit of speaking aloud what I might write in my notebook."

Her red-gold crinkle-waves brush at his cheek like angel's hair. The light from her gray-green eyes dives down into his soul and washes it warmly. He feels that he holds in his arms not just a lovely woman but a farseeing one. Suppose she's a witch? His life, God knew, could use some of that — redemption by magic, by miracle. Margaret, he remembers, had warned him about this — attributing special powers to a woman. But surely he's right to recognize what he has found in Hannah! He hugs her — his salvation — tight.

◆§ §◆

In a rush of feeling, full of his own joy, full of awed pity for Charlie, Paul reports at lunch time to Edgar the latest news about Charlie and Sylvia. "He really did it this time, Bunky, he finally managed to strip away his last support!"

Edgar, in turn, recounts the story in the evening to Ellen, who unwittingly makes matters worse. She briskly responds that such things happen every day, that it is no cause for alarm, that in fact this little sexual interlude may be very good for both Sylvia *and* Charlie.

"Millions of people," she authoritatively says, "have extramarital affairs!"

Edgar thinks of the note fraying in the breast pocket of a little-used jacket. He feels something between a sob and a laugh rising deep in his chest. The more he feels like sobbing, the more he feels like laughing. How has he managed to turn his life into an Italian opera, despite science and a New England wife? *Ah Guiseppe!* He whispers inwardly the name his mother had protectively tucked between the two Americanized ones.

But how often he and Ellen have scornfully dismissed such notes! They have become formula: whenever an employee leaves — quitting in disgust at a physical process repeated so many times, or fired by Edgar for anything from incompetence to too little sympathy — often the vicious note comes. Vulgar. Awful. Sickening. Sick.

"See to your wife, Bianky! While you're so busy scooping it out of other men's wives, they're pouring it into yours!" Or, "Your wife and the big black orderly. At night. In the assembly room they're getting it together."

And worse. Much worse. Coarse and filthy. It always goes the same way. An employee who can no longer stand the sight of aborted fetuses will often lash out killingly at him, as if there were no known way of connecting feelings for these early cell clusters with compassion for the evolved human being.

How often Ellen has come upon a note in his pocket, brought it to him torn to pieces on her upheld palm. "Did you want to show me this?"

But *this* note, fraying in the breast pocket of his little-used jacket, she has not found. Somehow, as long as she does not find the note, it may be true. So — he says it to himself with disgust — why don't you put on a baggy white satin costume with big red pompons and walk down the corridors of the Center in it? Pagliacci!

Ellen, all unaware this time, goes on lovingly, scoldingly, as Edgar sits in his handsome Japanese-style bathrobe of rich burgundy velour. It is her own present to him. Her choice for herself in bathrobes is tailored navy flannel.

"How many new aides can you put on? Soon you won't be able to move in that place!"

"Don't you understand vigilance? Don't you — ?" Edgar works at his large, square hands, cracking the joints, the right-angle-knuckled thumbs spread in loose strength, as if ready to receive a thrown ball.

"Oh, I know what you think," Ellen dryly goes on. "You think that because of what's happening to Charlie and Sylvia, somehow your silly fantasy of Genevieve X is going to suddenly jump into reality. Believe me, it isn't. So what if people's lives are a little complex? It's all, really, useless worry!"

Ellen's calm-featured face composes all difficulties. Her pure white skin shines at him from flat cheeks and a high domed forehead. Her intelligent nose — English — arches and then lengthens at him consolingly.

But then even Ellen's temper gets the better of her and she bursts out, "Oh, I hate this reign of terror!" though she catches herself and repeats, "But it's all . . . darling . . . useless worry. You don't *need* another aide, but do it, darling, if it will make you happy . . ."

Book Two

Talking of the common remark that affection descends, a gentleman said that "This was wisely contrived for the preservation of mankind, for which it was not so necessary that there should be affection from children to parents, as from parents to children; nay, there would be no harm in that view though children should at a certain age eat their parents."

Johnson. "But sir, if this were generally to be the case, parents would not have affection for children."

— The Table Talk of Dr. Johnson

... No. 5 ... one more tiny voice to swell the vast human wail rising perpetually to the skies!

— Alice James,
Diary

1

ALREADY TWENTY-TWO? Surely younger than that? Twenty, say — Mimi's age? No, there is no duplicity in that face. Amy Netboy is, since she says so, twenty-two years old. Gray eyes unusually clear. Light brown hair twisted into a long loose braid shining alertly at her back.

It is not because of Amy's youthful look that Edgar tries to discourage her from taking the job. There is something else — and at first he can't quite place those odd sensations he feels during their interview.

He tests her. "You're in favor of what we do here, but what about seeing hundreds of procedures each month? Will you think there's something immoral about ending so much potential life? What do you think about" — he recalls a phrase from a brochure — "the sanctity of the seed?"

She smiles a healthy broad smile. Her voice softly burred, like a child's, with that suggestion of energy so abundant that it overpours itself, roughening its own edges. "I don't think about it at all. My thoughts are with the women who want freedom to choose."

She speaks the phrases that by now — with all he knows — are almost a mockery to him. She says she believes in "the autonomy of women's bodies." In "free choice." Her lips, fresh and sweet-smelling — he catches the scent of them from where he stands facing her, with a shiny colorless gloss on them of the kind young girls use as their first makeup — shape the sounds as if savoring them. As if the words are sweet in her mouth, like ice cream flavors. *Freedom. Women's bodies. Choice.*

That is the first time, alone in his office with her, after hours, that Edgar thinks he is having a heart attack. And of course he is. While he sits facing her he feels it: it pounds, it flails, the motor in his chest, not like the machine it is but like a live being. Edgar rubs his hand in circular motions over his deep chest. His brown broad hand with its square nails — they look ivory-colored and strong; the skin tanned and unpierceable — circle his breast and nipple, to soothe. But the inner tumult persists.

Amy's braid gives an alert twitch to one side and lands on her shoulder. Its fine wavy hairs gleam at him. He wants to reach out to touch it — an overwhelming need! The doctor's discipline of attitude, the athlete's discipline of muscle — both nearly fail him. He calls them smartly in like margin notes in a market plunge. But though he keeps his hands either at his sides or rubbing his chest, circle upon circle, he feels a bankrupt.

"Some women want it and don't at the same time!" Edgar makes his voice harsh, disapproving. "They're the ones who need special attention." Should he tell her right now, he wonders, about Genevieve X? Even to consider it feels like a betrayal of Ellen. She is the only one to whom he directly and openly speaks of it. What the staff knows is only leakage and rumor.

With eager energy Amy replies that she understands all that.

"Religious scruples" — Edgar growls it at her — "give problems!"

All too easily, she responds, "I haven't any." When she

comes to live in New York she'll stay — at least at first, she says — with her grandmother. Who was born a Jew but became a humanist and social reformer when young. Amy has heard from certain relatives, she explains, that her mother had been attracted back to religion, but that might have been in rebellion, like her marriage to a Roman Catholic, Amy's father. "In any case" — the smile does not shrink so much as dim — "both my parents were killed in a car accident when I was a baby — I don't even remember them — so I was spared the next round of reaction."

Foolish, prattling child, Edgar prepares to tell Ellen. Though he sees that the smile is brave, not foolish. Meanwhile the pain in his chest pierces even deeper. An orphan, too! The congestion, the swelling, is terrible!

"Don't talk frivolously, then, about things you haven't experienced." He shocks himself with his own brusqueness. "More to the point now" — thrusts a hand under his white coat and rubs at the left side of his shirt; he sounds to himself hard, razor-voiced — "This job will keep you from your studies. You may feel it's a service to women and it is that, but I assure you it does not lead to the profession of medicine!"

Amy pronounces the word again — *choice* — delectable on her tongue. "This is my own choice, freely arrived at." She has finished undergraduate work. The Center is now more attractive — "a thousand times!" — than further theory in some graduate department of social work. "Dreaming about better worlds — I don't want to do that anymore. Only work that's practical and immediate."

Her healthy open smile flashes and flashes at him like signals: "Stay — Come." Those first terrible deaths have not dulled the life that shines forth from her person. At that very moment, how deeply it touches him! He had forgotten how the expression of full, direct feeling gives pleasure; is aware of a second betrayal of Ellen when he thinks, Tight, Protestant control — it's drying up my life!

But Amy's innocent faith fills him also with sadness. She makes him think of Mimi. Yet also not Mimi.

"Now it appeals!" Edgar forces himself to insist on it harshly. "You'll do a service for women but you won't make a way for yourself in the world! On top of that — come with me!"

He strides toward a procedure room, flings open the door, and points into the silent emptiness. The powerful vacuum assemblage looms over the immaculate white cot — the glass tanks, the loops and loops of coiled tubing, poised there like a pillaging army.

"There it is!" Edgar turns to her almost viciously. "On this machinery, with this procedure, by these hands." He holds out his own two brown and broad-nailed ones but sees the faint tremor and quickly pulls them down. "And the eyes of every kook, creep, woman-hater and baby-sentimentalizer in the world are focused here. They'd blow us up in a minute if they could!"

When he turns again to her he sees tears.

"Dr. Bianky, I have my own strong reasons for this decision!"

She's had some dreadful experience, Edgar thinks. Some painful, dangerous, frightening humiliation of an abortion, it must have been. Poor child, poor girl, poor woman!

The tumult in his chest does not subside. And although he has already early that morning been to the New York Health Club, where he had undergone carefully supervised stress tests and been pronounced fit to perform on the exercise bicycle, jogging treadmill, weight machines — everything, in fact, including the squash court, as long as he does not indulge more than once a week — he has the distinct feeling that his heart is failing.

"I'm dying," its message comes. "Already lost." And this young woman I barely know, he thinks, will have to watch me fall and cradle my head and breathe into my mouth and call the authorities. A moment later he sees, This is the third thought that betrays Ellen: now I've taken my death away from her too! He is suddenly, fiercely angry. The injustice to Ellen seems an emblem of the cruelty of all life. *It's absolutely unfair,* he thinks, with an indignation that removes it far from his doing and brings with it a sense of the miraculous appearance of evil — for, although it is true that he is doing it, *why* is he doing it?

"You'll start in three weeks' time," Edgar says hoarsely to the upraised child-face of Amy Netboy. She nods and smiles in anticipation. The man in the white doctor's coat looks to her by no means on the point of death. She sees a handsome man of solidly built middle age, care and kindness mingled in his face.

She notes with surprise her own grateful tears and wonders if she had wanted him to see them. She feels dimly aware that an inner movement of spirit is going on, without her full consciousness and without, certainly, her permission. It is oddly familiar, though it has not happened to her before. It is almost frightening, and she catches her braid in her fist for comfort. It is sudden, but feels too considered to be precipitous. With a kind of "deliberate speed" there is a sort of inner reaching and stretching. Edgar is being *placed* — is being accepted as a figure who can illuminate a dark corridor of her childhood's imagination that has stood void. His great strong bulk is effortlessly lifted and set down again among the archetypal figures in this inner pantheon, within the empty niche where (she nearly, from stress of feeling, mingles nervous giggles with her tears as she thinks of a Victorian mustache cup with Gothic letters painted in black) the word "Father" is carved.

There seems to be no end to the cavernous halls of spirit that receive this effigy — roomier than the cellars she has read about in the Metropolitan Museum of Art, where the great romantic statuary is stored, and where stone friezes of horse and chariot plunge on for several glorious, out-of-fashion feet.

⋖ ⋗

In the next days, Edgar sees Selig busy at her scribbling. He peers in passing, imagines what he might see: "A pretty young woman is coming as an aide. Paul will fall in love with her and I will have no chance."

He hears Paul make one of his jokes: "I hear Bunky's hired a new one. How old this time — ninety? With a rocking chair? The ladies can abort in her lap, how's that for supportive?" Then Paul bites his lip. Edgar bites his own.

Even Charlie has time to comment before he leaves: "Netboy's her name? Good. I hope she'll draw the net tighter." He means the opposite of what Edgar intends, which is to sieve out disaster. For Charlie the net is to catch and keep all.

Edgar at first urges Paul to take a vacation. Failing at that, he turns to Charlie. He would send everyone away if he could. Foreknowledge grips him of the time when Amy will arrive to be greedily loved by all.

▪ ▪

Every day someone on the staff is sure to stop Edgar in the corridors. "When's Dr. Brodaw coming back?" Why, he wonders, is Charlie so missed? What is it about the sight of his slender, sick body? Elegantly clad in trousers of pearl- or charcoal-gray, with double-vented blazer of navy blue — what does he contribute to the well-being of nurses, aides, and orderlies? Charlie has the mysterious power of someone who needs to do nothing but show a sardonic smile. Yet it must make them uneasy, that smile, Edgar thinks. It is a smile of judgment, after all — you can count on Charlie for judgment. No one at the Center, or out of it for that matter, would want to admit that judgment is more welcome than indifference. Yet Charlie is missed. By people who do not like the work they do to go unremarked. They do not want to experience the loneliness of the undetected. Better to feel surrounded by Charlie's sardonic commentary as they garbage the fetuses, is that it? When Charlie returns, he will judge, with his smile, everything that has happened till then and will also, by his smile, show how little else could have been expected.

Edgar is used to it now — the sense that something has curdled. Disappointment has crept around the edges of these light-filled rooms. Everything has changed, yet not everything has. The quality of life has improved — a segment of humanity relieved of misery — but in another way has deteriorated — a million fetus-killings a year. A numb pain seizes society after some great technical or legal innovation is celebrated. What — are we still less than perfect? Can't we ever advance?

These thoughts come to Edgar with Amy's arrival. Often when he sees her through the open door of one of the conference rooms, she is talking quietly to a small group of women. They hold questionnaires, drooping, in their hands. Personal data. They have to be convinced information will be kept confidential. Her braid moves, animal-like, along her back, arching high out from her head, held by some kind of clip. He would like to undo the locked plait, each link as strong and smooth as a limb. Pass his fingers along the freshly parted, intimate edge. He is already jealous, though he can't tell of whom; already guilt-ridden, though he has not acted.

Now and then when he thinks he is unseen Edgar stands and stares a moment and draws a full, painful breath. I'm going to die, he tells himself for the third or fourth time that week. My heart won't take this.

❦ ❧

Connected by office phone to Charlie's ski lodge in Canada, Edgar projects an encouraging tone into his urgings. "No need to leave!"

"I hate to, without t-t-trying, Bunky. I didn't want to spoil the first week, so I haven't had a t-t-talk with Daniel yet."

Paul had refused Edgar's vacation offer — he couldn't afford to let Margaret think he would skip visits with the girls, he said. But Edgar had been able to persuade Charlie to go away with

Daniel, he — childless Edgar — advising, "Best way for father and son to get close. After things settle down at home, I mean." With an attempt at delicacy his concern made impossible, Edgar surrounded with a bear hug the impending event: Sylvia was moving from the grand, ornately furnished house in Harrison to the simple, charming Greenwich Village apartment that she and Charlie together had found for her. Fearfully she had responded at last to Charlie's insistence that less in her life would mean more.

"Daniel would like to get far, not close. I can't have everything, Bunky." Charlie had answered in his deep but dry voice. Not forgetting to smile.

But Daniel, though he at first sneered, "What's this, Be Good to Dropouts Week?" accepted, finally, the offer of a trip to Canada with his father. Daniel is enjoying the skiing, Charlie says on the phone.

"We've got the new aide now." Edgar's lips shape themselves soundlesslly about her name. But he does not utter it. "By all means, take another week!"

The moment the phone leaves his hand he is off in search of her, is always looking for her now. The pressure of the work justifies it. But this is a different need. How can he not admit it? He has seen too many men stride to center stage, hands pressed against hearts. He has heard too many arias not to know the name of this one swelling in his chest.

❦

Selig is scribbling, scribbling.

Do your worst, thinks Edgar.

In fact, the ceaseless diary-filling has flooded over its boundaries. Selig has now resumed letter-writing as well.

"I beg, Rabbi Pinchas," she writes — the beseeching tone is late nineteenth century — "that my silence will not be construed as unfriendly. It is the result, rather, of my readying a longer communication in the form of a journal."

She stops to think. Writes more rapidly, carelessly. "But now I need your advice. Is that the best way to explain? How should I do this, then? Like *Uncle Tom's Cabin?* Scenes of abuse? Abused children. Belts, sticks, whips, hot oil, boiling water, candle flame, burning enema — 'Oh, please, no, Mommy dear! No, Daddy, Daddy, I'll be good! I'll be good!' Can I do that? Must I, gagging and retching, write about that?

"Or trace one family. Too many little ones. Thomas Hardy's *Jude the Obscure.* The oldest boy hangs the children, then himself. 'Done because we were too many.' Ruined hopes. Ruined bodies. Ruined lives. Oh, it's hard, it's the hardest story of all.

"Or women dying? Mutilation, blood, terror, despair. Must I? Oh, I'd rather not!

"Tell me, please, what you think is the best way to explain my life now to those people who have known me since I was born. Despite your disapproval, you will be generous, I know, with advice. You had the reputation, with my parents, of wisdom. You will understand that questions of morality are also dealt with here every day."

She sees Edgar passing and weaves him in: "The head doctor here, for instance, a moral man till now, is being tested by youth and beauty in the guise of his dead sister. What could be clearer? I will keep you informed of his progress.

"I hope that all goes well there, and that your cesspool problems are over."

She is tempted — tempted — to copy out, right after that, burning words from her notebook: "I have gone in too far and can't get out. In my arrogance I shouted my challenge as loudly as I could. Now the answer comes and it will break my heart."

Instead, she humbly signs herself, as if the recipient combines the attributes of Maimonides with a lovelorn-adviser's, "Perplexed Hannah."

2

Y OU'LL DO ME a favor, Paul, if you come to lunch. It's at home today, with my grandmother. You have to tell lies for me."

"Little Red Riding Hood!" He could kick himself for that joke. If that's who she is, what are the rest of us? "Amy — what lies?"

"Nana doesn't know yet where I work."

"Doesn't *know*? Maybe she shouldn't."

Amy protests quickly: what a strong feminist her grandmother had been in her day; how astonishing it is that Nana had taken so terrible a dislike to what they do here. "I had to let her think we only give out contraceptive devices, like the old Margaret Sanger clinics. I hate to deceive her. I know she'd accept if she heard in the right way. Meanwhile, will you help?"

"I'd be a fool to try to fool a smart old lady like your grandmother."

"Oh, Nana's brilliant. She once made speeches and led demonstrations. In the thirties and forties. She was a mathematician, like Grandfather, but he taught at the university. Nana tutored children in hospitals."

"Sounds like an awesome lady."

"You'll come and see? And help me? Please?"

"I'll do it because I'm courting you for my friend, my associate — Charlie Brodaw. You know that, don't you?" The old-fashioned term pleases him and he repeats it, "I'm courting you for him." He feels prompted to add, "You know why I don't court you for myself, don't you?"

"Why should you when there's wonderful Hannah!" She laughs.

"I speak for Charlie even though he doesn't ask it. You don't ask it either — but you seem very much on your own in the world."

"What makes you think Charlie would like *me?*"

That, of course, is the best question in the world. Paul thinks it possible that Charlie will not want to like Amy. He is perverse. He is self-denying. But as for Amy — she seems already half in love with Charlie. Paul is astonished at how well he has done his job.

"There's no one whispering in his ear about my supposed virtues, the way you are in mine about his."

"He'll see them himself."

"Maybe he won't be susceptible."

"If that's true," Paul says passionately, "then he's a dead man! But it can't be true. How could it be? He'll see what you are." For the moment, he believes it.

They pass the lunch room on the way to get their coats. Paul sees Hannah writing. Beside her sits Bomstein, large and impenetrable, a yellow boulder, coming to her own conclusions — the opposite of Hannah's. On Hannah's page at this very moment, Paul imagines there are words like "hope," and "change," and "renewal." On Bomstein's, only words that reveal the nastiness and self-delusion of the poor wretches they describe. Paul shudders. Unlike Edgar, he believes in the existence of their books. Between these two views — one, angelic visions; the other, dust and ashes — where, Paul wonders, will I find myself? The thought of what Bomstein's appraisal of him might be depresses him, so that he turns away without waving to Hannah, as he'd meant to do.

◦§ §◦

He would not have imagined the mathematician would care much about cooking, but Amy's grandmother serves a delicious home-cooked meal: fresh vegetable soup, followed by baked avocado stuffed with flaked halibut, and a dessert of wafer torte lined with crushed hazelnuts and chocolate cream.

She looks like a grandma, too, with kinky gray hair and a big saggy bosom in navy blue with a silver pin stuck through it. He thinks to himself, That's what her mind is like, also — a heavy sack of ideas fixed with a big pin.

He is uneasy all through lunch, wondering what the grandmother makes of him. And then he has to pretend to be a practicing gynecologist, giving himself a few unwanted pangs. The grandmother, keeping up, asks him eager questions about the latest techniques for saving premature babies.

This won't help me, he thinks while glibly answering, when the truth finally comes out. She doesn't look the type who goes for irony.

"So now how young? Six months? Five months?"

"By weight, actually, Mrs. Landau. As little as one thousand grams now, and we are all working toward reduction of the amount."

"Good!" She is a large woman, with a heavy, impatient, downright speech. "Then there will be no deaths at all soon! We are at last beginning to be interested in the women who want to have pregnancies and cannot hold them . . ."

She gives him a broad, encouraging look. Not that her fierce earnestness would emit something so commonplace as a smile. But it is as if he has been gathered in by an aura of approval — as if a large bronze Buddha set in the middle of an ancient temple had given a nod and a wink. It is over in a second, himself the only witness, asking himself if he has been hoodwinked ("hoodwink" being the kind of wink it was if it was a wink at all — a wink under a hood, veiled, mysterious, compelling) by his own senses.

Amy ends the moment by getting up to clear away the dessert plates and coffee cups. She kisses her grandmother's cheek. "Thanks for the wonderful lunch, Nana. We've got to think about getting back to work now."

"Very mysterious, your work," the old lady says shrewdly. "Are you C.I.A.?"

Amy sends Paul a look and he inwardly groans.

"Nana, I know you were a rebel, weren't you?"

"I like to think so."

"You told me how you demonstrated for Margaret Sanger. To allow women the right to contraception."

"Oh, yes. I don't mind admitting this in front of your friend Dr. Sunshine. I was one of the first. It's not thought about much these days. But all those women who go into medicine and law, and who hold jobs and run for political office — there's not one could do much if she had to have a baby every year!"

The old lady lifts her head, pulls her bosom up after it, and begins to intone: " 'The basic freedom of the world is woman's freedom. A free race cannot be born of slave mothers.' "

"Oh, Nana!" Amy claps her hands with pleasure. "You still know all that by heart!" To Paul she says proudly, "It's Margaret!"

Paul has a bad moment until he realizes she means it is the great crusader, Sanger, who is the author of the grandmother's noble declaration, and not that his ex-wife had preceded him like a seven-league-booted giant to pass out speaking parts to everyone playing a role in his life. These powerful Margarets, he inwardly mutters.

Now the great bosom swells up like a blue sea; the silver pin rises with it like a caught fish. The deep voice rolls out again over the green mint dish and the scattered cake crumbs.

" 'When the last fetter falls, the evils that have resulted from the suppression of woman's will to freedom will pass . . .' "

The old lady goes on reciting, nimble-brained. Her wrinkled, heavy-browed face seems to smooth itself into a much younger one — Paul catches a glimpse of a serious-faced, handsome young woman shouting through street-corner tumult: steel-rimmed glasses, leg-of-mutton sleeves —

" 'Child slavery, prostitution, feeble-mindedness, physical deterioration, hunger, oppression and war will disappear from the earth!' "

"Nana! I think about that always. Now women can have abortions too — that's a continuation of her work."

Nana's face wrinkles with distaste. "No, that's different. Abortion — that's a different matter."

"But important for the same reasons, to give women free choice!"

"Dear child, I go more slowly now. There are idealists who want to kill you if you refuse their efforts to save you. Even Margaret, sometimes . . . that kind of energy, that zeal . . . it tramples others to reach its goal. She made reality of one of the greatest dreams in human history, but she broke many lives, I know that. Let's stay with what we have — diaphragm and foam and pills and uterine loops. What more do they need? Why bring it to the ugly stage of killing? I know you're not talking about — about . . ." Her look loses its sharpness. It turns inward, in momentary confusion. "Of course, in certain circumstances . . . If a rape, or if children . . ."

Amy hurries into the breach. "Or if the men won't allow them. I know people used to say if women don't want babies, let them use self-control. People used to think those devices were immoral! Now it's the same with abortion, Nana. For a while there was one heroic doctor, Dr. Spencer, who lived in Pennsylvania. His own daughter died from a bad, illegal abortion. He devoted his life and his practice to performing good, safe abortions for anyone who came to ask him. And the police and the courts never touched him, everyone respected him so much! And there were even a few others" — she rushes on — "Paul knows a doctor who risked himself in the same way, with so much courage . . ."

"No — I'm sorry — it's different." Her grandmother wrinkles up her face and her old skin bunches and then sags. "I can't even talk about it. It makes me sick to my stomach."

He can see how disappointed Amy is as they leave. In the taxi he says, "What can you expect? She's too old to take in any more new stuff. Though I noticed she was willing to make some allowance for rape, or conception by children."

"Oh, don't you know why, Paul? Can't you guess?"

She grabs nervously at her braid, bringing it quickly around from the back to a place on her right shoulder as if it were a small child snatched to safety.

His bowel grips him at the sight of her sad young face. He is conscious, too, of a shrinking, a premonition of disappointment on Charlie's behalf. Though Charlie is sick and worn out, he had imagined for his friend a young woman of innocence and cleanliness. Maybe it was unfair, but that was what he had hoped for his friend.

"What is it, Amy? What's the trouble?"

"You know my parents died in an accident, don't you, when I was very young?"

"Yes, Bunky told me that. Terrible for you."

"My grandparents brought us up — my brother and me. It was worse for Matt because he was the older one. He began to do things."

He makes himself ask it: "What things?"

"He set some fires in people's garages. He stole. Don't hold it against him. He was a kid. Grandfather couldn't — wouldn't — deal with Matt. He was too broken up from my mother's death, I suppose. It was Nana who had to think about it. She'd cry to me, 'What should I do? If I don't punish him he will get wild. But I know he is suffering and I don't want to add to it.'

Then she decided. 'You and I will go to the movies and Matt will stay home.' 'You and I will go to the circus.' 'You and I will go downtown to a restaurant and Matt will stay here. Till he learns his lesson.' The two of us would go downtown and suffer through the movie and the meal. And Matt — he didn't learn anything but bitterness, Paul. How could he?"

"As it turns out it wasn't such a good idea, but it might have been. Anyway, what choices did she have, an old lady faced with all that by herself? Who said she should have the responsibility of figuring out your brother's nutty behavior? She was a mathematician, not a child psychologist!" He marvels at his forbearance. He had not been able to understand his own mother as well. He feels a rush of warmth spreading in his chest at his own words.

"And maybe what she did had no effect on your brother anyway."

"I was cruel to go along with it," Amy says sadly, "but I did. We felt impelled, Nana and I, by ideas we didn't believe in — wasn't that dreadful? I vowed never to do it again — never to believe that love wasn't enough to cure sickness of soul."

He begins again to say "After all, how could you — ?" when with a deep sigh she breaks in, "When I came home I would try to make it up to poor Matt."

"How do you mean" — foreboding seizes him — *"make it up?"*

"I hugged him and loved him," she says simply.

"For God's sake, you didn't sleep with your brother, did you?" he demands hoarsely.

She gazes at him, startled. "Not my brother. He had a friend — Mickey. Matt didn't have many friends. He was too unhappy."

"You did that" — Paul stares — "for your brother?"

"Matt seemed to want me to go with Mickey. And I felt — if it keeps Mickey for Matt . . ."

Her look is open, simple, reasonable. Above all, she wishes to give herself, the look says, where she is most needed. It is the pragmatism of an idiot — or a saint.

"My God, you were — how old?"

"Thirteen."

He shudders. So close in age to his daughters! A child's sacrifice. "What happened then?"

"My poor grandmother had to find an abortionist. It nearly killed her. She sent Matt away to school. That and the abortion nearly killed me as well. I developed an infection. And poor Matt suffered in other ways. Later I was told I could probably never conceive again."

"Poor girl," Paul murmurs. And adds to himself, Poor Charlie. She's not what she seems. Suddenly he understands the grandmother — the old woman scared in the old female way under all that authority, grasping on to him as a dupable prospect for Amy, besuitoring him while she disarmed him . .

"Tell me more about that doctor I haven't met yet!" Amy suddenly bursts through her own sadness. "The one who says no one is thinking of the good of the fetus. Who says we protect the rights of the unborn by what we do at the Center."

Her wide gray eyes are still troubled as she turns her healthy heart-shaped face to him. He sees along her jaw the faint raspberry rash of emotion.

"Charlie" — his voice begins to shake with zeal, with feeling — "Charlie is one of the most idealistic men I've ever met. He was born to privilege and could have rested on it. But he struggled all his life to do what seemed honorable and right . . ."

He begins again the story — so well rehearsed in his head through so many procedures — of Charlie's courageous act that evening in May years ago. The fifteen-year-old Maria, the risk, the rage of Charlie's father, the refusal of any fee . . .

He sees written on Amy's face, youthful and clear, the stirrings of hero worship. Good! It is possible, by lifting out of Charlie's life the best and most ideal of his acts, to restore him to the hero he ought to have been. So every life, Paul thinks, if only we could cut away the selfishness and rot, is heroic — and why not his own? Surely Hannah sees his life, writes his life, that way in her notebook!

When they return they find Edgar waiting like a Sicilian father — arms folded across his broad chest, creased cheeks facing the door.

Amy takes one look — everything Edgar wants her to know about the anxiety accumulated in her absence is in his face — and hurries to the waiting room. Edgar grabs at Paul's arm with one enormous hand.

"Where the hell *were* you?"

"What's the matter, Bunky, trouble? Jesus, I'm sorry. Amy and I had lunch."

Edgar's voice seems to snag and choke deep inside his chest. "I want you to — leave her alone!"

"For crying out loud, Bunky! What is this?"

Paul peers at Bunky's face, then grasps at enlightenment. "Oh! You think I'm playing two against each other? Hannah and Amy? Oh, no! My God, Bunky, don't you know me yet? Let me tell you, that's not for me. I've never been unfaithful to a woman in my life. Not even Margaret. You want to know my faults? I'm nasty, impatient, and rough. But faithfulness is my *need*, for God's sake! All I have to improve" — he begins a self-deprecating laugh — "is my goddamned character!" Edgar's glare wipes the laugh away. "It's for Charlie — don't you see?" Paul earnestly now tries to explain. "I'm doing a Cyrano de Bergerac number, sticking my nose into Charlie's love life till Charlie comes back!"

"Get your nose out! Get it over to the schedule desk! Do you think I'll let this place turn into — ?" Edgar chokes on the rest, then turns his back and leaves Paul staring in bewilderment. Edgar, retreating, hunches, as if his still-folded arms carry the heavy load of unsaid words.

What can Bunky think the place is turning into now? Paul

wonders. He forgives the outburst. Bunky's bad nerves deepen Paul's sense that by some kind of miracle he has floated from his own sea of troubles to a life raft from whose safety he, unlikeliest one of all, stretches a hand to other drowners. He has something at last to offer Charlie, after all these years! He hurries to find Hannah but not to tell her yet what he plans. That, he instinctively feels, would not be a good idea.

3

TILL THIS MOMENT Edgar has had no time to read Charlie's letter. Busy morning, chaos barely under control. He thrusts a meaty hand into a crumpled white pocket and removes crumpled white pages. He plants his feet broadly in the bustling herb-sauce-scented lunch room. Laughter and bright strokes of anecdote pass in and out of his awareness with the tact of lasar beams. He knits his concentration around the noise.

"Reconciliation postponed. Talk at dinner — skiing conditions." Charlie's letter style hurries along as if he feared his pen might slip into stutters. "I am tolerated. Sylvia wanted to come. I urged Daniel, but no. Furious. 'She wanted to leave!' Nothing changed in that department."

At that moment, the penetrating lasar beam swerves millimetrically from its accustomed path and the lunch room talk — "I bore and mothered three sons and lost a daughter" — spills over into Edgar's attention. He hears Mary's brogue like a fine oil upon which her words slip effortlessly along: "The daughter is never off my mind. I had her out of wedlock, as we said in those bad days, and raised her myself. Held waitress jobs and far worse, I don't mind saying it now. She was seven when she died, poor thing; it was of the world's neglect, not mine — of loneliness and knowing how different she and I were from the rest. An obliging polio germ came along — I think she must have whistled for it — and twenty-four hours later she was gone."

"I'm so sorry, Mary, for the grief in your life." Amy is speaking, and Edgar finds it hard to go on with the letter.

"Not a day goes by that I don't miss her," Mary continues. "If there had been a Bianky Center, wouldn't I have been right to take advantage of it?"

"You'd have been spared the suffering." Paul chimes that in. He is casting sidelong looks at Amy's lovely face.

Edgar catches those looks and feels astonished. The fellow in the baggy white satin suit is ready to go for Paul with a knife! Edgar bites his lip and listens.

"I don't think about that," Mary says. "And I never think — but then my little daughter would never have come to me at all! No, what I think is that she might have been saved up. She would have come to me again. That's what I tell the women." Her broad, weary form, cheerfully clad in yellow, with the gray grandmotherly curls above, shifts its authoritative weight: "At a proper time, when I could have shielded her more."

Charlie's snow-crisp sentences seem to be melting away in Edgar's hand. He wrenches his attention from the hot hearts of the lunch room and returns it to the snowy landscape.

"Yesterday I saw how fast the second week is going. I made up my mind to talk. The sight of all those skiers too — toiling up, skidding down. Like life. I watched Daniel descend. In his ski clothes he looks like an armored mercenary. Feet clamped to skis. Shiny molded boots. Body in a swollen sheath. Hands in gauntlets twice a hand's size. Brutal look — how he wants me to see him, too. It was either pass on my father's silence or speak. I aimed one blow — it took all my control — into that bulk. 'Daniel, do you know how much we both love you?' He looked shocked. His face crumpled. He began to cry. Said he did know. Hated himself. 'Why did I act so shitty? Why?' I kept it up. I showed no mercy. 'And you know your mother loves you deeply?' He knew, he said. 'And Mom had every right to go off and be happy with somebody if you don't mind. I'm not a baby. I don't have to live with my mother!' "

"The trouble with the world" — Edgar hears Warner now, her voice that of a good mother or schoolteacher, caring enough to take on a scolding edge when she sees the damage whoever is in her charge is about to do to himself — "the trouble with the world is pride!"

"May be that but more, you know, it's the technolo*gee.*" Joe, the Jamaican man who is chief orderly, gives weight to his meditative voice with end-syllable emphasis. "It is moving too fast for our powers to understand de nature of humani*tee.*"

"That's what the book's got to be about too," says Warner. "Whoever writes it." Her dentures click lightly at the ends of sentences. It is as though she were already tapping at the typewriter. One of the nurses, Boyer, adds emphatically, "That's it!"

Edgar had missed whatever "that" was, but doesn't concern himself. He has heard all their talk of writing books, seen Selig when she'd been here scribbling in a battered blue looseleaf. He takes it all for harmless outlet. It is never to be realized; wells out of people who feel themselves forced too full of other people's lives. They dream of "the book" that will bind up for them the broken pieces of their days.

His glance searches out Amy. She listens, her lips parted in an unconscious smile, with a child's attention. Edgar decides that what it is about her face that so affects him is her chin. Rounded and soft — a child's chin. It points itself with certain puckerings when she is thoughtful, as now. He is aware of feelings in himself almost too powerful to contain. Is that the way things might go now? And then one day Ellen will begin to receive notes about him and Amy? What will she do? Hide them stoically? No — she will stab a knife into Amy's breast and then, before the eyes of his astonished staff, will hurl herself from the window of the Center as easily as if she were Santuzza in *Cavaleria*, flinging herself down the cathedral steps. He tries desperately to combine Amy's image once more with Mim's. How in God's name had she separated herself?

"Well, it seems so clear." Warner's voice is taking it up again. "We come into this world without enough development. Is it possible we're meant to linger in the womb another nine months? And spring out a toddler of a year and a half? No bigger in size but in spirit?"

A favorite theme is being taken through another variation. Paul draws off a cup of coffee and sits beside Amy. Edgar doesn't catch his words. They cause Amy to turn to Paul with a look of deep interest. Mixed with Edgar's jealousy is fear. At the Center — there is no safe place for such wild emotions as he is feeling now!

"Figure out for yourself how nature might have managed it" — Mary takes it up — "as nature manages everything. The opossum's pouch. The kangaroo. How do we know what was meant to be? Or even — how it was? The first baby we know was Cain. No spiritual giant. My guess is Eve aborted him before full term, upset as she was by the move from Eden. And burdened with guilt. 'No need for guilt,' I'd have told her. 'You are the instrument of mankind's mission.' I could have reassured her."

Amy smiles with enjoyment. "I wish you could have!" It is half joke, half wistfulness.

"Not that I condone everything, but once a thing's done, go on from there, I say! So poor Eve was made to feel guilty, and she aborted, probably. Interruption of the eighteen-month term. And who knows what forms it might take? First it's a fish and then a frog or a bird or a reptile or any of those early forms before it's what we call a baby. Well, then, maybe after it's a baby it's meant in its next nine months of development to turn angel (the bearer would feel lighter!). Then after wing-molt, maybe Devil — red-hot and sharp-tailed. A mother might have bad heartburn in the thirteenth month. Then saint. Empathy and floods of tears for suffering humanity. The mother urinates like crazy. Then its ready to come out. It's been scalded, flooded, a soul burned into it."

Amy applauds, laughing. "It would be worth carrying that long to achieve it!"

"Oh, the mothers would only do it once. And after that it would be practically ready to take off on its own, strong on its legs like a baby elephant. But it would feel for every human possibility. It would have at least as much empathy as a porpoise. It would do what it could to make life on earth more bearable. But as for the case with us now — you see how it is. Aren't we all abortions? We don't have what it takes to live in peace and in goodness."

It is Paul who now puts down his cup and applauds. Amy turns to him. "Did that doctor," she asks, "the one who's on vacation, say that too?"

Edgar is irritated and depressed by such fancy weavings. They show a dimming of appreciation for the act they perform here. Amy's question now reminds him that Charlie's letter is in his hand. He returns to it.

"I kept on at Daniel. 'You know your mother doesn't love you less because she went to live near Simon. She thought you were set with school and sports and friends, but that she had no time to lose. She planned to see you every weekend you could come.' 'Except I was a shithead,' Daniel kept saying. 'I refused to see her!' The minute I saw I had an edge I didn't let up, Bunky. 'And you know that I love you?' I said. 'You don't have to say that, Dad,' Daniel said. 'I always knew it!' Daniel's tears by now were falling into the snow. *I* couldn't go that far — I couldn't cry, even to carry out my plan. Besides, there were enough tears bouncing over the snow and the ski equipment to take care of everybody — Daniel and Sylvia and me and even my poor father, I suppose. I do these things — administer doses of love like antibiotics. I look at my son and ask myself like a diagnostician: Now what is lacking to the emotional balance here? Then I shake out a pill or two: 'You know I love you.' 'You know your mother loves you.'

"You'd think that synthetic emotions wouldn't do any good, but my pills seem to be just as effective as the ones produced by Pfizer or Squibb. So it's possible to say them anyway — those wonderful and mighty words — love, cherish, care, love, love, love — and get the same results. I tell this only to you. With Daniel I'm careful to act like a believer."

After this there is a space. The letter resumes in pencil, in a rushed scrawl. "Something terrible has happened!"

At the very moment Edgar comes to those words, he is paged on the loudspeaker. He breaks at once into a heavy sweat, as if the "something terrible" that he carries always with him has erupted. He hurries to the receptionist, expecting to find — even though no one is operating now — Genevieve X in a coma. But it is only a routine question: his notes for the afternoon had not been entirely clear to the typist. He glances automatically at the appointment pad. Filled to capacity, even with the inevitable nervous postponements — an Alexandra White has canceled — he stops himself from reading further.

He looks again at Charlie's letter in the corridor, away from the clamor of the lunch room.

"Daniel came to me this morning. 'I think you're some kind of saint, Dad. You try to give people happiness but you can't have any yourself . . .' I began yelling like a maniac. My damned impediment came back worse than ever. I must have sounded mad. *'Don't call me a saint!'* A maniac fending off canonization. One gap's been bridged, but a worse one opened. I have to begin all over again with Daniel. I have to do it differently. I can't leave him a legacy of suffering father!"

On his way back to the lunch room, Edgar meditates on the

business he is in. What does it mean, he asks himself, to be the instrument through which a large part of the population of the world (in potential) is destroyed? He has no sentimental notions about being a murderer; he doesn't compare an abortion clinic to Auschwitz or Birkenau. He is too intelligent and too honest for that. He and his Center fill a human need. But there are implications, reverberations. He finds that his mind, instead of dealing with those implications, veers off — no better disciplined than the minds of his staff members — into fancy and metaphor.

Abortion. It meant that things — projects, persons — were begun but not completed. Abandoned. Destroyed. It meant that a father-son relationship that began in natural love could end grotesquely mutilated, yanked from its protective human cushioning. That a twenty-year marriage — ripe with experiences, associations, possessions, even if not with children — that should stretch itself over the couple's span of life to the grave, could be torn apart by the appearance of a younger woman. He circles his broad palm over his chest. It's true! A fountain of youth had opened up in his inner life, his vitals! To feel it gush and not to acknowledge it, not to cup the flow in his hands at least and bring it to his lips to drink — ! He breaks off his meditation abruptly. Sweat pours down his back as if he had been pickaxing in a sun-parched Sicilian field. When he thinks of Amy he feels: To love and not express it, that's an abortion of the soul! But when he thinks of what that would mean to Ellen he feels: That would be an abortion of her life and of the whole meaning of mine.

Edgar returns to the lunch room, draws Paul outside, and in the corridor wordlessly shows him Charlie's letter.

"Good for Charlie," Paul says. "He sees a future again! I hope he *can* do differently."

"Differently how?"

"Gain some happiness, I mean. Suppose some pretty young woman — maybe Amy — suppose she and Charlie . . ."

But Paul stops short. Something in Edgar's face prevents his going on.

꿍 ꕤ

Nothing stops the chorus of chatterers.

"When you think of it — amazing! Everywhere making use of the local product, like *vin du pays.* In China, rice paper; in Ceylon, palm leaf; in certain Middle Eastern countries, I read, a paste from the opium poppy or a bit of camel dung. In a few parts of Africa maybe they put monkey fur to some good use, and had the sense to keep the missionaries from getting wind of it."

"I don't want to think about that — ugh!"

"Why not? It's a tribute to human ingenuity, the great creative urge to free oneself. Free from the crushing wheel of nature rolling over everything, obliterating and replacing endlessly."

"In that case I'd say the wheel won, hands down."

"Oh, sure! Why else would we be in our present employment?"

"But after all the creative urge to free oneself must be in conflict with the other urge — to join the creativity of the wheel."

"Of course."

"But then after you join it you see how impossible it all is — to replace yourself and also go on living, like digging your own grave."

"Some would rather not . . ."

"That's why we're here . . ."

Circling and circling . . .

4

T HE RECOVERY ROOM with its fifty beds filled with sleeping women beginning to bleed, beginning to return to a cycle that pregnancy had blocked, the outer rooms filled with silently waiting women — what satisfaction can they offer? But Charlie says, "It's a relief to be back."

"It is?" Some of the staff look doubtful.

"No further complications." Charlie smiles. "The terrible human web unwoven at last, right here!"

They can relax now, into the familiar uneasiness. They laugh. They know where Charlie stands.

"You look rested," says Edgar, who wonders if he will ever rest again.

"It's the snowtan. But of course I am fine. I am also out of touch." A smile for the understatements in both cases. "No news reaches the ice slopes. What's been happening on the home front?"

"Bad news," Paul answers. "The antis are mustering strength. They have contacts who supply them with fetuses the way some people have wine purveyors. At their rallies they display second-trimesters. Bunky thinks it might be a real problem to get insurance soon. Someone tried to get them on incitement, because of the fire bombings . . ."

Amy stands with a shy, eager gaze, and Paul reaches out an arm. "Here is someone you haven't met. Amy Netboy." He is conscious of bringing something about, of being an instrument for good.

Charlie seems to rock slightly back, to lean languidly away. "What brings you here, Amy?"

Proudly: "The women's movement."

"It sounds like" — Charlie is beginning to smile his half-smile — "a labor pain. It sounds like a vast uterine convulsion through which you have passed" — he pauses and peers in an exaggerated way at her face — "unscathed."

Paul winces, but Amy accepts the teasing. She looks at Charlie with widened eyes, someone she is prepared to like, but who baffles her.

"You heard some eloquent woman speak, in some hall, of freedom of choice," Charlie says, "and you came to the Bianky Family Planning Center?"

"Yes." She is quiet. She nods.

The sudden rushing movement is Edgar; his large bulk jostles several of his staff. "Amy!" He cries it over his shoulder.

"I have to check the waiting room. I'm glad you're back looking so well." Amy's smile lifts her round cheeks. The whiteness of her neck rinses itself in blood. Her light-filled gaze lingers on his face a moment and then she is gone, her long lively braid swinging out behind her.

"Really a beautiful girl," Paul says encouragingly.

"In that case," Charlie replies, smiling, "we can expect to see her one of these days on the procedure table."

"My God, Charlie — !" Paul begins, shocked, then checks himself, remembering Charlie's protective ironies. "Relax and admit it!"

"Let's see this paragon at work" is Charlie's answer. They pass through the waiting room. Amy sits beside a woman in the corner whose feet nervously twist themselves in and out of their shoes. She keeps her gaze fastened on Amy's open, speaking lips, on Amy's intent gray eyes. Light from the wide windows strikes Amy's round cheek.

Charlie stops and stares. Paul, peering, imagines that while Charlie gazes, he sees what that woman sees — a new world of possibility opening up. Yet looking again at that all-weather sea of females, Paul feels a slight depression. What does it mean, he asks himself, that I am in the abortion business though I wanted to be in the baby-delivery business? That the world has more need of removal than replacement? Absence more than presence? Emptiness more than fullness?

He peers curiously again at Charlie's face. A mask conceals everything.

The next moment he catches sight of Hannah crossing the waiting room. Amy has by now stood up and is moving in Hannah's direction. They link arms and talk in an animated way as they walk together toward procedure. It hadn't occurred to him that they might become such intimate friends. Paul is startled and wonders why he does not feel more pleased.

❦

Staggering like François, the Haitian orderly who brings in the daily fruit to the Center, Paul climbs the smelly stairs to Hannah's apartment. His arms are loaded with department store boxes — filled with blouses, filled with fine cotton turtleneck shirts, with tweed skirts from Scotland with blue and green nubs in them to go with the blouses and with her eyes. He had prowled through her pathetic closet for sizes. Now, with great satisfaction, he opens the first boxes. All of it in the best taste, expensive but worth it.

"Let me dress you," he begs, beginning to undo the buttons of her worn orange (orange!) shirt. She stands patiently while he zips and buttons and ties. He had even bought shoes. Black calf pumps, with a gilt shell ornament. He likes the idea of the tiny shells at her feet — she is Venus rising from them. She has, he'd discovered with excitement, elegant slim feet to go with the slender ankles.

Dressed in a silk shirt of midnight blue, an emerald-green cashmere cardigan, and a blue-and-green tweed skirt, and with a dreamy expression on her face a million miles from what she's wearing, she looks like one of those *New Yorker* ad queens — a hunt club lady with a book of poems in her hand. He is filled with awe.

Now he opens box after box, dumps wools and silks into her lap.

"Thank you for so much generosity." She sounds, however, doubtful.

"You look marvelous in clothes! In *good* clothes."

"I can wear only one blouse at a time."

"Change off. That's the whole idea!"

She says quietly, "Please take everything back."

"Back? Why? Not on your life!"

"If I ask you?"

"What's the idea?"

"I don't like show."

"Where's show? These are just clothes! My God, everybody wears ten times as much as this . . ."

"I am not everybody."

"Do you think I don't know that?"

She draws him down to sit beside her on the bed.

"I became — with pain — who I am. I can't change it. Not even for love. Even for you. What you gave me, what I am wearing, that I will keep. One blouse. One skirt. One pair of shoes. Nothing more."

"Do you want to hurt my feelings?"

She looks away.

"Then take!"

She shakes her head. He cannot believe how much all this

upsets him. A sensation of anger passes through him. He had knocked himself out!

"And I bought furniture too." His voice quivers. "They're sending it."

"Furniture? What kind?"

"A kitchen table, for one thing. A nice round wooden one, instead of that chipped enamel wreck. And chairs to go with it."

She smiles with real pleasure. "That I will accept! Oh, you are wonderful!"

She throws her arms about his neck and kisses and praises him. He feels baffled but better. Encouraged. If she'd accept the furniture and one outfit, it wouldn't be long before he could get her to go along with the whole thing, would it? One Saturday they'd go shopping together and they'd both get new clothes. He'd make an appointment for her at one of those salons where she could get a hair-styling, a makeup session, the works. She'd be a stunning woman. All he had to do was go a little slow and give her old-time scruples a chance to fade.

Just before he leaves, Hannah stuns him with news: "I will have to go — away." She stumbles over the words, as if they are hard to say.

His breath fails him. "Away? Where? When?"

She has difficulty expressing it. "To — for — a visit. As soon as Bunky says it's all right." She looks away. He makes a quick guess about where she is going — the reason for her uneasiness — and hastens to reassure her of his tolerance for her attention to this old, backward, superstitious part of her past. "I don't mind," he says. "Though I miss you already."

"I know you will get used to it," she says, then slaps her fingers to her lips.

"What is it?"

"For an instant I wished the words snatched back into my mouth!"

"Don't worry — I don't want to get used to it." He encircles her long slender waist with his arm. "But I have an idea that you are going to talk to a certain person there — is it to the rabbi? — about me! To get his blessing? I don't mind, sweetheart!"

She makes no reply, only fingers the pleats of the new blue-and-green tweed skirt. He marvels that these moments of shyness still return — she is still his wild girl, oh, lovely!

"Give the rabbi my regards!" He pinches her cheek, teasingly.

He is still dazzled by his luck in love. Yet he feels its strangeness: to be rewarded so handsomely and so swiftly! For the merest gesture toward a woman! It almost makes him uneasy. He feels like the knight in the fable who is obliged to marry a crone (not that Hannah was ever that — but once she had been only *Selig* to him, when he had not yet *seen* her — or when he had seen her only in her rigid, traumatized state, eyes staring, cheeks drained of color, lips bitten bloody) and is then rewarded by her metamorphosis into princess. He feels he has hardly earned this metamorphosis. But why quibble with fate? His luck has come to a turn in the road. Like the knight in the fable, he gallops toward his reward.

When Hannah interrupts his reverie, he is startled to see that she is still fixed on words he had already dismissed.

"After I said I wished my predictions back again, this is what I thought about my parents and Rabbi Pinchas and the whole community. They were trusters in God. When the world persisted in evil though they were good, they told themselves it was their part still to find and open the door through which they would perceive the link to God — to goodness — unbroken. To perceive is to make real. They did so. Perception, prediction, prophecy — ensures enactment. Even though a bitter past suggests a failed future. How guard against it? They did! They were Jews! They believe in a prophetic and messianic future. Believe in virtue, not because it follows the best model but because it is active; it brings God nearer the world and the world nearer to the goal of goodness . . ." She bites her lips shut after this lengthy speech, but then bursts out again: "When I said you would get used to my absence, I wondered how much of fact would be conjured by prophecy!"

In all this welter of words he grasps at the thing he thinks he understands — her anxiousness underlying it all. He replies as if conferring a gift: "Of course — didn't you know? — I'm a Jew like you, like them!"

She shakes her head. *"We* don't struggle to re-create the foundations of the world every day! You are not like me, I am not like them."

To which he silently adds, Amen!

5

AS HE SMOKES a cigarette between procedures, using Bunky's office as a place to relax, Paul hears Amy's voice, the familiar sandy texture of it. It is as if her whole sweet being, having cast impurity off like a kind of sediment, then decants it into her voice, making it slightly hoarse.

At first he thinks he is hearing her voice in his head. Then he hears an unfamiliar male voice and wonders, Who is Amy talking to?

Probably Lal. He rises with the intention of joining them. Then he begins to make out some of the words and stops.

"I asked you not to come here." That's Amy, trembly.

"Why not, damn it! It's the only place I'm sure of finding you without *her*. Who can I turn to when I need help if not you?"

For Charlie's sake, Paul goes on listening through the wall without shame.

"You could make money." The man's voice goes on. "You're stubborn. And naïve. They exploit you. You're my sister — I want you to have the best."

Paul feels relief — the man speaking so intimately and urgently is Amy's brother. All the same, now that he has begun, he goes on listening.

"There's nothing else I want to do. I can help here. I know how to talk to these women — why shouldn't I know? I'm well rewarded. I pretend I'm saving Mim, Dr. Bianky's sister. Or I pretend I'm saving myself."

"Save *me!*" The brother's voice roughens; for a second it is like Amy's.

"You're not in danger."

"I am. If you knew."

Silence. Then Amy, hopeful, shy. "If you wanted an abortion for Renée I could arrange it for you."

"I don't need an abortion for Renée. Renée is goddamn infertile!"

"Then I can get her an introduction to the best fertility doctor in New York, and Dr. Bianky could . . ."

"I don't give a damn if her womb stays zipped up till she dies. That's not what I want!"

"What do you want, Matt?" Amy's burred voice shrinks to a papery whisper.

"I want in. Get me in."

"How?"

"I want to be a partner. I'll borrow money to invest."

"But Bunky doesn't need another partner, Matt. Why should he want someone — even if he wanted someone — who's not a doctor?"

"I can do books. I can advise about investment. Christ, there must be barrels of money! Women opening up, one every five minutes, their cunts stuffed with cash!"

A long and *terrible* silence, Paul feels. Then the brother in a different, wheedling tone: "Of course I think of Mim, Amy. Don't you think money would have saved her too? She could have gone to a five-thousand-dollar man instead of a five-hundred-dollar one. Damned straight she'd be alive today.

You're alive, Amy! God — the amount of blame I took — and nobody died!"

Amy still silent. Again the wheedling voice. "Everything in *my* life is aborted! My God — hopes, dreams, plans. Look at me. I can't get started. I need help. Help me."

"Go to see Nana, Matt." Now she is pleading with him. "Tell her you're sorry you wasted the money she gave you last time. She'll help you again. She never meant any angry thing she said to you."

"Never. That's what she said. It's you she always liked, not me."

Paul, in the next office, hears the dry hard sound of male sobbing. The sound fills him with fear.

As soon as he hears a door slam, Paul hurries into the next office. Amy sits at the desk, crumpled tissues near her hand.

"You look a little down," Paul begins, cautiously. "Anything bothering you?"

She shifts to him the candor of her large gray eyes. "A little." Anyone else would have guessed he had overheard.

"I would love to help. If there's anything."

"My brother's awfully eager to get a job in the Center somehow. He's got it into his head it's a good place to be." She looks unhappy rather than embarrassed. "I don't know what he could do here. But he wants to come."

Her openness touches him. To hide that he'd overheard, he jokes, "Why — is he pregnant?"

"He thinks you're getting rich here." Her clear eyes are neither ashamed nor angry — only amazed.

"I am. I am," he says generously. "That's the curse of our idealism. It makes us rich."

Meanwhile he says to himself, It's true, what a business women are! Their wombs, their breasts, their varicose veins! Their skins, their backs, their noses! Women are gold mines! On top, he thinks, seeing this too, suddenly, of their being witches and goddesses and everything else his ex-wife accuses him — and every other man — of foisting on them!

"Leave it to me," he says. And goes off, hardly understanding his own urgency, to try to find the "something" that he has promised "will work out."

◄§ §►

At first Bunky argues uneasily against it: "I try to trust my intuition on these things. When Amy introduced him I felt there was something a bit shifty there." He cracks the knuckles of his big right hand in the thickly cushioned palm of the left.

"On the contrary, Bunky." Paul hears his smooth lie with some surprise. "I was really impressed with him. He seems a stable and clever fellow. And look at Amy, after all. And it's her brother."

The creases in Edgar's forehead deepen. "Does she want it so much? For God's sake, then, keep an eye on him!" He agrees to put Matt into the orderly training program.

Paul himself feels frightened. He had half-relied on Bunky to resist. He puts that out of his mind as, all evening, he tries Charlie on the phone. At last he reaches him. He had stayed late in town to visit Sylvia in the city.

"I'm telling Amy you arranged it, Charlie. What's the difference? It can't hurt to give a hand to the brother."

"The brother is a crumb," Charlie says. "I wouldn't give him a hand in p-p-poker."

Next day all the same, when Paul tells Amy the news and sees her flushed, openly gratified face, he whispers her benefactor's name to her. "It's Charlie's doing. But don't say a word. He likes to do favors in secret."

"That's like him." There are tender tears in Amy's eyes. He is grateful when she adds, "And I know you helped too, Paul."

◄§ §►

" 'My bitch of a mother hid my birth control pills because I flunked my exams!' A fifteen-year-old said that, Charlie. And a woman in menopause asked me, 'Can you see me having a baby the same age as my grandchild?' "

At lunch and at coffee break, with shining eyes, Amy recites for Charlie the lists of the relieved. What Amy does now with her excellent memory, inherited from nimble-brained Nana, is to collect fragments of confession and gratitude. She saves them up for Charlie.

Amy's clear skin flushes, heated by emotion. Her pleasure in the work is great. She watches Charlie's face to see if she can increase *his* pleasure as well.

"And a married woman whose husband wanted a divorce. She decided to make a baby to stop him, but then he didn't come back. She'd have been left with a child she didn't want! And a woman who desperately wants children some day when she's married — she said she would have killed herself if she couldn't have come here, Charlie!"

Because she would like to draw forth from Charlie what his half-smile withholds, Amy allows her rough, burred voice to reach toward insistence: "A *fourteen-year-old,* Charlie, raped by her father. The misery her life would have been!"

She waits, then, to see her reward — the full radiance of Charlie's smile. Instead, Charlie corrects her in his unemphatic voice: "The misery *its* life would have been."

He smiles his unfinished smile. The tide of blood rises again in Amy's cheeks. These episodes, bits of evidence, confidences blurted in tears and pain — these glimpses from a dark disordered world — pass through Amy's young lips with more of Amy in them than of the dark world. Meanwhile, Amy watches Charlie closely. Edgar is another observer — his forehead knit in anxious concentration. Paul, too, looks on, with the intense interest of the matchmaker. Once, to his surprise, a nudge of matchmaker's guilt jogs him. He quickly reasons: But to other eyes, *Hannah and I might seem unsuited!* Maybe someone like me — failed at marriage, with two children — might seem to a stranger not worthy of Hannah's youth and integrity. Fiercely

he lashes out at that imagined stranger: We need them! —
these young, forgiving women — we *need* them for our second
chances!

Hannah, when present, is the final observer who watches
Edgar watching Amy watch Charlie, watched by Paul. Sometimes she writes rapidly in her notebook. More often she looks
over the heads of everyone into some inner vision, as note-
book-keepers do.

❦ ❧

Amy's voice, when she speaks to Charlie these days, has a
coaxing lift to it. And occasionally, these days, the mocking
half-smile is absent from his face.

"Were you always this way?" Amy asks it with a little shiver
in her voice.

"What way?"

"So — so dedicated? As a young man, Charlie, were you
dedicated?"

"I'm old now."

"I didn't mean that. I never think you're old."

"Will you admit you're young?"

"Not that young."

"And you're romantic."

"Because I believe in idealism? That's not romantic. I believe in your idealism, even though you like sometimes to
speak like a devil."

Amy lifts her chin. Her braid slips from her shoulder.

"You're romantic because you're attracted to me," Charlie
says quietly. "Cancer and death would scare you off, otherwise. I'm not an idealist the way you mean. Maybe what I am
is vengeful. I cling to certain ideas because everything else is
gone. Ideas, even empty ones, can be squeezed for meaning
if you need them to be. I'd show no mercy to anyone who
stood in the way of them."

She stands stubborn ground: "Paul told me once — you said

Sylvia was sacrificed to Daniel's happiness. How many men would see that, or care?"

"Statement of fact," says Charlie. "Sick s-s-society — happiness at another's exp-p-pense — involves an act of c-c-cannibalism."

Paul wishes Charlie would not take that dry dead tone when talking of love and happiness. But Amy moves past his fears.

"I understand, then, why you don't pursue happiness for yourself! I see you plainly, Charlie!"

"The way to see me," Charlie calmly adds, "is as an aging, probably sterile man."

Paul is again afraid that Charlie will scare off Amy. Until he sees how vigorously she shakes her head in denial. The gleaming braid sweeps side to side like the luminous train of a young animal. "Oh, no, Charlie, you don't even know yourself!"

"You ought to run from me. You're young and healthy. You believe in happiness. Light is your element. Why do you let yourself be attracted to the dark? I ought to beat you with sticks to make you run away." *Beat* is the word that most troubles his tongue, and must be recommenced many times.

She steps nearer, past Paul. "Too late," he hears her say with a laugh. "I already love you. I loved you right away. You remind me of someone who's very unlike you . . ."

"I told you — a romantic."

"If I am, then let me do this — " She kisses him on the mouth.

Charlie takes it lightly. "You should be kissing my son, Daniel. Much nearer your age."

"But it's you I want to kiss!" In demonstration, she throws her arms about him, kisses him repeatedly on his lean cheeks, his finely lined forehead, and lastly on his thin smiling lips. "I'll convince you that you're worthy of joy!"

"I suppose Daniel would be glad" — Charlie muses when she is done kissing — "to think that his father is loved."

"Of course he would!" Amy at once enters into the spirit of Charlie's words, half-murmured to himself.

"If Daniel knew you'd come into my life, Daniel wouldn't have to pity me, would he?"

"Tell Daniel he doesn't have to pity his father!" Smiles. Kisses. Tears.

Paul exhales a rush of breath. Like a spectator at the circus who feared the high-flyer would fall, he finds his relief is mingled with a tiny, horrifying disappointment.

6

T O T H E D I S T R E S S of everyone at the Center, and most of all of Amy, Matt occasionally and quite suddenly bursts out of the bored shadowless sounds of his ordinary speech into the flowered rhythms of Joe the orderly's Jamaican accent. Is it parody? If so, what will Joe do? After a time of nervousness, while the staff wonders if Joe in his dignity will reach out a huge fist to grab Matt's jacket, they see what Joe has understood. Not parody but accolade — an imitation of depths of concern by someone who cannot, with his own habitual sounds, summon shadings of feeling or thought, and who can therefore be said to be, in charity, not pitiless but languageless.

The Jamaican dialect — strong and manly in the mouths of Jamaican men — becomes in blue-eyed, frightened-eyed Matt a kind of baby talk: "I goin' to de lounge now. I goin' to fix de basket dem fruits for de ladies!"

Amy turns her normally head-on gaze partly to the side as if she would like to cut down sensation by half.

Just as suddenly, Matt leaves off. Hard flat sounds, then.

"Sometimes I think they've got something, those right-tolifers!" Matt holds forth in the lounge with the swagger of the uncertain.

"Wrong name," Charlie replies, his voice quiet and dry. "There's no *life* in them. They never give a thought to life once it's born. They're not for social reform. They're not against war. On the contrary! You'll find them lined up behind the artillery every time. *Save the fetus!* And when it's old enough, send it to the front. Abortion at eighteen years is the tragedy, not at eight weeks!"

Though the sound of Matt's voice always quickens Amy with love, it has begun to make her ashamed. Why does she hear whining behind the swagger? Has it always sounded that way? Is she hearing it now for the first time only because Charlie, so stoical, is listening too?

From the start of this conversation, Amy has begun to move about restlessly. Up to the bulletin board, straightening the messages, fastening the tacks, looking sideways over her shoulder, twisting her body one way, her head another, and then reversing the movements as if her brain is issuing two conflicting sets of directions. Her braid wags slowly like the tail of a puzzled, imploring pet.

"Sometimes, though," says Matt, "I think there's just too much easy life for dames now."

"Then maybe you shouldn't work at the Center." Charlie's tone is paper-dry.

"I believe in it," Matt whines. "They ought to have this place to come to. Freedom of choice, okay. I'm talking general philosophy."

"I hear a lot of that — general philosophy." Charlie leans back. He takes a deep, controlled breath as if he is inhaling a cigarette. But he has been forbidden to smoke now. "It only takes nine months of general philosophy to ensure catastrophe. We say we want to save the fetus because it belongs to God, or to society — or to anybody but the bearer. But let it be born, and we abandon it to the bearer, however inadequate, who may in turn abandon the baby again to a stranger-parent or an institution. But as for society stepping in, that's never more than in a detached, legal way, often when the baby's near death. And as for God — no, no footstep's heard there!"

"Look — I believe in this, I told you! Would I work here if I didn't? I'm like Amy! Even Bunky has nightmares about some woman, some Genevieve X dying on the table and the whole place going crazy. Ever ask yourself why? And what about *your* nightmares, Charlie?"

"I don't have any," Charlie answers steadily. "Numbers don't bother me. I know they're in the millions. I don't think, Look what's happening to mother-love. I think, Look how many catastrophes there would have been. Uncared-for children are the only sin."

"So you're one of the few with no second thoughts?"

"No second thoughts. I'm always eager to do an ab-b-b-b-b..."

Matt smiles sneeringly, as if Charlie's stutter is proof of his fear. Amy puts down her coffee cup and comes closer to Charlie.

"Don't pretend to be tough." Her voice trembles.

"Who's pretending?" Charlie thumps himself on the chest with his thin fist. "Iron man." Charlie sips his coffee and quietly alternates his attention between Amy and Matt. The half-smile he suppresses and the half he presents are in strained, precarious balance, like brother and sister.

◆§ ৯◆

Paul, again watching, sees how Matt, older than Amy by only a few years, resembles her. The same physical beauty is there. The same full lips, luminous unshadowed eyes, clear, rounded brow. But light is not there. Matt is closed, sullen, resentful. A grievance Paul uneasily recognizes as male (what is it? the warm tit torn away?) stitches up his look. Paul feels a kind of shame for both Matt and himself. Why are we both so desperate for help from women? Why so surly when help's delayed?

What a prick her brother is, he thinks. Then with no warning he wonders, Is he sent to reflect me to myself, is that it? Amy's brother, my glass-gaper? What am I — getting like Hannah? God's sending me messages? Throwing down pieces of mirror into my path, in human form, for me to shape up by? Why do I even think that way? Let me go back to simple things. Amy is an innocent darling. Her brother, Matt, is a shit-heel prick (nothing to do with me); Bunky is an anxiety case who's driven Ellen to adultery, probably; Charlie is an idealist madman I can never live up to, so let me not waste time trying. Hannah is — Hannah — She is not sitting with them in the lounge. He is unable for the moment to complete the thought. He stubs his cigarette, pops a Sen-Sen into his mouth, tugs at the wave of black hair that all his life has fallen like bad news before his eyes, and, as soon as Charlie leaves the lounge, strolls over to sit beside Amy.

But Amy's attention now is riveted on Matt, who, in a whining tone, is saying to Joe the orderly: "But look, it's all changed now — no man can plant a seed anymore! It's a game of Put and Take. Any damned woman can get rid of any man's trace. Yank you out like a tonsil, grind you, crush you. I wouldn't be surprised to see men all going impotent — all like Bunky . . ."

"You got de wrong mon, mon!"

"Any time soon now. A sailor used to be able to brag he had a kid in every port. A soldier sprayed the enemy's women. What the hell other way is there for a man to stay alive except by knowing what he planted? All work and no reward. Even a seal they throw a fish to. A monkey gets a banana. What's there for a man? What the hell do they think is such a thrill in a bang? If you can't nail it in so it stays nailed . . ."

"What is that, mon — you are a lover or a Roman soldier? Lord, it's a crucifixion!"

Matt persists even when Edgar enters the lounge; he needles: "I hear the Senate's making noises again about withdrawing funds. How many of our women are on welfare and can't pay without Medicaid, Bunky?"

"I don't keep the numbers in my head," Edgar coldly replies.

"You'd better, Bunky. It could mean a big revenue cut."

"No one" — Edgar glares — "will be turned away for lack of funds!"

"Better check the books, Bunky. Welfare patients don't pay the rent."

Amy abruptly stands and pins a letter to the bulletin board. Turning her back to it, she recites from her excellent memory: " 'I thank you for my life. I thank you for not making me feel ashamed.' " Her voice lifts with emotion. " 'I am going back to school. God bless you.' "

For a moment, because Charlie is not there, Paul has the startling illusion that she recites for him.

◦§ ु◦

It is impressive, electrifying — a natural wonder. Paul is awestruck by his own handiwork.

"She's picked you, Charlie!" Paul blurts it out, astonished. "Amy picked you!"

"No one's been picked. I am not for picking." Charlie smiles his crooked smile. The side that glides down cancels the side that rises.

"Why him? Why Charlie? Why," Paul asks Mary, "does Amy pick *him?* I know I suggested and encouraged — but I only could do so much, after all! The rest — the rest is sort of unbelievable, that's what I think!"

Mary places her hands on her hips and regards him soberly. "Oh! I could write a book about love, Love!" The zipper over each breast grins at him like a flinty smile. "From the 'why' backward to 'A,' " says Mary, "and forward to 'Z.' Oh, could I!"

Gen-Lee also has his theories, which he clips off in neat

Oriental arrangements: "For a certain type of woman, Paul. Illness, need of some kind. Aphrodisiac enough, you know?" Gen-Lee delivers his wisdom with smooth conviction, clicking out reasoned reasons like abacus arithmetic. *"Because* circumstances unlikely! *Because* without usual pressures. Therefore sensual nature is freed, you know?"

"Out of your own mouth, Gen-Lee! I wouldn't have dared to say it myself. You've just proved women are perverse, if not actually insane!"

Paul wonders what has got into him.

"Society, you know, inflict these restraints, Paul — "

Ah, here's this fled Korean lecturing him about society . . .

" — Women forced into them, maybe sometime their spirit jump out like wound spring at odd place, don't you think, Paul?"

It's easier to go on taking his poll than to think.

"How come, Warner" — he catches her flying toward the recovery room — "Amy picks Charlie?"

"That? You're asking about that? Men and women? Please! It would take a volume to answer." She pauses, a large yellow shape with a bosom for weeping on. "And I should. One of these days I really will . . ."

She pauses another minute to gaze at him with chin sunk toward her chest, as Mary had done. As if the weight of knowing about them all — Amy, Charlie, himself, and several hundred others — is too great to bear.

Paul collects himself. No one knows any more about Amy than he does. What they think may have less to do with Amy than with themselves. Maybe they translate a skinny experience into a fat generalization. Who says he has to buy that? Who says he'd read their books if they ever got around to writing them?

෴ ෴

At night, in his apartment, Paul faces the truth: My old, old affliction! What Charlie has I have to crave! Why now Amy? *Because Charlie's got her.* But you — idiot! — have your own. Happiness with Hannah. *Charlie has better with Amy.* Scum! I wash my hands of you! *Scum yourself, I'm the only hands you've got.*

Before sleep, he gazes with shame at the pictures on his night table, the expectant faces of Karen and Helene. Every night they look out of their frames, waiting for their father to grow up and get better. They smile encouragement. But every glinting wire of their braces, each perfect pigtail, is loaded with what they know about Daddy.

"What can I tell you, my darlings?" He speaks with bitterness. "Daddy has a gene for weak character — which you didn't inherit," he hastily adds.

In the morning he dreads waking, and fearfully pays out consciousness inch by inch, like a man feeling psychic limbs for fractures. He opens an eye. Karen. Another eye. Helene. They smile reassurance at him. Miracle! — he feels himself whole. Sanely himself again. Full of love for Hannah, happiness for his friend Charlie.

He kisses the dear, wise faces of his daughters. "You kept watch over me!"

He sits up in bed and feels, as if with a boy's joy at first long pants, "I grew! I grew up in the night!"

7

D O Y O U K N O W that there's a lively trade in babies
going on in this city?"

Ellen, whose pale handsomeness is wonderfully set
off by the dark fur of her coat, has carefully conserved this
information until after their dinner, when they are taking a
turn along Madison on a clear evening.

"The antiabortion people make contact somehow with the
clinics. Siphon off the women there, so to say — put them in
touch with a middleman, who pays for confinement and ar-
ranges for adoption. The contact at the clinic then gets paid
off. I heard this at the hospital today. I suppose it wouldn't be
so terrible if people were properly screened, but I doubt they
are. The antis aren't in the screening business, after all."

Ellen then makes one of those conversational leaps that
originate in innocence but that deliver to the listener a sense
of heart-freezing omniscience.

"Who is this *Matt,*" she asks, "this orderly? When did you
hire him?"

Edgar has not said that Matt was hired for Amy's sake. Has
planned never to mention Matt at all. But since he's developed
the habit, God help him, of pouring out what plagues, Matt has

slipped into the cornucopia of cares, the horn of harassments, that Edgar intrudes into Ellen's consciousness each evening like a metaphysical phallus.

"I don't know why it is" — Ellen switches again suddenly — "that the description of this baby-seller's contact — short, blue-eyed, and speaks with a Jamaican accent — strikes me as familiar. It's — you won't be hurt if I mention this, will you, darling? — somehow so reminiscent of the Portuguese fisherman with the white Cadillac! Why are these people, who ought to be in hiding, always identified with some eccentricity? Like racetrack touts. It's almost as if they wanted to be found out. It's almost — if it weren't so awful — funny!"

Oh, yes, funny, very funny. Oh, hilariously, gargantuanly funny — calling for the blood-vessel-bursting laughter of Pagliacci himself! If, after years of heart-crippling care, I have, by hiring Matt, caused this catastrophe to descend on the Center and on me. "Oh, God!" Edgar groans aloud.

Ellen looks intently at his drained face. She puts out a loving hand — then suddenly withdraws it.

Edgar, from the corner of one reddened eye, glimpses the receding of that reliable love.

Days earlier, Edgar had seen other certainties withdraw. And had begun to ask himself: After all this while, where are they — nobility of ideas, hopes for the future of the race, dreams, plans for a better world? By now life has stressed and overstressed the crude equations. Edgar knows them too well: the Bianky Center, light-filled, on the one hand; the dark places of heart, mind, soul on the other. The large life-principles were what he had been after. Now he is forced every moment to stop and think about self-betrayals, the small pulls that enlarge till they are out of control. He had wanted to stress the grand principles, but must face instead the petty intrigues that spring maddeningly from the surfaces of life like toadstools after a rain.

That's human life, he had been telling himself: it sinks at the moment it aspires. "Human, all too human," that cry which springs so easily to the lips, is a cry of resignation, not pride.

None of these reflections has helped. One evening, therefore, very soon after Edgar hired Matt despite his better judgment, and despite further warnings of that same judgment, Edgar had confided certain carefully selected feelings to Ellen. Afterward, he sensed that he had somehow begun to upset a marital balance that, like the snail which is said to live at the center of the world, has kept his life intact.

"Pursuing her," Edgar had said to Ellen. "A girl a good fifteen years younger than himself — saying it's for Charlie! A girl out of school! And Paul's a man with two daughters and a destroyed marriage."

His voice passionate, grieved. Ellen searched his face to see if she could discover any private interest in the girl. He knew she guessed that he thought of Mimi. But what besides?

She teased at his heavy sincerity, as it had always delighted him to have her do. "You men do that. Hardly ever women."

"Why should anyone?" Edgar sounded angry.

At that she bristled a little. "If men take unfair advantage, it's hard not to want the same for women."

"I thought the point was supposed to be fairness for everyone?"

"Are women to have all the high ideals and men the low benefits?"

They had never discussed such ideas seriously before — much less in anger.

Now as they walk after dinner, Ellen searches Edgar's face, remembering that Amy is sister to Matt, who appears to lack any other credential. In an unconscious gesture she brings her flat open hand to her belly and presses it there as if in hunger. Although the belly is packed full — of tissue, muscle, organs, and just now as well of good food — Ellen, moving her hand to her lower belly and pressing there, feels, despite palpable fullness, that it is empty.

She is forty-four. The question that had till recently been posed each month by womb to woman is now answered. Neither question nor womb will ever be reopened. Not so for Edgar. "Let's not preach water and drink wine," they had agreed when they married. "We don't need children; we have work." Now she hotly imagines this: He will rid himself of the old barren wife. Will embrace this young sister-sweetheart, pouring into her jet after jet of his milky stream.

"Take this wine," he will say to her. "I no longer preach."

Her hand moves now upon her rising belly, which fills and fills as she draws in the heavy breath of understanding.

◄§ §►

"How many in such-and-such a year?" — Hannah is writing — "How can I find out? What were the resources? Little pink pills? Advertisements? Female Complaint a Specialty. Irregularity. How much must I do? Where will research end? The Salons. Back Rooms. Spurious Apothecaries. In 1890? Boarding Houses. Seaside Resorts. Astrologers. Fortunetellers, Chiropractors, Masseuses . . . In 1914? In 1953? Home remedies. List them: hangers, knitting needles, knives, candlesticks, pot handles, vinegar, lye, caustic — that's enough! I am making myself sick . . .

"I'll do dates, then. Clean and cold — except that soon enough the months and years become stuck with bits of human tissue like the bayonets of soldiers in those Goya drawings. Is there nothing that won't make me sick?"

She looks up from her letter. She seldom receives an answer now. She wonders if Rabbi Pinchas can be keeping a journal instead. The light wood of Paul's new table is inset with long striations of varying shades and grains, here and there flecked with chevrons. The patterns suggest the variegated stippling of literary styles. For relief, she chooses an older one of curlicued cross-patterning:

"I count on your advice, dear Rabbi Pinchas. Though you are not, I know, a *popular* writer, your little book on marital purity, if it had been mass-paperbacked, would no doubt have affected the spiritual development of millions. Is it possible for you to inquire among some of the older women in the community what they remember hearing of such things?"

She pauses, bites her pen, looks up. Then in one hectic moment she bends and writes quickly. "The beautiful young woman has arrived. Dear Rabbi Pinchas, she is here! Paul does not recognize his love for her yet. He hides it from himself, disguises himself as John Alden, the Puritan who wooed Priscilla for another man. Though I fight against the thought I can't escape it — sent more for me than for him? How childish and harmful it seems to me now — my 'war.' Now I am on the run. But as I run, I can also right a wrong. Poor Amy, too, is caught in a by-blow of all this. Now and then I wonder — is this, too, a misunderstanding? Can Paul's love for me be after all a hint of reconciliation? But my own self cannot pry loose the tightened fingers of the fist I have made of my own being."

At the last minute she hastily scrawls, "It has been a relief to address my questions to you. Should I have confined them to my journal? Forgive me if I have confused one with the other. I have been accustomed to replies of a very different sort from the one I anticipate receiving from you. Replies not to letters but to acts, and they have all but crushed me. I thought I did not mind — they were all the more proof of what I sought. But now . . . ?"

As she licks the letter shut, she feels that her heart has unexpectedly grown lighter. She places the envelope in the center of the new table and contemplates its varied surface. It is as ribbed with ornament as the plan she is at this moment devising.

Book Three

. . . If, on the one hand, the character of a person, the way in which he reacts, were known in all its details, and if, on the other, all the events in the areas entered by that character were known, both what would happen to him and what he would accomplish could be exactly predicted. That is, his fate would be known . . .

The destructive character lives from the feeling, not that life is worth living, but that suicide is not worth the trouble.

— Walter Benjamin,
Reflections

1

NANA READS in the old high-backed needlepoint-covered chair, and Amy can see that she is remembering. She gives a little sort of jump in the chair. Her breasts quickly rise and then drop — her very flesh leaps. She sits quiet a minute or two, pretending — clearly — still to read. Then, nearly crushed beneath her ponderous voice that once could project, through traffic and without microphone, past the jeers of street-corner hecklers, whole paragraphs from Margaret Sanger leaflets, comes the eager yet unwilling question: "Your brother, Amy, dear — how is he?"

The pain of memory can cause your flesh to move. Her grandmother has not seen Matt in years. Of course she remembers everything just as clearly as Amy herself. But her grandmother does not have the same reason Amy now does to rejoice at her clear memory.

Amy is grateful that her memory is good, as good as her grandmother's. She suffers because of her good memory, of course — the wrong things float to her sometimes, lying in her bed in her grandmother's apartment. Living with Nana now and working with Matt, she thinks of the old days even more often than when she lived at college. When she knows Nana is remembering them too is when she sees Nana's flesh give the little leap.

"He's fine, Nana," Amy warmly replies. "Matt does well in the new job. Everyone likes him." She cringes at the lie.

"And his job is to write the brochures about birth control that the clinic gives out? I'm touched that he would go into that line of work. It means that he doesn't bear me any — " She catches herself up. Her pride allows no outcry against the pain. "Why haven't you brought some to show me?"

"I will, Nana — I keep forgetting."

When she goes to her bedroom, Amy sees in the mirror the face others praise her for: clear, open, light-struck, rinsed with health. She compares its reflection with the evening's reflections; she thinks of her thoughts. But the image before her is unwavering, as though no pebble has ever been flung into this pond.

The sadness of people in their thoughts, she thinks — we cannot know. Her heart is at once flooded with Charlie. Matt is in shadow on the shore. For Charlie — break down stony suffering, let feeling flow. For Matt — stem the poisoned river of self-pity, infuse Charlie's splendid stoicism. Missions of cross-purposes.

She undoes her hair. It breaks into a hundred *s*'s from the continual braiding. My hair is stuttering, she thinks. Charlie's tongue has got stuck in my hair. S-s-s for suffering. But I will give him joy.

ᐧᔦ ᔦᐧ

Though Charlie also sits at the table drinking coffee, it is Paul whom Amy addresses.

"I have wonderful news!"

Her eyes moist, the iris darkened with emotion.

"Five weeks old! And I want it — for Charlie and me!"

Amy's cheeks flare with excited color. Her brow, her cheekbones, her chin — all radiate the same message. But Charlie is a dead spot in all that radiance, reflecting nothing. Amy is a stream pouring over rock. Her excitement rushes about Paul and Charlie. But Charlie is a stone.

"Everything's going to be all right, Paul!" Amy sits very straight in her slender canary-colored uniform. Charlie's face has gone gray; he ages while she speaks. Amy grows younger. She looks no more than fifteen.

"I know Charlie loves me, Paul. I hope we'll get married. I want us to."

Paul nods at every sentence. His luck, his role. He has to be present. Without him, messages can't get through to anybody. He is beginning to feel like a filter. All poisons lodge in him so that essence can pass purely to the other side.

Slowly, his voice dragging — it is like the dragging of his father's voice — Charlie replies, "I can't do it."

"Happiness? Love? Me? A new life? What can't you do?" She laughs up at him coaxingly.

"Devour others to give myself happiness."

"No one will be devoured! Think of it" — she is shy, almost embarrassed to be using the old clichés again — "as giving life."

"But Daddy has no more life to give." Charlie smiles again his half-smile, shows the crippled sweetness of it.

"No, Charlie, that's over and won't come back!"

"No guarantee. Suppose three years? Suppose five? It's cruel to think of doing it."

"I know it won't come back. You won't have any more misery in your life!"

Amy flings herself on him with a kind of whoop — "Oh! Oh — Charlie!"

Paul quickly shifts his gaze away. But not before he sees the look on Charlie's face. It is — isn't it? — for a second? — a sunburst of joy! Paul feels a heady triumph.

Quickly, Charlie disentangles himself.

Amy throws her head back suddenly and laughs. Her soberness takes off like a bird and flies back with joy in its beak.

"Look at us, Paul! The two of us — Charlie and I — had given up on ourselves! And look what we've done!"

"How seductive procreation makes itself." Charlie has recovered; his dry, intelligent voice breaks in. "No one remembers the child." He lights a forbidden cigarette and stands apart from Amy — a small, elegant figure, as if carved from material that is very fine.

"Charlie — Charlie — don't smile that little half-smile," Amy calls to him. "When did you ever smile a full, happy smile? Oh, Charlie, prepare yourself! You're going to live a happy life!"

Paul, in a trembling voice, gives them his congratulations. Incredible — he has engineered another person's happiness! — he, who had never even known where to look for the stuff! He feels sacred, shamanlike. To be a fully grown man means to have magical powers — what else is it like but magic, to give happiness to another?

Hannah had begun to mention doubts about Amy and Charlie. Telling her will hardly do justice to this, and he hasn't her knack of putting things on paper. He wishes Hannah were here this minute to see it all.

◈ ◈

Nana is already asleep by the time Amy gets around to washing her hair. When the doorbell rings, she wants to run and get the door before the ringing can wake Nana. Yet because of a foreboding that never leaves her, she is moving too slowly.

It is late. This is a ringing she always expects. She pictures Matt's fist outside the door, on the bell, clenched on trouble. Whether it's Matt or not she forces herself to move quicker. Hastily wrapping a towel around her sopping hair, she runs to answer.

Someone in a dark hooded coat frightens her. Like a stage figure of Time or Death.

"What is it?" she demands of the hidden-faced figure at the door. There comes a voice from under the hood, startling. She peers another moment into the shadowy covering, then bursts into a laugh.

Deep inside the gloom of the hood, Selig's face is all but invisible. Her eyes, only, catch the light from the ceiling fixture in the hall and gleam at Amy. She thinks how beautiful they are. The intensity of Hannah's eyes is never visible during the day, when pale face, stricken mouth, give forth their own impressions.

"Come in!" Amy, in relieved surprise, embraces Selig and leads her into her bedroom.

"Your room surprises me," Hannah says.

"Nana decorated it for me when I was growing up here. She thought that if you put girls in pink the fight would go out of them. Brown was as far as she could get from pink, so I would have no excuse not to fight for what I wanted." She laughs quietly. "Poor Nana. She didn't think that I might want to fight for what she thought wasn't good for me."

Hannah looks about. Sees puppy pictures on the muddy walls. Kitten pillows on the somber bedspread.

"You like helpless animals, I see."

"I love them. But Grandfather was allergic, and Nana didn't like the dirt."

"Also they don't evolve."

"How can you say so, Hannah? They all develop characters — even souls!"

"Never mind. A prejudice I have. Maybe it's because they can't argue."

Amy caresses a puppy nose. "I painted the room yellow when I came back from school. But I think it will take a hundred more coats to drown out the old darkness. I want this room to be gayer for my baby than it was for me."

While she goes out to fetch cups of tea, Hannah sits in a desk chair taking in the message of the room with its coarse brown-

and-green-plaid draperies. She studies the infant dogs and cats.

Amy returns with tea, smiling. "What is this about, Hannah?"

Selig sips her honeyed tea a moment, then sets it down on the dark dresser top. "Why should you take on the burden of a baby all by yourself?" she asks. "You should have a willing partner."

"Don't jump to conclusions, Hannah! Charlie is working things out. He'll speak to Sylvia. He's not in favor of having the baby — not yet — but I know he'll come around." She smiles in hope. "I'm waiting till it's all arranged before I tell Nana."

"I didn't mean Charlie."

A startled silence. Amy's hand, holding a cup, stops midway to her lips.

"Do you expect me to look in the street for a man with the right qualities" — she tries to make it a joke — "now that I'm expecting a child?"

"You don't have to look far. Don't you notice, Amy? Are you so busy memorizing that you don't see that Paul follows you, drinks you in with his eyes, wants to do much more than that?"

Amy turns an astonished face. "You're not serious, Hannah? If Paul is sometimes with me it's because of Charlie. You know his devotion to Charlie. It's you — "

"I believe" — Hannah takes up her cup and sips between phrases — "he uses Charlie — as an excuse."

"There's nothing between us, Hannah. I know Paul loves you!"

"Maybe once."

"You don't think he's stopped!"

"He soon will."

Amy stares. Hannah sits on the brown bedspread in her tan jumpsuit. Her brilliant hair stretches out on either side of her head like information-charged filaments.

"How can you think you know that?"

"Don't ask how," Hannah hastily answers. "I haven't time to tell you what a long story it is. Only that it can do good — to you and to him. Really, I meant to speak before this. Only I have — put it off. One learns very late the weakness in one's own character."

"And your good? And Charlie's good?"

"My good is another story, which would be too long. But what would happen with you and Charlie would be, I am afraid, a very short story."

"What does that matter!" Amy passionately rebukes her, causing Hannah in turn to cry out, "Your love for Charlie is too unlikely! Don't you see? How other things must be at work?"

"Hannah, it's the human heart at work. That's enough without seeking other causes." As if she suddenly feels the wet weight of the towel, Amy with one hand snatches it from her head and throws it down. Her damp hair, too, seems darkened by the room.

"Women like you truly need no babies." Selig's voice lags, figuring slowly. "You find men whose cries — even if silent ones — open the glands as fiercely as a three-month infant in your arms . . . Cynicism, it must be," Hannah goes on softly, "attracts the innocently altruistic mind. One lure is to want to change the cynic to something else. The other is to want to give in, fascinated, as if cynicism tapped a deeper vein of life of which innocence can have no knowledge . . ." She catches herself up, abandons her musing tone, and says sharply, "But these are surface reasons only!"

"Don't call me innocent!" Amy's gesture rocks her cup. She steadies it. "You've forgotten what I told you about my life. And you, Hannah! You withhold your secrets from me!"

Selig glances quickly at the titles of the books in the brown bookcase. "No Bible here? That's where you'll find it — sick old men with young women — for whose benefit? For old men, pleasure; for young women, protection. From what does your love protect you?"

"No — no — Hannah, that's not good enough! *Why* do you tell me to go after Paul? *Why* won't you be happy yourself? I'll tell you, if you won't speak! Do you think you are not as known to the Center gossips as everyone else? Do you think no one has dared to peep into the pages of your notebook? You think you are going to be punished — made to suffer. And your pride rushes to give up first what you fear will be taken away! Isn't that so, Hannah? Isn't that the truth?"

Hannah has stumbled to her feet and spilled her tea — brown on brown. The ends of her wide-waving red-gold hair seem to tremble and reach out, confused. Her narrow white fingers — palms flat open as lily pads — flutter at her cheeks.

"I don't know — I wanted to do — what was needed — to help you . . ."

A deep woman's voice calls into the room from another part of the apartment to inquire whether Amy has a visitor. Amy calls back that it's a friend from the office who's leaving soon, Nana dear, good night . . .

Amy presses Selig's hand and kisses her cheek. "Thank you for coming, Hannah. Don't try to help me. I'm happy. I know what my love protects me from — all the sadness I would feel for all the happiness I never could give anyone before."

2

Hannah remembers how day after day it had gone on while she watched in fascination. How at each door the slats of a louverlike arrangement, controlled from inside the room, were turned to show colors that symbolized the activity within. She had astonished herself with her own quick learning.

White dots on yellow — anesthesia being administered. Red dots on yellow — procedure in progress. Blue on yellow — patient taken to recovery, and green with white stripes — the room prepared fresh for the next one.

When they broke for food — doctors, orderlies, nurses, aides — there was quick, light chatter. Weekends, past or coming. Families. Weddings. Children. As much celebration as could be crammed into half an hour. Hannah had listened hungrily. Such things had vanished from her life.

Seeing Paul, hearing his poor jokes, watching his awkward progress through the corridors, Hannah had felt so moved she had had to press her hand under her breast. From happiness. From sadness. Though it was hard to translate to this world what she had known in the other. He followed no rituals, kept no days. Prayers? No. How? But he was good. He cared about patients. She had seen him seek them out. He was skillful in medicine.

She has had to learn to recognize adaptations of what she was taught was virtue in her closed, safe world. In the great world outside, there are no safe places for virtue. She marvels that people have not torn one another to pieces, like the wild beasts. Yet this is where she wants to be. Where there is no safety for morality, and where souls must nurture themselves in the jaws of danger.

This struggling man, she had thought — he wants to do good and to love. She would have liked to tell him even then that he must go carefully, stealthily. Every desire, she had wished to say, carries its own death.

Stay away from me, she thought she ought to cry out. I am watched and mined . . .

She rings the bell at Paul's door. Hearing Amy's words: You rush to give up what you fear will be taken from you. She had thought the words outrageous, meaningless. Day and night since then she has struggled against them. Why, at this moment, with her finger on the bell, should they seem penetratingly true? Why is she here?

She wants to run away, but the door opens. She enters in her too-big blue duffel.

"Sweetheart — " Paul extends his arms to help her. "God," he says, "the ugliness of that old coat! When will you let me buy you a new one? But anyway I have affection for it. You wore it the first night you came to me."

She steps back from his help, refuses to remove her coat.

"I am here now," she says, "because during the day there is no time to speak. I came to tell you there is a way to show your friendship to Charlie."

"How?"

She catches sight of herself in the mirror on the opposite wall. The blue hood has slipped back. One vigorous red-gold thrust of hair looks angry, quivers or beats there. Why? she asks the image. Why do I follow this course? Why can I not stop now — this minute?

"How, what's the way?" Paul repeats impatiently.

She sees in the mirror a convulsive movement, as though the mirror image has fled. The Hannah who remains says dully, "Marry Amy."

He starts to laugh, sitting beside her on the sofa, then catches the look on her face.

"Are you crazy? Charlie's girl?"

Her gray-green eyes seem to gaze with no emotion, nothing in them but their own message. Is this, Paul thinks, the pure, cold way angels speak?

"Although you also are older than Amy, you are healthy. You are already attracted to her."

She sees the sharp sweep of anger through Paul's body.

"Thanks!" He is choking. "Thanks for looking me over like livestock. Thanks for your concern. You ought to have mentioned it sooner. It's a little late! I mean *pregnancy* is a little late!"

One minute he feels he is boiling with rage, the next he is close to tears. "Hannah, my God, you make me feel like some cast-off, twenty-year wife — *After all the love I lavished!* I don't know what the hell you're trying to do. Is this supposed to be for Amy's good? My good?" He turns his eyes from her strict, celestial gaze. "Damn it, I don't *want* to!"

"Such an idealistic young woman." Something driving her to complete what she has begun. "Her idealism comes at a time when you are all losing your own. All of you refresh yourselves at her, as if at a spring. Bunky, too, I see. He, who's never found in one spot too long — he *lingers* near her. And you — "

"I don't — not me. Hannah, you're wrong! Hannah, it's you . . ."

"Charlie can't be a father to this child. Help your friend Charlie. Help Amy. You will also benefit" — he hears how coldly she says it — "a beautiful young woman — perhaps you meant to speak for yourself in the first place . . . ?"

Paul, who has jumped up, presses his back to the wall for support. "Hannah, I want to tell you the truth! I admit — once — I might have thought — I was jealous of Charlie, my old affliction. But no more! You talk about change and growth, my God, can't you allow me mine? Hannah!"

He turns from that frighteningly neutral glance, as steady in its sockets as the light-colored liquid in a carpenter's level. He feels giddy, and reaches his forehead toward the cool wall. Instead of resting, he beats it there, crack! crack! She hears his forehead and the plaster smack against each other like thin mocking handclaps after a poor performance — her own.

"See what you make me do? Hannah? See?"

She is perfectly free now, when his eyes are closed and the damage has been done, to run away.

*

On Saturday, Hannah from her open door sees Sorita on the stair landing.

"Come in, Sorita." Her voice is pitched only for Sorita's hearing. The man who sleeps behind the door must be left undisturbed. "Bring the baby with you."

Sorita throws a quick glance over her shoulder at the flaking, once-green door, now peeled to its iron. She speaks in Spanish to her children in the hallway, grasps the baby, and follows with hurried shuffling movements into Hannah's hallway.

"Do you see?" Hannah points to the new table. "We have a good place to talk."

The surface of the table, clean and bare, gives the impression of being adorned. Hannah slides from their places two of the new chairs, their backs curved and hammocked with straw-colored cane. Sorita sinks exhausted, grasping the baby. She smiles uncertainly at the new things.

Hannah begins hastily, fearing interruption. "In the place

where I work, women like yourself can come, who have no money . . ."

When they hear footsteps in the hallway, Sorita cringes in her chair. She seems to be trying to melt her body into the baby's body. Hannah, too, waits in fear. Now that I long to be free of my old delusive idea, she thinks, will every act of mine be answered by instant reprisal? Will everyone be punished whom I try to help?

But it is only José, who walks through the open door looking for his sister. He stares at the table, at Sorita, with his dark puzzled eyes. His wide, flat, yellowish face is turned slightly away.

The women say nothing.

José slides a chair out from under the table, silent as a duenna. Like Sorita, he quietly moves his fingers over the wood of the table's surface.

Now and then the old refrigerator and the plumbing behind the sink give off sharp reports, like pistol shots. Boys playing in the street beneath the windows shout like commandos. All the same there is a feeling of peace in the room. The baby dozes on his mother's neck. Sorita's pretty face with its tired, dark-circled eyes, her thickened, factory-working fingers with the blood-red nail polish, also seem to be at ease. Even the frightened expression on José's face does not interrupt the feeling of brother's and sister's timid resting here.

"Do you think" — Hannah begins again — "because you are religious, that what I am telling you about is a way of murdering God? I think the opposite! Because the world is not yet fit — we are incapable of receiving all our children. Do you understand?"

Sorita sits rocking her baby softly on her left arm. The thickened fingers of her right hand rest lightly on the table. Now and then she rubs, as if with secret pleasure at the contact.

"The priest," she says dreamily, "says I'm gonna burn in

hell if I do something not to make a baby come. He says I better go to that meeting that's coming here so I can see myself what they make some women do."

"I'll go with you," Hannah says, "to that meeting." Hannah rouses herself. She goes to the old refrigerator, whose door groans open, and brings a bottle of apple juice and a plate of dates to the table.

Brother and sister shake their heads in refusal.

"Please."

After a shared glance that is like some signal, each slowly and with delicacy unsticks a date from the pile and begins to bite at it.

Hannah leans back on her chair. She no longer hears the sounds, the pistol shots, the commando raids outside in the street. Her kitchen seems immensely quiet. Peace fills it like some delicious scent. It binds the occupants with sleepiness, like bewitchment in an old nursery tale. José's eyes are closed; he appears to nap. Sorita gazes, heavy-lidded, at her child.

The caul of rest is suddenly snatched from the room.

Sorita clutches her child. Her short-cut black hair, not well combed, stands out from her head in chunks.

Julio, Sorita's man, has thrown open the door Hannah left ajar for Sorita's children. It crashes against the iron jamb.

"Venga!"

Sorita scrambles up with her child, smiles an instant's apology at Hannah, and shuffles out in her bedroom slippers with a kind of Oriental quick-trot. José instantly follows.

As if her own words have made her restless, Hannah goes downstairs and into the street. Men and boys lounge in the store entrances. She looks toward the interior of the *bodega* where she buys cheese and bread. The woman who owns it is friendly to her, never failing to greet her when she passes. But the woman is quarreling angrily now with one of the young men lounging at the door and doesn't see Hannah.

She walks several blocks, to the building that was once a

synagogue. It is a medium-sized edifice of dark stone, which would have been ugly were it not for an exceptional set of leaded windows, azure blue, with rounded white shapes — like heaven filled with loaves of light. The synagogue had for a while been converted into a community center till funds ran out, then into a pentecostal church. It is now abandoned, the windows pierced by stones.

A Star of David, carved over the front door, had been overlayed by a painted cross on a large piece of canvas. It is torn, and flaps in the wind. Now and then its corners lift to reveal the stone Star beneath.

Before the synagogue she shuts her eyes and sees her father and mother, the rabbi, the whole, once-flourishing congregation leaving after the Ne'ilah service at the close of Yom Kippur. It is a chilly fall night, in which the first three stars shine purely in the dark autumn sky. The people who emerge are faint with hunger, with confession and mourning, but also buoyed by forgiveness and the promise of renewal. They walk quickly toward their homes, calling New Year's greetings to one another.

How could this pious, injured congregation, Hannah had asked herself over and over, take seriously again the message that prayer and charity would avert evil? The question had bothered no one else. It was nothing compared to the assurance, reaffirmed, that the watchful, caring God hears all, forgives all, is eager to renew His covenant. Year after year, Hannah had seen the deeply passionate union take place. Always, she knew, the cold, inexplicable withdrawal was bound to come. There would be, at the very least, the thefts — the loss of the few remaining possessions cherished by those from whom so much had been taken; there would be the attacks on pious old people. And finally there was the brutal murder of her own parents. Those patient God-loving people, who had already lost everything, lost a little more.

The young women among whom she had grown up, all by

then married, many already in pregnancy, had come to comfort her. They came uneasily, not knowing how to be with her anymore. She had begun, by her questions, to separate herself from them in school. She saw their uneasiness and had refrained from saying aloud what she thought — that Onan, that reneger against the promised union — must be another name for God.

She returns to her apartment and is assaulted by an odor that instantly causes her to gag. She covers her face with her hands but can't shut it out, so familiar that it seems to come from within her — meat grown rancid, rotted to cheese. There has been none in her kitchen since her parents' death. So the odor, it must be, is seared into her nostrils.

She lifts the sash of the kitchen window and strikes matches to fill her nostrils with the acrid sulfur smell. Better the scent of Satan than the foul odor connected with deeds in a place where God's invocation had been on the doorpost and God's presence faithfully acknowledged in every pot and pan.

She lays upon the new table the battered blue notebook and opens to a fresh page. She means to write out what Amy had told her about herself — "Your pride rushes to give up what you fear will be taken away." But the words are too terrible — she cannot.

ᲓᏅ Ꮕ

The auditorium is by now almost unbearably hot. The damp chill of the hall has been blotted up by an hour of heated words: "Hemorrhage." "Toxemia." "Shock."

Specialists preside on the platform. Like Amy, they can recite by heart: "Melancholia." "Frigidity." "Permanent infertility." "Irreversible insanity." Words leap down from the platform like tigers to mangle and destroy. Flaming mites swarm and burn and give no rest: "Guilt." "Shame." "Remorse." "Nightmare."

Specialists abound in the audience, too, passionately interested in the creation of miniatures. These miniatures are known by the name of "baby." There is only "baby" in the air — there is no "person," there is no "man," there is no "woman"; there is only "baby." These specialists are like guild members who learn industry forecasts and fear that miniatures may go out of production entirely. Like any miniature-lover — of, say, metal Eiffel Towers or porcelain puppies — they do not much care what happens to the article after it is manufactured and, so to say, "placed." If it is broken or lost or hidden or sold at auction or displayed in some institution or smashed in a subsequent smash-up — that is not their concern. What they want is to ensure that these miniatures will go on being produced.

Every now and then Sorita trembles and utters a little groan of fear. Hannah puts her arm about her at once, yet she looks at Sorita in wonderment — so many hot tears for these embryos on display, so many slaps and screams for her own brood of children.

Sorita tries hard to suppress these noisy groans. She has already been warned by her neighbors that she prevents people from hearing the speakers. But there is little danger in the case of this speaker. The woman's voice is clear and full, embellished by the careful enunciations of the Middle West. The blown *h*'s of "where's" and "when's" impart to her speech the stability of the unslurred. Though some in the audience lose composure, like Sorita, the speaker herself does not give way; the sentences come crisply. The rhythms are curiously doggerel-like, as though the talk, largely autobiographical, has become a well-rehearsed recitation.

"I heard the news that Joe, my husband, who was sent to fight in Nam" — there are patriotic cheers from the audience — "was killed" — sympathetic applause bursts out. "The child inside my womb seemed too much burden with Joe gone." Light booing. "But at the very last I changed my mind." Applause again. "Through cowardice alone and nothing else!

Ever since that day I've thanked the Lord. I know it was the Lord who sent me fear. I pity all those women who are told that there is nothing wrong with what they do." Boos. "They think they're free to choose but they are not! Their murdered babies all will — "

But Hannah cannot hear what the murdered babies will do. Sorita is for the moment overcome. "Maria! Jesus! Maria!" She tries to muffle her words between the baby's little yellow cap and sweater, which Hannah had bought for him. Fortunately the baby, as if Sorita's groans are lullabies, relaxes into deeper sleep. The baby appears to project a dream of itself onto the wall, where a slide of a giant curled fetus expands into focus.

A man now takes his place at the microphone. His voice is rapid, matter-of-fact; a doctor's voice, or a policeman's, bored with these elementary facts:

"At three months a baby's fully formed. Heartbeat, brain waves, fingers, toes, genitals. If you try to penetrate the uterus with a needle you feel the fetus repelling it. When the suction nozzle goes in, you can bet the fetus is grabbing for dear life to the sides of the uterus with its fingers. What's our excuse? If we can kill life at this end, why not the other? Why not the helpless old? Why not the crippled? The retarded? Why not brown-haired children if you like them blond? Why not girls if you prefer boys? Remember Kitty Genovese pleading in the street for help? No one came. These babies scream for help. They have no words, but something in them is screaming, you can bet!"

As if in illustration, Sorita's baby lets out several sharp screams. A man behind them complains loudly, "Why don't these people learn not to bring their brats along?"

"Or if they must," a woman nearby replies, "why can't they learn to remove them when they make a disturbance?"

The baby subsides; a new image flashes on. Sorita begins her muttered prayers again. A new voice speaks, once more a woman's, while a new giant fetus wobbles on the screen. "The baby in my womb didn't look any different than this at six months, and neither did yours. Except this child was strangled with salt." The normal aggrieved infant-look takes on poignant meaning. "And here" — she rests her shaking voice while the image wavers and jumps — "is the hardest thing for me to talk about. But I feel I can go on because God is with me on this platform."

Hannah leans back with a pained expression.

The image changes again. Now the art of visual aids outdoes itself in compression. The screen is crowded with the bodies of the naked dead. Economy has been foremost. Ten are squeezed into the place of one. Familiar as these stick figures are to the inhabitants of the age of advanced technology, the moment comes when viewers squint in puzzlement. Can these, after all, have been human beings?

"And here," the woman is saying, "is what happened when people thought everything was permitted."

Hannah, sitting tensely in the crowded hall and stroking Sorita on her shaking back, sees the Nazi soldiers. They are posed for the photographer, arms crossed, grinning, at the side of the grave where adult men and women, the stick figures, are so economically piled.

"You mustn't — " She feels, the moment she cries it out, that it will be hopeless. "You mustn't use them like that!"

In the audience people turn and call for quiet. There is some booing.

"Their poor bodies," she cries up toward the platform, "you mustn't *use* them. Don't you know they were killed for being Jews?"

Near Hannah someone demands, "Why do Jews think only of themselves? Can't they see the implications for humanity?"

Hannah is baffled by the word "implications." What implications can the thing have that is itself the utmost?

"Those who did it," she cries up toward the platform again,

"do you think they would kill their own? No, they *cherished* their own. Killed other people's children, fathers, and mothers, while they cherished their own. Don't you see? It isn't love for fetuses you ought to teach. You accomplish nothing here."

The baby, wakened by the commotion, starts to wail. Several people turn angrily. "Can't you shut the brat *up!*" Sorita jumps from her chair and starts quickly up the aisle, holding the crying baby. Hannah follows, heading after her down the long aisle. The bored man, having told them how to vote in the next election, now counsels them to become detectives and track down women about to make a mistake. He recites a telephone number, uttering the separate digits in a frightening urgent monotone as if the slow progression is meant to end in detonation: "Four–eight–three–four–two–one–zero . . ."

Hannah loses sight of Sorita in a crowd of milling people at the end of the aisle but catches a glimpse of someone else, hurrying in the opposite direction, moving forward as if drawn by rope toward the bored man. It is Matt. Hannah is about to call his name, to ask him to help her find Sorita, who will be confused in all this crowd, when she feels her shoulder grabbed from behind.

It is the last speaker, panting a little from having trotted in the aisle to catch up. Her plump body is dressed in a suit the color of rusty blood. A manicured hand, with nail polish to match the suit, clasps her own cheek as she trots, as if to quell permanent outrage.

"I must speak to you." She pants. "Because you're a Jew. Can you guess about me? German descent. My parents born there." Her speech, elliptical with panting, becomes more German-sounding. "I give my life to this. You Jews — I don't understand you. Indifferent to your own seed — you carry out Hitler's will — don't you see!"

Hannah looks around but sees that she has lost him too; she has lost Matt now as well as Sorita.

"I see that if Jewish women do or don't do something because of what Hitler wanted, they give up their freedom, volunteer to be slaves, still victims of Hitler . . . Where can they be?"

"Astonishing idea!" The woman hurries along. "I admire this — as idea only — " For a moment she drops back. Hannah sees Sorita, far ahead. Her bright orange slacks cling to her heavy hips, her upper body bends ahead of her legs; she flees crouched, as if she expects stones to be flung. But the woman surges forward again, vehement. "Or do you say this because you don't trust me? I know what you must think!" She is panting and hurrying alongside Hannah, who is nearly running now. "You think it's easier for me to love a fetus than an already born human being. You think that no complete human being is abstract enough for me — isn't that it? No sooner is the baby born than it has a history — a religion, a color, a sex. But unborn, in the womb — there is the perfect nonspecific humanity I long to love. I know — that must be what you think. Oh, the unborn, you think — the most generalized of all protoplasm! You think I hate them once they're formed — that I can't love Jews or black people or yellow."

"Excuse me," Hannah says, "I am trying to find a woman — with a baby."

"You won't find her," the speaker says testily. "She'll have got rid of it! Why don't you tell me the truth about what you think about me?"

"I think you believe it — about God on the platform with you."

"But I know you think it's a delusion." The woman is almost running now to keep up with Hannah. "I know what you think. You think I think they're sweet and helpless, floating in the water. You think I think of comparisons, that they're like the baby Moses in the bulrushes, waiting to be rescued! You think I want to be Pharaoh's daughter! You think I think no one can call me anti-Semite if I can think of comparisons like that! Don't you! Don't you!" Her hand presses now against her bosom.

"No, no!" Hannah cries over her shoulder as she runs.

"Why should I think that? I was interested — you said — on the platform — "

Hannah is running as hard as she can, but Sorita, baby and all, must be running even harder. Finally Hannah catches up with her. She has stopped and stooped amid the crowd to retrieve the baby's fallen yellow bootee. Hannah leaves the speaker behind as she sprints, red hair flying, bobbing up and down, massed and electrical.

"What you fear can't happen, Sorita!" Hannah breathlessly says, taking the baby from Sorita's arms to rest her. "Men sometimes give women babies against their will." Sorita looks away and Hannah looks away: they don't speak of the muscular ploughman who sleeps all day in Sorita's apartment and then at night ploughs and plants his woman's body, as industrious a farmer as ever feared the failure of a crop. "But they can't — they couldn't — take the fetus away from women against their wills. Only when you don't want it doctors know how to take it from you. Now that you see both sides you can choose."

In reply, Sorita reaches again for the baby, clutches it tight as if to underline what she has already said: once she has it she wants it. The trick is then for Sorita to catch herself at some time when she is not already pregnant — and that is very hard to do.

❧ ❧

At home, Paul is waiting at her door. "I came to remind you I am for you," he says. "You are for me."

They embrace — it is an extra sweetness to her — on the old wide bed of her parents, and it is transformed from a hollow-centered tear-soaked pallet to a couch of love. May this joy, she thinks, ease their memories of me.

Paul never spends the night, for fear Karen or Helene might suddenly need him and he would miss the call. But it is late when he leaves.

"Don't tell me ever again about marrying somebody else.

It's you I want. I'm only waiting now for you to meet my girls and get to know them. Will you, Hannah, sweet Hannah, my love?"

Afterward, though, Amy's words again. Pen poised, Hannah writes to sort out confusion. How confused all her actions have been!

For weeks after the death of her parents, she remembers, she had come home to her apartment almost believing she would find that nothing had happened. She believed she would open the door and see that her parents lived. She would see that God had sent a ram to sacrifice in place of her parents, as He had sent a ram to Abraham in place of Isaac. God had sent two rams for her two parents, two gagged rams. And God had deflected the blows of the killer from her parents to the rams. Like Ajax on the Trojan battlefield, the killer had slaughtered livestock, not people, and when he saw what he had done he ran and killed himself. So she would turn the key and imagine that her parents — by God's intervention — lived. But they had not lived. She had begun her punishment of God for not sending rams. Punish and punish, because no ram.

Those two old ghosts, her father and mother, had come to her in dreams. She thought they cried through bruised throats for vengeance. Not against the crazed murderer, a hireling of his own depravity. But against the not sending of the ram. Nothing had come from Nothing. "Revenge!" her ghosts had cried.

So she had in her madness thought. But when thought of again, less mad, the dream was simpler. Two loving ghosts had come to kiss farewell.

The cry for revenge had been her own.

"I declared war on Almighty God," Hannah writes, "and an obliging angel answered my challenge by laughing and flinging a handful of dust in my eyes."

If there had been no ram, then what had there been? The bitterness toward God did not last. It simply melted. Time passed, birds sang in the city trees, she and Paul made love. And though no ram was sent, it was as though a ram had been sent! She had no heart to punish anymore. Even if there had been no ram, hadn't there been *something* that caused her to think now with awe about the lives of her parents, that even caused her — yes! — to thank God that they had never suffered ugliness from within, but only from without, had never returned evil for evil? Such gratitude as she would have scorned before now seemed realer to her than any rage. To suffer bitterly and yet the soul not die of its poison — that was the ram.

"Then I needn't — !" She speaks the beginning of a sentence so wondrously powerful that it pitches, first her pen from her fingers, and then such a flood of happiness into her heart that she might be Sarah herself beholding Isaac, after an eternity, come home.

3

WAITING FOR CHARLIE, Sylvia feels proud of looking slimmer and younger. She is calmer and more attractive, she knows, than she has been in years. Certainly she feels happier. There is a good deal of unhappiness to subtract from her happiness, but still the sum left over of happiness is a tidy and reassuring one.

It is natural for Sylvia's thoughts to take an accounting turn when focused on her life with Charlie. Her earliest association with him had been as his father's bookkeeper, and there remained something ever after of the debit and credit side to her thinking about her marriage. "With Charlie, I don't have this or this or this, but he gives me that." Too timid by nature to oppose Charlie successfully, she had for years used her figuring mind to counteract Charlie's pressures and to do what she wanted to do, which was to love him.

When Charlie stands in her new, independent doorway and says, "You look wonderful, Sylvia," in a quiet, smiling, selfless voice, she tries not to feel such idiotic delight in her own well-being. For Charlie's sake, on this visit, she tries to keep her happiness subdued to a degree of gravity. Yet she feels delight at looking so well. Delight at having worn her new, fine-fitting gray wool slacks with the white silk shirt. Delight in the small scarlet kerchief knotted at her throat. And she knows her delight is increased because it is Charlie who sees it.

"It would make me look even more wonderful" — Sylvia smiles — "if I could see *you* looking happier."

It delights her to give him a brandy and coffee in her new brandy glasses, her new blue-and-white Arabia cups. She has made her small Village apartment colorful, comfortable. Her job in the registrar's office at New York University enables her to sit in on courses there. Texts and notebooks are piled on a round table covered with a fine paisley throw she had discovered in an antique shop. Charlie has brought a bunch of red carnations, which stand now among the books in a blue-and-white Staffordshire milk jug.

"I'd hoped," Sylvia says comfortably, "to hear by now that Paul and Hannah had come to some understanding. She came to see me here, you know. I invited her after she wrote me a sweet note when I first moved in. She gave me advice on living alone, told me to keep a journal. 'Some day it will be a book to give to Daniel,' she said. 'You will be relating your life to him even when you're away.' I think she meant that 'relating' to be a pun, I'm not sure. I'm no good at writing down my thoughts, but it was sweet of her to suggest it." Sylvia laughs indulgently, safely, savoring her delight. "Just one woman for Paul. Not his usual procession. I'd hoped to hear by now that he was ready to start a new life . . ."

"Instead," Charlie says quietly, "it's me. I'm the one."

Sylvia had just brought her brandy glass to her mouth. It jogs painfully against her gums.

"You, Charlie? When? Who? Where did you meet her?" She suddenly knows without being told. "At the Center? And are you — what? — in love with each other?"

Sylvia puts down her glass. She refills Charlie's coffee cup with a steady hand and automatically thinks, Look, I'm still ahead. Once I wouldn't have been able to do that. Then there slams into her chest something that feels as hard and heavy as the carriage of an electric typewriter, office model.

"She claims to be in love," Charlie is saying. "Foolishly. She's young . . ."

"How young?" She demands it sharply — she has to know. Charlie's half-smile shows he understands how ridiculous it is: "Only twenty-two."

"Nearly Daniel's age!"

"I thought that myself."

Sylvia pulls at her neck scarf. To the left, the right, the left. She feels she is choking. But a calm, civilized voice — hers? — is saying, "I want you to be happy, Charlie. But I don't understand. Are you asking for a divorce?"

He shakes his head, smiles half a smile. "I'm indifferent." His long, finely shaped eyes seem almost to smile at her as well, as they draw her intimately into this absurd confession. "Amy wants it."

"Let me think a little, Charlie." Sylvia is trembling. "I hadn't expected . . ."

She breaks off, walks to the window, and stands gazing down at the street. She feels sick to her stomach, chilled and fevered, as once she had felt at the onset of her periods. She remembers Genevieve X, Bunky's nightmare woman. By her own indecision, she was supposed to bring doom on herself and the Center. Sylvia wonders now if her own timidity had similarly marked her for catastrophe — as if the very elements of her own self-protectiveness could, nightmarelike, thrust forth tentacles to drag her down.

Genevieve X doesn't know what to do, she thinks, trembling. The stupid woman can't make up her mind to save her own life . . .

A young woman in a brilliant orange sweater is setting up her music stand in the street. When she begins to play her violin, phrases of music — rapid, ornate — tear into the room. A white-haired man passes. Sylvia sees him bend to drop coins into the open violin case. She turns abruptly back to Charlie.

"What am I to think of this match? Is it suitable? I mean for you. I'm thinking of you, Charlie. You were so generous to me." Her eyes fill with tears. "I have to think of you now!"

Charlie says lightly, "What sort of judge am I, Sylvia? Terrible at such things!"

Again Sylvia turns to the window. The young violinist is wholeheartedly absorbed in her playing, oblivious of the noises of traffic and argument. An older woman, passing, stumbles over the open case on the sidewalk. Still the younger one plays on, unnoticing.

"Charlie!" Sylvia whirls as if rescuing her own feet from a stumble. She feels the blood surging into her face. "I see what it is! I see what's happened!" Sylvia begins to pace and to clasp and unclasp her hands in excitement as she works everything out aloud.

"You've been lonely, despite what you say. And vulnerable. You don't want to disappoint this girl who thinks she loves you . . ."

Charlie listens in silence, his half-smile giving a strange sweetness of expression to his face. Once, while Sylvia talks, he looks over at the flowers on the table.

" — Who *does* love you, Charlie, I'm sure she does; why shouldn't she? But I left you exposed to this — to be drawn into a life that you're indifferent to and that would exhaust you. And there's no need!"

She has forgotten, for the moment, that he had been indifferent and exhausted when they shared a life together. She no longer thinks of Genevieve X. She is filled now with the sense of her own well-being, and feels endlessly strong. I've gained so much in my new life. I could never have talked this way before!

"Charlie, I'm ready to come back!" She holds out her hands. "It isn't a sacrifice at all for me."

"What about Simon? What about" — no one can make the phrase sound more desolate — "your new life?"

"Simon's not the same to me as you, Charlie. How could he be? It's not the same as how I love you. Newness wears off. Then what's left? We have no old associations — no family life."

She has untied her scarlet scarf because it suddenly choked her, and whips it nervously through her fingers while she speaks.

"If I thought, Charlie, I was holding you back from happiness, I wouldn't do it. And if you still want a divorce, you can have one. But if not — at least right now — then I want to come home. And I think — when Daniel leaves — we ought to move to the city. I like my job, and it would be a new life for us both . . ."

She turns partly away. "I am asking if I can come home, Charlie."

"You don't have to ask. It's your home. Come whenever you want to." His expression of quiet sweetness, when she turns to look, is, mysteriously, a torment to her.

"I will" — she lifts her arms — "my dear husband! — I will come home!"

She is stunned by her words a moment after she has uttered them. The sounds of the street violin must have bewitched me, she thinks, must have made me think I know my mind. Her slacks feel constrictingly tight. She loosens the belt a notch, but does it up again too quickly, and it bursts apart when she breathes. She feels she is coming undone.

"Give me a little time, though!" Flushed and trembling, she begins to arrange objects on the paisley-covered table as if nothing at all is in its rightful place. "Don't be hurt by this, Charlie. I want to be fair to Simon and — and" — here she begins to tremble violently — "and to myself."

She bursts into tears. Charlie, rising, places his hands on her shoulders. "Take your time," he soothingly says, before he leaves.

She rests her back against the door, turns a blind face to the empty room. Something is putting itself together in her mind. Something the teacher of her Ethics course had quoted. She forgot who had said it: "Please yourself; that way you'll be sure at least one person is happy."

Her thoughts whirl endlessly. What pleases me? What pleases me? She cannot decide. She has lost — or never had the chance to learn — the pathways through her own nerves and blood that can lead her to an answer now.

◄§ §►

Outside the assembly room, Amy detains Paul with a hand on his arm. "Oh, Paul, I have news! Can you guess? I'm pregnant!"

He stares. So much for good memory! Can she have forgotten that she has already told the news? Now he sees that she had, all the while he thought she was talking to him, been addressing herself so fervently to Charlie that she had actually forgotten Paul's presence.

"What does Charlie say?" Paul goes along with his supposed ignorance.

"He says have it out. You knew he'd say that, didn't you, Paul?"

"I don't know anything these days!" He says it a trifle testily.

"Charlie says his wife wants to come home. She doesn't want to give a divorce."

"Is that what Charlie says?"

"Yes. So that's another reason. It wouldn't be fair to the baby."

Her lip trembles. Tears stand in her eyes.

"What are you going to do, Amy?"

"Me? Nothing. Charlie's going to do it all." He sees that she is crying. "I'm going to have it out by one of the best. Like a tooth."

It is the first time he has heard irony in Amy's voice.

"I'm so sorry, Amy. Did you think a baby would bring Charlie off the fence?"

"I admit it, Paul. So Charlie was right after all. I was just another woman using some poor fetus to manipulate life."

"Well — I'll admit too — I'm disappointed, Amy. I thought that with you Charlie would allow himself a new life. Never mind — you'll still have each other."

"Yes." Her eyes shine with tears. Her voice quivers as it had quivered that time he had heard her through the wall being bullied by Matt.

4

LIGHTHEARTED at Bloomingdale's, she looks at the tightest pants. The snuggest vests buttoning under and over the breasts. Two buttons, two breasts, two months — no, nearly three now.

Lucky, lucky, luck! To be living now, this decade, not some other. She catches herself thinking that is her own smartness, and has to laugh at herself. Alexandra! What did *you* have to say about when you got shoved through?

Crowds of women push. She pushes good-naturedly back. When some poor stretched creature passes on the escalator, she nearly laughs again. *You not goin' up, you goin' down, girl!* No time before her appointment to try things on. But her mood calls for something new. She can buy a scarf to throw over her shoulder, show how she feels. She can hardly believe that she had been scared enough to postpone the appointment till now.

She's fine till she gets to the counter heaped with silks. She turns one over and feels under her fingers the exact touch of the cool flesh of her mother's arm.

"When you give birth to your first child, I'll be there with you, honey. That's what a mama is for."

A hell of a thing to hear that now! Poor Mama — worn out,

and no wonder! Dead of heart failure at fifty-nine. Who sits by an abortion? No one. A machine does it. So what? *So what!*

She leaves without the scarf. A sudden panicked feeling that she will be late and miss her three o'clock appointment makes her tear down the steps — the escalator is too draggy — and flap her arms in the street. A taxi sidles lazily up. The cabby's voice is ironic and slow. "You *really* flyin'!"

Then, when she gets there, one look at the scene stops her in her tracks. She has stepped off the elevator into a floor-through length of waiting room, where women silently sit. It's as if she had never seen *anything* when she came for her checkup.

She wants Brody. That skinny, blond girl sitting next to the skinny youth in a brown leather jacket, his face sullen, she envies her. Her man, her boy, is with her.

Three lines of women stand before the reception desk. She adds herself to one, behind a girl no more than seventeen. She's a kid and all alone, Alexandra thinks. Most everybody here is alone.

Wanting it to be all over and be healed and back in Brody's arms — laughing about how scared she was, or crying about it, or whatever it is she is going to do. How can she tell? Everything inside her is quivering.

Suddenly, again, her senses betray her. How can Mama be here? Someone in the line must be using that same old powder Mama had used, when she thought to use any. Alexandra fills her lungs with the smell. She sees her mother sitting by the radio in the evening, in her cotton print wraparound, sewing.

In all this scene of pregnancy, nobody sews. Why should they sew? Her glance roves the room again and she feels a shock, as if she had willed this to be: there is someone! Her eyes adjust. Not a woman, though. A guy, his hair drawn back to a pony tail. He is working on a hoop, his needle plying in and out of canvas, the long tail of blue wool lifting into the air and sinking again. The needle pierces the fabric from below.

His hand emerges from beneath the skirt of the hoop, darts up, seizes the needle. His muscular fist clenches, pulls, lifts it free of the cloth. It is a miniature birth. The thread plants another stitch in the fabric; it leaves its mark.

Now the young man lifts a tiny embroidery scissors and snips the thread. Innocently, he pantomimes one of the Fates. At that very moment, with his consent, the life of his child might be going to be cut off!

Alexandra feels faint, dizzy. She feels an arm encircle her back.

"Let me help you." A young woman's voice speaks quietly into her ear. Alexandra turns and looks into clear gray eyes. She feels herself escorted to a seat. The young woman brings a card on a clipboard. She sits beside Alexandra in a gold-colored outfit and begins to ask questions in a slow, thoughtful way.

Looking around, Alexandra White sees other women filling out such cards by themselves. She understands that because she has shown some telltale signs of unease and faintness, she is being given special treatment.

"Will you give me your name, please?"

She gives it.

"Address?"

"Why do you need to know?"

"We keep our records absolutely private," the young woman says. She wears a name plate set into a rectangular gold-colored pin.

Alexandra again glances around. They are here in all sizes, ages, shapes, these women. Some with faces of innocence, some marked with roughness. Some in quiet clothing, others in the sleazy loudness of poverty. They are all managing to wield pencils by themselves.

"Amy Netboy," Alexandra reads aloud. "Is that what you are? Someone who retrieves what can't make it over the net? You make me feel I'm dreaming."

Netboy lifts her pen and asks softly, "Is this your first time?"
Alexandra nods.

"And how do you feel about it?"

"Godawful!" She is amazed to hear truth scrambling for dear life from her lips, as if she were a burning building. Truth having opened the locked gate, a long-imprisoned sob escapes too.

At once Netboy is on her feet. "Please come with me." Her voice is firm and neutral. Netboys don't laugh or cry. Netboys keep things moving. They enter now a private room with a desk, a few chairs, tasteful wallpaper — bamboo stalks leaning into a beige sky. Netboy sits beside Alexandra.

"There is a note on your card. When you came for your checkup you were very upset. You don't have to answer," she says in a gentle voice, "but I'd like to ask if you are married to the father?"

"No."

"Is the father willing to marry?"

She is older than this young woman, this Netboy, probably by thirteen or fourteen years. Yet she is answering questions like these. How dare Netboy think she is unable to handle her own life? She attempts to gather her fragments together.

"He's already married," she says as coolly as she can manage. "We've worked it all out."

"Could you handle a child yourself?"

"Of course! But I don't want to."

To her horror, another sob breaks loose. "I beg your pardon," she says, as if she has yawned or sneezed.

"No doctor here" — Netboy's careful manner is suddenly broken in on by a thrust of pride — "will do a procedure on someone who's not one hundred percent sure. In fact" — she jumps up, her slender figure in the light golden uniform is full of purpose — "Dr. Bianky will have to consult."

Alexandra wants to protest. Yet will-lessly she watches the young net boy go. She waits with a certain dull interest for a new element to enter her mind. Pictures the braid wagging down the hall.

The door opens. A slight young man in a white coat enters. An exceedingly handsome young man, who seems not to know that he is and who looks as furtively around him as if he were ugly and disfigured. As if he needed to know, in any room, who might be there to observe him, before he dared come in.

He shuts the door behind him. Shifts nervous eyes to every corner of the room. Alexandra wants to giggle. She feels a touch of hysteria about her own hilarity. He looks like an abortionist! He stands blinking, giving off a strong scent of lotion.

"Are you the doctor who wants to see me?" Contempt now controls her nerves. She stands, poses her superbly groomed figure against his shifting, dissolving one.

"Yes, I am de doctor." His whispery voice has an odd foreign lilt she can't place.

"I'm fine! I was a little nervous, but I'm sure that's normal."

"Do you know what it is you want?" His voice is still whispery, his eyes blinking and shifting. His skin is thickened in places, like Brody's.

"Yes!" Her defiance cracks her voice.

"Are you sure you know how to get what you want? De other ways? I askin' for your good."

An iciness creeps into her bones. Her knees tremble. Abruptly she sits down, silent.

He looks over his shoulder; he seems to be expecting someone. "Hundreds of couples — lookin' for de babies. Any baby can live."

She remembers now that she had had an uncle — her mother's oldest brother — who had spoken in that lilting voice. She sees her mother surrounded by babies, babies in her arms, at her breasts. Her own breasts and arms feel the weight of babies. She sees in the young man's handsome frightened face the helplessness of babies. Sees babies rotating in the air above them like lost planets. Hundreds of couples below with hands outstretched.

"Here I am!" she longs to cry out to them all — to the one who is her special one. "Here! I am a safe place for you! Here, my darling! I am here for you!"

He looks over his shoulder, expecting someone. "Hundreds of couples," he repeats. He startles. Listens behind him. Draws a piece of paper from within the white coat, folded, and thrusts it at her.

"Call them. You won't regret it. Have some pity, please! You don't have to kill. Everyting nice and secret. Tell them you are from here."

He puts his finger to his lips one moment before the door opens and a stocky man in a sweat-wrinkled white coat and a worry-wrinkled, forward-thrust face enters. Obviously a person in charge.

"What — ?" he begins, seeing the young man. "Matt?"

The young man scoops up a blue glass bowl in which there are a number of brightly colored paper-wrapped candies.

"I came in to check the refreshments," he says in an ordinary, flat, American voice. All trace of charming, coaxing, foreign lilt has vanished.

"The stuff goes like there's no tomorrow."

He leaves swiftly.

The heavy person in authority turns to her. Alexandra bursts into nervous tears. Better that than to guiltily cry out, I didn't take any candy!

◄§ §►

Edgar gives himself a second to sort his confusion. He had pictured her differently — his nemesis, the woman he had called Genevieve X, the one who was to destroy his clinic by her death, her breathing failure under anesthetic caused by extreme emotional trauma. How he had worked it all out, tortured himself with details!

He had pictured her dressed shabbily. Or with too much makeup. This woman is well dressed, in a wine-colored suit with a matching beret. Her ankles are slim, crossed; her feet in neat black pumps. Her handbag is in her lap and her hands are resting on the handbag. Otherwise, it is all the same. She is wringing her hands. Her face is almost distorted by her fears. Her nose has the small bump at the bridge, from some childhood bruise, exactly as it does in his waking dream. He stares. She moves her head; a wave of hair slips off her forehead. A tiny scar travels into a corner of her hairline. He had not foreseen that, but now it seems, like everything else about her, to be inevitable, ordained. He had imagined her deathly pale. This woman's skin has a light brown tint. Yet underneath must be the pallor that drains the blood from the brain.

Alexandra White wipes her eyes and stares as if through mist at a forehead deeply furrowed. The white coat pulls across the heavy chest. He seems to be breathing with difficulty, choking over his words. She feels she will faint. *You don't have to kill.*

"I have only one thing to say to you. What we take out, we can't put back in again. So be very sure." He is slow and explicit, as if to an idiot. "How far are you?"

"Nearly twelve weeks," she whispers. *Thousands of couples. Any baby can live.*

He stands over her. His words beat down, press down with those other words. *Do you know what you want?*

"Then if you wait and think it over — which I strongly advise you to do — you can't come back here for procedure. It will be too late. You'll go to a hospital for saline injection, unless of course you decide against doing anything. I just want you to be clear about it."

"I don't want that!"

"And I don't want to do a procedure on anyone who's too upset to take anesthetic safely." His slow voice affronts her.

"I'm all right!" Her hands are shaking. She tries to hide them beneath her purse. Hold on!

Netboy enters. He turns at once: "Postpone her to four o'clock and check again. If she's not sufficiently composed, cancel for today."

"You can't cancel!" She cries it out deperately. She does not want to wait. To think. *You don't have to kill.*

"Just so much can be cleared up in a few minutes' consultation, Miss" — he glances at the card — "White. It might be better for you to consult a private therapist." He turns back to Netboy. "Stay on this. Check it out. Cancel her three o'clock. Or" — he hesitates, flushes darkly — "if you're busy" — his frown engraves itself a little deeper — "pass the details on to one of the others."

As Edgar walks down the corridor he feels like an innocent man reprieved from judgment. The relief lasts one second — then the questions begin.

Where has the burden shifted now? To the doctor who will abort in second trimester if she only postpones? To the adoption agency if she goes full term and gives the baby up? To the child itself if the woman decides — bravely, foolishly — to keep it?

He is not a literary man but he remembers, from high school reading, the queer little daughter of the Scarlet Letter woman. Little Pearl. Burdens, like matter, are never lost, only shifted elsewhere.

He thinks of Ellen. Of Amy. He has wounded the first without winning the second. Wounded the first in hoping for the second, yet the second — he draws on some hunting idea from the old days when he was always outdoors, either with a ball on the field or a gun in the woods; when did he ever stand still and simply endure, as now? — the second has bounded away into the forest. He cannot even tell if the second is wounded also, there is so much blood from the first. And all of this without firing a shot! What had he said? Nothing! What has he done? Nothing. Yet Ellen knew, and therefore this blood was shed.

He is full of protective love for these wounded gazellelike creatures with which he has filled his mind's eye. Against such a background he sees that Genevieve X is not what he should have feared. Not that ordinary frightened woman. Then what? Some deeper disaster, like the promise of death in every birth.

◆§ §◆

"That was horrible!" The imposing, crumpled-looking man is gone and Alexandra White cries out shakily, "Why did he do that?" Then, more assertively, "I have a right to have it. The law says so!"

"We have to be sure," Netboy says, "for *your* sake." Again the pride thrusts itself.

"Listen to me," Alexandra says. "I worked like hell to get where I am. My job, my clothes, my lover, my life! There's no way I'm going to blow it now. You think I'm going to pass up my turn because some doctor with no guts gets scared if he thinks somebody else is scared? That's his problem. Don't worry about what's for my sake. I'll take care of that!"

She silently thanks Brody for this tone. She has heard him — often — blow up like that and face down whoever opposes him. It's a world where people step on the meek, he tells her over and over. "You *take* what's yours by right!"

"It's three o'clock now," Netboy answers quietly. "You have an appointment at four. If you still want to go in then, you can."

"I want to go in," she repeats.

"I'll be back later," Netboy says. "You can tell me then."

After the door is closed, Alexandra picks up a magazine and stares into it blindly, at the perfectly dressed mannikins — alone or with men, but never with a child. Her breath comes short. Icy cold, she feels, close to fainting. A couple wants her child. She feels it already in her arms, sees herself put it away from her breast, giving it into darkness. Darkness. Coldness. Loneliness. She senses that the door is opening, even before she sees it is. She shudders, expecting the return of her first visitor, already smelling the strong scent.

But it is Netboy who has come back, her eyes stretched wide open.

"I want you to know — because I asked you all those questions — I feel you have a right to information about me too. Maybe it will help you resolve your own feelings. I am doing the same myself. This afternoon. At the same hour you are rescheduled for, if you decide to keep it. I thought you should know that about me."

Even more than this: tears stand in Netboy's eyes.

"Are you" — it is involuntary — "all right?" Alexandra asks.

"Yes! I feel sad but I am all right. I know I am all right."

Alexandra extends her hand. Netboy grasps it. "Still your decision," she says as firmly as before, and leaves the room.

Alexandra White looks at her watch. It is three-ten. She wonders if she can have dozed off at three o'clock and dreamed it all.

ᘓᏄ Ꮔᘔ

Edgar means to take care of Genevieve X himself — though he has learned her name, she is still that to him — but at the last minute, falters. He frantically tries to gauge which is the better safeguard: his knowledge or another's innocence?

In the end, he chooses Gen-Lee for the job. But at three-forty-five Gen-Lee comes to him. "I think I got flu, Bunky. Hundred and three temperature, I just checked. Hands are shaking."

Edgar stares.

"I suppose I better go home?" Gen-Lee inquires patiently, despite his hundred and three.

Struggling to move as if through nightmare, Edgar now debates whether he or Paul ought to replace. He finds Paul, sees his oddly grim expression, thinks of telling him who this woman is, then abruptly changes his mind.

Edgar's terror is upon him again. The moment of clear calm — as when he was a boy on a hot field, aiming his pitch — has vanished as if never existing. He grasps Paul's arm. "This afternoon, Amy . . ." His beautiful baritone cracks like a dropped dish. "And Genevieve X," he means to add, but he will be taken for a lunatic. "I want *you* to do Amy instead of Charlie," he impulsively says.

Edgar sees a vein bulge in Paul's temple, under the dark hair tugged aside. Paul stares back, dumb as a new orderly with no English. Edgar feels the thickening of his own blood pounding in his head. Enraged at refusal, he glares. "I thought you would see it!"

Paul can't — won't — say what he sees.

"A man to abort his own child!" Edgar whispers fiercely. "Where is this thing taking us? Poor Mimi!"

Edgar remembers then: it was Paul who he had once thought would be his rival for Amy, not Charlie. That day seems long past, dim, nearly forgotten now.

Edgar's fingers search his creased forehead for the exact spot of pain. A blinding chop comes down like a cleaver between his eyes; he can feel them crossing. Nauseated by headache, he says, "Never mind. Leave Charlie alone. You replace Gen-Lee!"

◆§ §◆

Planting himself in the exact center of the corridor between two doors, fastening his look on the louver slats outside each door, Edgar feels he would give anything to telephone Ellen at her hospital now. To say "It's happening — the worst! Genevieve X in one room. Charlie aborting Amy in another!"

But Ellen hardly speaks to him these days. The very words with which he might protest his innocence would betray all that he had hoped might happen. So he stands alone in the corridor and pictures the scene behind the door where Paul operates.

Tears are streaming down her cheeks. "I want to get off," she will whisper.

"You want to get off ?" Paul will distractedly say, too aware of what is going on next door. Next door are Amy and Charlie! Paul will learn another lesson from his hero. He will think that women love ice in a man.

"You want to get off ?" Paul will attempt playful repetition. Paul will joke. "You mean you want to not pay any price for anything?"

"I want to get off! Off!" She is shuddering. Can't Paul tell her thighs are trembling by the way the sheet keeps rippling like a sail in a breeze? Her arms and ankles are already strapped down. No one else is present but Lowry, the anesthetist. True to his speciality, he sees and hears nothing but what his machines monitor.

"This is easy and painless." Paul's grin is riveted to his cheeks. "The new way is, everybody gets off."

An aide comes in. It's only Warner. If it had been Amy or Mary or Hannah, they would have sized up the situation in a minute. But Amy is strapped down in the next room. Hannah and Mary are doing double duty elsewhere.

Paul nods to Lowry, who instantly eases the clamp on the tube.

The woman turns her face to Warner. A track of tears drives past her temples and into her hair. A mumble escapes her lips.

"Patient consultation?" Warner looks puzzled.

A faint gurgle-groan comes from the patient's open lips. She is under.

Paul lifts an instrument from the ringing tray. "The procedure has begun," he says.

Next door, Paul is thinking, *next door!* The soft, hidden tissue has no protection against sharp scrapers or the suck of the machine. Next door Amy, whom he could have had for himself but wooed for a friend, is now, by that friend, being scooped out like a sleeve of coal.

Edgar clutches his chest and fears he will fall. Moments pass. He is paralyzed; he whispers, unheard, "Stop! Stop!" Light blasts into his eyes from the opened procedure room. The patient is slumped over as she is wheeled out in the wheelchair, groggy but awake.

When Paul emerges, Edgar emotionally claps him on the shoulder. Paul looks startled. To cover himself, Edgar says, "I heard there was some complication?"

"No," Paul says. "All routine."

Even while relief is pouring, as if his full heart had tipped like a pitcher, Edgar thinks, Of course — she wasn't Genevieve X! He resumes his watch. The second door does not open.

When Mary passes he calls out, "For God's sake, where's Amy?"

"Amy's here." The answer comes from behind his shoulder. Edgar turns, dumfounded, to see Amy in her golden uniform approaching, with her wide-stretched eyes, her clutched braid. She has never entered procedure at all!

"You see — how it all works out?" Amy's face shows signs of tears, but her eyes shine at him, and she is smiling. "I changed my mind. I made my free choice. You should be proud. You've given Mimi this wonderful gift!"

She quickly and with the same trembling smile speaks to the figure close behind her. "Don't worry about me, Charlie!"

But whether concern for Amy is one of the feelings at that moment reflected in Charlie's small smile would have been hard for Edgar to say. Careful watcher of his staff's emotions, he for once feels he does not want to know more. He feels, in fact, strangely preoccupied. He is giddily aware that the change he had prayed for is happening. The panic of events, it may be, like the blow on the head that cures blindness, has somehow made a stereopticon of his inner vision. Amy and Mimi, arms outstretched, slide toward one another from opposite ends of the void until they again merge and form one figure, embraced in his battered heart.

◆§ §◆

At the end of the day they briefly meet in the coatroom — Edgar and Charlie and Paul. Edgar forbears to mention the eight-week fetus growing in Amy's uterus, at a stage somewhere between fish and pig, but so great is his agitation that he is actually unsure of whether anyone else mentions it.

Shortly before, Amy and Hannah, departing together, were close in conversation. With a little effort, Edgar might have overheard. But he has a lopsided headache that crashes in and ebbs out like an ocean. With whom can he talk all this over? He nearly staggers with longing for his lost companion.

◆§ §◆

The slamming of the door announces that Nana is home from her evening meeting. Nana's bulk moves down the hall. Amy prepares a smile for her grandmother. She sees herself smiling and smiling. At Bunky, at Charlie. Why has she chosen for herself the role of the child-woman with the cheerful, reassuring smile? She has never been able to ask that question of unsmiling Nana. Now that she is going to be a mother, she must ask it of herself. Why am I always saying, I am fine, don't worry about me? See? I am better!

Are there many people like me, she asks the new self who is going-to-be-a-mother, who feel guilty if they are happy? Who can only be happy with someone the world says is no good for them — that's their only chance for happiness? "My parents were killed when I was very young, so they had no chance to be a bad influence." That's what I said to Bunky the day he hired me. And smiled. That's what I always said. Cheerfully. Why? I never mourned my parents that I can remember. That much is true. Never thought of their pain — the car, the terror, the crash, the moment, the impact. Did they cry out, "Dear God, the children?" Such deep pain that I never felt it. The knife too sharp. But Matt's pain, Nana's pain, Charlie's pain. Cheerful girl. Make them happy, make all well. The parents are two tiny creatures held in the palm of the hand and guarded from all harm. Tiny as embryos, tiny as my baby. I am going, going to be a — "

Nana knocks at Amy's door. Slowly, the fish-pig fetus is raised from the bed, where Amy has lowered herself to rest and think. She opens the door. She tries to subdue her voice, but happiness is pounding in her throat.

"I have something to tell you, Nana."

Her grandmother's bosom lifts, heaves; it seems to want to leap from her body. "About your brother, Amy dear?"

"It's about me, Nana. I'm afraid you'll be disappointed in me. It's not that Margaret Sanger failed me. I failed her. But I didn't believe it was possible that it could happen. Nana, I'm pregnant. I'll probably never marry the father. But I love the baby already and I want to keep it. Forgive me, Nana, darling. I won't stay here. I know how it would upset — "

"Do you think" — her grandmother's deep voice cuts through — "because my life has been logarithm tables and graphs" — with some effort she raises her heavy body from the chair into which she had allowed herself to sink — "that I don't want what everyone wants?"

The old woman propels herself at Amy with a force that makes them totter, and they cling with arms around one another for balance. Never before has Amy seen Nana weep. Loss has always brought stiff dry-eyed resolve — to *do* for the survivors. Now Nana shakes down tears like a thawing mountain.

"A *wanted* child!" Nana's voice is heavy and rough with sobs. "That's all Margaret ever cared about. Oh, to be understood!"

"I want it, Nana."

"And I want it, darling. You must stay here — and let me

help you. My poor child, what have I ever been able to do for you?"

Amy, in her happiness, is calm. A mother who gives herself fully to her child, Amy is thinking, is giving only what is needed. Why did that never occur to me before? Because poor Nana tried to keep it from me. This happiness I long to bestow, this giving and loving and doing are no more than what a mother does. I can be happy with no guilt when I love my own baby.

After a little, Amy laughs, because Nana is already planning out loud for the child a comfortable, brown nursery, free of culture-spoiled associations.

"But darling, brown can be charming," Nana protests seriously. "Teddy bears are brown."

◆§ §◆

"You are pretty." She stands alone and naked now before her mirror. Nothing shows yet. "You're pretty." She says it again, aloud.

She wonders for a moment how it would feel to be in love with a handsome young man with a whole life ahead. She sees a faint face in the mirror — as if summoned on Halloween by apple peel flung over the shoulder. It is certainly not, as Hannah suggests, Paul! No, someone she has never seen. A handsome, gentle look, a strong, tender face. No sadness in its gentleness. Happy loving eyes gaze back for a second, then the mirror goes blank.

5

SELIG'S clumsy duffel coat is unevenly fastened in its coarse toggle closings. She hurries by subway to Sylvia's smart little apartment on Charles (she calls it Charlie's) Street. Packing boxes stand about in the living room, unfilled. A man is having a drink with Sylvia. His hair is gray-flecked, but his face and manner are filled with a kind of stubborn mild optimism or innocence. He leans his cheek on his hand and watches with interest — Hannah glimpses how his eyes are magnified by thick lenses to youthful largeness — as she blurts, "Can you come into the other room, Sylvia? For two minutes, to talk?"

"I am just leaving anyway," the man says, rising with a smile from a denim-covered chair. "Should I open this for Daniel?" he adds to Sylvia.

"This is Simon Pinsker." Sylvia touches his sleeve. "He teaches evening classes at the university. In Business Accounting," she says proudly, then adds in a more intimate tone, "No, Daniel's not coming tonight, Simon."

"I am delighted," he says to Hannah. His speech is slow and deliberate, his handshake more ceremonious than most. There is about him in general, Hannah sees, an unhurried air. He seems to linger with the faint wistfulness — oh, she recognizes that! — of the unattached. "I see you are looking at me with a certain curiosity," he says amiably. "Were you wondering what kind of guy I am? An ordinary one — not a home-wrecker! I happened to be in the right place at the right time, that's all! *I* was a student, *she* was a student. In another class, you see. Her marriage was at the breaking point" — he seems anxious that Hannah should not overestimate his charm — "that's all! As for me — an elderly bachelor, that's my category. Never married. You could look at me and conjecture: How come? I'm no worse-looking than millions." He laughs and comments in an aside, "The Kon-Tiki" — he palpates all around his mouth and chin a small oval-shaped beard — "I added for Sylvia because she thought it would look distinguished." Then he flings up his hand in earnest puzzlement. "Yet — I don't know — I was not easily satisfied. I was never *eager*. Eagerness — do you understand me? — is an important element. Unless there is that *eagerness*, that feeling that . . ."

Sylvia captures his waving hand. "Don't miss your class, Simon."

He smiles at the interruption. "You see now what I mean by *eager!*" Then soberly again to Selig: "And also you see packing cases here. Believe me, I am honored to be partly the reason a woman is torn about whether to return to her sick husband. Personally, I am a believer in loyalty, even though I never married. But in this case my opinion is she should not go back. Who am I to say it? I have — as we say in business — a vested interest here. So" — he responds by a wave of his hand to Sylvia's admonitory headshake — "so I don't say it. Although" — here a charming, joke-sharing smile at Hannah — "you can imagine that I am eager, *eager* to do so!"

"Simon, darling, you'll be *late.*"

He tips his pepper-and-salt beard downward, lays the flesh-colored parting upon Sylvia's fingers, appears to want to linger there, then slowly straightens, bows again to Hannah, and leaves.

"Isn't he amazing?" Sylvia asks. "You can see for yourself what kind of man he is — eager, his own word, eager for love, and he's older than Charlie!"

"In fact I wasn't sure whether I would find you here or in your house in Long Island by now," Hannah answers.

"I guess I'm a little behind schedule." Sylvia brushes at a pleat of her navy skirt. "I haven't exactly rushed back, have I?"

"Are you sorry you said you would?"

"Sometimes. I forget now why I did say it. It was a fit of jealousy, I think, about that girl at the Center. Charlie came here and told me about her. I said to myself, Suppose she gets pregnant? That was the first thing I thought of. Though how can that even matter, working where she does?"

"Did Charlie say Amy was pregnant?"

"He said nothing about that, but what I think is that Charlie didn't want to face his responsibility to her; that's why he told me. He never wanted to face his responsibility to me, either — I made him do that. If I came home it would make everything easier for him. He played on my jealousy. But it was foolish and petty of me to respond that way. In the end I punished myself. I said I'd go home. And the whole thing, I think, was because Charlie must have been afraid this girl would make demands on him. Don't you think that's what it all adds up to?"

"Or because his purpose with Daniel was accomplished."

"What purpose?" Sylvia asks sharply. "What has Daniel to do with this?"

"He didn't want to burden Daniel with pity for him after you left."

"But why would he want to make me jealous — he knows me like a book — so that I'd want to come home? Why, Hannah? What is Charlie planning?"

The question so agitates Hannah that she jumps up from her chair, then sits down again, beating her palms at her cheeks.

"I think you know, Hannah. You know as well as I what the reason must be. That girl must be pregnant. And she must be determined to go through with it. You know Charlie's views on such things! So I'm to be transferred to another square on the checkerboard, because it suits him now. He wants me home so that girl will see it's hopeless — Charlie won't be able to marry her and then of course she won't think of keeping the child."

"Won't she?" Hannah asks. "Does that make you want to stay or go?"

"I don't know what to tell Charlie. I know I'm sick of being manipulated."

She has brought Selig a glass of wine, which remains untouched. She refills her own glass and lights a cigarette. Before putting out the match, she shifts its flame behind her glass and gazes with melancholy pleasure at the red illumination in the wine.

"Tell me about that girl at the Center." She nervously smokes, though without inhaling. "Would she be devoted to Charlie?"

"With all her heart."

"Oh!" Sylvia puffs. Then: "Why did you come so urgently? Was that the reason? To tell me that? That she will be good to Charlie? You don't know how welcome that news sounds. I rejoice over that news. Thank God! Then he won't be lonely. He'll have someone, and I — "

"Would you do that?"

"Do what? Leave him *finally?* Yes, if I thought he'd be taken care of. I do feel responsible. But does that mean my whole life has to be his?"

Selig is silent.

Sylvia moves to the window. Under it is a handsome cabinet for records and hi-fi components. She moves her fingers across the record album spines, bends as if to choose one, straightens, and lets her arms fall to her sides. Without turning around she speaks in a low voice.

"Charlie was right. My whole life was an immolation. If I go back I'll spend the next years — five, ten — nursing a dying man. After that I'll be old." Sylvia stops — her face reflects her horror of that — then bursts out again: "She must be one of those women — if not Charlie, she'd find someone else to sacrifice herself for, wouldn't she? Otherwise why? It's a pattern, I tell you, with certain women. I ought to know! There probably can't *be* anybody else for her!"

Selig continues to watch her back, which lowers itself suddenly as Sylvia begins to cry.

"Oh!" After a bit this comes muffled. "You came to tell me I ought to return! Didn't you? But why? Who says a man has to die in his mother's arms? I won't have the chance to do that, will I?"

"No, no," Hannah says hastily. "How could I advise you? I came to ask something else."

Sylvia turns slowly. "But you must despise me because you see I don't really want to go back. I'm only torn because I can't bear the idea of someone else having Charlie — for whatever time is left. You see me here writhing like a worm. I feel like a worm. For years Charlie tormented me because I couldn't make up my mind to leave him. Let me honestly admit it about myself now, when it might at last help me. Hannah, I can't! I can't make up my mind to go back."

"You misunderstand me. You don't know why I am here. You are right, Sylvia — Amy is pregnant. Charlie wants her to give it up. I only want to ask you. What do you think Charlie will do if Amy can't be persuaded?"

"Can't be persuaded?" Sylvia laughs bitterly. "When did it ever happen that Charlie couldn't persuade a woman to do something? Don't be foolish," Sylvia says. "Charlie will prevail!"

Sylvia wipes her eyes with a tissue, then flings it onto the table. "How stupid we women are to wear eye makeup," she says, "when we're so often in tears! Oh, it isn't fair! I can't tell you how my life has changed! It isn't just Simon. I'm not the same person. I'm awake now. Maybe I've gone to the other extreme, to just selfishness, I don't know. All I do know is that I was sleeping — or dead — before this. Charlie was right! But I don't want to think he's right about other things!"

"Are you still going to think over your decision?"

"I think everything over, Hannah." Sylvia wipes her eyes more carefully this time, though her tone is still bitter. "Haven't you noticed? I'm a suggestible woman!"

◦§ §◦

From Hannah's departure till Simon's return, Sylvia spends the time, not preparing the term paper that is due, but remembering Charlie's visit days before. Afterward, in her panic, she had telephoned Daniel. He had matured, was a man now. All this pain had been worth something; it had transformed her son.

Daniel understands her best. "You don't *have* to do anything at all until you're sure how you feel, Mom," he had said. "Dad's doing fine. You have every right to change your mind. I've changed mine. I've decided to resume school in New York — Columbia, if they'll still honor their acceptance of me from last year. I'm going to stick around. I'll be on hand."

And so, despite the painful feelings aroused by Charlie and Hannah, the packing boxes may stay unfilled forever . . .

◦§ §◦

Slim, elegant Charlie, by despising himself, has achieved a detachment whose bloom is the style of all styles. He passes Hannah with an aureole of cool removal like a parade saint handed, with faint smile, over the suffering crowd.

She detains him, touches his navy sleeve.

"I have a reputation — in Paul's eyes — for seeing the future."

Charlie smiles. "I don't believe in it."

"The future? Or my seeing it?"

"Let's say — for conversation — the latter."

"I don't believe in it either. But one may know things by knowing the person."

"And you know me?"

"I know myself — we are alike in some ways."

"Through s-s-suffering?" His deliberate smirk takes dominion away from the word.

"It may be. Some suffer and then almost suffer the death of their own souls afterward."

"Are you making predictions about me?"

"In my notebook. Sometimes."

"What do you say?"

She watches him carefully. "Writing is a better expression for me than speech. I can show you — if you like — what I have written down."

Hannah feels dizzy and dazzled; the air glitters where their two gazes meet.

"You want to tell me that you are watching me, Hannah? You want me to think twice about what I do because you are watching — is that it?"

She does not move her gaze.

"Like God? Do you watch like God?"

She had never heard him laugh before. It is like a cough.

"It never occurred to me — God keeping notebooks! Writing down predictions, checking them when they come true, crossing out and revising when they don't. Sending them off to the printer, getting them p-p-published! Bad reviews all the time, but what does He c-c-care? Unlimited f-f-funds, He can back His own p-p-promotion. Circulating them among the angels — all of them r-r-reading away — reading about us and f-f-forgetting about us!"

He gasps for breath and presses a handkerchief to his mouth.

"I will bring water," Hannah says.

He grips her arm to prevent her while the other hand covers his face with the handkerchief. Still gasping, he shakes his head, as if refusing, in one gesture, all water, all watching, all words.

◄§ §►

"You know, don't you," Ellen says to Hannah, "that I know about Edgar and Amy?"

"Sometimes we make the mistake of knowing more than there is to know. Sometimes I wonder if I am making such a mistake."

"I *know* — as clearly as if someone at the Center had sent me a note. I mention her name and his lips go white."

"He is not married to her name. He is married to you."

Ellen's hand rests on the trayed tubes. This Sunday she is on duty here at the lab where Selig has come to find her.

"I modified every aspect of my life to his well-being. Till now."

Hannah shivers at the hospital smell, cold and chemical, with its suggestion that everything human will be suppressed, along with germs, for the sake of a goal. The shuddery hospital feeling springs from perceived coercion — the sting of its smell — as in acid-soaked memories of certain schools. No one would want a permissive hospital, where germs are allowed to express themselves freely, but no one can repress the shudder either.

Hannah had written to Ellen to ask if she could meet her here, the place that seemed most private. Now she feels imprisoned by the smell, and for once speaks without jumping restlessly from her seat.

"Can there be joy in an affair — for revenge?"

"I'm not after joy, Hannah!"

"If you hope for a child, then why not Edgar's? Or is that revenge too?"

"Some expert or other has suggested that Edgar's infertility is psychologically induced; it was either the trauma of seeing his sister, or it's what he sees every day. It's a bit late for me to become pregnant now. But it was theoretically possible and possible also that the child would not be deformed or mongoloid."

"If you became pregnant, that would be a way of letting Edgar know your feelings. Is that what you thought?"

"That part hardly seemed important. But I'm not going to be pregnant. Not by Edgar or Sorenson or anyone."

"And are you angry at Edgar for that too?"

"That would be a waste of energy, wouldn't it?" Ellen returns question for question — amused, detached. But her hands, Hannah sees, are clenched white about the sides of the tray. "The thing with Sorenson has equalized us. I don't suppose Edgar actually slept with Amy, so I suppose I've overequalized us. It's not important. For a while I enjoyed the irony. Suppose I *did* become pregnant, I thought! I knew where to go. I tested my urine and began to think it would be better to make all babies in test tubes, where they could be monitored. I even thought, If Sorenson's made me pregnant, I'll insist that he abort it. That would be a way of making a man share in the trauma! But I said nothing. I only gave him secret gloating glances."

My voice, Ellen is thinking. My voice, my tone, my toes, my fingers — all cold, cold — the very tip — there! She presses the center of her cold palm to the point of her nose — it's freezing cold, a tip of iceberg, and at the root leading to the brain, God knows how many fathoms deep of ice! She feels an ice avalanche of rage falling upon Edgar. He has stolen away his warmth, put a stop to her own grateful crossing of cold with hot. Haughtily she thinks, Peasant! How many times he would have torn his life to pieces with his huge peasant hands, have burned and blistered himself with his own fire, made a cauldron of his blood and brains without her steady snowfalls, her cool and steady weight, flake by flake, of snow. She is buried in it now. Nothing stops it — over the lintel, the sill, the roof — her house, and she in it, are buried in ice.

Still she hears herself, detached and reasoning: "It's strange — the connections between sex and procreation have almost been drowned by modern life. Once in a while, like a deformed child born with the fetal split down its face, something of the past reasserts itself."

Suddenly she is on her feet and crying out, "Marriage is terrible! Character-destroying! It hands you a scapegoat the way wealthy parents once bestowed on a bride or groom the gift of a slave for life. Edgar will blame me for keeping him from Amy. I blame him for keeping me from whatever I might have been if only . . ."

"What might you have been?" Hannah, leaning forward, demands with passionate interest, *"What?"*

"There was no doubt" — float on, iceberg, Ellen thinks, resuming her seat — "those times when it seemed I might be pregnant — that the thought of it intrigued me. Sometimes I wanted it. Sometimes yes, sometimes no. Which is sufficient grounds for action? Neither one. Equivocal, ambiguous — oh, very modern feelings! There was no 'had to' about any of it. Whichever way I decided, I'd wonder how life would go if I had decided otherwise."

Hannah, unanswered on the edge of her chair, watches the pale face compose itself, watches Ellen's swift, fastidious movements among the tubes and charts.

"Charlie would have said I had no right to summon a human being, would already have condemned me to abortion. For all I know the way I felt was how Genevieve X herself felt. Not knowing even at the eleventh hour what one wants to do. Always with that astonished, ironic sense that comes upon some women and never leaves them — 'Who, me, a mother?' When I felt an emotion like physical movement, some inner pull, I tugged it down, weighted it with more irony. I could go away, I thought — a foreign study and work grant — to India. And have the baby there and bring it back. To a family, a healthy Idaho farm family, something like that. I could send money and visit every first Sunday of the month, like some French or Italian servant girl in the old novels, hiding the child from public eyes. Not to pretend at sexual, but at political, purity. I am a charter member of N.O.N.E. — No Offspring Now or Ever — after all! I kept smiling at the self-parody among the test tubes, Hannah, I found enough to amuse myself." Ice, ice, she is thinking. Words like icicles form and break off. The clatter of test tubes is like their glassy sound.

" — Or keep it, bring it home? Explain to Edgar, the master of contraception, how contraception failed, how the baby must really after all be his. I saw us all as if we were daguerreotyped — Edgar, the child, myself — woven into a fabric very different from the loose threads that dangle about our lives now . . ." At those words, at "our lives now," she hears a desolate cry from her frozen heart.

"This is not what I see for you."

"Don't! Don't talk like a soothsayer to me, Hannah. I have no drop of mystical blood in me. Everything that's ever happened in my life — I have *made* it happen!"

"No one can make that statement. But I didn't come to argue, only to tell you — Amy is now pregnant, with Charlie's child. Or do you already know, from Edgar?"

"Edgar and I tell each other nothing now. From everything to nothing, a quantum leap backward."

"God knows what will happen."

"Only God?" Ellen asks it mockingly. "Don't you have some ideas, Hannah?"

"I know what I hope for."

"What do you hope for?"

"Too much to tell."

"What do you hope for us, Hannah?"

"That what will make one happy will also do the next one

good. If — " She stops, her hair-ends tremble, her thin fingers flutter at the sides of her face.

"Don't stop now, Hannah. If what?"

"These are Amy's 'ifs.' If Amy persists in wanting to give birth to her baby. Would you want to adopt it? Would you come forward now and say so to Amy and Charlie?"

"You're mad!" Ellen cries. Yet why, now, does Ellen's frozen heart send to the tip of her frozen nose a sudden, melting thaw, so that she must grope in her stiff pocket for the fine lawn handkerchief with a minute E.B. embroidered into a pale blue corner?

"Otherwise," Hannah is haltingly saying, "it may have to be Paul."

"Paul?" One bizarre statement after another. "How, Paul?" Ellen searches that stricken face. *"Chagrin d'amour,* everywhere one looks." The remote, distanced voice is recovered; the infusion of Edgar's heat might never have been. He is like a transplant her spirit has rejected. "A strange notion, isn't it, Hannah? Because a man and woman loved each other once, that they should raise children!"

"But *would* you?"

Ellen bites with perfect white teeth at a corner of her lower lip. That fusion of their two selves, *that* had been their child, as close-woven as the cells of any blastocyst. Now — she shifts the x-ray films — bones stare back, a skeleton world that has rid itself of flesh. "The fact is — I have sometimes thought of adopting. But why must I wait for Amy? And how do we know what Amy would want? Why get entangled in all that emotion when I can work out some painless, anonymous arrangement? Why should I do things the way you see them, Hannah? Why must I take on Amy's 'ifs'?" Proudly, bitterly, she draws tighter her garment of coldness.

"But why *not?*"

Hannah burns with her own fire — her hair, her look. Ellen reflects again. "It's strange" — she says it wonderingly and more softly — "I almost have the feeling it might be Edgar's. I almost feel I could say yes. But that's only one possibility."

Hannah palpates the air — grasps, fastens on, Ellen's hand, the other hand too: "Possibilities also can save!"

◆§ ट◆

Joy is now like a recurrent disease. It has patterned itself into her body like malaria or bronchitis and without warning flares up again among the old traces.

Sitting on the edge of her subway seat, Hannah says aloud, "All may be well. All may be well." A smile flits across her face. The apprehensive elderly couple, sitting opposite her in the corner, coming up from Brooklyn to an afternoon concert at Lincoln Center, nudge one another while the wife whispers, "Such a beautiful girl, what a shame!" And the husband replies, "Don't you notice how many people talk to themselves in Manhattan?"

Hannah emerges from the station to wander in the city with the nervous energy of the old days, visiting the haunts of the old, lonely times. In the evening she is going to Paul's apartment.

As she leaves the Museum of Modern Art she catches sight of the tall, handsome woman, just entering, who threw such a scare into Bunky that day at the Center. It is the woman who was supposed to have been Genevieve X, before it became clear that no one can fill that part now but Amy. We can all prevent it, Hannah thinks, as Bunky and the others prevented it for that woman!

◆§ ट◆

All morning she had told herself not to go. Sundays are always hard. Unless Brody's wife is visiting her family, Alexandra never sees him then. Sometimes weeks go by and Brody can't break away to see her. It's been that way this time.

She remembered having been taken with her class as a child

to the Museum of Modern Art — a ghetto kid exposed to the finer things. Fascinated, she had stood before the canvas that had seemed to her, then, gigantic. This morning as the taxi drew closer to Fifty-third Street, she had told herself how stupid she was being. Yet it summoned her — the canvas she hadn't thought about in years.

She leaned back, closed her eyes, breathed in the chemical smell of vinyl. Behind her eyelids always a scene of carnage now. She snapped upright. It's nothing! she told herself fiercely.

She asks herself now, at the museum, what it could mean to anyone — demographers, perhaps? charters of populations? revelers in distributions of numbers? — that fetuses are killed.

The horror of the operation itself — dragging the tiny bodies out, broken-boned, chopped to pieces — that itself is nothing. In earlier centuries, where cultures were humane, fetuses were smashed in the womb to save mothers' lives. There had been instruments to crush and drain the skull . . .

No, the horror is nothing. Has to be done. All operations are horrors. And if doctors, nurses, aides, orderlies, are known to be sickened by the sight of so many little chopped-up bodies sucked or scraped from wombs like so many raw eggs by some egg-sucking monster — what difference can that make? It has to be done. A witness at an operation on the brain or the bowel might feel as sickened. A spectator at a splendidly performed leg amputation of a six-year-old child might experience as much pity and rage and horror and — But why go on, she thinks. Isn't it plain? It has to be done! She runs her palms over her hair, whose neat round form rises again from the flattening. Her eyelids squeeze down in anguish. Her thin body is slightly curved forward — she is losing weight — and she clasps her belly like a woman with menstrual cramps. Having said to herself, "It has to be done" and "What could it mean to anyone but population-watchers?" she is overcome by a sick wave of knowing what it does mean.

The high heels of her blue calf pumps click on the marble of the museum floor. She must ask the guard to tell her what level. "The Tchelitchew. *Hide and Seek.*" A small crowd is gathered before the canvas, just as she remembers there was when she had come to look as a child. What is the fascination? It is not so overwhelming in size, not so gigantic, as she remembered it. But large, very large. A large canvas with the dark form of a great old tree rising in the center and spreading its huge limbs into every corner of the painting. All around the tree the canvas is drenched with varying shades of green, with light-filtered, unfathomable depths of leaf, bud, and fine-twigged branches. Here and there the small figure of a boy or girl, vastly dwarfed by the tree, is painted nearly flat against the trunk. Only after seconds can one discern what moves in the leaves and branches. Round fetus heads, traceries of vein and blood visible, burst through everywhere like transparent chrysanthemums. Through the branches, smaller fetus skulls cascade like thistle heads streaming on a breeze, borne away like milkweed seeds to implant themselves — where?

The tree is alive with the unborn, even the unconceived. They are souls already in being! The thought stabs into her. It is not only to children that the folk tales ring true: "You waited up among the stars (in the great tree?) till mother and father were ready to receive you." Or, more urgently, "You called out, you wanted to come to earth. Mother and father came together to let you be born."

The horror of it, when the fetus is scraped out and thrown away, is like the horror felt by the visitor to the House of Usher when the still-living sister, nailed into a coffin, bursts out with a deathly blood-soaked screech!

"It can't be helped!" she groans aloud, so that people in the little knot of viewers turn, apprehensive, to look. She bites down on her lips and goes on, silently, It means less, so much less, that a fetus with no consciousness except maybe for that pure greenness splashed with yellow and red, that light-and-shadow-penetrated interplay, that mingled-with-tree-branch sense of life and mystery — which might be the same sense that a flower or a blade of grass has of its being — is killed, than that wholly developed human beings with all their consciousness and with the message "I am dying" formed clearly and in words — that they should die, as they do, most horribly and every day.

Don't have to, Alexandra thinks, talk about *war* or *crime in the streets!* Just one worn-out black woman who had too many children, too little money, and no man to care for her, and got sick and old before her time . . .

"Help that woman!" someone cries.

She is doubled over — feels a grabbing at her heart and her entrails at the same moment. She staggers. With a supreme effort, she straightens. "Thank you. I am fine."

Her heels click across the marble. She is leaving.

6

PAUL sometimes accompanies Charlie to his office on Saturday mornings. Charlie tosses a white jacket at Paul, brings him along into the examining room, and casually introduces him: "My assistant." Paul's heart, at the thought of it, leaps up like a dog after a ball; he feels that a grin of mongrel-longing must be fixed to his face. The already nude and sheeted women never think of questioning.

Or sometimes, as now, Paul merely fits his narrow bottom into the broad, black-cushioned oak chair next to Riva's desk and opens his ears. Riva, with her strong, big body and slightly popping eyes, gives the impression of being solidly filled with opinions. Riva's sardonic comments on life have been oddly comforting to Paul. Even though she had once said in her positive way, "Charlie won't get really involved with Amy."

"How would you know that?" Paul had asked curiously.

Riva gave him a meaningful look. "I don't say there ever was — but don't you think, if Charlie was susceptible to a woman now in that way — that there would be, close as we are here every day, something between *us?*"

Riva had lost some ground with Paul over that. He was astonished to find that even she — sardonic, disillusioned Riva

— could be further proof of Charlie's effect on women.

He is startled now to hear her say, "Your friend Hannah told me that Amy is pregnant and wants to hang on to it."

"Hannah? My God, she gets around! I had no idea you knew her."

"She wrote me a note and we had lunch. Nice girl, but a picky eater. She asked me what I thought Charlie would do. I told her I'd bet her any amount Charlie will see that Amy changes her — "

The possibility of Riva's further expert opinion on the event is cut off by a sound of weeping from Charlie's consulting room.

With instant presence of mind, Riva swiftly slides shut the front glass window between her desk and the waiting room to block off the sound. At the same moment she props wider the back window between her office and the corridor to the examining room.

"I don't think the soul comes in yet, do you?" A woman is sobbing the words. "Not till after it lives in the world?"

"S-s-soul!" Charlie spits it out with contempt. "I don't begin to think soul for a long t-t-time!"

"When do you?"

"When it s-s-smiles at its m-m-mother."

"I can't bear this anymore!"

"You bore it s-s-six months. Where were your b-b-brains?"

"I thought — that man said — there would be people — lovely fine people — waiting for a child. They would give it the best care, he said. I know they must have paid him to say those things, but for me it meant not killing. I thought that would be better. Now I can't bear the idea. Now it seems more a killing of my own child if I — have it and give it away at the end. If — if — it doesn't come into the world now — maybe there's a chance — it will come to me again . . ."

"Don't talk nonsense," Charlie says sharply.

"But how do we know — ?" the woman pleads.

"All right, talk nonsense if you must. So long as you *do* the right thing!"

Charlie comes out grim-faced to tell Riva to book the woman into the hospital right away. To Paul he says, "Here's your chance to w-w-watch third trimester. It s-s-stinks, but it works!"

⋖§ ও⋗

The immensely long needle sinks through the swollen ball of the belly. Amniotic fluid, a substance so nourishingly perfect that if by chance the umbilical cord should be blocked the fetus might survive on absorption of the fluid alone, is extracted. In its place, Charlie injects the saline solution.

They had found the woman already booked into one of the labor rooms by the time they arrived at the hospital.

"I won't leave you to the floor nurse," Charlie tells her. "After work tomorrow I'll be back to stay with you."

Feeling he needs the experience, Paul goes with Charlie to the hospital next day and settles himself into a corner, keeping frightened watch. "I'll stay too."

Once or twice the woman screams out before anything begins to happen. "I feel it drinking in the poison!" She holds her belly in her arms.

But during the contractions, the actual labor, when the uterus clenches itself roughly and repeatedly, and the sweat beads on her brow and soaks the gown above her breasts, she bites her lips and utters no sound.

It is a well-formed big boy, its body blue and stiff, genitals swollen erect. Its furrowed brow gives an impression of elderly sorrow, as if life span had been telescoped at the moment of death.

To keep himself from going sick, Paul forces professional words through his sour throat. "Very effective method."

But Charlie is too busy to respond. He works out the afterbirth and sews the cut. Then he thrusts the small body into a green garbage sack and takes it out of the room to the disposal bins in a closet at the end of the hall.

Paul bends over the sweated, exhausted woman. "It's okay. You're fine now. You did the right thing."

She slides her eyes over his face. Very softly she whispers, "Why don't you all cut your balls off — bastards!"

He rears back from that murderous hiss. When Charlie returns, Paul watches for a new attack from the woman, but none comes.

Charlie says only, "This is a sedative." He plunges a needle into the woman's arm.

Humbly she asks, "Will I have another chance?"

"Ch-ch-chance after ch-ch-chance!" His teeth chop at the word, as if to say "Better without."

But when a woman decides to be grateful, Paul notices, there is no stopping her. "Thank you," she whispers. "You're very kind, for a doctor."

Charlie shakes his head. "No kinder than the rest. I respect you for not passing on the misery."

She closes her eyes. Tears slide down her cheeks. "If I didn't pass it on, it must all be in me."

He lays his hand on her forehead. "It will go away."

Not through all that night or early morning when they leave the hospital does Charlie say anything that prepares Paul for what happens when they get to the Center.

Charlie enters the lounge and, without breaking the measure of his elegant, dancerlike walk, approaches the sofa where Matt sits with Amy and Mary. He grabs Matt's uniform in both his slender hands and with all his might hauls Matt to his feet. "Bastard!"

Matt's eyes shift from side to side. With his white jacket lifted up around his ears, Matt tries a smile.

"Charlie!" Amy puts out her arms toward Matt.

"Mon! — get off me — you cra*zee?*" Matt's impersonation croaks out.

"Charlie, Charlie, please stop this." Amy turns desperately to Paul. "Please stop him."

Flabbergasted, Paul turns to Charlie, but he has already released Matt.

"Pick up your stuff and get out. You can't work with these people." Charlie's voice is even, without stammers.

"But what reason . . . ?" Amy's gray eyes are shocked.

Charlie's stutter erupts. "P-p-persuading women to go ahead and give b-b-b-birth! S-s-s-selling b-b-babies!"

"He's crazy! He's lying!" Matt has pulled himself up out of his fright and out of his borrowed speech. "You better ask yourself, Charlie," he sneers, "about your own death trip. You dig out life and junk it."

"Matt!" Amy now rushes to Charlie's side.

"I have asked myself about it," Charlie replies.

"I guess you don't understand yet that you want the whole world to drop dead like you. The rest of us still put up a little fight because we have warm blood in us!"

"Stop it, Matt!" Amy swings her head from side to side, her flushed face turns to each of them again and again, her heavy braid flails against her shoulders and back like a flagellant's scourge.

But Charlie is calmly replying. "I've given it thought. I'd like to know that about anybody. If a person suffers too much, can he still be a good person? I don't think so about those unwanted fetuses. If they're not loved, they can't come to any good or do good. All the same I hope for myself that though I s-s-s-s — had a hard time — my motives are good. I'm not just a death-dispenser! I think that l-l-l-life at its s-s-s-strongest is what we're p-p-p-passing on here!"

A long statement is a series of compromises for Charlie. He has to keep settling for words that are not what he wants in the first place. Matt comes back with strength.

"You don't pass on a thing! You rake in dough because this business is legal now. If a family wants a baby badly enough to pay for it and somebody else supplies it, what the hell? Make that legal too. Don't I perform a service that way? I save a little baby's life!"

Silence after that. Stares from every part of the lounge. Amy's braid has come loose. She weeps into her spread-out hair.

"The antiabortion madmen," Charlie says, "found another madman they could reach." His glance finds Amy. "You are a pair."

"I didn't know what was going on, I swear it, Charlie!" Amy cries.

"But you know what *you're* doing, don't you?" Charlie says bitterly.

Amy manifests for the first time the protective hand-to-belly movement of the pregnant woman.

"So what if they did reach me?" Matt says. "What if they're right? People are supposed to pass on to the next generation and the next and the next one, for whatever reason, whatever is supposed to be there! And here in this place we end it. We put out the torch. And what if there was some plan to it all? And what if we ruined it?"

"If there were a plan," Charlie says dryly, "it would have figured on the suction aspirator. Your plan figures on money."

"Charlie the Puritan! Charles the Pure! How is it my fault? When there are people who want a baby so badly they'll pay almost any price . . . !"

"Pick up your stuff. Get out! Don't dare come back. What we owe we'll mail you." Charlie's stutter returns to chop at his final words like emblems of damage done: "We'll p-p-pay for m-m-misery i-i-inflicted!"

Matt makes a grimace of small-boy revenge that twists his features up as if into a sponge to sop the tears of fury that stream down his face. "Pay? I'll tell you who wants to pay! Like to know? Like to know who?"

As if in answer to Matt's question, the loudspeaker blares:

"Dr. Bianky! Dr. Bianky!" The urgent cry overlays to perfection the name that Matt pulsatingly repeats.

                ❧ ❧

In the evening at the Pigeon Roost, Edgar says humbly to Ellen, "All my fears about Genevieve X were unfounded. You were patient and you knew, all that time — Darling, I want to tell you that I know. I understand."

"Will you have the fish tonight?" Ellen asks.

"It doesn't matter. I want us to *talk* — "

"I won't have fish. I'll have veal. By 'us' you mean me, I suppose. But I'm tired this evening. I'd like to keep the conversation light, if you don't mind. A boiled egg. Conversation as invalid food; you ought to know the feeling."

"What do you want me to admit?"

"Nothing! Please, I only want a conversational boiled egg."

"I've hurt you, my darling. I'm so sorry. It wasn't anything, really — wasn't so much — a flurry — call it my midlife crisis — a bit of nostalgia — a longing for my youth, my childhood, my sister. Is that so terrible? I saw my dead sister in — "

He stops himself, and begins again. "I see how it was. Your own intuition sent you a note about Amy. And you who never wanted a child — never needed one — your profession absorbed you, and rightly so — you thought that now you wanted one for that old, old reason. You thought" — he has now come to the most painful and dangerous part — "it would secure our marriage, but you should have known that what we have is far more — "

He stops again because Ellen is leaning forward and the look on her face is a look of such blood-filled rage that he can't recall ever having seen it before on the face of anyone, unless maybe it was his father that time that Mimi —

Ellen is perfectly silent. Yet a curious thing happens to Edgar. He has the impression that she is screaming.

Though their waiter, the one who knows so well their preferences in food, their wish for tranquillity during dinner, is hov-
ering near enough to observe it all, Ellen, or someone in
Ellen's impeccable clothing, looks out at him with his father's
rage-filled eyes and — he has the impression — coarsely
screams, loud enough for all the waiters, even those in the
farthest corners of the elegant room, to hear: "Do you think
I give a *shit?*"

He shuts his eyes and sees — unbelievably — an image of
Hannah. She is writing. For a moment, while his eyes are shut,
he prays that the chaos that is overtaking him does not really
belong to his life but only to Hannah's invention.

Why in God's name couldn't she have invented better for
me?

◄§ §►

"So now I must try again. All possibilities have faded. Ellen has
had her revenge and has no more need of a child — Amy's or
anyone else's. Sylvia remains with her packing crates and
Simon's love. Amy still has hope. There is only Paul. He must
act! Or else what is the meaning of the knowledge I have been
given? This time there is no mistake, no misread message.
There is only what everyone who looks can see. Thank God I
have been able to look."

Tears burn her eyes at the thought of what she must re-
nounce. Paul . . . But astonishment for the moment dulls the
pain. That she should praise God's mercy toward herself! She
remembers the prayer of thanksgiving — for having been allowed to live to behold a new thing. But she does not utter it.
Dear God, this new thing is too hard to bear!

She writes, then sleeps at the table. The phone rings once
and wakes her. She senses it is Paul and doesn't answer. The
ringing croons to her. "Come." "Dear." "Help." "Love."
Ring. Ring. Ring.

She lifts the receiver and softly says, "Yes?"

"Hannah, I must have wakened you. I only wanted to say good night." She is silent. "Hannah? Hannah?"

"No." She reproduces Sorita's shy, whispery syllables. "No Hannah. Hannah ees no here."

"Now," Hannah writes, "how do I dare visit Amy and Paul again with the same proposal? I will be accused of crying wolf too many times. And how can I trust my own idea on this? Haven't I led myself astray more than once, betrayed myself with pride? Who will believe me now? How can I believe myself?"

◄§ ৡ►

"Do you know what a Levirate marriage is?" Hannah asks Charlie.

"I have a vague recollection. Something Biblical, Hannah, isn't it? Never far from your mind. A man marries a dead brother's wife in order to raise up seed to his name, isn't that it? Always the preoccupation with seed!"

She waits. Charlie's eyebrow has lifted, but he is otherwise impassive.

"In the same way," she begins carefully, "only somewhat altered, a friend could marry the wife of a brother who has already planted his seed but who fears he will not live to raise his child."

Charlie says nothing, only sucks in that deep, whistling breath as if he is drawing on a forbidden cigarette. He suddenly looks away.

"Such a brother who had knowledge of this would feel reassured about the safety of his child, wouldn't he? He wouldn't have to do — anything — drastic — to prevent its birth. Isn't that true, Charlie?"

Charlie has recovered his old, distant manner, his fixed half-smile. "Who am I, Hannah, to argue with the wisdom of the Bible? Unfortunately, society doesn't provide" — he calls it out lightly, striding off in his slender immaculate white coat — "such reassurances."

Hannah stands looking after him, absorbed in thought. When he is long out of earshot, she is still formulating her reply.

◆§ ξ◆

"You simply want, Hannah, to be a martyr," Amy accuses her. "It's tiresome!" They are speaking in passionate whispers late at night in Amy's dark room with its kitten- and puppy-tinged overlay of brightness.

"Never! Far from that! I want happiness! I think about the women with whom I grew up. Never did I envy their lives. But now I think — the certainty, the loving, the simple, orderly family lives. I cannot be what I am not, and I cannot deny what I fear. I told Sorita, 'Men can't rape babies away from women.' What made me say it? When I know that in this open world *everything* is possible! Would you want me to suppress that knowledge?"

"Of course I would!" Amy replies fiercely. "Since it has nothing to do with me and certainly not with Charlie! And why must you drag poor Paul into it? If you want to be a saint go and work with the poor in India. My baby and I don't need your protection. It's all arranged. We're going to be fine!"

"Whose sin now is the sin of pride?" Hannah cries. But then they must both hush and pretend all is well, for Nana's heavy steps and heavy voice can be heard from the hall.

"What is it, Amy? Is anything wrong?"

◆§ ξ◆

A ring at Paul's door. It is late, after midnight. Selig enters in her blue duffel.

"Sweetheart!"

She steps back from his help. Retains her coat. Sits on the edge of a chair.

"I came," she says, "to tell you you must offer marriage to Amy."

"Oh, no" — he groans — "not again!"

"This is different. This is worse."

"Hannah, you can't cry wolf again."

"I'm not. This time believe me. I won't say it again. It's different."

"Different and how! Amy's going to hang on to that baby. Maybe I shouldn't have meddled. I did her a bad turn, putting her in with Charlie, a desperate character. I admitted to you already that I was jealous — once — for about five minutes, okay? I wanted Amy for myself. Kid stuff! And over fast, thank God! She's not my type! I don't *want* a cheerful baby-faced girlfriend. I want you, Hannah! You know my worst and my best. Even if you do think every goddamned thing that happens is a special thunderbolt meant for you!"

"You are right about me. I am already punished for referring everything to myself. But this is not about me! Listen — this is what you must do. Tell Charlie you will marry Amy. You will be a father to his child. That is a beautiful act you can do for a friend! And you must mean it. Amy will accept you after a while, I think. You are already her friend and she will want security for her child."

"Friend isn't lover. Not to mention being father to a child no one ever consulted me about. Hannah — my God, what am I talking about! What are we? Chess pieces?"

She responds as gravely as if hyperbole were no more outlandish than truth. "This can only be done freely. But maybe Charlie would see that in so-and-so many moves ahead — one way or another — he can be checked. And maybe then he will be."

"Checked at what? You can't come in here like this and not say what! Checked how? What do you think Charlie is going to do?"

"Destroy everything. Amy ought to run away, but she won't."

"Don't frighten me!" Paul says. "Hannah, my God!"

He thinks that lately he is always seeing her like this —

disappearing through his front door with her bright red hair flapping up and down like wings, waving him goodby.

◦§ ﻌ

Night after night in Paul's apartment the phone repeatedly rings. Then stops. Then rings rings rings again. The band about his head tightens, loosens, tightens. He refuses to answer — braves anxieties about Karen and Helene to let it ring on. It can only be Hannah, telling him to do his duty and win Amy away from Charlie.

After that the doorbell. Short separate buzzes at first. Then one long unbroken cry. He pictures her, his blue-hooded conscience, standing alone in the hall.

Usually after that he finds a note under his door. Now, for the first time, one that is formally typed. Weary as a man picking through garbage pails for his dinner, yet desperate to rummage, he bends down to it and reads: " 'If we are to call for the attribute of *kindness,* infinite pardon, through our unbounded deeds, it is because *lo samnu* — we are not perfect. The last word, *samnu,* may mean, 'They are not concluded . . .' "

Then, in Hannah's tiny handwriting, as if she is imparting secrets: "These are a rabbi's words, yet think of Mary's idea about needing more time in the womb!" Again, typed: " 'A little abortion of a man . . . hastened before us.' " Hannah's hand: "This is Nathaniel Hawthorne! Do not think I am making my old mistake of supposing these are messages meant for me. Did you speak to Amy yet? What we all might become, Paul! We will not always be as we are!"

Tears come to his eyes for a greatness of spirit that so far exists only in Hannah's notebook.

He rushes to his door and looks hopefully down the long empty hall. The green corridor carpeting curls like a tongue to the arabesqued wallpaper, the brass wall sconces upraised and winking like sentinels at a revel.

Cancel the revel. Selig is not there. The depth of his disappointment wrings him. Oh, lovely girl! And she understands me better than I do myself . . . While he mourns her in his thoughts, he hears a second envelope rustle under his slipper.

"Bomstein's quotes" — the second note says — "believe me, don't talk about perfecting!" He feels a sinking of the heart. And a hatred for Bomstein, that uglifier of human aspiration who won't give him credit for wanting to be better, even if he's up to his ass in worse.

7

L OOKING OVER Hannah's shoulder in the lounge, Paul
reads: "We rebel against a God we're taught to think of
as a father and are enraged when we suffer, when the
father doesn't protect. But what is God? Do we know its combinations? Into our idea of God we may put also a mother who
loves and weeps, like Rebecca, and a lover who tests the love
of the beloved. What is that like? Unfair! Everything taken
away, reneged on. Evil triumphs, but also goodness is reborn.
Enough of goodness to dazzle . . ."

"At it again?"

Hannah tries to shut the book, but Paul weights one side
with the palm of his left hand while he moves the index finger
of his right down the lines of script on the other side: "Why
else would God have scattered greatness, have burst the forms
with grandeur, if not for this — to see us gather God-frag-
ments forever? The Lover tries the patience of the beloved
with every betrayal. The beloved is by now very weary. But the
Lover's energy? Cruelty? Injustice? Endless! Ask any domestic
relations judge about the demonic inventions of love — "

"Or ask anybody here at the Center, how about that?" Paul
snaps. Yet he won't allow the blue cover to close: "God de-

mands from us proof that we exist! Demands that we restore ourselves and the world to goodness. The joy of knowing that this task can have no end! Those who are bored with life have not begun to understand its meaning!"

Paul riffles through the pages — pages — pages. "Don't you ever get tired of the subject!"

He is in a sour mood these days anyway. Margaret has let him know that she is taking the girls on a trip west with her new boyfriend next vacation.

"No," Hannah answers. "But you do. Look how different our tastes are. Soon you'll want to avoid me altogether."

She utters this prediction with a kind of sober energy, which irritates him more than anything else so far. Because of his bad mood, Hannah's words remind him of an old vaudeville turn in which a man accidentally knocks the hat off a pedestrian and then announces in hopeless paranoia: "Now you're going to hit me, aren't you? Go on, you bully, hit me!" But then he is appalled at the association. He does not want to think about himself thinking about hitting anyone.

He rouses himself to take measures.

"Hannah, Hannah — I know what the trouble with us is! We've never, I realize, appeared in public together."

"Here where we work — it's a public place," Hannah says reasonably.

"Not the same thing. So bring clothes with you tomorrow. You can change after work, before we go out. Wear the new shoes. With the black velvet top, okay?"

There is no girl to match her in that blouse, Paul is thinking. Her long neck and pale face with the streaming red-gold hair float above the velvety black like blazing jewels.

"This will be our first time out. There's something in that," Paul says, "of a public declaration."

But when Hannah emerges from the ladies' room the next evening, he is astonished to see that she is wearing an old blouse from before his time — peach-colored polyester —

that drains her skin to yellow and turns her hair on like a neon sign in a pop art gallery.

"Why not the black sweater?"

"I forgot."

The lethargy of her voice irritates him beyond words. "What happened?" He snaps at her. "Did you give the new clothes away to José's sister's children — whoever they are?"

"Yes, I did," she answers in the same maddening drawl. "I wanted them to go to good use."

In the restaurant she is less sure of herself. She seems almost frightened when she asks, looking like a small child on the red leather banquette beside him while the tuxedoed waiter hovers nosily, "Do they sell cottage cheese?"

"Steak! For God's sake it's a steak house, the best!"

She seems to turn a shade yellower against the red leather. He brusquely orders for them both rare sirloin, baked potatoes with sour-cream-and-chive dressing, and salad with Roquefort. That done, he questions her about José, of whom he feels jealous, and annoyed with himself for feeling that way. Especially since — as he tells himself — it's combined with how critical he feels about her appearance. Tonight, under the restaurant's concealed fluorescent lights, he finds her looking like some pathetic creature instead of the magnificent one he thought he had discovered. He had wanted to bring her along on Saturdays to get to know Karen and Helene. But it was clear he couldn't trust her — she'd come dressed like some polyester clown, and the girls would report to Margaret — no, he couldn't bear that!

"Don't toy with your steak," he says after it arrives. "Eat it."

She broaches the subject of Amy, her favorite one these days, and remarks that a sympathetic person would mean a great deal to her, after so much tragedy.

"We could all use sympathy. We've all got tragedy. Eat it, for God's sake, don't stab it to death — it's not a bullfight!"

She obligingly bites down on a piece, swallows, then bites

and swallows another. He grumbles on, "Tragedy? How? That's the original Sunshine girl. Nothing can dim that light." He hears an echo of his words. Sunshine girl? *His* girl?

He wonders whether the moment has come again when everything will be shattered. Hannah is ghastly pale. She speaks stiff-lipped, as if afraid of too much movement. "Why should you tie yourself to me? In my life there are complications — you see how many — too many. There is the past weighing on me. How is it you don't think of Amy for yourself, such a beautiful girl?"

"Amy? Are you crazy? Amy belongs to Charlie!"

"She gave herself to him. She can take herself back. You wooed her for Charlie. You can woo her for yourself."

"It so happens she's pregnant, if you've forgotten!"

"She can take that back also, or share it with you."

"Do you think that's what my love is? Something that can be returned in a box like a sweater? I gave it to you. Keep *that*, for God's sake, don't hand it back."

"You are right. It is like a sweater. It doesn't fit me."

"You love me, Hannah. I know you do."

"My love doesn't fit you either."

"It does. Like a glove. Like a warm sweater that I wear on my heart. Goddamn it, Hannah, what are you doing?" He feels angry tears start at his lower lids, but Hannah's eyes are as dry as truth. He rouses himself again. "My God, Hannah, don't make me into a failure at love. I failed once and have been trying hard ever since. I can't go the same way again. I can't lose you."

"People lose people all the time. It's even, sometimes, a sign — "

"Don't start that God stuff now! I warn you!" He feels his head get hot. His eyes seem to be pushing from their sockets.

"You see — I am not right for you. My brain is filled with God stuff. I can't be a sweetheart." She reaches her hand to him. "It depends on you — if you persuade Amy — then

Charlie won't — " Deadly pale, she grips his arm. "I feel sick."

"You really made up your mind to spoil things, didn't you," he says between his teeth. After another glance at her face, he pays the bill in haste. Outside it is pouring rain and he has a bad time convincing a cabby to drive them to Brooklyn, but he is resolved to take her back to her own apartment tonight. With white face and clenched teeth, Hannah endures the ride.

At home, she does not want to lie down. She faces him across the new kitchen table. "What will happen if Amy is determined to keep the baby and Charlie is determined she shouldn't? Why won't you speak up — put your claim before Amy — declare yourself to Charlie? Otherwise, I see — terrible!" She clamps her hand to her lips against impending words or sickness.

"You know what? I'm getting sick myself. I'm sick of your seeing!"

His rage whips up and overtakes him at last. "There's someone else, isn't there? That's why you shove me off onto Amy! Who is it — José?"

"Yes," she answers, pale. "It is José."

"You bitch, all this time!"

His arm — of itself — pulls back and smashes his hand into her face. As if they are engaged in a pantomime of gift-giving, she, after the first recoil, plunges back toward him. The sickness she had suppressed at last jettisons its stream: he feels it hot on his chest like the unwanted claim of some deepest visceral touch. His anger does not subside even when she topples and the chair goes over too, as if tied to her.

She gags in vomit on the kitchen floor as if re-enacting the primal scene of parental death, yet meanwhile struggles to say "I see — I see . . ."

He hastily wets a cloth and cleans her face. Then he lifts her to her bed and covers her. She is pale, eyes closed. He goes back and wipes the kitchen floor.

"Forgive me," he says brokenly. He is standing at the

foot of her bed. Her pale face has turned to him at last.

She closes her eyes wearily. Sick of himself, afraid to stay longer, he tiptoes from the room. "Try to sleep," he says. "I'll be in the kitchen. Call if you need me."

"Speak to Amy . . ." Her hoarse whisper follows him to the door. "Declare yourself to Charlie . . . Don't wait . . ."

"All right," he mutters over his shoulder, to stop it. "I'll look in on you."

"Soon . . . !" Her whisper trails after him and he cannot tell whether in persuasion or prediction. "Soon . . . !"

He buries his head in his arms on the kitchen table and at once falls into an exhausted, dreamless sleep.

But Selig dreams that she is writing in a kind of celestial blue notebook whose pages are white and puffed. She hears herself read aloud, from what she has written, to a black-robed demon.

"Wait! Hold it! Not that stuff again!" the demon protests.

But Hannah is on her feet, unstoppable, arms out, narrow backward-arching fingers stretched to the light fixtures, reading and reading.

"Idiot! Madwoman!" the demon cries. "There is no task! There's nothing! Only happiness or unhappiness! And you blew it!"

He raises his hand to strike her. A second figure hurries in, his robes white but in disarray, as if hastily put on. To stay the demon's hand he lifts his own. Hannah wakes, filled with longing for Paul. She listens, mistakes the silence, and thinks, Better that he is gone. She lies quietly weeping. She remembers that when his robe opened, it showed the naked rising phallus, the vulnerable aspiring flesh.

◆§ ξ◆

"The whole sex thing too," Ellen Bianky says laconically in bed at the lunch hour. "Between men and women. So unsatisfactory, really."

She wants Sorenson to hear how little she values it. "Inconclusive. Unfinished."

"Really?" Sorenson is taken by surprise. It is a thing he never tolerates. It makes him quite angry. He is naked and angry.

"I thought you enjoyed it," he says tauntingly.

"I meant the feelings. The relationship aspect," she says severely. She draws up the sheet. She regrets her own nakedness.

"Oh." Sorenson in his irritation with this topic is barely polite. "I didn't get your meaning."

"You didn't and you don't and you can't!"

Edgar goes on with it till strength and imagination give out. Sometimes the man isn't Sorenson; it's someone else. Ellen is present grudgingly, reserving true love for *him*.

I didn't know I was like Selig, he thinks with weary amazement. I didn't know I would try to retrieve disaster with hope.

Book Four

A babe in a house is a well-spring of pleasure.
—Martin F. Tupper,
Of Education

In one pocket of your coat keep a slip of paper on which is written "Dust and ashes." In another pocket keep another slip on which is written "Little lower than angels." Take these out and read them often. Remind yourself of what it means to be human.
—from a Hasidic legend copied into Selig's notes
under the heading: *For Bomstein, for her book*

I

NOW THEY ARE like dancers in a square, honoring partners and corners all, in a moment of stasis before some furious new reel strikes up, and a brand-new pairing off begins. Amy and Charlie keep formal distance from one another; Paul and Hannah do the same.

Paul hurries about the city, paying visits, unwittingly tracing some of Hannah's footsteps.

At Sylvia's apartment: "I don't want to go back there, Paul. I don't want to be a martyr. I've told Charlie he owes me nothing. I also feel I owe him nothing. We lived together a certain number of years and gave each other what we could and brought up a son to manhood and now that's over. A new phase has begun. At first I thought, If he got sick again a young girl wouldn't nurse him the way I would. She couldn't be his mother."

"And now?"

"Now I think, What difference does it make if she's his mother or his daughter or his paid companion or whatever? Who says a man has to die in his mother's arms? I told that to Hannah, too."

At the mention of Hannah's name, Paul clears his throat

loudly. A lump there won't go away. "Do me a favor. Don't talk about dying. I've got too much to do."

"You have Hannah now," Sylvia says. "I think she's your salvation. She has a core of something very strong and good in her. Of course she's like an immigrant to the modern world, poor thing — someone who's come all alone and in steerage from the old absolutes of religion. Oh, it will save her, too, Paul, your loving her back. She's one of those rare creatures whose good hold of the old wisdom enlarges her capacities to learn the new. But she can use a little loving help."

Paul feels himself blush. "It's not set, you know — don't jump to conclusions. She wasn't very nice to me — I won't go into it. As far as I'm concerned, it may be all off."

"Hannah? I can't believe it! I thought she was close to saintly."

"She took you in, then!" He hears himself feigning anger and thinks, My God, I used to have to sit on myself to *control* temper! Is everything authentic in my life leaving with Hannah?

"She used to send me little quotations from her reading because she heard I was lonely. She lived in loneliness and poverty and wanted to comfort me. I thought she was a good soul, a clever girl, and would make you a devoted wife, Paul." Sylvia gives him a long look. "She has a lot to give someone. But she *needs* desperately, too. And besides that — I wouldn't be surprised if she has a saint complex. What do you call it when Jews have it? Maybe she wants to be one of the thirty-six righteous ones. A female one, whatever you'd call that."

"Look, I see her problem! If I knew of a decent therapist, I'd recommend she go there. Even Margaret, believe me, if I thought Margaret could possibly help anyone."

Oh, you are fallen, fallen, Paul thinks. Not a word of truth comes out of your mouth. What happened to your inner evolution? Back to the slime for you. But I will get what's mine!

◦§ §◦

Charlie reports to Paul that almost every night Matt telephones him.

"How's the death trip, Doc?"

"Okay for everybody but you, right, Doc?"

"You didn't kill your own, but you can justify the other killings, right? If it was anybody else, you'd be screaming at them to do something about it. But your case is different, right, Doc? You can't marry my sister and you're going to die. You'll have the pleasure of a kid for a few years. What you don't see after you're gone can't hurt you, right, Doc?"

"The lousy bastard!" Paul says. "A walking illustration of Mary's theory. He could have used another good six, eight months in the womb, shaping up." Me too, dear God, Paul thinks; me, too.

"Even a bastard can be right" is Charlie's dry response.

◄§ §►

"Any time my mother wants to come back is great." Daniel sips wine gravely when Paul and he have dinner near Columbia. "I respect them both. I was so wrong about my father. He gave my mother her chance at freedom. If she wants to go on the way she's living, that's okay, that's her choice."

"She wants to be near you, too."

"You don't have to add that, Uncle Paul. I understand. I'm not the same person I was before. I'm almost glad about everything that happened. The painfulness of becoming a better person is that you have to see how awful you were before." Daniel has piled a stack of newly purchased philosophy and history paperbacks on the chair beside him. Topmost is Bronowski's *Western Intellectual Tradition.* He lays an eager hand on the cover. "I'm learning a lot from these guys. I'm also learning something from women. From their bitterness, their terrible anger. We have to pay attention to them. We have to learn from what they're saying, painful as that may be."

Paul shifts uncomfortably as he reaches for the check. He suspects he's being preached to, but of course that's only

paranoia — Daniel's face is filled with innocent thoughts
of self-improvement. Paul feels an unbecoming envy of
the spiritual advantage of the young. Me, I've got no more
leisure for soul-shaping. Hustle. Get what's coming to me
now.

Pacing his apartment at night, Paul thinks that it is surely
Hannah's fault that he has been put into one false situation
after another. Yet Hannah's ideas after all may be right. Amy
should have been for him in the first place. He recoils from
thinking about his friend's illness. But Hannah has harped and
harped on it, hasn't she? So has Charlie. All right then, if that's
the accepted wisdom of everybody! Can he be accused of
opportunism when it never was his idea in the first place? *His*
idea had been selfless. But time after time he's been hit on the
head with this other thing.

His fault, he reasons, pacing, is that he has, out of too much
respect, picked women of ideas. It's time to admit he'd be
happier with a docile woman. Like Amy.

He doesn't have to do things the way Hannah sees it —
jump into the breach now, talk to Charlie, win over Amy —
that's a hare-brained scheme; it would be damned *embarrassing*.
It would be goddamned inconvenient to take on another
man's child. Margaret would see him for a sucker. Karen and
Helene would have every right to feel resentful. No — he
doesn't have to take on Charlie's child. It's a matter of time;
Charlie will prevail.

Yet even though he has paced it through, a bitter disappointment overtakes him. To his horror he sees that
when passing the photographs of Karen and Helene he
had somehow, without realizing, turned their faces to the
wall.

❧ ❧

"Where's *Hannah?* What do you mean, where? On vacation.
Don't you *know?*"

Edgar sends Paul, from under his lowered brows, his intensest stare, which Paul avoids by gazing urgently at his watch.

୶୫ ୧ୢ

A divorced woman named Roberta Weinstock and her ten-year-old son, Kevin, sit beside Karen and Helene and Paul at a Sunday afternoon Young People's Concert. Roberta is cheerful and attractive, if a little on the hefty side. Yet her round face falls into sad expressions now and then, and when Paul asks, during intermissions, how come, she says she's sad for Kevin, her little boy. He misses his father, who has headed west, a footloose Irishman. She wants no more part of him and has taken back her own family name. Nobody talks about love or redemption or evolving or soul-making when Paul and Roberta go to bed. Paul tells himself that his unmoored feelings, his strange, almost apathetic detachment, are relief at sleeping with someone who presents him with nothing more than, so to speak, the raw flesh. Roberta seems to be mad for it. He sometimes suspects that she pretends. That the leaps into erotic bliss from which she draws forth joyful yelps and hooked-fish shudders are faked. He accepts her plagiarized pleasure: What, after all, does she counterfeit but her own former love? Paul does the same, though less detectably, he feels. In Paul's bed the name Roberta sobs is not his. "Jamie! Jamie!" she cries. "Hannah! Hannah!" Paul's soul responds. His arms seek out, in Roberta's robust flesh, the delicate shape of his love.

I've got to break myself of this, he thinks. Body reflex. He had it after the breakup with Margaret, too. Give in to it, and a man enslaves himself to women.

One night, instead of simulating gay abandon while playfully crying "Fuck me, lover!" as soon as she has got inside his apartment door, Roberta stoops to retrieve a sheet of paper from the carpet. Before he can stop her, she is reading aloud.

"Paul and Bunky come up together in the elevator as always

Into the empty waiting room like a beautiful ship floating on waves of sunlight. They hear cries, hurry toward them at the back. Charlie slumped in a chair. Amy wrapped in blood-stained sheet. Mary, always first in, is screaming, 'You raped her of her baby!' Bunky folds up his heavy body like an empty bag and sinks to the floor. Paul says, 'How come you did that, Charlie?' "

"What's this, in God's name?" Roberta asks.

He snatches the paper from her fingers. "A friend of mine — trying to write a play — coincidence there's a character with my name. . . ."

"He or she?" Roberta asks slyly. He is relieved she is back on sex. It gives him a chance to take in that Hannah has returned — or never left? Now a raving maniac? He cannot get it out of his head. His hero's disgrace, idealism's distortion and death. And Amy, sweet Amy — what then, after this catastrophe?

Hannah's Gothic fantasies have given him a headache and he does not perform well in bed. To his surprise, Roberta abandons her coarsely joking approach and becomes relaxed, quiet, almost tender. He appreciates the kindness and wonders if she is not secretly relieved.

Sleepless, he ponders his own character. He is not among the saints. He doubts he's a devil. Harder than that to classify. He decides at last that he is simply someone who thinks himself so misfortuned that only other people's disasters can bring him luck. What name is there for that? His face colors darkly and his innards grow weighty with shame.

When he can, he slips out of bed and telephones Hannah, but no answer. In the morning he tries again from work, gets a phony Spanish imitation, and snaps, "You take a good man for a model and malign him in your imagining! You twist everything. What the hell do you think you are, a witch?"

Selig drops her disguise long enough to protest "Can't you tell? It's from Bomstein's book!"

Amy hurries by, catching Paul by the elbow as she heads toward a procedure room.

"Everything's fine! Charlie and I are having our first dinner together again." Her smooth-haired braid swings round her shoulder like a bell-ringer's rope.

If some bell were tolling for me, I'd know it, wouldn't I?

Amy's joy moves by him fast — she radiates while she hurries. *"Celebrate* with us, Paul!"

2

PREGNANCY agrees with Amy. Her skin glows more brilliantly than ever. Her eyes seem to swim in joy — a sparkly liquid that fills up to the brim and occasionally overflows. Her palms are stained with the rich red of motherhood.

Though Charlie as usual says little, Amy talks with excited happiness all through dinner.

"Charlie now wants the baby as much as I do!"

"Is that so, Charlie?" Paul glances at him. He is quietly eating his salad.

" — Though he doesn't talk about it as much." Amy kisses Charlie's cheek. A bit of lettuce has fallen onto Charlie's lapel. Amy tenderly peels it off.

Paul eats his steak. "That's a big change."

"And we've already picked names," Amy goes on.

"What are the names, Charlie?"

"Sarah if it's a girl," Amy answers, "for Charlie's mother. Saul if it's a boy."

Amy brings a forkful of food from her own plate to Charlie's lips. "This is delicious. Taste some, darling!"

"Have you changed your ideas about fatherless children

too, then, Charlie?" Paul cruelly says it. Anything for a response.

"But it won't be that! Charlie will be with me," Amy bursts out proudly, happily. "Even though Sylvia refuses a divorce."

This is the restaurant where Paul and Hannah ate their ill-fated dinner. It is Amy's choice — the good food, the celebrational décor. But to Paul there is a glumly familiar glow in the red of the banquettes and table candles. He feels like a habitué of hell.

By the time they are at coffee, Paul confirms what he observed at the beginning of the meal. It is Amy, not Charlie, who is now making all the assertions. When they leave, Paul hails a cab for the three of them.

"I'll drop myself off at Eightieth," he says with one hand on the door handle, "and you two can take it on up to Amy's."

"No, we're going downtown," Amy says quickly. "We're going to the Center."

"How come?" Paul asks it with sudden sharpness.

"Nostalgia," Amy replies, smiling happily. "We return to the scene of the beginning."

The cabby makes restless noises. In a kind of dream, Paul says to them, "Go on, then, you take it — I'll catch the next."

And why shouldn't I believe it? Paul asks himself at the curb. At dinner, Charlie had kissed Amy's hand, eaten from her plate, cautioned her to use little salt, then tenderly lifted her coat to her shoulders when they left and tucked her wrist into the crook of his elbow. He had acted the part of a man in love and full of protectiveness toward the woman who bears his child. *Acted?*

No, Paul thinks, watching the red retreating lights of the taxi as it sweeps Charlie and Amy away from him, I suspect nothing, nothing at all! Why, then, does his recollection linger over the way Charlie dropped into Amy's wine a nourishing potassium capsule, first ceremoniously holding it aloft like the King benevolently displaying the jewel before dropping it, poisoned, into Hamlet's cup?

All that night, Paul sits wrapped up on his balcony. He is stiff and cold and unable to move, except for the cigarettes he keeps bringing to his lips.

What should I do? What Charlie might or might not have planned is not my business. How is it my business? How am I responsible? Any more than I could be responsible for Bunky's Genevieve X nightmare coming true. I am either too soft or too brutal with women. And each at the wrong time. How do I know what is right or wrong about what Charlie might have in mind to do? Charlie's the one who has the way with women. How do I know that Charlie has anything in mind? Hasty words, hasty scribblings — Selig's or Bomstein's — are no proof of anything.

And even if I did know, what could I do about it? Should I have tried to warn Amy? Hannah must have tried, with no success. How could I? How could I warn without making monstrous accusations against Charlie? Wouldn't it look as if I hoped to profit from them? Altruism is for the noblest souls only! At lower levels, always tainted with self-interest.

And if he does nothing? He might stand also to profit, but how is that his fault? He shudders from the cold, and tries not to picture the scene in the recovery room of the Center. But he's trained himself to be a Charlie-watcher. It's hard now to leash his imagination, keep its nose out of that vast room, empty save for those two.

◦⧫ ⧫◦

Amy's arms around Charlie. She hugs him like a child.

"You can't think what a good mother I'll be! I have the gift of making other people happy, Charlie, I know I have!"

"A common delusion." Charlie is smiling, though, when he speaks.

Amy has chosen their original recovery cot to make love on

again. Now she lies there naked, smiling at him. He removes his clothing, drapes his jacket carefully over the back of a chair. He is too slow. She comes to take him by the hand. Then reaches for his other hand and closes it over her small belly. The tip of her braid hangs over to tickle the back of his hand, and in this way, cross-armed and joined at every finger, they glide like warm skaters over an icy pond.

When they embrace on the bed she puts her fingers to his eyelids. "Those are tears of happiness, aren't they? I told you — I told you, Charlie! Oh, I have to brag to you now — I *said* I'd bring you joy!" Then, when his face is buried in her braid-loosed hair, which falls in soft *s*'s — "You've never held me so tight before, Charlie. I want to hug you just as tight! I want to take your breath away, too! I never loved anyone as much as I love you, because you let me make you happy."

Drowsily she murmurs, "I'm filled with everything — with life, with happiness, with you."

While she sleeps her deep sleep, he rises, moves a chair next to the bed, and gazes down at her. Round face, round breasts, round belly — worlds within worlds. He lives his new life. Amy is his wife. The fetus in her womb has become his child. It is a girl. His mother's blue eyes look lovingly from her small face. He names the child Sarah, his mother's name. He takes little Sarah by the hand. He runs on the beach with his child, holds her warm, sandy, nearly naked body close to his chest, feeds her chocolate ice cream, licks where she licks. The delicious custard runs in streams down their warm tanned bodies. His little daughter laughs and hugs him. He runs with her and makes her scream with joy — "Daddy, Daddy, oh!" — into the booming ocean. The waves rear up and pour down nets of foam. He shelters her with his body, binds her up in the net of his love . . .

Naked, he walks across the icy tiles, past the ghostly cots, to where his clothes are thrown on a chair. City moonlight paints a stripe across his belly, with its whitened scars. His body seems embalmed in moonlight — waxy, dead.

He retrieves from his pocket the needle he had filled in the bathroom. He returns and holds it over Amy's unconscious form.

◦⋛ ⋚◦

Shivering on the balcony, Paul thinks that some of Hannah's notebook-scribbling clairvoyance might be passing through him. No — how can I know what it's like to be Hannah, or Hannah know what it's like to be Charlie! But if we *could* all know, as Charlie seems to know what it's like to be some sobbing woman at the hospital, then my God, my God, why couldn't we all do better with our lives and our sympathy and our knowing?

Excited, he jumps up. The wrappings fall from him and he stands exposed to the cold wind of the balcony. Slowly, he sinks down into the chair again and draws the blankets over him.

3

A T THE DOOR of the waiting room, Edgar sucks in a
deep breath before he throws his glance over the
place. No woman waits there yet. Every morning,
though, Edgar enacts this ritual. And every morning Paul, who
enters with him, waits for Edgar to sweep round with his ceremonial look, his glance ticking like a clock past blue upholstery, beige pillows, flax-colored drapes, crimson and lavender
flowering plants.

This morning Paul's heart hammers so violently that he
imagines Bunky must hear it. Deathly pale, Paul claps a hand
to his chest.

Edgar catches sight of this in his ceremonial sweep, and is
touched. This is some sign of enlargement in Paul's spirit.
Deep forces of empathy must have broken through, Edgar
feels. For Paul is reflecting the exact gesture which, at that
moment, Edgar himself enacts, moving his hand to his shirt
pocket where he keeps the envelope marked URGENT! and PER-
SONAL. Every day for weeks he has been transferring the envelope, nearly ragged now, to a fresh shirt. He is unable to
destroy it and has no idea where else he can leave it, with its
cruel crudity. A small photograph of Ellen's face, torn from the

page of a medical journal, smiles within the envelope in his pocket. It is mounted at the mouth upon a phallus, possibly traced from life. Below the drawing, the same hand has printed: "Who's this kissing your wife?"

As Edgar moves quietly on toward his office, unaccustomed sound begins to disturb the air. Again, Edgar pauses, puts trembling fingers to his shirt pocket. Paul does the same, in perfect unconscious mimicry. In the next second, Edgar shoves heavily forward, then quickens, then runs, slamming into corners and doorways as he hurls himself on.

By the time Paul arrives, rushing after, Edgar has already flung open the door of the recovery room. Paul, peering aghast under Bunky's upraised arm at the terrifying tableau — Amy, Charlie, Mary — manages only partly to lessen the thundering crash — Edgar folding up his heavy body and, in slow-motion, like a breaking, toppling tower, collapsing downward — of Edgar's fall.

Wildly and absurdly Paul wracks his brain while staggering with the afterstrain of Bunky's weight: "What did Hannah say that *looked* like?"

Then he whispers to the air, "How come you *did* that, Charlie?" and fails to remember where he's heard that before.

◄§ ĝ►

No answer. Not from Amy or Amy's grandmother, though Paul has been telephoning nearly daily. Have they gone somewhere for Amy's recuperation? Then he asks himself, What recuperation? Women danced away from that procedure! Yet he can't think of anything that's happened without also thinking, though he'd like to avoid Margaret's jargon, of terrible psychic scars. Have Amy and her grandmother shut themselves off like a pair of grim females in an O'Neill play?

At last one day Amy's grandmother answers the telephone. Paul is able to ask, without knowing how much to betray of what everybody knows, "How is Amy?"

"Very, very bit-ter," comes the old lady's ponderous tone. "Very full of hate now, full of hate." Her voice dawdles sadly over the words.

Paul says he is sorry to hear it, having to clear his voice twice to make it audible.

The old lady's tone rises a bit in hope. "It might help her to see some friend."

"Would she want to see me?" He asks it doubtfully.

"Perhaps not." She says it shortly and, he feels, with little sympathy for his feelings. "But you will come all the same to see? Even if you are greeted with bitterness?"

He thinks of Amy's open young face now closed against him, against all men. *"Why don't you cut your balls off, bastards!"* It echoes softly, killingly, in his head.

"You will come?" the grandmother urges.

"I want to — of course — as soon as I can. Just now it's hard to get away. I have my children with me. My ex-wife is on vacation." Not exactly a lie. His children are always with him in his mind. His ex-wife is always on vacation from him. "Also, we're short-staffed at the Center . . ." *That* sounds as if he blames the victim for making it impossible for him to visit her.

He hangs up in sour judgment of himself. Still, a bitter woman! For that he has already had Margaret, hasn't he? And Roberta. And fifty more. And soon, no doubt, Hannah, too. All bitter women are the same and fill him with revulsion and fear. Why should he go and stick his head in that acid?

But to be able to *do* it! He would like, somehow, to be the person who might have been able to do it . . . Charlie. Charlie could do it. Charlie before his fall . . .

◦§ ৡ◦

Charlie, too, is in retreat since that day, having disappeared that same morning from the Center and from the house in Harrison. No one is there to answer the phone. Daniel is living near Columbia, reading at the library, making up for lost time, preparing himself to be a dedicated student when enrollment begins.

From Riva, Paul learns that Charlie made a single phone call to cancel all appointments with private patients.

"He told me to take the month off, with pay, and then sent me a fat bonus check besides. He's taking a well-earned vacation. I have a *feeling*" — Riva nevertheless grants it the assertiveness of knowing — "that this is his way of cutting loose from that baby-faced aide. He never thought that much of her."

"Charlie aborted Amy's pregnancy," Paul says brusquely into the telephone. He lowers his voice in sudden fear that the woman waiting to use the phone, wearing a smartly styled raincoat and with a Lord & Taylor shopping bag on her arm, will hear him and start screaming. "Without her knowledge or consent." He breaks into a sweat. He is calling from a street booth, and the heavy urine smell makes him feel that he has lost control of his own functions.

"I don't believe it," Riva yells into the phone. "You're eaten up with envy, you always were — !"

◄§ §►

Without understanding why, Paul feels compelled to find Matt. He hunts him down, traces him landlady by landlady, discovering that he has moved three times since leaving the Center. Matt's new address is a brownstone in the East Seventies, where Paul waits for him one chilly evening, on the front steps. Judging from the outside, the apartment he rents must be elegant digs.

"How's Amy?" Paul yells it over a distance of fifty yards, jogging in place and massaging his frozen fingers as Matt approaches.

Matt shrugs an expensive fawn-colored suede coat more comfortably up on his shoulders. He wears, also, a deep-brimmed suede hat with a cocky green feather. Money is coming in from somewhere. Maybe he has found a way to manipulate the unborn-baby market after all, Paul thinks.

Matt waits till he is within inches of Paul, then drawls through a cigarette in the corner of his mouth. "Well, after what she went through — Charlie ought to go to jail for that. Unless she settles for a bundle of dough. That's their business, though."

Paul fights down revulsion. "So you know, you talked to her — how is she?"

"Her grandmother will take her on a nice trip, that's what I know. She's got dough. She loves to spend it on Amy."

"Is that all you feel after what happened? The fact is you did your share, didn't you — goading Charlie?"

"Me goad him? Christ, he should have thanked me! He had no choice. He knew that himself. Without me, he might have lost his guts. Amy ought to thank me too. She's free. Isn't that" — he finishes bitterly — "what dames all want?"

"*Thank* you! You wouldn't even dare tell her you had a part in this."

"Why don't you go ahead and tell her then?"

Paul sees himself sitting at the bedside. *"Why don't you all cut your balls off, bastards?"*

Matt grins, his handsome empty face pushes closer to Paul's. "But I don't think you will. I think you'll profit from the way things are right now!"

Paul puts all his gangly strength behind the punch, but it seems to do no more than unmoor his own feet. Matt comes back at him with his swift muscular wallop and Paul goes down.

He sits on the sidewalk with his hand to his eye. With the other eye he sees a blurred figure strolling away. He had not even knocked his green-feathered hat off.

Profit from that son-of-a-bitch? He groans. Am I that low?

Paul's eye hurts for days. The bruise feels as if it spreads all through his head, down his neck, and into his chest — his whole body inhabited by the ache. It seems to blend with the other ache, the one he has been haunted by since that day at the Center.

All that day, the swift and stunned activities had gone on. The "how" was never clear to anyone. How each scheduled procedure was got through. How the staff was too busy for once, or too stunned, to talk. How Edgar was white-faced but controlled. How aides and nurses buzzed in groups and broke off. How Paul had stared at Selig's note, carried in his pocket. How work was blessed. Even such work. It brought them through the day. At some point, Warner and Mary took Amy home in a taxi. And no one was sure exactly when, but at some point Charlie disappeared from the Center.

On that day also there was an ugly commotion in the waiting room. A perfect couple, perfectly matched in grimness — she with a deep black pot of a hat with a pleated colonnade going around it like a soufflé mold, as though underneath it her brains were steaming and rising into pudding; he with a long, silent, hole-eyed face and a dark-spotted shirt, menacing as a hyena — came for their sixteen-year-old daughter.

"You have no right!" Mary said, as they pulled the girl by the hair toward the door, and the only other sound was the high whinnying whimper that came from the girl's throat. The waiting women watched in disbelief, someone cried out indignantly, "Call the police!" but meanwhile steady progress was being made toward the door.

"I'm her mother, *that's* my right," said the woman whose brains had been steamed into a dish.

"I'm her father, that's *my* right," said the hyena.

"Think what you're doing to your daughter," a waiting woman pleaded. "How having a baby now will ruin her life!"

The perfectly matched couple looked back in perfectly matched hatred.

"She'll take her punishment," said the hyena.

"She'll get a good lesson," said the pudding-brain.

So it was terribly odd how, on the same day, someone who had wanted to be rid of a fetus had been forced to keep it, and

someone who had wanted to keep hers had been forcibly rid-
ded of it. No one asked the woman what she wanted. Other
people perpetrated their ideas upon her. Paul saw that and, in
a moment of horrified empathy, he felt it, and shuddered
deeply.

Even after the last patient was gone, the staff had kept silent.
One by one they followed Edgar's example, retrieved their
coats, and silently left. As soon as he reached the street, Paul
telephoned Hannah. He made up his mind to let the phone
ring, if necessary, till neighbors called the police. When at last
she answered he said hoarsely, "My God, are you really a
witch?" and let her know what he had called to tell her.

"It's only from watching so much," she pleaded. "What do
I have to do but watch? I have so small a life! I look, I watch
other people. And sometimes it comes to me — when I write
in my notes — how they will behave when I am not looking at
them!"

Tears filled her voice. "I didn't wish for this evil. For you,
in my notes, I see only good deeds . . ."

"Don't give me my fortune now!" he shouted at her.

But she was unstoppable.

"Look, look — how quick!" — her ragged speech had no
time for the elegant turns of her bookish notebook style —
"how easily a good person can do a bad thing! Much easier
than a bad person can do a good thing!"

He felt himself teeter in the phone booth, sway on some
knife-thin borderline of good and evil.

"Live to make a difference . . . !" Her voice had leaped
through the phone, to push him off balance.

"I'm not noble!" His voice came out hoarse and thick. "I
started out cheated by life and want my share. Go out to New
Jersey if you're looking for a just man. Not here! Not me! Even
Charlie couldn't be a saint!"

"Humility in the just man is also spoken of." Exhortation
rose up through the receiver. He pictured Hannah gesturing
toward the ceiling.

"Even Charlie couldn't be a saint!" He yelled it again and then hung up, feeling sick to think of how she thought of it, that he was somehow to blame, had not lived to make a difference.

He had called and called the Westchester house, then called and called Daniel's apartment. Let Daniel be the one to tell Sylvia and hear that bitter woman-screech, not him! When Daniel finally answered the phone, he said that he had been at his mother's; they were worried because they could not reach Charlie.

"Is anything wrong, Uncle Paul? Anything involving my dad?"

It had been harder to tell than he had imagined, and for many seconds there had been no response. Then Charlie's son, in a breaking voice, had slowly said, "He's gone somewhere to die, then."

◦§ §◦

"There is someone to see you, darling!"

Nana — fat old Nana — calls again outside her door.

"Don't say his name!"

"I won't, darling."

"I don't want to see him."

"He is very patient. He waits every day."

"Tell him there's nothing to wait for! No baby will be born."

Nana listens and creaks in the doorway. A sorrowing hippopotamus who once saw visions with Margaret Sanger: "What is the goal of woman's upward struggle? Is it voluntary motherhood? Is it general freedom? Or is it the birth of a new race? For freedom is not fruitless, but prolific of higher things."

"Tell him," Amy screams. "Tell him!"

"I will, I will, darling. Please don't upset yourself!"

When she draws the draperies of her granddaughter's room, she is thankful that they are dark-colored, that all is somber, that there is nothing anywhere to suggest the lies of the nursery.

4

THERE ARE TOO FEW at the funeral. Daniel, Sylvia, an apologetic Simon, broken-hearted Edgar, Ellen, Paul. The Center staff stays away. Riva weeps copiously but surreptitiously, for fear the widow might suspect a new rival. Paul keeps his fascinated tear-blurred eye on Charlie, into the grave.

Sylvia's face is swollen and red, so that grief looks like anger. When the little group returns from the cemetery to the house in Harrison, she bursts out, "Was it my fault he did these things? I didn't tell him I wouldn't give him his freedom. I only said I wanted to come home. And I certainly wasn't rushing back. But I suppose I was the last straw!"

Simon argues, reasonable and conciliatory at the same time. "How could it be your fault? Certain events combined with certain other events! The fatality of history! Are we responsible for the bullet at Sarajevo? Remember our course, Modern Events and World Collisions!"

"He's right, not your fault, Sylvia," Paul adds. "How could anyone have been the last straw in Charlie's life when it had nothing but last straws in it?"

She recounts obsessively what she had learned from police reports about how Charlie had put an end to everything. "Sat in a hotel room like a drunk or a derelict. Like one of those literary types, Delmore Schwartz or Dorothy Parker, and how they died . . ."

"It's true." Simon nods. "Creativity and Suicide in America, Tuesday night, eight to nine-thirty, a real insight!"

" — Stopped going for treatments, stopped taking medicine. It *was* a kind of suicide. It wasn't literary — what did he leave? He destroyed himself and he destroyed that poor girl. How could he have wanted to kill everything that way?"

"He couldn't stand the combinations, Sylvia. Amy was determined to have the baby. He must have felt desperate."

"But I told him, go ahead and marry her!"

"Then the kid would've been fatherless another way, and soon, Charlie must have thought. Everything he believed in was at stake."

Sylvia's eyes widen as if she is just now taking it in. "The arrogance of it! He — *he* — was the one who had to have the last word! And all because of an *idea!*"

Sylvia had ordered food sent in, which is now being set out on the long table in the dining room whose brilliant blue-and-gold Portuguese tile flooring sends up a solid "clunk" with every footstep. The caterer's men are dressed in cheerful red jackets. That morning Sylvia had been nearly paralyzed by the thought of returning, after the funeral, to the house. In the end she had decided she must face it — it was the only way to do it, to live there while making arrangements for its sale. She had hastily thrown clothes into a bag and had dressed herself without being aware of what she was putting on. In the bathroom she had been astonished to see that she was wearing a pale green wool suit with a wine-colored silk blouse. She had meant to wear something black.

Suitcases, hers and Simon's, stand in the hall. She pushes at them impatiently with her shoe, then bursts into tears. At once she recovers herself and repeats in a trembling, contemptuous voice, "Because of an idea!"

Paul hopes to leave in a hurry so as not to see the jumble of collapse that will surely follow. But Daniel detains him. "You think this person, Amy, was really damaged by this, don't you, Uncle Paul?"

"I don't know how she feels. She wouldn't see me," Paul lies. Daniel's mouth trembles downward. Say something more, Paul exhorts himself. Create something good for Daniel! Speak well to the living of the dead, my friend Charlie! But whatever words there might be won't come forth.

Daniel stares for a silent second. Then he himself speaks, rushing the words out as if the firmness of his voice might collapse at any minute. "I don't think my father would ever have done what he did to Amy if he'd been in his right mind. Who knows what all those drugs might have done to his brain chemistry?" It is Matt's sneering notion, transformed by love. "And who knows what the thought of a person's coming death can do to his psychology?"

I should have said that, Paul thinks. I should have spoken those words for Charlie. And if I couldn't do that, then why can't I at least nod my agreement now?

Charlie's son, with all the energy of youth and health, pitches himself into sickness and fatality and snatches out his father's laurel. "Not that my dad didn't care," he cries, "but that he cared so much! And he took his own life when he felt too sick to do any more good."

Sylvia has been listening, red-eyed. "I won't say a word to him," she tells Paul after Daniel moves away. "Let him go ahead and weave fantasies about his saintly father. If he needs them I won't rob him of them. But I don't like it. If he doesn't feel enough the crime against a woman that his father committed, if he can't see that, then he'll never be a complete man."

"Oh, as for that" — Ellen, walking toward them, catches the tail end — "don't wish for the moon. Daniel is already a fine young man, but no man feels the woman's part, or ever will."

She glances across the room to where Edgar stands, with one arm thrown about Daniel's shoulders.

Ellen sees how Edgar's handsome head is shaken sideways by tremor — No! No! — as if in perpetual denial. Sees how his broad-backed hand — the tiny tremor is there, too, cherished in the deep creased curve of the palm, the angled thumb and high-knuckled fingers — brushes, flicks at air. As if those motes were thoughts, Edgar's terrible thoughts, all unmerited, all taken upon himself because the world craves oblivion . . .

She feels the sensation of her heart "turning over," and it is as if earth is turned. A moist richness, a heat under the crust, is released. It is a whole vast farmland, her heart, germinating, fertile, Nile-nourished! She feels rising in her a wave of pity for Edgar so towering that she fears its breaking will crush her. It breaks, and it crushes her: she is drowned in pity for his fine, shaking head, his great, trembling hands . . . She wants to scythe and scythe at the fields growing in her heart, and bring armfuls — armfuls! — to Edgar, of whatever will nourish him. What has he done to deserve these blows? Noble, noble! She stumbles forward, tear-blinded, with armfuls torn from her heart. She thinks of Amy. A second later, of Mimi, and discovers, to her astonishment, that she had hated her. Now she forgives Mimi and with that forgives Amy also, forgives both women for having been there, in the way of Edgar's affections, no guiltier than flowers or mice. Humbly, she raises up some of the fallen sheaves, broken and trampled, and rushes on, toward tremoring Edgar. But doesn't move, only stands and flickers, trembles in her own body, and pulls down over everything a sleeve of caustic: "I suppose that's the reason" — crisp, seeming to give it all away now that the secret's so clearly out — "Genevieve X turned out to be a very different sort of catastrophe from what Edgar imagined." Charlie's death, they will all think, has brought perspective. What, after all, has Edgar been guilty of? Adultery in the heart — that brilliant backdrop against which fidelity sharpens its blurred outlines.

He has wrestled, poor man, they will all think she thinks, in his blind way . . . "With all his sympathy, even Edgar doesn't like to go very deeply into any of this."

"My God," says Paul, "how deep must we go?"

No one answers him. The question hangs in the air, gathering weight.

Sylvia kisses Paul her thanks as he prepares to leave. "For everything, Paul, for all your help." She astonishes him by adding in an undertone, "Think about taking over Charlie's practice," and squeezes his hand.

He hears a woman's voice, slightly flat and Brooklynized, with an overlay of dreamy poetry from much reading. He lounges in the doorway, leaning a little, eager despite himself for the sight of pale skin and wild red hair. Even for the sight of the wintry blue duffel coat — she hasn't noticed the approach of spring.

"I am sorry I am late!" Selig embraces Sylvia. "Though it is not possible really to be late for an ending, only a beginning. And I am here — you see — for that."

She pauses before Paul, who stands apart. "I took wrong turns in my car," she says. "And wrong turns in other ways."

He stares at her face, then stammers. "You — you can't think any of this — is my fault?"

"Now you will have a clear way that costs you nothing," she says quietly. Then, after a pause: "I have visited Amy."

He sighs. "How is she? I heard bitter."

"How should she be anything else? But when you are young, grief sometimes doesn't mark you."

He waits for more urging, one way or another, but Hannah is silent. He misses the moral prodding. Feels chilled, and says, meaningfully, "I guess I'll be leaving soon." But she, mistaking him, answers that she, too, will be leaving the Center. "I will come and go for a while only until Bunky can find someone."

Meanwhile, as she offers no ride, he struggles home by train and taxi. On a downtown street he is greeted by a flock of vultures with closed wings and hunched shoulders, their heavy heads sunk forward like Boss Tweeds of the bird world. They sit in driftwood trees, morose and single-minded — everyone carrion, no body tastier than any other — and stare at him in knowing, grim assembly.

A young man in faded denim pants and jacket attends them, his sun-bleached bangs raking his forehead. He is as cheerful as if he had created an aviary of singing canaries. The bodies are black mussel shells, he explains to a skeptical couple passing by. The wings are pairs of blue-tinted mussels, and the beaks are crab claws. His blunt-end, paint-and-glue-covered fingertips are pointing to his chart.

"Ribbed mussels, blue mussels, horse mussels, then rock crab and lady crab and green crab and fiddler crab and horseshoe crab."

"My God, why vultures?" Paul is peering, close up.

"They're maligned. They're misunderstood. What they really do is pick the world clean. They protect us."

Paul's heart pounds. Either he is encountering the Devil disguised as a smooth-faced, born-again beachcomber, or a true innocent — to him a vulture is the best of what a vulture does, a kind of ungainly nanny in a black apron. Does this sculptor leave the vulture-shudders to some other sculptor? Name of Bomstein?

An awful nostalgia fills Paul. For what — vultures? "All right. Okay. I see how well made they are." He backs away.

"It's not easy," their creator calls after him, "to get people to see them my way."

At home he finds a registered letter from Margaret's lawyer, informing him of Margaret's plans to remarry. Everything gives him a pang these days, so why shouldn't Margaret's marriage do that too? But at the same time he thinks how odd it all is, as if life is turning a page for him.

He thinks about stepping into the shoes of his hero, Charlie, who once had everything going for him, but who blew the whole thing.

Charlie's practice. Charlie's life. Charlie's girl? Bitter now. But maybe she won't be marked.

That night, his sleep is full of dreams. Charlie's father appears, shackled with chains, in a ridiculous parody of Old Marley's ghost. He clanks and cries, "Deliver me!" Paul watches while Charlie approaches. At a touch of the nozzle of the vacuum aspirator, the chains disappear. The old man then springs up, plucks at his wrist where the chains have galled a wound. He sprinkles Charlie with a few drops of blood and departs.

What is it? I want his father's blessing, too?

◆§ §◆

He keeps on — drilling at his job, turning off other people's children, taking his daughters to the park and to the movies and to Saturday afternoon concerts and musical comedies. He has got into the habit, after bringing them back to Margaret's, of drinking a glass of whiskey at home so that he can sleep, a thing he'd never had much trouble with before.

The women in the waiting room, ever-changing yet fixed, have sat all winter like a regiment in boots; now they thrust their bare toes into sandals. Seasons shift, and neither Selig nor Amy is here. A stout, sixty-year-old ex-nurse with gray hair expands inside her yellow uniform, replacing with double age and girth the two lost ones.

One night, Paul dreams of an old crone with a beautiful voice who, when he kisses her, turns into a lovely young princess. Who was that, he thinks when he wakes. Hannah, after years of childbearing at the community? Amy, dried like a prune after what's happened? And has he such great powers?

Another night he dreams again of a princess, this time without initiation fee. No more old crone. He sees her from behind, dressed in sparkling fairy-tale robes. But when she turns around, he sees that her face is plain.

"That's not so bad," he hears himself asonishingly say, "Goodness is beauty." That, he supposes, is Hannah. On the other hand, it could be Amy.

One morning at the Center, Bunky intercepts him. "Paul — I want to warn you so you'll know ahead of time . . . She's back."

"Hannah?"

"Amy."

Paul's heart begins to knock. "Is she so changed? Is that what the warning is about?"

Edgar edges away. His movements have grown heavier and slower since Charlie's death. He seems to flinch from Paul's excited questions.

"I meant — I know how attached you felt. I thought you'd like to be prepared . . ." He trails off.

"Prepared for what, for God's sake? Is she a man-eater? What is it?"

"Maybe I shouldn't have said anything." Abruptly, Edgar turns and walks off.

Paul finds her drinking a glass of milk in the lounge. She is wearing the trim canary-colored uniform, her hair in the same long loose braid, her gray eyes clear, her skin radiating its healthy strawberry tinge just above the rounded jaw line.

For a moment, he stands stunned in the doorway. What had they all been talking about — her grandmother? Matt? She is unaltered!

He sees, with a pang, how young she is. But he feels powerless to stave off his greed, since Fate has worked in his favor at last.

"You're back!" he cries.

"I couldn't stay away for long."

It is the same sweet smile.

He knows he should go easy, go slow, but he can't help

himself. She is looking at him clear-eyed, patient. He thinks how remarkable it is — the grandmother was entirely wrong. She had not lost a drop of her sweetness, her freshness. She is the same lovely girl, somehow — in spite of all the horrors.

He would like to say a mitigating word against any bitterness there might still be, but how can he? Suppose he tells her what he knows about her brother's role in goading Charlie? She might turn on him for maligning her brother.

He sees her lovely and restored. All that time I wooed her for Charlie, he says to himself — not a thought for me. It's my turn now. He is afraid someone will come out of the shadows and steal her from him. He talks swiftly.

"I'm sorry about everything that happened, Amy." The words rush out. "I know you can't — won't — open your heart so fast. All that pain — Charlie was my friend — He turned out to be a Class A bastard! Such a terrible thing, the insult, the harm. He cut himself out of you with his own hand!"

He smells the stench pouring from his mouth, but Amy gives him a very pure look of wonder and then reaches in among the garbage of his words and lifts out a question.

"Don't you really see it at all? Don't you understand, Paul — yet?"

"Of course I do."

"Why Charlie did what he did?"

"I know why. Of course — it's Charlie's tragedy too. His tragedy was that he let an idea, which at first was *for* human good, become more important *than* human good." He feels he is betraying his friend with some grandeur.

Tears creep to the brim of her lids. One emerges, slowly spills over her lid — a kind of tear-birth — and lowers itself, plump, full, down her cheek.

"It was in order not to pass on the loss. Not to stab his need into someone else's heart . . ."

"But your heart! What about your heart? What about your need, your loss?"

An inner tremor begins. Along the peristaltic walls. Then the pancreas seems to flutter, organs to leap from their accustomed places as if informed the old shelters are no longer sufficient. A new bedazzlement takes him. This power of women to forgive . . . !

At that moment, a familiar, yet to him astonishing, figure enters the room.

"Daniel! What are you doing here?"

"Hello, Uncle Paul." Daniel smiles handsomely and offers Paul a vigorous shake. "Bunky's letting me help out the orderlies and learn my way around during vacations."

In the most natural way, then, Daniel moves to Amy's side and places an arm about her shoulders.

"Without Daniel, I couldn't have recovered."

"Without Daniel?" He repeats it stupidly.

"When I wouldn't let him talk or sit with me, he sat with my grandmother. Once I threw a glass pitcher full of orange juice at him!" She leans up and kisses his forehead. "See a scar where it cut him, poor boy! But he always came anyway."

"Daniel came to see you?"

"Yes, every day. Little by little I got over it. Used to it, I suppose. I came back to life. I think because of Daniel. I thought about a lot of things while I was lying around the house, wanting to be dead." The husky clarity of Amy's voice and gaze holds no trace of self-pity. "I thought about how life sucks things out of you. Just like the Bianky Center. Life processes you, scours your insides. And life makes sure you give birth to no surprises. But why shouldn't we? Why shouldn't we, Paul? As long as they are surprises of the good sort, surprises that open the heart and the mind, the womb of our lives?"

Now it is Amy preaching at him. She might as well be Selig. *Selig?* He clutches at a vanished certainty. Then feels a groan being torn from him. But it is a wounded sneer instead that bursts from his lips: "You lost a baby and you found Daniel!"

They regard him without blame, like visitors to a sickroom. "It's true I'm a few years younger than Amy, Uncle Paul. But she was decades younger than my father."

"I think Paul means," Amy corrects him quietly, "that first I was with your father and now I'm with you and that can't seem right to him."

And first, he wants to sneer, *your brother pimped for you and now you're with your dead lover's son!*

But his feelings — jealousy, grief, loss, a terrible unforgiving self-reproach (Hannah! Hannah!) — are churning together too harshly for words.

"As lovers we may be unusual, but we're not immoral," Daniel says. He wears the gold-rimmed aviator glasses so favored by youth, and his handsome face is sober. He seems to climb up minute by minute to a responsibility beyond his years, taking upon himself the need to understand what Paul might feel.

"Maybe you think we're just being selfish in love without caring about obligations, Uncle Paul. Neither one of us wants that."

"Daniel is sharing his inheritance from his father," Amy says. "There's enough for both of us to go to medical school. I know my job at the Center is important, but I'd like to go on and study so I can do more. If I can prepare myself and get accepted . . ."

"Of course you can — you *will,* with all your training here," Daniel says proudly.

" — Then I'll be a doctor a few years earlier than Daniel. I'll open an office and later he'll join me. Obstetrics and gynecology — all aspects! But mainly I'd work with fertility." Pride battles modesty and sorrow, rushing red over her throat.

"Pretty dreams!" Paul hears his own voice sneering. "Too bad he's underage. His mother no doubt will have something to say!"

"To tell the truth, Uncle Paul, it's all mother's idea. She says she'd send herself to school too, if she were ten years younger. Mother's the one who's going to open an office for us."

"With a chair?" he mutters. "With an oak chair? And with a cushion? Oh!"

A furious longing seizes him for youth and altruism, so strong it brings him almost to the edge of fainting.

"Why couldn't it work?" The words burst from his lips in a kind of low moan. "Why won't life bear me up? When will I be happy?"

They all note now a swift movement of red-gold hair past the doorway.

"That's Hannah," Amy says. "I haven't told her yet . . ."

Her timing terrible as ever, Hannah bursts in.

"I came only to pick up my check — I heard you were here — I heard the news!"

She hugs Amy and Daniel and gives double-cheek kisses like a Lubavitcher at a *farbrengen*.

"Shall I tell you now that in the Bible there exists just such a case — only with differences — how a childless widow made herself into a harlot in order to have intercourse with her father-in-law because he withheld a son from marriage to her? That was Judah. It was Tamar who made herself a harlot. I hope" — she interrupts the excited recitation — "you will excuse this language!"

"Oh, Hannah!" — Amy, half-laughing, half-crying, hugs her friend — "I don't mind!"

The conflagration of Hannah's hair burns brightly beside her pale cheeks, but the excitement and fire of her speech have all burned out by the time she turns to Paul; nothing for him but ashes: "What cost you nothing brought nothing . . ."

Remarkable how the ache spreading over his entire thorax attaches itself to this, to Selig's leaving. He notices, quite dully, that Amy goes after her. Then Daniel begins.

"Uncle Paul, I can quote to you something my father said to me at a time when I could only think of my own unhappiness.

I think you heard it too, but you may not remember. He said that seeing someone else's happiness is reassuring. It means the possibility exists in the world even if it's not your turn right now. And I think, if you don't mind, Uncle Paul, I'll stop calling you uncle. I feel a bit old for that. You and I will be to each other whatever we create for ourselves from now on. You and I and Amy. Just like, for that matter, everyone else out there."

He shifts his gaze to the wall, sea-blue. Paul follows him there and beyond it, back of it, to the throng he can picture, the silent birth-blocked multitude that waits in honorable candor to surrender lives to which they can not offer life's due.

Something in his chest seems to give way at that, seems to burst an iron seam. Hannah! He sees her face in the distance like a pale gold coin. His head aches and he longs to place it in her lap — she stroking his brow and reading to him from her notebook, her version making sense of everything. Goodness streams from her like her red hair . . . Only, his body seems to be frozen in immobility as if he were a woman in the waiting room. Yet the more paralyzed his body becomes, the more feverish the activity in his brain.

Clear, Paul thinks. Everything is clear! The way as clear now as if a voice in the wings directed him. But where was this narrator before? Drowned under the clamor that said nothing was required of him, all was due to him. Multitudes of voices saying that. Yet all the while, those absolute tones were there, unaltered, like the deepest sostenuto at the bottom of a choral pile-up. Too late, as if a conductor had pointed his fingers, the upper voices are fading by groups. And there, all the while, is the underlying note.

But when at last he rushes out to the hall she is gone.

He finds Bunky. "Where's Hannah?"

Edgar jerks his thumb toward the elevator. "I suppose she took off. She only came for her check. Amy couldn't find her, either."

"Did she leave any message" — Paul has a sudden, desperate inspiration — "or a notebook for me?"

Bunky's look finally alters from impatience to sympathy. "No. She had it hugged up tight under her armpit when I saw her."

&§ ?»

"Bomstein, Bomstein! The book! The book!" Paul frantically cries it out when he finds her, boulderlike in her massive uniform.

"Hook? Why a hook? God," she says, "what's happened now?"

"*Book!*" He mouths it as if to a deaf person.

She stares unyielding at him.

"Your book, Bomstein," he pleads. "Merciless. Unrelenting. All our sins laid bare, but at least a point of view! I swear to you I won't complain . . ."

"My what? All your what?"

His frantic, inflated purposefulness begins to slowly sink as if air were being let out of it.

"Aren't you writing a book about us, Bomstein?"

She is galvanized into her lunch room brag.

"Oh, I could really write a book! The things I've seen. I'll write it all some day, I'll write it down!"

It dawns on him there is no book. Bomstein's book — is what they are living . . .

He runs to find Bunky again.

"Selig must have left something for me! A *leaf* from the notebook! For God's sake, Bunky, will you check your office?"

Edgar swears again there is no notebook. However, later he says there is a lumpy envelope addressed to Paul that he has overlooked.

5

HEARING EDGAR APPROACH, Paul quickly thrusts the little box under his sweater. Selig will be in trouble soon. At first, when he saw the paper-gray fist that matches the paper-gray fingers and toes in the assembly room, he marveled. How cleverly she had constructed it — an origami fetus hand! Then he sucked in his breath at the daring. Not paper!

Bunky would never forgive her for tampering. There might be some panic pretty soon around here. He can't stop to worry about that now. He feels pressed, pressed to move.

It pleases him to have made a kind of womb for it there under his shirt. The little quill seems to jab at his insides. Quickening. Prick of life. Gets him moving at last. He begins strolling past Bunky, toward the door.

"Where are you off to?" Edgar looks at him sharply. "Going out? Away? Leaving? I'm to count on no one then?"

He is not yet aware of how Ellen will sail to him over a sea of departing traffic, and feels for the moment bereft.

What can Paul say? Anything would be too complicated to utter now. And poor Bunky would get even more upset if Paul lifted his sweater to show him. But without the hand and the quill how can he begin to explain?

"Off to find Selig," he mutters, moving rapidly.

But where is Selig? Back with Rabbi Pinchas? Which Rabbi Pinchas? Suppose he can't find him? Where in New Jersey?

He thinks of that raw new settlement. Imagines woods and flooded roads and outdoor privies. Sweltering in summer, frigid in winter. Beards and babies their specialty. The men grow one, the women the other. He sees himself there — in the settlement. He is delivering those babies by the dozens, in the cold and ill-lit bedrooms, on the kitchen tables.

"Busy morning till night till morning again! Runs all the time!"

Could he do that? Why not — if Hannah's there? He could! He could! He only has to tell her that he is not for Amy and Amy is not for him. And that this decision became absolutely his free choice the moment he understood that it had already become fact, with an epistemological rightness he would defend to the death.

But first, because the little hand that writes has prodded him into reading his own aspirations, he goes to find Amy and Daniel, to give them his blessing.

"Life should give birth to surprises!" He kisses Amy on each healthy daughter-cheek. "Wonderful, loving surprises like yours!"

Daniel he hugs, fatherly, about his broad shoulders. "Son — you opened the womb of the heart!"

Afterward, crossing the waiting room, Paul sees Mary, Warner, and Bomstein, all coming from different directions. He waves a farewell to each, and they, not suspecting that he is about to give birth to a new self, hardly in their hurry signal anything back.

❦

Warner, Mary, and Bomstein, crisscrossing the waiting room from different directions, all catch sight, at the same moment, of the woman they had once believed was Genevieve X.

Though her last painful visit was a while ago, it would be hard not to recognize her. She enters wearing the same smartly cut plum-colored suit she had worn before, but flamboyantly this time, calling out over the heads of the waiting women to the receptionist at the desk, "Anybody find a beret" — she taps her shoulder, reaching across her breast with a long and graceful finger — "about this color?"

The receptionist having rummaged in a drawer and then handed her a maroon pancake, she flaps it jauntily in the direction of the silent, seated throng, who follow with their eyes.

"Good luck!" She cries it out to them all.

Her slender high-heeled feet seem to dance over the carpet, her body to float over her shoes. No one can doubt that she rejoices to be free of a burden. Yet even the shrewdest guessers among those who watch her now cannot imagine what that burden could have been, or the relief she feels that makes it possible for her to return to this place to fetch her hat. She had let time pass so it could all sink in, and so that other thing could sink in, too — the telephone call to Brody.

"It's over," she had said.

"Good enough," Brody replied. "Nothing to it, like I told you, babe."

She had nearly choked with disgust. "That's not what I mean is over. That happened weeks, *weeks* ago. I never told you when it was and you thought so little about it that you never asked. You don't see me enough to know my dates."

"What the hell, baby — you blaming me?"

"Nobody's blaming you. I'm talking about feelings. That's all we ever had between us, right, was feelings?"

"I feel the same as I always did, babe. I love you. You can't tell me that was such a big-deal thing that it went and changed all your feelings!"

"I am just telling you what I found out. Now *you* think about it. What's over is us . . ."

Now she dances, positively dances her light body over the carpet and into the elevator and out — free! — into the street. It is not the child gone from her she celebrates. She knows it — that is a sadness that will never leave her, as if sadness replaced the stuff that was sucked out. But oh, oh! — to be shed of the tormenting man!

ᴥᖶ ᖲᴥ

Amy and Daniel, drawn at first by an outcry in the assembly room, remain behind after the others have left. They embrace and passionately kiss, leaning against a counter on which fetal parts are neatly bagged and labeled.

Boyer, unnerved by the hullabaloo, returns and shoos them out.

"Of all places to make love," she complains to Gen-Lee, who comes in a moment later. "But nothing stops lovers, I know that. Garbage bags or satin sheets, it's all the same! I could write a book about lovers," she says bitterly.

Gen-Lee smiles his friendly smile. "We all could write such a book. Garbage bag, satin sheet. Dead body, sickness, confusion, war. Nothing stop anybody. It really is the same in Korea or China — you know?"

6

WHILE SHE CLIMBS the stairs to her hallway, Selig thinks about how Paul will open the envelope. There had been so little time in which to do everything.

In the assembly room she had told Boyer, the nurse in charge then, that a phone call had come for her. With Boyer gone, she lifted up a tiny fist. Then she had to hurry. In Edgar's closet she snapped a single corn straw from his clothes whisk. Between thumb and forefinger of the tiny right hand — the skin wrinkled and gray — she fixed the quill. The corn straw from the clothes closet, the small rectangle cut from a sheet of paper on the desk, the clip box from Edgar's drawer. She inserted the paper, the fist, the straw. She thought the fist looked calm, mature, judgmental. She was satisfied that it gave the impression of a hand that wrote, that recorded. She placed the whole thing then in an envelope addressed to Paul.

Going home now, she thinks about Paul opening that. How will he take it — her last message? There will be no more from her now, because she is leaving; there will be only Bomstein's book. She is seized with terrible foreknowledge of the loss she will feel when she is finished with message-sending. No more to Paul. No more to Rabbi Pinchas and the community in New Jersey. All the retained messages will be a kind of acid burning away within, hollowing out her life.

At the end of her hallway, Hannah sees José's figure in the shadows. He is watching Sorita's babies, scattered over the hallway and stairs.

"Today I am saying goodby, José," she calls out. He casts a frightened look at Sorita's door and breaks into unaccustomed, raspy speech: "You gon to wait to tell her, no?"

"Oh, yes, I will."

She unlocks her own door and enters. One battered suitcase will serve. She will not need very many things from home. A picture of her father and mother dressed in Shabbos clothes for the photographer, he seated, she standing, her anxious hand working at his twisted collar — and the collar and the hand blurred. No more notebooks. She must contrive to find some wrapping for them now and mail them off to the community in New Jersey, this long letter to them about her life in the world. Without surprise, they will pronounce her life a failure: How could they imagine that it might have turned out otherwise? The rest — the old, serviceable clothing.

After a while Sorita knocks. They have a brief conversation, they embrace, Hannah gives her keys, Sorita leaves. Hannah attempts to go on with her packing but feels so tired suddenly that she throws herself on the big broken bed in the bedroom and is at once asleep, imprisoned in a dream of terror.

She dreams that she is walking down the hallway of a house in a strange city. She turns a key in an apartment door and feels a man's embrace from behind. With his powerful arms he grips her about the neck, cutting off her breath. She cannot cry out. And besides, no one will know her or answer her cry. Who, among strangers, would hear her, or run down the stairs to aid her if they heard?

He forces her inside, this unknown man who waits in some distant city, from the little entranceway straight into the kitchen and then, by shifting the pressure on her throat, down onto her knees. With the other hand he grabs her hair and pulls her head up. Then, still pulling her hair, he releases her throat and steps in front of her. He has opened his pants and wants her to put her face inside. All this she recognizes, having read of such forcings in the magazines on Forty-second Street.

She tries to call up to him. He holds tightly to her hair and stretches her neck back so that she cannot speak. From the pocket of his pants, with his free hand, he removes something and shows it to her. A knife.

She wakes in terror. What is in store, in strange cities? The little hand she sent to Paul now seems to write her own fate. What she had wanted to tell is that all acts are judged — to remind him of that. But also to remind that his life is not yet finished, not sealed — still being written: he can free himself, under the very point of the pen that harrows his skin, onto a fresh page, a new entry, a redeemed life.

Will he see that? Or will he only see — the thought makes her heavy and sad — a parody of notebook-keeping? So that he will wonder at the sense of it — a mad girl who mocks herself?

Again her eyelids drop. Now behind her shut eyes, a miraculous scene. Mama and Papa stroll along the streets of the new community with Rabbi Pinchas. He talks excitedly — about her, she knows. She hurries to join them. Why should she not explain herself in her own words? But only Rabbi Pinchas possesses the power of speech.

She has the happy thought that her parents can read her notebook and understand everything. But when she looks, it is gone. She sees it in the distance on a muddy road, trampled under heavy shoes. She screams silently for Paul, who comes running. He heals the throats of her parents. Now they are all about to walk under the wedding *chupah*. It collapses and falls, crashing like chunks of stone to wake her.

Is Rabbi Pinchas really there? She sees him, real and solid, his blackness welcome as light — a burly man who seems strong, though he pants for breath, often, as if he had had a heart attack once, or smoked too many cigarettes. She had said to him, "I won't be back. This can't be my life anymore." He had answered with one of his coaxing jokes (oh, there was no end to the number of variations he could make on his one theme of remember your father and mother): "So then when I have to go to the city, I'll pick myself up and I'll visit you."

She hears him panting hoarsely — the effort it must have cost him to come! She seems to see him whirling now about her kitchen, beard flying, heavy black shoes skidding and scuffing, like some ancient, exorcist rabbi . . .

The rabbi and José are locked in an embrace, whirling about her kitchen, uttering hoarse grunts. Why? Is this a dream too?

Throwing in hasty armloads, she snaps the suitcase shut, lifts it off the bed, and moves past the struggling men, their eyes shut with awful effort. A knife glints and spins on the kitchen floor, as unreal as the scuffling shoes and the grunts of the men. Yet the knife and the shoes and the grunts are all real. Before she is aware that she is thinking it, she has already had this thought: Surely the knife will never be used on either one? Surely God will provide the rabbi's ram?

She stands a moment in the shadow of her doorway, while the men, blind and deaf, whirl and scuffle. At least, then, until the ram arrives . . . She stoops and lifts the knife from the floor and leaves it, safely tucked in the pages of her notebook on a table beside the refrigerator.

Then she wants to cry out, Oh, stop! Stop! to the men. But if they stopped what would she say to them? It would be impossible to say anything. They are locked in enmity as if Israel and Ishmael have been brought face to face before her. Each of you is my friend, she could say. But sadness, lassitude, the thought of her journey silence her.

As if she herself is a dream image, she passes unseen

through the front door and down the stairs, quickly. At the corner of her street she turns back. A cab has pulled up before her door. Out bursts Paul — running, running for the stairs. How angry he must be! Running in anger to confront her with her own message to him. He has felt nothing but anger for her for so long. Yet suddenly she feels a small smile begin at the corner of her mouth. How beautifully Paul's anger carries the rabbi's ram upon its back! No harm will come to either of the men who struggle in her apartment. Great emotion builds itself inside her chest at this idea. She feels the linkage of life — how desire and act in each individual affect the survival of every other.

She raises her hand in farewell to Paul, who has already disappeared into the house, and with the same gesture hails the cab, which slides along the curb until the door handle reaches her hips.

As she opens and enters, banging the old suitcase against the seat, she feels a startling release of pleasure. This setting out on her travels! This adventure that she had so often promised herself when a girl!

The cab moves toward Manhattan and Grand Central Station. She will adventure first in stages — train, not plane. Hannah reflects with further pleasure on that last-minute reflex in her room: she had packed the remainder of her best new clothes, Paul's gifts. Fine, even ceremonious clothing! Despite the battered suitcase — perhaps she will buy a new one — she will not go forth as a mendicant. She ought not!

In the women's lounge at Grand Central, the attendant helps her out with coins for the dressing room. When Hannah emerges, the attendant sees an impeccably dressed woman: soft-haired tweed suit under a topcoat of light, supple wool, neat pumps and a polished leather shoulder bag. Except for a slight imbalance in the matching of wool weight with warming weather. Oblivious of the tilt of the seasons at best, and always a bit on the chilly side anyway, Hannah carries the wool suit and topcoat with an elegance that would have made Paul proud if he could have seen her.

Hannah washes her hands with the small cut of white soap that the woman carefully places on the sink for her, then turns to put money in a dish on a counter. The attendant is a peaceful-faced elderly black woman with a slow, off-center walk, who has taped to a wall news items of mankind's help — acts of rescue from near-drownings, from burning buildings; recovery of lost relatives embracing under the beaming smiles of airline personnel. Hannah feels a surge of recognition, as if they might have met before. "Thank you, thank you!" she cries.

She then walks eagerly into the resounding space of the great hall, under the arching constellations. High up on one wall the names of cities turn themselves over like cards as if for her delight. She hears the slight shuffle-clatter of the spinning letters above the general low-booming noise. A smell of smoking cheese strudel wafts like gauze and evaporates; a peppered pizza drives a spear of scent past the nose, then drops. What endure are the odors of arrival and departure, high, crisp, pervasive — leather, wool, fur, cold — in this perpetual, moving, self-replenishing world where joy and despair are trussed for travel and must wait to be unpacked elsewhere.

She feels her heart expand like some warm, delicious fruit. She imagines that her spine, flexible and young, is strengthened with sweet-smelling sheaves of willow. She sees now what the ancients had meant by that: her own being will be a stopping place for her in her dangerous and desirable journey . . .

High in the air the letters spin and permutate, all intelligence in their combining.

A young man carrying a potted palm from florist to train track moves ahead of her. The broad leaves nod and spread their cloud of color; the trunk holds itself firmly upright, a pillar.

Smiling, she follows. These echoes, she thinks. This light from stars already extinguished, these accidents, aping portents! Yet how seductive they still are. How expectant she feels, how eager!

Now and then she looks about, as if she might still see Paul running to join her. . . .

She boards her train.

7

GOING TOWARD the elevator, Paul suddenly broke through his mind set. Why insist on imagining that Hannah has returned to New Jersey? Why not to her apartment in Brooklyn? He can try there, can't he? Not telephone — she might not answer. Simply go, as she had once in the old days simply come to his apartment — arrived — risking that he might not be there or might turn her away. All the way down, crowded among women leaving the Center, Paul held against his belly the embryonic fist safe in its little box.

In the street, Paul was startled to come upon an ugly scene. An unknown man with a cap pointed to him and snarled, *"He's from there!"* Two other men and two women, raising signs, then began to scream "No more murder!"

Paul ran, holding his belly. At the next street, he flagged traffic for a taxi. "Between you and the pregnant woman over there," the cabby drawled, "I decided you look closer to due date."

Climbing the stairs to Hannah's apartment, Paul braces himself. Suppose she has really disappeared? To some hidden place? He feels, at the thought, a depth of sadness that shocks and terrifies him. The sadness he has felt till now has had a false bottom. Suddenly it opens downward.

He stops on the stairs, dragged. Gravity has increased its pull by a ton. He hangs on to the cold, greasy bannister and tells himself, cajolingly, as if he were his own child, that no one can really disappear forever. Though he remembers that his life has been full of such disappearances, and that probably, with the exception of his father (and maybe even there, even there!), he has been in some part responsible for them, he goes on.

Up and up he climbs, through sickening smells, dampness, dark rotted halls whose walls sprout a fungus of curse words, runny names, swastikas. His heart feels near to bursting with pain at the sight of this dimness and filth — nothing of this had entered his consciousness before — through which Hannah had walked each day toward him, offering love.

To calm himself while he climbs, he thinks about where he will go, in case he can't find her right away. He fingers in his pocket the clip box that holds the tiny bit of protoplasm and that before this had been clutched to his belly. Why not, then? Go off to some small town somewhere — South or West — where the state fathers were even now grimly decreeing that no woman could have an abortion just because she wanted or needed it. She'd have to be dying first, and have a note from her doctor saying so. He would be that doctor. He'd write the note and then he'd do it. For whatever the patient could pay. If nothing, nothing. If there were no Medicaid funds, he'd manage without them. He would work so honorably and openly that no one in the state would touch him. The police, in gratitude, would bring their own daughters to him. They would help him in his search for Selig, tap along the network of police hotlines from city to city. When Hannah next beheld him she'd find — with joy, he knew — a changed man. He would free himself from the pages of Bomstein's book, that damned scoresheet of botched reality — it exists! He would become worthy of Hannah's notebook's finest aspirations for him!

Karen and Helene would be sad. They'd be losing the old daddy at the very moment, he supposed, they were gaining the new one. But they would have more than Saturday afternoon musicals to talk about when they grew older.

"Remember when Daddy went away?" They'd recount it to each other. "It was to take risks for women. And the whole human race got better."

For a moment he has an almost giddy perception, as if drunk, of the conflict of his two dreams. First as deliverer, then as suppressor — of a million babies! How could either way ever get him out of Bomstein's book?

Never mind that! he tells himself. Now he's flying up the stairs, three at a leap. His head is light, he realizes that he's almost hyperventilating. Never mind if these thoughts are oxygen-crazed. He rises on them, soars up freed from the pages of Bomstein's book like some Kabbalistic spirit ascending from letters of ink.

Selig's door anticipates his arrival — like the gate of heaven, it stands open for him. Breathing hard, his vision blurry, he's unable at first to take in the scene before him.

It is a bizarre sight. A stout bearded man wearing black hat and coat, struggles, with forehead purple, to hold by the lashing arms another man who, in shirt and trousers only and though small, is fiercely fighting. The two — big bearded one and thin wire-muscled one — careen around the room, knocking against chairs and walls and emitting short, anguished grunts.

"*Gevalt!*" the bearded man gasps at the sight of Paul.

"*Ayuda!*" calls the other.

Two intruders?

Paul looks bewilderedly around, sees with joy that Hannah's notebooks are on the table, so she can't have left, but where is she? That odd gleaming point that protrudes from one notebook — he with horror understands it now — a knife! He springs forward to grab it and shoves the wicked blade between the two men. The wiry one subsides at once, freezes rigid against the wall. With a groan, the other totters to a chair somewhere behind Paul. He hears it creak under the man's weight.

"Vey is mir," he moans.

"What in God's name is happening here?" Paul holds the knife, wavering, pointing at no one. "Where's Hannah?"

"Geshtorben die meydele." The old man weeps.

His breath held in fear, Paul backs up until his vision is in line with the refrigerator. He flinches, expecting to see a bloody figure slumped — but there is nothing.

The small wiry man begins to spray out an excited jumble of broken language from against the wall. "I see he push — he go in. I come help — she ees no here!"

"He came to help Hannah?" The bearded man shakes his head bitterly. "God should help her from such help — with *knives* they help!"

"Where is she?" Paul asks the wiry man. "Who are you?"

He shrugs sullenly. He demands his knife. "That belong to me!" He saunters out, exaggerating slow steps, when Paul refuses.

Paul sees a pregnant woman with a baby in her arms peeping around the door jamb. "You know me!" he cries. "I'm Hannah's friend. Where is Hannah?"

Sorita shakes her head and looks with sudden attention at her baby.

"For God's sake, she'd *want* me to know," Paul cries. He advances on the woman, who retreats, then pelts him suddenly with words.

"She take a suitcase. She din' tell me where she's goin'. She give me the key, her car, everythin'. She pay her rent till two months, leave all the furniture in the whole place to me — " She looks as if she thinks she will not be believed. "She say I

can sit here by myself sometimes before I sell it. I must have
leave the door unlock, this guy come and push himself in! So
then José . . ."

The bearded man's chest still heaves.

"My God — that's José? Took a suitcase where?"

She shrugs.

"She left a message for me, then! Paul? Paul? You can trust
me!"

But Sorita will only silently regard her baby.

"I am Elias Pinchas." The bearded man's breath comes
painfully back. "If you are who I think you are — I ask you"
— he spreads a trembling hand over the bone button at the
breast of his black overcoat — "save at last — this poor girl's
life!"

❧ ☙

At one in the morning his phone rings. He springs to answer,
but it is not Hannah. It is Ellen, weeping and nearly incoher-
ent, though he has a second's wild mad hope that she is Hannah in disguise, putting on Ellen's accent as she had once put
on Sorita's, as Matt put on Joe's. But it is really Ellen.

"The bastards — they finally did it — Edgar's already there
— go there, Paul! I'm getting dressed, my fingers won't move
— Edgar's there alone — he wouldn't wait for me. Oh, Paul,
it's like a death!"

❧ ☙

Edgar keeps smelling something delicious. It is there, among
the other odors, the delicious smell. If it is not madness, then
he thinks it must be the smell of all the fruit in all the bowls,
baking. There is a sweet aroma of cooked apples and pears and
bananas, rising up like a last hosanna from the Center, of
which nothing will be left. It will all go. The rooms gutted and
blackened, the equipment melted down in the flames, amid the
blare and stench and the insane, consuming wildness of the fire.

He is nearly blinded with smoke and tears. Is roughly pushed back, back, behind the barricades, by the firemen who wearily tramp through the doors of the building, beneath the ladders scaled to the seventh floor. A long pink suction tube has wrapped itself about the black boot of the fire captain, and trails like an umbilical cord as he approaches Edgar. "You run this place?" He looks so weary and grim that Edgar thinks he is going to shout "Good! This filthy hole will burn to the ground!" Instead he says, "I'm sorry to tell you the damage is pretty total. Whenever it's incendiary like that it's hard to control. The machinery's all wrecked. The place is a mess. Of course you got to be glad they picked the nighttime to do it — nobody got hurt. But I call it a goddamned shame. You people did a decent job here. The daughter of a friend of mine, I know, came here."

Edgar thinks wearily that it was probably the fireman's own daughter. He looks at the crowd. How many of their daughters, too?

Extension ladders crank up, wobbling. Firemen are hurling chairs through smashed windows to the roped-off sidewalk seven stories below.

"My God, look at the furniture they had in there!" a man on the sidewalk comments to his neighbor. "They certainly made it nice and comfortable! If it was up to me I'd tell those women to find some back alley to do their dirty business in. That's what they'll have to do now. I don't hold with violence at all. But I can tell you I see why the people who threw this bomb got ticked off. It turns my stomach!"

The woman beside him turns with a look of loathing. "And if it was *your* daughter, would you say that?"

"I don't *have* a daughter."

"You don't have a *mind* or a *heart!*" the woman says through gritted teeth.

"What happens now, Bunky?" Paul asks over the turmoil of the engines and the crashing and the shouts and the droned instructions of the fire captain to the men aloft on the ladders.

Edgar turns reddened eyes. His head thrusts itself from the turned-up collar of his raincoat. There is the suggestion of a pajama shirt below. His feet, beneath hastily pulled-on trousers, are thrust into moccasins, sockless. His head swings from side to side like the head of a wounded bull.

"I'll start again."

"Will you, Bunky? Really?"

Edgar shudders. "Smaller scale." He shudders again, convulsively shaking. Paul thinks of Humphrey Bogart in *The African Queen*, shuddering with revulsion and walking into the leech-filled water a second time.

"Just not so grand-scale this time, that's all!" Edgar says. His fists are bunched inside his coat pockets. "Maybe the numbers will diminish. Maybe no more millions. Maybe only thousands. Then hundreds. Then none. Maybe some drug company will come up with something that will work without damaging tissue. Maybe sex education in schools will start to make a difference. Maybe people will start to change . . ."

Edgar seems suddenly to see him. "You'll be all right, Paul. You can step into Charlie's practice. I can arrange something for you at another clinic. When I'm ready I'll want you back with me . . ." He has to shout, over the noise. Tears are pouring down his cheeks.

"Thanks, Bunky, thanks very much. Don't trouble your mind with that now. I'll — we'll talk about this later."

He sees Ellen pushing through the crowd, weeping. Paul pushes toward her and embraces her, then makes a way for her to Bunky.

Ellen pulls away from him and reaches out for Edgar.

◄§ §►

Paul walks along Forty-second Street. He thinks of Bunky, nobly wishing himself out of business. But then, Bunky may not have read the movie marquees lately, may not have seen these crowds walking with Paul.

The streets are thronged with men and women, boys and girls. They look incredibly young to him. The boys are almost smooth-skinned. The girls — the girls are all Maria — high heels, tight jeans, short nylon or fake leather or painted satin jackets. Their long hair is streaked blond, the front curled back like a ruff about the face. Or cut boyish-fifties-short and plastered smooth, some with a dye of yellow at the brow. Hours and hours spent on hair-processing. Beads and bangles woven in, too. When they stand still they do narrow dance steps, stamp their heels and shiver. They are cold, cold, seeking heat somewhere within the society that makes hot sex endlessly available to the young but that freezes them — freezes them all the same.

What would Charlie say about Bunky's noble dream? Charlie would say that if the number of teen-age abortions goes down it won't mean the world is getting wiser. It will mean they're keeping them, making babies some kind of teen-age badge of attainment.

❦

The place stripped, Sorita standing among the empty rooms in a stretched red sweater that does not reach the waistband of her purple slacks, the fingers of her left hand clutching at one inflamed cheek, as if she's been slapped: one week after Hannah's leaving, there is still no word for Paul, and now no Hannah's furniture, either.

Now that it's gone, he sees it vividly — massive and old, with a medallion of pale crackling veneer at the center of each drawer and of the bed's headboard, like circlets of faded cemetery flowers. The floorboards are gouged, as if human life could bite like an ax into wood. The removal of the furniture strikes at his heart with all the stunning melancholy of a magician's pass — vanished! Water drips from the kitchen faucet with the starved insistence of an abandoned animal. Otherwise, silence. The floors rake to the open door like a chute down which all life has swept. The small, shabby rooms shout their emptiness. He sees, smells, hears — as in the roar of an empty seashell — how great was the force with which Hannah filled them.

Meanwhile, Sorita is weeping. "My man took all the money, too!" But Sorita has in her possession a treasure beyond price, which she shows to Paul. A postcard from Hannah, whose swift hand penned a single line: "God bless your new child."

Heart hammering, Paul scrutinizes the postmark, almost obscured by thick cancelation lines. "Cleveland, Ohio? For God's sake, *that's* her idea of a place to go? Did she say she was heading west? *West?* If you help me I can help her!" It's become reflexive for Paul to ask Sorita questions she can't or won't answer. But this time Sorita, after casting a heartbroken look about the empty rooms and then giving him a deep stare, at last nods yes — yes, west.

On the card's obverse side a thick red column rises into a spacious sky: "The Old Shot Tower." He wonders for a second whether Hannah might possibly have seen the joke of choosing, for an emblem, this other proliferator of messages. No — not possible; so why should he?

"I hope," he says gravely to Sorita, "Hannah will put a lantern for me in the tower."

◦§ ৡ৯

Ellen rips and centers and rips again the notes and envelopes. She fills a wastebasket with them. Then she sits at her desk and, with the same concentration she bends upon her test tubes and x-ray films, she begins to decipher a way.

My good man Edgar! My good man Edgar! She has always known he is that. She wants to retreat from these random sexual episodes. Boring. They've become boring.

At the thought of Edgar and the terrible fire, a long, sharp pain cuts through her upper body. She feels it in Edgar-language: it is a musical pain, a coloratura attack, with trills, above a diffuse, menstrual, alto ache of the lower part. Extraordinary — how the events of the past weeks, which have brought Edgar back to her, his very way of thinking, have also brought back menstruation, as if her body must be young and energetic now, ready to begin again. She thinks of it that way — energy, not children. She has no more desire for a child now — hers or anyone else's — than she did when she and Edgar had first married and pledged childlessness to one another.

She begins to doodle a headless figure — torso and legs only. In response to the coloratura pain, she fills in rippling lines across the chest. Guided by the alto ache below, her pencil scores dark vertical strokes at the groin. When she becomes aware of her drawing, she sees she has achieved an odd female figure — modest lace at the bosom, combined with bold pubic bareness. Which is — *what?* Emblem of some tragic split? But why tragic? Rich duality, perhaps, problematic only if so perceived.

At that moment, it comes to her that she could arrange her workdays so that, if she planned efficiently, a taxi could zip her up to Edgar's new Center — wherever it might be — at lunch times and back to her own hospital. She would be on hand to do biopsic analysis of the extracted tissue. It could be an extra service provided by the new Center — wherever it might be. Edgar had often said he wished it could be done. Nothing would make him happier! Nothing could reassure him more about how she spends her time!

She thinks further, moves her pencil rapidly. She realizes that she would in essence be holding two jobs. At that thought, she feels positively uplifted — eager, zestful!

With her pencil she has reproduced, now quite consciously, several of these little female figures, but more and more abstractly. Finally there are only three wavy horizontal lines above four bold downward strokes — a flat pattern that she continues to see in its vertical arrangement, only the design she is making now appears to be the surface of a playful sea over fathomless dark depths.

Two jobs! Two jobs! How could she so have misunderstood herself! What she ought from the first to have sought out for her salvation was not the moonlight of secret sex, but of secret work!

She draws a broad moon over the surface of the sea that plays upon the dark depths.

8

HANNAH'S NOTEBOOK. It is one of the first things Paul unpacks when he arrives at a hotel or inn.

Even when he tries, he can never feel proper remorse for having stolen it from the community. Hannah had written across the top of the first page that it was for them. But without it he felt he might not be able to go on living. That was important, wasn't it — the moral obligation to sustain life? His need of it was greater than theirs.

Besides that, he had an excuse, a reason. Now the first words out of his mouth could be "Hannah, I found your notebook!" When he finds Hannah.

Sometimes Paul curses himself for looking so long. Sometimes he thinks he sees her. Sometimes he has to come up close before he is disappointed. He is traveling west. And cursing himself each time he is disappointed. But other times he feels great hope that he will find Selig. He sees other women better-looking and, God knows, better-dressed. But it is only Hannah he wants. Only Hannah can give him the feeling that his real self, asleep for so long, is now awake.

As he travels west through cities, through the most densely populated parts, taking short-term jobs in local family planning clinics if there are any, or health clinics if there aren't, always he hopes to find on the staff a slim pale beauty whose crisply waving red hair rises layer on layer till it stands out from the sides of her head like wings. Botticelli angels had such hair.

Being willing to work odd hours, having no private practice or life to press demands on him, Paul is instantly employable on any clinic staff. The question of how Hannah fares, with no credentials of any sort, often fills him with anguish. Can she find the only work she knows? But then how does the rest of her life go? She will search out the library and read there. But she is on the move and can hardly build much comfort about herself. She hasn't, to sustain her, Paul's own sense of running, arms outstretched, after the thing he most wants in life — which is to begin his life. When is life truly, viably life — at thirty-eight? Forty-eight? He will begin his life when he is united with Hannah and so with himself.

He pictures the bright rays of her hair moving westward like a sun. Is she completing her education, like any ordinary mortal, seeing America? Or taking another kind of journey, hoping to encounter again, in some lonely pass, her old, thrilling adversary? Or leading *him* on a journey? Teaching Paul Sunshine how to travel through the world — light, compassionate, dedicated?

Or sometimes he pictures Hannah stationary — an archangel at the gate to paradise. She brandishes a sword to keep him out because he has, unbelievably, broken the only promise there was to keep, but it is the same flashing sword that marks the way back.

Wherever she is, is Eden.

The clinics where he finds work often fall sadly short of Edgar's vision, though many are clean and correct and sometimes even employ people of compassionate sympathies, so that the women upon whom they perform their services do not seem to them like so many butcher shop loins of meat to be processed with impunity under the law. Such medical practitioners and attendants do not appear to feel they are working on boring assembly lines, evacuating and deconstructing worthless trash. Instead, they seem capable of believing that each fetus unblessed into life is a sacred promise to the generations: "That you may enter a fuller (because less crowded with the emotionally crippled) humanity." His standard now, for the best, is a place where, among those who work with most passion and dedication, there is still no hint of the arrogant ideologue who says, "I will *impose* this on you because I know better than you how to live your life." And "choice," that simple lovely word in which echoes the sound of "rejoice," is truly in practice.

Now he is fairly into the Midwest — and no Hannah Selig listed with any telephone information he has consulted between here and New York. Soon he will be coming to the rusting chastity belt of the United States, the grim badlands where a woman is punished for her sins in the grand old style. If she is poor and ignorant, there is no hope for her — she goes down in shame and delivers her child into a legacy of ignorance, poverty, and the sum of the two, violence. If she is determined to free herself at all costs from her trap, then she submits herself to mutilation, as the trapped animal will gnaw off its own leg to be free.

Sometimes at night he walks past the local downtown movie houses and bars, and recognizes Forty-second Street — jackets, jeans, boots, shirts, hair styles, all interchangeable. Teen-agers dance the same freezing street-corner dance — stamp! stamp! turn and stamp! Or they snatch an hour's warmth in the movie houses, little Paolos and Francescas, who do not read about love, but who watch love being made. After the movie, the fifteen-year-old boy with the carefully combed wave over his forehead and the dark-haired girl with the platinum roll at her temple snatch another hour's warmth in the back of someone's car, and neither of them suggests the use of a contraceptive, for that would mean premeditation, a whole system of morals other than the one they think they live by.

As Paul arrives at each new city he carefully prints his address on a postcard with a colorful picture on it: "The Capitol Building in the City of M —— "; "A busy intersection in downtown P——." He addresses the card to Sorita, in Hannah's old building. Always the message is the same: "If you hear from Hannah, tell her I am here." He blesses the practicalness of Hannah's concerns — what greater priority for a message-sender than to have taught a nonreader to read?

In city after city Paul opens, at night after work, the door of the small furnished apartment he rents near the local family planning center. Sometimes it happens. Then he almost feels more than hears it: a shudder passes upward from the sole of his foot, there is a faint movement of paper beneath his shoe. Trembling in every limb he bends to the carpet to retrieve the folded note and opens it to read that there is to be no hot water. Or elevator service.

One day without warning he catches a glimpse of Hannah standing at the curb only yards ahead of him. He sprints madly along the crowded sidewalk and then, just before the bus pulls up, he catches her around the waist from behind — feels her slender body again in his arms, presses his lips against the back of her head where some springy wisps of red hair peep from under a beret of brilliant yellow (who else would wear it?), and cries, "I've got you!" He hears a tremulous moan, and then a terrified face strains itself about, with an inch of white hair showing at the tam's rim. He backs off, runs, the woman's terror digging so deep into him that it feels like the spur of his own panic.

Yet it is only weeks later that he retrieves a note from under his door and reads, "What might we all be . . . ?" His heart nearly stops at the sight of Hannah's tiny, all-generous script. There is no signature, no address. It is as if she had taken up an old and irresistible habit, but had then lost heart and broken off. Two days after that he sees her, in the very clinic where he works. On a fragile hunch he had rearranged his schedule, and arrives there at an unexpected hour. She is so startled when he comes rushing at her in the vestibule that she drops a clipboard and, still dressed in the aide's white jacket, turns and runs through the opposite door. She runs, he runs.

"Hannah, Hannah!" He speeds after, crying recklessly through the corridors, "I am for you! It's not because I couldn't have Amy! Stay and yell at me — anything — but don't disappear! What might I be, Hannah, with you!"

It's no use. She vanishes from the building, the street, and, for all he knows, from the city of M——. He senses that she has moved on. But was it Hannah at all? Scared out of her wits and never came back — it could have been anyone. Even, the director of the clinic finally convinces him, the redheaded Irish girl who had actually worked there, not Hannah in disguise.

Thereafter, though, a new element enters into his pursuit of Hannah. Now when he arrives at a city, moves from hotel to apartment, and takes up a job at a clinic, he leaves careful instructions with the person at the switchboard. "Give my address to anyone who asks for me. Here, I'm putting it in writing: 'Dr. Sunshine's address not to be withheld.' " That's in addition to the mailed-out messages, one to Karen and Helene, the other to Sorita.

Now in each city where he makes such an arrangement, messages arrive. Sometimes they repeat the messages of old: "What might we all become . . . ?" Or they are new and cryptic. Yet he feels that if only she would explain the context, he could understand.

When the messages stop for as long as a month, he knows it is time to move on. There are no peaks or valleys to the graph of their travels, his and Hannah's. They make a blade-straight incision, more or less, across the belly of America, keeping to the capital cities. Where will Hannah travel after she has reached the sea? South? Toward the fertile groin of America and back to the East again, weaving her thread of promise? He will follow.

He has shamelessly taken to mailing money orders to Sorita, which he encloses in envelopes along with the illustrated cards. "Rent a room in someone's apartment," he prints, "so you can be alone when you need to be." "Buy yourself a table and set of chairs." "Tell Hannah I will always register at a clinic so she can find me. Tell Hannah where I live, so I can help her." Help *her?* If he told the truth, he would sound like Rabbi Pinchas. "Tell Hannah to let me find her so she can save at last this poor boy's life!"

Now and then there enters into his imagining of Hannah not the frugal saintly life of the Williamsburg message-sender, but something flamboyant. He sees her as the traveling factotum attached to a mystical rock singer who takes her red-gold hair to be a sign of special luck or favor. So vivid is this imagining that he actually pictures Hannah on stage dressed in a shimmering white satin dress, her breasts all but shaken out of its V by her wildly gyrating body. He searches frantically and vainly in *Rolling Stone, Disc, The Beat* for news of her.

And what else? Some California empire-builder finds her with her incredible looks, her amazing repertory of sexual delights . . . Paul scans more magazines and newspapers — *Movieland, People, The Inquirer,* and *The Star.*

But if not there? His imagining has no resting place. When you went out into America you fell into the absurd. He reads that a woman bumped off an abusive husband, and the whole family of thirteen kids, all abused too, helped to bury him. A fourteen-year-old son recited the graveside prayer. But then a daughter marries a man indicted for child-molesting and he, having heard from her about the murder, confesses to it, hoping that it will get him off. But that's not all: the daughter, to save him, accuses her mother publicly of the deed.

Where is Hannah in all this?

He gazes up at the sky: from the rear end of a plane little bursts of cloud emerge. They cuddle themselves into babyish shapes, then disintegrate. "W-h-a — " The snowy-white writing gracefully spills its loops onto the pale blue cloth, and a tiny silver bee works overtime, pollinating all the letters. "W-h-a — " But there is nothing more. The sky swallows up message and bee — too much can't be revealed.

Sometimes Sorita herself sends him cards with hints printed on them: "You just miss her." Or, "She was their already." Are they valid? True directions? Or has her husband grabbed the letters and money and slyly directed Sorita to lead him on with false clues? For that matter, are they the authors of the notes he receives? Delivered by members of the local Puerto Rican community, all provided with matrix alphabets traced from Hannah's handwritten postcards to Sorita? Then it hits him like a thunderclap! — maybe Hannah is back home after all, has another job and apartment, and by making use of Sorita manipulates his meandering: Is it seven years, or forty, that he must wander? Can she think him purged, cured, sufficiently weathered and refined in anything less than that? Two years he hopes for, something like a Fulbright. He prays he will not become paranoid in Peoria. In his best moments he feels sure that the messages are Hannah's and that she is never far away from him.

He feels how Hannah is teaching him — leading him — preparing him. Just one town and one message more and she will be his, he feels — one day. In each city he registers and receives his message. Once, to check, he does not register. No message — it is very frightening. He almost loses touch.

He is moved to tears of gratitude by her great caring, her willingness always to be in search of him. Yet she eludes him.

He pursues her. But for how long? Till those red-gold filaments, which plunge outward from her scalp into the universe around her like eager feelers, have turned to the metal-gray of the transmitters and receivers whose idea they resemble? Until his own black locks, which fall across his eyes and which on bad days he makes the metaphor of all his missed joy — until those have traveled so far up the front of his skull and down the back that they are like ghost-colored Jacks and Jills enacting, in the bland euphemisms of the nursery, the erotic mishaps of men and women?

Such predictions are beyond the scope of telling. Only Selig might have attempted it — and Selig, for now, is precisely the one who can't be found or heard from in this matter.

✌ ઠ✆

In contrast to Paul's wandering, one fixed event can be recorded — a wedding. Amy and Daniel married and stayed faithful to their plans for working together, which may be one reason they remained happy in one another's company. There was, however, a complication: Amy's womb, once opened, stayed that way, and she found herself with an unexpected pregnancy when she was midway through her final year of medical school, and Daniel still an undergraduate. They held agonized conferences, then.

"Financially we might manage," Daniel said. "We could probably afford to have a woman come in most days during the baby's first year, and Sylvia and Simon and your grandmother I know would help us out on weekends. I'd get by at school. But you wouldn't be able to keep up with the kind of stamina and undivided attention that's called for. Be honest and admit it. Wouldn't you resent your own child for making you sacrifice everything now? Wouldn't it be better to see Bunky?"

At the newly re-established Bianky Center, he meant.

But Amy cried out that she couldn't see how! She upheld every woman's right to do exactly that, but she herself, because of her own personal history maybe, or maybe not — how could she tell? — could not bring herself to do it. Though maybe after all she should listen to what he was saying, because she did not ever want to resent her own child or do anything but lavish love and teaching on it.

She went on at her exhausting studies, tormenting herself, until one night in her third month she awoke, feeling a strange premenstrual ache in her lower belly. She went to the bathroom to see, and there it happened that a perfect, tiny female fetus expelled itself by miscarriage. Amy screamed for Daniel and collapsed. Then the old anguish dredged up again. She cursed her former lover and father-in-law. She cursed herself, too, her ambition and selfishness, and said she had caused the death of her own child. "I didn't love her enough," she wept. "Not enough, not enough. And she knew it! She knew it!"

Daniel, pale and frightened, again set himself the task of staying near and listening to a woman's bitter words. After Amy had been absent for a week of medical leave, he began gently to argue that nothing could be accomplished by her collapse, and to remind her of all they had planned to accomplish one day in their own clinic. There was so much work to be done in the country and in the world, he reminded her. This terrible experience could, if she would allow it, serve to deepen their understanding of the men and women whom they hoped to help. Finally Amy returned to her studies, gradually regaining strength and interest. A few years later, after she had completed her internship and half of her residency in obstetrics and gynecology, she began a new and wanted pregnancy. It was timed so that she could deliver her child one month after finishing her hospital work and one year before Sylvia financed, as promised, the opening of Amy's office, which would eventually be the clinic run by Amy and Daniel. And so it turned out, this carefully timed event, exactly to the week, for a wonder. Amy gave birth to a baby boy, whom she and Daniel knew from the beginning they would name Charles.

Baby Charlie resembles every other healthy baby who ever lived. He has fat creases at the wrists and thighs, soon a sharp blue gaze of incredible attention, and not too long after that, a swift laugh of generous humor. He appears, like every healthy baby, to have come ready and waiting for heaven knew how long to embark on his corporeal adventure. Soon the baby begins to take on characteristics that show how its own particular constellation of time and place has seized its fate. There is a shape to its head and to the bones of its limbs that seem to show the boy is not going to resemble Charlie or anyone else the couple knows. It may be moving in the direction of some forebear whose genes, no doubt, had stored up strength for this moment — maybe even the feisty old grandmother's grandmother.

Nana herself stands with tears of joy at the cradle. She bears her gift of a large brown teddy bear (it has a music box in its insides that plays the old nursery tune about a male and female child who went off somewhere together — a concession to nursery sentimentality that she finds to her amazement she cannot resist for this first great-grandchild). She remarks — without the faintest self-consciousness or awareness that she has fallen into the unscientific and merely self-comforting frame of mind she so thoroughly despises when she encounters it elsewhere — that there is something in the shape of the long, sensitive baby fingers that puts her in mind of Amy's mother, who had been a gifted musician.

Other friends visit the newborn, bringing gifts — Edgar and Ellen (she uses the occasion to reassure them both once again that a child of their own would have been a mistake), the aides, orderlies, physicians, and other staff members from the old, now the new, Bianky Center. Ellen has been working harder than ever and is even slimmer than before; Edgar, as if to truly distinguish between the old and the new Centers, has grown a short beard, which has come in entirely gray.

Everyone expresses regret that Paul and Hannah cannot be there to greet the baby. Their absence, however, has taken on the overtones of one of those prolonged, old-fashioned, trips-around-the-world honeymoons, even if there is some indication that these lovers may travel separately. No one doubts that their joy in the new baby would be great, and their surmises as lively as anyone's about his character and appearance. What might this same child have resembled — an aide wonders aloud — had it been conceived one year before its actual time? Or one year after? Or a month or a week earlier or later? No one cares to risk a response. The answers to such questions rest with the unknown. Why this form, not that? Mightn't it have been such-and-such, rather than so-and-so? Again silence. The reply to these conjectures likewise remains a mystery — a mystery, however, to which the happy couple give not one single thought, and in this they resemble the condition of happy parents everywhere.